"...the extension is endless, the sensation of depth is overwhelming. And the darkness is immortal."
—Carl Sagan

PLEASE STAND BY	TOM ENGLISH	3

SPECIAL FEATURES

THE BEAST SURFACES	GREGORY L. NORRIS	17
THE FAMOUS MONSTERS STORY	JOHN M. NAVROTH	68
THE ARCHAEOLOGY OF ALIEN	THOMAS KENT MILLER	176

STORIES

THE FOG HORN	RAY BRADBURY	11
THE NIGHT STALKER	GREGORY L. NORRIS	28
AMOEBOID	WILLIAM MEIKLE	39
THE BALA WORM	JAMES DORR	49
THE SPECTRE SPIDERS	W. J. WINTLE	61
BLACK ICE	KURT NEWTON	89
LIFE'S BLOOD	JASON J. McCUISTON	100
THING FROM A NIGHTMARE	TOM ENGLISH	115
SMOKE AND SPRITES	VONNIE WINSLOW CRIST	121
THE RING OF THOTH	SIR ARTHUR CONAN DOYLE	128
THE DUNWICH HORROR	H. P. LOVECRAFT	146
DRACULA'S GUEST	BRAM STOKER	195
THE PURPLE TERROR	FRED M. WHITE	204

COMICS

REPTISAURUS RETURNS!	CHARLTON COMICS	214

COVER ("THE FOG HORN"): ALLEN KOSZOWSKI
INTERIOR ILLUSTRATIONS: ALLEN KOSZOWSKI
UNLESS OTHERWISE CREDITED
EDITOR AND PUBLISHER: TOM ENGLISH

Black Infinity: Creature Features (Issue #10, 2023) is published semi-annually by Rocket Science Books, an imprint of Dead Letter Press. *Black Infinity: Creature Features* is copyright © Tom English and Dead Letter Press, PO Box 134, New Kent, VA 23124-0134. All rights reserved, including the right to reproduce this book, or portions thereof, in any form including but not limited to electronic and print media, without written permission from the publisher. Dead Letter Press has endeavored to source and credit the copyright of all stories, photos, and artworks used in this volume but would be glad to right any omissions in the next available issue. All stories, art, and film and television images are copyright © the relevant writers, artists, producers, or studios, etc. The publisher adheres to the "fair use" policy of using photographic imagery, artworks, and other material for critiquing purposes.

www.DeadLetterPress.com   www.BlackInfinityMagazine.com   ISBN-13: 979-8986230726

Invasion of the Saucer-Men
American International, 1957

CREATURE FEATURES FEATURED CREATURES

WE DIDN'T HAVE CELL PHONES OR TABLETS. THERE WAS NO INTERNET, NO WI-FI, no desktop computers. No home video or gaming systems. No microwave popcorn or pizza delivery. And most of us didn't even get basic cable until around 1980. We had to settle for three network-affiliated broadcast tv stations, and the programming on these local stations often ended not long after midnight. If you were an insomniac, your best friends were the cheap paperback novels sold at drugstores, and the mute Native American chief depicted on RCA's Indian-head test pattern.

But for all we lacked in technological advances, those of us who grew up in the 1960s and '70s were well compensated with, and bound together by, a golden era of pop-culture that gave us the Etch A Sketch, Spirograph, Creepy Crawlers, Hot Wheels and ... a new age of superheroes.

We could buy comic books at any convenience store for just a handful of silver coins, stuff them in our back pockets and trade 'em with our friends. When we got to school, we were all talking about the same television shows that had aired the previous night, or the latest, made-for-TV *Movie of the Week*.

And better than just about anything else, we had *Creature Features*.

CREATURE FEATURES was a package of horror and science fiction movies produced between 1930 and 1960, bundled together especially for television syndication. Locally produced programs airing this package of films began in the early sixties, and the term "creature features" soon became the generic name for all such shows featuring vintage "monster movies"—*Chiller Theatre* (1961), *Creature*

Godzilla, flossing between meals, in director Ishirô Honda's *Gojira* (*Godzilla*, Toho Studios, 1954)

Above: Mattel's 1964 Creepy Crawlers kit.

Previous page: Monster movie hosts Maila Nurmi (as Vampira) and John Zackerle (as Zackerley; from "Night Harbingers of Horror" in the May 4, 1958 issue of *Life Magazine*.)

Features (1969), *Svengoolie* (1970), and *Doctor Madblood's Movie* (1975), to list just a few. Most of these shows were hosted by colorful, humorously ghoulish characters such as Chilly Billy, Count Gore de Vol, and the Bowman Body.

Screen Gems had previously bundled all the old Universal Horror movies as a package called "Shock!" with the films airing on *The Vampira Show* (1954) and *Shock Theater* ('57), hosted, respectively, by Vampira (American actress Maila Nurmi, 1922–2008) and Zackley (American stage actor and radio personality John Zackerle, 1918–2016). But something was missing...

The Creature Features movie package may not have been the first, but it was the best, thanks to the inclusion of Universal's creepy sci-fi films of the 1950s, as well as Japanese Kaiju monster flicks such as *Godzilla* and *Gamera*. Sure, we loved *Frankenstein*, *The Wolfman*, and *The Mummy*, but we hungered for giant ants, spiders, and grasshoppers, not to mention invading aliens and hideous mutants from outer space. And where else could a monster addict get a free, weekly dose of radiation-drenched insects or thawed out dinosaurs?

Six o'clock news flash: *Creature Features* features creatures!

Screaming through the airwaves, rampaging across the small screen, leaping or crawling right into the home—it was all too wonderful, and it was all ours!

Our parents, however, fully understood the childhood dangers of watching so much monstrous mayhem on the tube—so they never let us sit too close to the TV. *It was bad for our eyes!*

The Creature Features films included several giant-sized threats, from movies such as *Them!* (1954), *It Came from Beneath the Sea* ('55), *Tarantula* ('55), *Rodan* ('56), *Beginning of the End* ('57), *The Amazing Colossal Man* ('57), *The Deadly Mantis* ('57), *War of the Colossal Beast* ('58), *Attack of the 50 Foot Woman* ('58) and the grandaddy of Atomic Age mutant monster flicks: *The Beast from 20,000 Fathoms* (1954).

Partly inspired by Ray Bradbury's classic story "The Fog Horn" (depicted on this volume's cover by artist Allen Koszowski), *The Beast from 20,000 Fathoms* paved the way for a decade of gamma-ray gargantuas. Gregory Norris discusses the film in his article, "The Beast Returns!"

And speaking of outer space mutants, *This Island Earth* ('55) gave TV audiences a superb example, from the distant, warring world of Metaluna.

Other sci-fi movies featured in the Creature Features package included Howard Hawk's *The Thing from Another World* (1951), George Pal's *War of the Worlds* ('53; cover-featured in our last volume), *It Came from Outer Space* (1953; based on a screen story by Ray Bradbury),

BLACK INFINITY • 5

A rapidly growing creature invades Westminster Abbey in *The Quatermass Xperiment* (Hammer Films, 1955). Page 5: Faith Domergue struggles with a Metaluna. mutant in *This Island Earth* (Universal, 1955).

Hammer Film's *The Quatermass Xperiment* ('55; aka *The Creeping Unknown*), *Forbidden Planet* ('56), special effects wizard Ray Harryhausen's *20 Million Miles to Earth* ('57), director Ishirô Honda's *Battle in Outer Space* ('59) and screenwriter Ib Melchior's *The Angry Red Planet* ('59).

And we mustn't leave out the monster movie classic *IT! The Terror from Beyond Space* (1958). In this issue, Thomas Kent Miller, author of *Mars in the Movies*, discusses *IT!* and the film's influence on director Ridley Scott's 1979 cinema classic *Alien*.

I could list scores of other great movies that filled out the *Creature Features* package, such as director William Cameron Menzies *Invaders from Mars* (1953) or Universal's *The Creature from the Black Lagoon* ('54), *The Mole People* ('56), and *The Monolith Monsters* ('57); producer-director Arnold Laven's *The Monster that Challenged the World* (1957); director-auteur Roger Corman's *Attack of the Crab Monsters* and *Not of this Earth* (both from '57); or... Ahem, but I think you get the picture: Television in the sixties and seventies gave us enough bug-eyed beasties to fill thousands of pages of Forrest J Ackerman's influential magazine *Famous Monsters of Filmland*.

I won't delay you any longer from diving into this issue's goodies—except to mention

BLACK INFINITY • 7

Still the greatest:
The Creature from the Black Lagoon (Universal Studios, 1954)

Opposite (Inset):
The Monster that Challenged the World (United Artists, 1957)

War of the Colossal Beast (American International, 1958)

that this tenth volume of *Black Infinity* is something of a milestone. Ten thick issues are about 9 more than I'd thought I'd ever be doing—typing with just two fingers.

I launched this retro-flavored SF book-magazine hybrid in October 2017, not really sure how readers would respond. From what I'm hearing, you guys are having almost as much fun as I am. Who knew?

And I hope we'll all be together for many more issues to come. The contributors and I have so many cool themes planned for the future; more creepy stories to tell; and more classic movies to celebrate.

Black Infinity wouldn't have lasted this long without your support. You guys are the best readers an editor could ever hope for. Okay, time for me to dry my eyes and get to work number eleven. Time for you to get cozy with a few creepy creatures.

What's that?

Do they bite?

Of course they bite! Probably scratch, claw, chew, and drool, too. Would you have it any other way?

Tom English
New Kent, VA

FIRST THREE ISSUES STILL AVAILABLE!

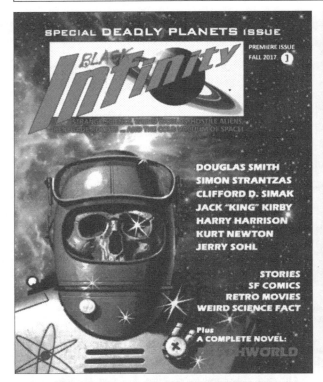

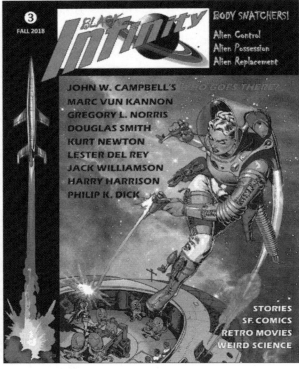

Purchase online at Amazon, Walmart, or BN.com—or order through your local bookstore.

Strange science, weird worlds, hostile aliens, renegade robots ... and the cold vacuum of space.

200 oversized pages packed with exciting stories, articles and art by some of the best writers of yesterday, today and tomorrow.

Black Infinity: Deadly Planets (#1)
ISBN: 978-0996693677

Black Infinity: Blobs, Globs, Slime and Spores (#2) ISBN: 978-0996693684

Black Infinity: Body Snatchers (#3)
ISBN: 978-1732434424

THE FOG HORN

BY RAY BRADBURY

OUT THERE IN THE COLD WATER, FAR FROM LAND, WE WAITED EVERY NIGHT FOR THE COMING OF THE FOG, AND IT CAME, AND WE OILED the brass machinery and lit the fog light up in the stone tower. Feeling like two birds in the grey sky, McDunn and I sent the light touching out, red, then white, then red again, to eye the lonely ships. And if they did not see our light, then there was always our Voice, the great deep cry of our Fog Horn shuddering through the rags of mist to startle the gulls away like decks of scattered cards and make the waves turn high and foam.

"It's a lonely life, but you're used to it now, aren't you?" asked McDunn.

"Yes," I said. "You're a good talker, thank the Lord."

"Well, it's your turn on land tomorrow," he said, smiling, "to dance the ladies and drink gin."

"What do you think, McDunn, when I leave you out here alone?"

"On the mysteries of the sea." McDunn lit his pipe. It was a quarter past seven of a cold November evening, the heat on, the light switching its tail in two hundred directions, the Fog Horn bumbling in the high throat of the tower. There wasn't a town for a hundred miles down the coast, just a road, which came lonely through dead country to the sea, with few cars on it, a stretch of two miles of cold water out to our rock, and rare few ships.

"The mysteries of the sea," said McDunn thoughtfully. "You know, the ocean's the biggest damned snowflake ever? It rolls and swells a thousand shapes and colors, no two alike. Strange. One night, years ago, I was here alone, when all of the fish of the sea surfaced out there. Something made them swim in and lie in the bay, sort of trembling and staring up at the tower light going red, white, red, white across them so I could see their funny eyes. I turned cold. They were like a big peacock's tail, moving out there until midnight. Then, without so much as a sound, they slipped away, the million of them was gone. I kind of think maybe, in some sort of way, they came all those miles to worship. Strange. But think how the tower must look to them, standing seventy feet above the water, the God-light flashing out from it, and the tower declaring itself with a monster voice. They never came back, those fish, but don't you think for a while they thought they were in the Presence?"

I shivered. I looked out at the long grey lawn of the sea stretching away into nothing and nowhere.

"Oh, the sea's full." McDunn puffed his pipe nervously, blinking. He had been nervous all day and hadn't said why. "For all our engines and so called submarines, it'll be ten thousand centuries before we set foot on the real bottom of the sunken lands, in the fairy kingdoms there, and know *real* terror. Think of it, it's still the year 300,000 Before Christ down under there. While we've paraded around with trumpets, lopping off each other's countries and heads, they have been living beneath the sea twelve miles deep and cold in a time as old as the beard of a comet."

"Yes, it's an old world."

"Come on. I got something special I been saving up to tell you."

We ascended the eighty steps, talking and taking our time. At the top, McDunn switched off the room lights so there'd be no reflection in the plate glass. The great eye of the light was humming, turning easily in its oiled socket. The Fog Horn was blowing steadily, once every fifteen seconds.

"Sounds like an animal, don't it?" McDunn nodded to himself. "A big lonely animal crying in the night. Sitting here on the edge of ten billion years calling out to the Deeps, I'm here, I'm here, I'm here. And the Deeps *do* answer, yes, they do. You been here now for three months, Johnny, so I better prepare you. About this time of year," he said, studying the murk and fog, "something comes to visit the lighthouse."

"The swarms of fish like you said?"

"No, this is something else. I've put off telling you because you might think I'm daft. But tonight's the latest I can put it off, for if my calendar's marked right from last year, tonight's the night it comes. I won t go into detail, you'll have to see it yourself. Just sit down there. If you want, tomorrow you can pack your duffel and take the motorboat into land and get your car parked there at the dinghy pier on the cape and drive on back to some little inland town and keep your lights burning nights. I won't question or blame you. It's happened three years now,

12 • THE FOG HORN

and this is the only time anyone's been here with me to verify it. You wait and watch."

Half an hour passed with only a few whispers between us. When we grew tired waiting, McDunn began describing some of his ideas to me. He had some theories about the Fog Horn itself.

"One day many years ago a man walked along and stood in the sound of the ocean on a cold sunless shore and said, 'We need a voice to call across the water, to warn ships; I'll make one. I'll make a voice like all of time and all of the fog that ever was; I'll make a voice that is like an empty bed beside you all night long, and like an empty house when you open the door, and like trees in autumn with no leaves. A sound like the birds flying south, crying, and a sound like November wind and the sea on the hard, cold shore. I'll make a sound that's so alone that no one can miss it, that whoever hears it will weep in their souls, and hearths will seem warmer, and being inside will seem better to all who hear it in the distant towns. I'll make me a sound and an apparatus and they'll call it a Fog Horn and whoever hears it will know the sadness of eternity and the briefness of life.'"

The Fog Horn blew.

"I made up that story," said McDunn quietly, "to try to explain why this thing keeps coming back to the lighthouse every year. The Fog Horn calls it, I think, and it comes...."

"But—" I said.

"Sssst!" said McDunn. "There!" He nodded out to the Deeps. Something was swimming towards the lighthouse tower.

It was a cold night, as I have said; the high tower was cold, the light coming and going, and the Fog Horn calling and calling through the raveling mist. You couldn't see far and you couldn't see plain, but there was the deep sea moving on its way about the night earth, flat and quiet, the color of grey mud, and here were the two of us alone in the high tower, and there, far out at first,

was a ripple, followed by a wave, a rising, a bubble, a bit of froth. And then, from the surface of the cold sea came a head, a large head, dark-colored, with immense eyes, and then a neck. And then—not a body—but more neck and more! The head rose a full forty feet above the water on a slender and beautiful dark neck. Only then did the body, like a little island of black coral and shells and crayfish, drip up from the subterranean. There was a flicker of tail. In all, from head to tip of tail, I estimated the monster at ninety or a hundred feet.

I don't know what I said. I said something.

"Steady, boy, steady," whispered McDunn.

"It's impossible!" I said.

"No, Johnny, *we're* impossible. *It's* like it always was ten million years ago. *It* hasn't changed. It's *us* and the land that've changed, become impossible. *Us!*"

It swam slowly and with a great dark majesty out in the icy waters, far away. The fog came and went about it, momentarily erasing its shape. One of the monster eyes caught and held and flashed back our immense light, red, white, red, white, like a disc held high and sending a message in primeval code. It was as silent as the fog through which it swam.

"It's a dinosaur of some sort—" I crouched down, holding to the stair rail.

"Yes, one of the tribe."

"But they died out!"

"No, only hid away in the Deeps. Deep, deep down in the deepest Deeps. Isn't *that* a word now, Johnny, a real word, it says so much: the Deeps. There's all the coldness and darkness and deepness in the world in a word like that."

"What'll we do?"

"Do? We got our job, we can't leave. Besides, we're safer here than in any boat trying to get to land. That thing's as big as a destroyer and almost as swift."

"But here, why does it come *here?*" The next moment I had my answer.

BLACK INFINITY • 13

The Fog Horn blew.

And the monster answered.

A cry came across a million years of water and mist. A cry so anguished and alone that it shuddered in my head and my body. The monster cried out at the tower. The Fog Horn blew. The monster roared again. The Fog Horn blew. The monster opened its great toothed mouth and the sound that came from it was the sound of the Fog Horn itself. Lonely and vast and far away. The sound of isolation, a viewless sea, a cold night, apartness. That was the sound.

"Now," whispered McDunn, "do you know why it comes here?"

I nodded.

"All year long, Johnny, that poor monster there lying far out, a thousand miles at sea, and twenty miles deep maybe, biding its time, perhaps it's a million years old, this one creature. Think of it, waiting a million years; could *you* wait that long? Maybe it's the last of its kind. I sort of think that's true. Anyway, here come men on land and build this lighthouse, five years ago. And set up their Fog Horn and sound it and sound it out towards the place where you bury yourself in sleep and sea memories of a world where there were thousands like yourself, but now you're alone, all alone in a world not made for you, a world where you have to hide.

"But the sound of the Fog Horn comes and goes, comes and goes, and you stir from the muddy bottom of the Deeps, and your eyes open like the lenses of two-foot cameras and you move, slow, slow, for you have the ocean sea on your shoulders, heavy. But that Fog Horn comes through a thousand miles of water, faint and familiar, and the furnace in your belly stokes up, and you begin to rise, slow, slow. You feed yourself on great slakes of cod and minnow, on rivers of jellyfish, and you rise slow through the autumn months, through September when the fogs started, through October with more fog and the horn still calling you on, and then, late in November, after pressurizing yourself day by day, a few feet higher every hour, you are near the surface and still alive, you've got to go slow; if you surfaced all at once you'd explode. So it takes you all of three months to surface, and then a number of days to swim through the cold waters to the lighthouse. And there you are, out there, in the night, Johnny, the biggest damn monster in creation. And here's the lighthouse calling to you, with a long neck like your neck sticking way up out of the water, and a body like your body, and, most important of all, a voice like your voice. Do you understand now, Johnny, do you understand?"

The Fog Horn blew.

The monster answered.

I saw it all, I knew it all—the million years of waiting alone, for someone to come back who never came back. The million years of isolation at the bottom of the sea, the insanity of time there, while the skies cleared of reptile-birds, the swamps dried on the continental lands, the sloths and sabre-tooths had their day and sank in tar pits, and men ran like white ants upon the hills.

The Fog Horn blew.

"Last year," said McDunn, "that creature swam round and round, round and round, all night. Not coming too near, puzzled, I'd say. Afraid, maybe. And a bit angry after coming all this way. But the next day, unexpectedly, the fog lifted, the sun came out fresh, the sky was as blue as a painting. And the monster swam off away from the heat and the silence and didn't come back. I suppose it's been brooding on it for a year now, thinking it over from every which way."

The monster was only a hundred yards off now, it and the Fog Horn crying at each other. As the lights hit them, the monster's eyes were fire and ice, fire and ice.

"That's life for you," said McDunn. "Someone always waiting for someone who never comes home. Always someone loving some thing more than that thing loves them. And after a while you want to destroy whatever that thing is, so it can't hurt you no more."

14 • THE FOG HORN

The monster was rushing at the lighthouse.

The Fog Horn blew.

"Let's see what happens," said McDunn.

He switched the Fog Horn off.

The ensuing minute of silence was so intense that we could hear our hearts pounding in the glassed area of the tower, could hear the slow greased turn of the light.

The monster stopped and froze. Its great lantern eyes blinked. Its mouth gaped. It gave a sort of rumble, like a volcano. It twitched its head this way and that, as if to seek the sounds now dwindled off into the fog. It peered at the lighthouse. It rumbled again. Then its eyes caught fire. It reared up, threshed the water, and rushed at the tower, its eyes filled with angry torment.

"McDunn!" I cried. "Switch on the horn!"

McDunn fumbled with the switch. But even as he flicked it on, the monster was rearing up. I had a glimpse of its gigantic paws, fish-skin glittering in webs between the finger-like projections, clawing at the tower. The huge eye on the right side of its anguished head glittered before me like a cauldron into which I might drop, screaming. The tower shook. The Fog Horn cried; the monster cried. It seized the tower and gnashed at the glass, which shattered in upon us. McDunn seized my arm. "Downstairs!"

The tower rocked, trembled, and started to give. The Fog Horn and the monster roared. We stumbled and half fell down the stairs. "Quick!"

We reached the bottom as the tower buckled down toward us. We ducked under the stairs into the small stone cellar. There were a thousand concussions as the rocks rained down; the Fog Horn stopped abruptly. The monster crashed upon the tower. The tower fell. We knelt together, McDunn and I, holding tight, while our world exploded.

Then it was over, and there was nothing but darkness and the wash of the sea on the raw stones.

That and the other sound.

"Listen," said McDunn quietly. "Listen."

We waited a moment. And then I began to hear it. First a great vacuumed sucking of air, and then the lament, the bewilderment, the loneliness of the great monster, folded over and upon us, above us, so that the sickening reek of its body filled the air, a stone's thickness away from our cellar.

The monster gasped and cried. The tower was gone. The light was gone. The thing that had called to it across a million years was gone. And the monster was opening its mouth and sending out great sounds. The sounds of a Fog Horn, again and again. And ships far at sea, not finding the light, not seeing anything, but passing and hearing late that night, must've thought: There it is, the lonely sound, the Lonesome Bay horn. All's well. We've rounded the cape.

And so it went for the rest of that night.

The sun was hot and yellow the next afternoon when the rescuers came out to dig us from our stoned-under cellar.

"It fell apart, is all," said Mr. McDunn gravely. "We had a few bad knocks from the waves and it just crumbled." He pinched my arm.

There was nothing to see. The ocean was calm, the sky blue. The only thing was a great algaic stink from the green matter that covered the fallen tower stones and the shore rocks. Flies buzzed about. The ocean washed empty on the shore.

The next year they built a new lighthouse, but by that time I had a job in the little town and a wife and a good small warm house that glowed yellow on autumn nights, the doors locked, the chimney puffing smoke. As for McDunn, he was master of the new lighthouse, built to his own specifications out of steel-reinforced concrete. "Just in case," he said.

The new lighthouse was ready in November. I drove down alone one evening late and parked my car and looked across the grey waters and listened to the new horn sounding, once, twice, three, four times a minute far out there, by itself.

The monster?

It never came back.

"It's gone away," said McDunn "It's gone back to the Deeps. It's learned you can't love anything too much in this world. It's gone into the deepest Deeps to wait another million years. Ah, the poor thing! Waiting out there, and waiting out there, while man comes and goes on this pitiful little planet. Waiting and waiting."

I sat in my car, listening. I couldn't see the lighthouse or the light standing out in Lonesome Bay. I could only hear the Horn, the Horn, the Horn. It sounded like the monster calling.

I sat there wishing there was something I could say.

👾 👾 👾

"The Fog Horn" first appeared in the June 23, 1951 issue of The Saturday Evening Post, *as "The Beast from 20,000 Fathoms." The story helped inspire the 1953 Ray Harryhausen film of the same title. "The Fog Horn" is copyright © 1951 by the Curtis Publishing Company, renewed 1979 by Ray Bradbury; and is reprinted here by permission of Don Congdon Associates, Inc.*

Author and screenwriter Ray Bradbury (1920–2012) sold his first story in 1938, when he was 19, to Forrest J. Ackerman's fanzine, Imagination! *Later that year, Bradbury launched his own fanzine,* Futuria Fantasia, *which ran for four issues, each with a print run of less than 100 copies. Bradbury wrote most of the fanzine's content. It's from these humble beginnings that the 20th century's greatest and best-loved fantasist started on his literary journey.*

Bradbury wrote habitually, rarely missing a day. Early in his career, he often tapped out pages on borrowed or rented typewriters, in local libraries or at the YMCA. Over the next 70-plus years, he produced about 600 stories and over two dozen novels and collections, as well as scores of film and television scripts. His work has been adapted for radio and comics, translated into over 36 languages, and has sold over 8 million copies. His most famous and critically praised work is Fahrenheit 451, *a cautionary novel depicting the perils of censorship.*

Bradbury once described his avocation as "a God-given thing, and I'm so grateful, so, so grateful. The best description of my career as a writer is 'at play in the fields of the Lord.'"

In 2005, Bradbury was awarded an honorary degree of Doctor of Laws, by the National University of Ireland. In 2007, he was made a Commander of the Order of the Arts and Letters, by the French government. And in 2009 he was awarded an Honorary Doctorate by Columbia College, Chicago. Not bad for a self-taught writer who never attended a single day of college, let alone earned a degree. But then, Bradbury never obtained a driver's license, either. Hence, for most of his life, he bicycled or relied on public transportation.

Bradbury was honored with an O'Henry Award as one of the best American short stories of the year, a Prometheus Award (for Fahrenheit 451*), an Emmy (for* The Halloween Tree*), two Retro Hugos, and both the Bram Stoker and the World Fantasy Awards for Lifetime Achievement. He was named the tenth SFWA Grand Master in 1989, had an asteroid discovered in 1992 named "9766 Bradbury" in his honor, and received a star on the Hollywood Walk of Fame in 2002. In 2004, President George W. Bush presented Bradbury with the National Medal of Arts.*

Ray Bradbury had the ability "to write lyrically and evocatively of lands an imagination away," wrote The L. A. Times, *"...anchored in the here and now with a sense of visual clarity and small-town familiarity." The Pulitzer Prize jury awarded a special citation to Bradbury in 2007, "for his distinguished, prolific, and deeply influential career as an unmatched author of science fiction and fantasy." (Want more Bradbury?* Black Infinity: Rocketships and Space-suits *reprinted three of the best of his early stories.)*

THE BEAST SURFACES!

DIVE IN DEEP WITH
THE BEAST FROM 20,000 FATHOMS

BY GREGORY L. NORRIS

The Saturday Evening Post, June 23, 1951. Previous: Rhedosaurus on the rampage. Movie images © Warner Bros.

FOR LEGIONS OF DEVOTEES, Saturday afternoons in the mid- to late 1960s through the 1970s meant appointment viewing on UHF thanks to weekly broadcasts of creature double features. Headlining that schedule was a trove of B-movie gems—monsters and outer space menaces, enough to fill the day and young minds with a mix of terror and imagination. And, occasionally, something cinematic that was pure A-list ran on boxy console TVs hooked to rabbit ear antennae—the original *Godzilla* (1956), the Quatermass classic *Five Million Years to Earth* (1968),[1] and the 1953 masterpiece *The Beast From 20,000 Fathoms* among that gold.

The Beast is a film with solid pedigree—creature effects by stop-motion wizard Ray Harryhausen and based, at least partially, on the classic short story by Ray Bradbury, "The Fog Horn." Originally scripted as *The Monster from Beneath the Sea*, Harryhausen brought it to producers Hal Chester's and Jack Dietz's attention that *The Saturday Evening Post* had just published Bradbury's tale, which appeared under the title "The Beast From 20,000 Fathoms," and that the two stories shared common DNA. Eager to cash in on Bradbury's popularity, they bought the rights to the story and renamed the project. The screenplay was co-written by Lou Morheim and Fred Freiberger. Freiberger would go on to write and produce for television on *The Wild, Wild West* (1965), *Star Trek* (1966), and *Space: 1999* (1975).

---

[1] The film's 1967 US release title; original, UK title is *Quatermass and the Pit*.

18 • THE BEAST SURFACES

"Born on the cusp of the Baby Boomers and Gen-X, I grew up on Saturday matinees filled with cautionary tales of assorted oversized monsters—classics like *Them!* and *Tarantula*, and classic cheese like *The Deadly Mantis* and *The Black Scorpion*," says author and editor Lane Adamson (*Robots Beyond* and *Times of Trouble*, Permuted Press). "But my favorites always seemed to feature the brilliant stop-motion animation of Ray Harryhausen—*20 Million Miles to Earth*, *The Valley of Gwangi*, and, in many ways the one that started them all, *The Beast From 20,000 Fathoms*."

Budgeted at $200,000, *The Beast* opens far north of the Arctic Circle in a frozen wasteland, where top secret Operation: Experiment is being prepped. It's X-Day, with less than an hour to go before the big event. At the rendezvous coordinates, atomic scientist Tom Nesbitt (Paul Christian) and military liaison Colonel Jack Evans (Kenneth Tobey) spot the plane carrying the operation's payload. The bomb gets dropped. Glaciers collapse and liquefy. Instruments in Nesbitt's monitoring station detect something enormous unleashed by the

meltdown—estimated at five hundred tons—but it soon vanishes from the screens.

Nesbitt and company head out to the forward observation points to take readings and get a look at the damage. They come upon a blockage of fallen ice and are forced to proceed forward on foot. The men separate to check radiation levels, and then, less than ten minutes into the film, colleague George Ritchie (Ross Elliot) spots the prehistoric horror released on the modern world from hibernation in the snowpack. So do viewers in a rare and breathtaking moment that bucks the usual creature feature convention in which the monster usually appeared only at the end of the movie.

The beast—the gargantuan Rhedosaurus—startles Ritchie, who slips over a precipice. When Nesbitt reaches him, Ritchie spouts on about having seen a monster. Nesbitt is skeptical—until Rhedosaurus's roar thunders through the blizzard, and the giant dinosaur unleashes an avalanche that nearly buries the scientist and seals Ritchie's fate. A delirious Nesbitt warns his rescuers that the monster is coming.

Nesbitt is airlifted from the frozen north far south to New York City and Hartley Hospital, where his story of the beast is met with disbelief. Even good pal Evans, newly arrived from Washington, D.C., can't back up Nesbitt's claim. However, far out at sea, unfortunate sailors navigating the rain-swept night learn otherwise, as Rhedosaurus rises up and sinks their fishing boat.

A forlorn Nesbitt stewing in his hospital room reads an article in the newspaper about a giant serpent spotted off the Grand Banks.

Nesbitt busts out of the hospital and heads to the office of Dean of Paleontology, Doctor Thurgood Elson (Cecil Kellaway). In Elson's lab, complete with towering dinosaur skeleton, Nesbitt urges Elson to organize an expedition to seek out the monster. Elson's pretty assistant Lee Hunter (Paula Raymond) attempts to voice reason, but Elson refuses. Then a second Canadian ship is sunk.

Nesbitt returns to his work, but when Lee visits, claiming to believe him, they pore through known dinosaur species, and he recognizes the monster. Nesbitt tracks down a sailor (Jack Pennick) who survived one of the sinkings, and who confirms the professor's claim about Rhedosaurus. This new evidence convinces Elson. Jack Evans is still reluctant to believe Nesbitt's story.

Another dark night arrives at a lighthouse located on a desolate rocky outcrop in the Atlantic. As the two keepers converse, the beast rises out of the sea, alerted to the light from the lantern room. In a truly horrifying moment, the monster peers in through the windows before tearing the lighthouse apart in an unforgettable scene that pays homage to the Bradbury story and earned the author his "Suggested by..." nod in the film's opening credits.

Also now convinced, Evans brings in the Coast Guard. Professor Elson tracks the latest destruction down to the Massachusetts coast and reasons the beast is following the Arctic current south to its former spawning grounds: the deep sea canyons off the Island of Manhattan where the only known specimen of a Rhedosaurus skeleton was discovered.

Elson makes the fateful decision to lower

himself down into the canyon in a diving bell to check out the theory.

A philosophical Elson descends into the deep sea. At first, the only forms of life spotted are a shark and octopus, who engage in a struggle to the death. Then Rhedosaurus arrives and devours both combatants. An excited Elson reports up to Lee and Nesbitt his observations only to go silent. When they attempt to raise the diving bell, the team learns the beast has claimed its next victims.

While Lee and Nesbitt mourn, the military mobilizes. Then, in broad daylight, dockworkers hear the fateful splash, and the monster rears its giant head up from the sea. The beast comes ashore and rampages into New York City, sending terrified crowds running and creating a swathe of destruction through the streets. In another of the movie's memorable scenes, the monster pounds along, flicking its tongue. A lone bold police officer draws his sidearm, stands against the horror, and gets devoured.

The beast crushes cars and pedestrians and smashes through buildings. It reaches the famous Flatiron as sirens sound and the National Guard is called in. As night falls on a shocked city, the military confines the beast to Lower Manhattan. But another deadly twist soon unfolds.

Soldiers fall ill and die unexpectedly. It turns out all that gunfire has splashed the city's streets in the monster's blood, which contains a toxic prehistoric virus.

Night engulfs the city. Soldiers man blockades, and the beast lurks among a canyon of dark brick buildings. Nesbitt, Lee, and Evans arrive to the blockade. The horror is targeted—the plan is to fire a killing shot through its skull, which Lee reminds is at least eight inches thick. The shot only enrages Rhedosaurus, who charges at the blockade. The men fire two bazooka rounds, and the beast tangles in live power lines, making for another stunning special effects display. It also splatters more of the monster's toxic blood around. The wounded giant storms off. The soldiers fan out, following the gory trail. They don't get far before most of the detail drops, sickened by the blood.

The military command post tracks the beast to the lower harbor. When Nesbitt, Lee, and Evans arrive for an update, a concerned doctor at the frontlines phones, warning that the monster is a deadly germ carrier—spilling more of its blood will result in greater numbers of casualties. If they continue to use

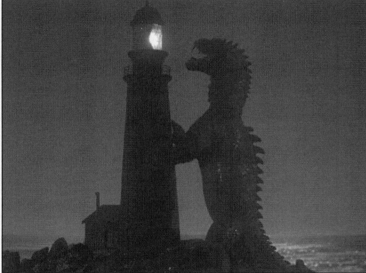

22 • **THE BEAST SURFACES**

shell-fired projectiles, the entire city is in danger of contamination.

As they ponder their next move, the beast comes ashore—at Manhattan Beach. Nesbitt claims the only way to take down the monster for certain is by shooting it with a radioactive isotope, thereby also destroying all that diseased tissue. Military vehicles stream into the

Coney Island amusement park, which is lit up like a chandelier. The monster is cornered among the tracks of the roller coaster when Evans and Nesbitt jump off their ride and into action.

Nesbitt's radioactive ordnance arrives while the beast chews through the tracks.

Evans assigns his best sharpshooter, Corporal Jason Stone (journeyman actor Lee Van Cleef in an early role) to fire the isotope grenade. Nesbitt informs Stone they've only got that single shot—the isotope is one of a kind. The beast devours more track, and the two men, suited up in radiation suits, head forth to confront it. Lee pauses Nesbitt long enough to peck a kiss to his cheek.

The two men approach the tracks. Stone can't get a clear shot. The only way to insure success is to take the roller coaster to the top of the tracks for a point-blank assault. Stone and Nesbitt board the roller coaster car and ascend. They stop at the top of the tracks. With the beast

CONTINUED ON PAGE 26

24 • THE BEAST SURFACES

growing more agitated by the second, Stone takes aim at the monster's vulnerable throat and fires. The beast shrieks and lashes out, its movements sending the roller coaster into a dive down the broken tracks. The car crashes, and flames engulf the structure. Nesbitt and Stone hasten down the tracks on foot to escape the inferno, which traps the beast from 20,000 fathoms. In one of the most memorable of all creature feature endings, the fire rages and the roller coaster tracks crash down as the monster succumbs to its mortal wounds.

"The grand finale at the Coney Island roller coaster is incredible—and clearly influenced by Harryhausen's apprenticeship with *King Kong* and *Mighty Joe Young* animator Willis O'Brien: always stage your climax at an iconic landmark," adds Adamson. "*Beast* is a creature of its era, pun intended. At the onset of the Atomic Age, no one understood what fission or fusion-based weapons might be able to do, so why *couldn't* one reanimate a frozen dinosaur? The Manhattan Project scientists estimated that there was a vanishingly small but very real chance that the first A-bomb explosion might start a chain reaction that would destroy the world. They still went ahead with the test. The innocence and naivety of the main characters in the movie is charming, even endearing. Hey, let's drop a diving bell in front of the enormous beast that's been sinking ships all along the northeastern coastline—what could possibly go wrong?"

This year, *The Beast from 20,000 Fathoms* celebrates seventy years since its original release. But its influence can still be felt in modern cinema. The movie directly influenced Ishirô Honda's 1954 *Gojira*—the first entry into the *Godzilla* franchise, which has produced a total of 38 films

26 • THE BEAST SURFACES

(the latest, *Godzilla x Kong: The New Empire*, is slated for March 2024 release).

"As for the movie's lasting appeal," says Adamson, "well, for one thing, Roland Emmerich basically remade the thing with his 1998 *Godzilla*—'Giant lizard awakened by A-bomb goes to New York to breed.' Am I the only one who sees the parallel? Maybe that's why I'm the only one who actually liked that film. And, let's face it—*The Beast From 20,000 Fathoms* fits the template for so many great monster films, and not just the giant ones. It has as much in common with *An American Werewolf in London* as it has with *King Kong*."

THE NIGHT STALKER

BY GREGORY L. NORRIS

IT HAPPENED IN THE 1970S. Then, phones were still attached to the wall, and you only stuck your finger in the rotary dial to call long distance after five p.m., when the rates were cheaper. My father, who worked at the airbase, wore paisley shirts with long collars in the ugliest colors of plum purple and burnt orange when not on duty.

After the gas dried up during the time of the second energy crisis, we stuck around our rural neighborhood, which might as well have been an island unto itself located far from the outside world. No day trips to Lake Winnipesauke or over the border of Massachusetts to Salisbury Beach. As the summer deepened, the tall pines and woods surrounding Armstrong Road seemed to press in like the dark forests from childhood fables, and the only news from the outside world came from the airbase—or the TV news, when we were lucky enough to escape rolling blackouts.

2

UNTIL THAT SUMMER, on lazy afternoons before the grass grew too long or after the killing frost knocked it down, I would lie on the knoll in the field across the road with my doll Tillie and stare up at the sky. Often, I'd hear the purr of a plane flying somewhere up there— not a jet, no; they screamed over the woods and Corbett's Lake on approach to the airfield. These were smaller planes, some wearing their wings on top, flown by private pilots out of the civilian airport located farther up Range Road, beside the cornfields. My Grandmother Rachel made Tillie for me the Christmas I turned six. Four years later, Tillie had visited Grammy Rae's doll hospital twice for emergency surgery.

Armstrong Road was a lonely place for a young girl during a tense, hot summer, devoid of friends apart from one made of cloth with yarn hair. Even planes with their comforting purrs had abandoned me. The skies were quiet and mostly empty save for clouds and the occasional screaming jet pulling duty over our heads, but even they were fewer between, given the crisis.

Our house was a tiny two-bedroom bungalow with a screened-in porch on the back. The porch faced the lake, with the stream that ran out of the woods cutting between us on its way to the water. I was hacked off again because my favorite variety hour starring the Osmonds, who were from a faraway state called Utah, had just started when the lights went out. And I'd just managed to get the rabbit ears perfect—the signal crisp, showing all those purple sequins in glorious, glittery clarity.

I dragged Tillie to the back porch and uttered a rosary of curse words that only adults were allowed to speak, the moonless night so dark that the trees, stream, sky, and lake could barely be told apart from one another. On that night, Armstrong Road in the town of Whyndom, New Hampshire might as well have existed on another planet, at the farthest end of the universe.

Heat rose up my throat and infected my face. I felt the caustic sting of tears threaten at the corners of my eyes but willed them back, which turned out worse than if I'd let them fall. I tried in vain to swallow down the lump in my throat. Everything around me had turned bad. Looking back, the sense that the world was about to go spinning off its axis was tangible, a shadow that dogged me from every direction and one impossible to shake.

Just how bad, however, had yet to reveal itself. That moment soon arrived low over the treetops, announced by a distant scream that whipped the hot night air into a frenzy, creating wind devils above the towering sap pines. All the oxygen seemed to vanish from my lungs, and breathing was no longer involuntary or even easy. I gulped down a sip right as the dark sky lit up. I saw the explosion before I heard it. Then, multiple trails of fire and smoke were plummeting over the lake, like fireworks gone wrong.

I must have screamed, too, because the footsteps in the dark, hot house all converged on the back porch.

"Mandy?" asked Theresa, my father's girl-friend.

My father said one of those adult words I'd recently gotten away with, his in the form of a question.

"We under attack?" Theresa gasped.

"I saw it," I said. "Over the lake. A jet exploded!"

I started to tell them about the wreckage, the pieces riding fiery comets out over Corbett's Lake. But they were already navigating the house's dark interior, headed toward the phone bolted onto the kitchen wall.

THEY USED FLASHLIGHTS despite that stern warning we all received in a leaflet concerning our responsibility as citizens to conserve batteries during the crisis. As search parties fanned out across the lake and shore, I carried the flashlight that had spent the summer in the kitchen's junk drawer but didn't turn it on. I didn't need to.

BLACK INFINITY • 29

Even on a night when not a single star chose to shine, I knew the stream, the woods, and our side of the lake intimately. I was a bored and lonely kid whose only friends were a doll made of rags and those my imagination created.

So, as a mix of military and civilians stroked the shores of Corbett's Lake with their flashlight beams and rumors spread, I walked with my father and Theresa, knowing where to step and what parts of the ground to avoid. My sneakers never plunged into muck. No pine roots riding just above the soil tripped me.

"It wasn't one of ours," said Mister Columbus, who lived next door in the green bungalow with the black shutters. "Jackson from the base says it's a damn Soviet plane, probably powered by high-test beet juice and vodka."

I stifled a rare chuckle. Laughter had been in as short supply as energy throughout that humorless summer. And I liked Mister Columbus, who, like my father, brought in an honest paycheck working at the airfield. I'd once remarked that with a name like his, every day must have felt like a holiday, not just the Twelfth of October.

"Damn Rooskies," my father sighed. He followed the sentiment up with another, more colorful adult word despite my presence and then checked his hunting rifle.

I realized I'd become invisible and tested the theory by dropping behind, back into the folds of the darkness. The righteous patriots searching for wreckage or the ejected Soviet pilot continued on ahead, their flashlight beams jiggling frenetically as they passed over uneven ground, or whenever one of their feet tangled in a patch of grabby scrub vegetation.

I sat on the Rhino, the smaller of the two boulders in our backyard set beside the Elephant along the bank of the stream, and studied the sky for other shooting stars. Though disappointed in my lack of relevance, I had to admit how charged my cells felt at the night's unexpected adventure. At least *something* had happened, regardless as to whether it pushed us past crisis to the precipice of all-out war. My heart was in a constant gallop and doing its best to jump up from my chest and into my throat. I choked it back down, considered joining the lights—now almost at the lake—but then I heard the crunch-slither of movement from the far bank of the stream. Footfalls, coming closer.

I resisted the urge to turn on the flashlight, which I caught myself twirling like a baton, and held my breath. The walker behind those steps moved without a flashlight, and with a kind of stealth that my young mind recognized as purposeful. We'd never seen a bear at the lake, despite the acres of surrounding woods. A lynx? One gray autumn morning, a bobcat had raced up the tallest oak in the backyard, which had both thrilled and terrified me in the same breath. On that day, I imagined the animal as part house pet, half saber-toothed beast from a bygone era.

Perhaps the lynx was back, a nocturnal predator on the prowl for its next meal. Only whatever was striding toward the stream walked on two feet, not four. My ears knew the difference. Was it the Soviet pilot that had everyone so incensed? I thought about switching on the beam, but my eyes had grown accustomed to seeing in the dark. I was part lynx. Someone tall made it to the edge of the stream. I sensed them hesitate before navigating down into the running current.

Two feet plunked into the stream, the sounds distinct. Then all the other flashlights returned, with my father calling my name.

"Mandy!"

I was no longer invisible—to them or that other presence cutting across the water. I slid off the Rhino, darted around the Elephant, and met the search party along the stream. "There's someone in the water!"

I pointed downstream. The flashlights tracked the direction I'd indicated. Not someone, no, but a some*thing*. The beams zeroed in right as the creature emerged from the

30 • THE NIGHT STALKER

water. Fawn-brown, with short hair and a giant head, a barrel for a chest, strong forearms and legs, huge paws, it was the biggest dog I'd ever seen.

"But—?" I started.

The sentence went unfinished. What I didn't tell them was that I was sure that the dog had been walking upright, on two legs.

3

ON THE SURFACE, a dog seemed the ideal solution to one of the smaller wars being fought that summer.

"A new friend," my father said, counter to Theresa's protests at having a dog—let alone one so beastly—in our small home near the lake.

And on the surface, I feigned happiness. All summer long, as the walls of trees pressed in around us, I'd bemoaned my lack of friends close enough to play with under the auspices of the travel restrictions imposed by the energy crisis. Underneath, my guts twisted into knots as the dog stood there, wet but not shaking himself off like a normal dog should. He allowed Mister Columbus to examine him.

"No collar."

"Don't the Hissocks have a big dog?"

"You mean Charlie? Put him down last year."

"Must be a stray," my father reasoned. "But stray no more."

I looked into the dog's eyes, which were glassy in the glow from the flashlights. He panted like a dog, looked like one, but my instincts told me not to trust appearances.

"I don't know," Theresa said. "It's so big. It'll eat us out of house and home. And it could be dangerous."

"It's not an *it*," Mister Columbus said. "If you don't want him, I'll gladly—"

And then in a moment of rare generosity, my father said, "No, he's Mandy's dog now."

4

THE DOG PLUNKED DOWN on the braided oval rug beside my bed. As the search continued well past the first murky light of the new day, I tried to sleep but couldn't. I heard the constant panting of the dog's breaths, smelled its wet dog smell, and realized my unwanted new companion felt more like an invader than a friend. All the while, my mind recycled my first impression: that the dog now walking about on four legs had arrived upright on two.

Another voice in my head, the one forced to view the world through an adult perspective, told me I was crazy. Worse, ungrateful—what kid wouldn't want a dog of her very own? Hell, I should have been happy with an aquarium filled with sea monkeys ordered from inside one of the lame comic books my father was always bringing home from the airbase.

A dog, yes. Just not *this* dog.

At a point right before the sun rose, I drifted into a state that wasn't asleep nor awake but somewhere in between. I sensed the dog standing at the side of the bed, staring at me with its wild golden-green eyes. When I forced my slitted eyes to open wider, the dog was gone.

SO, TOO, WAS MY FATHER. Called in early to work under the base's emergency protocol, I wondered if he'd gotten any sleep following the night's adventure. Theresa was passed out in their room, I saw, which reeked from the last cigarette she'd smoked. The house was eerily quiet.

I poured myself a cup of milk—a small one, given that world events meant fewer trips to the grocery store. We'd even grown our own garden to have fresh vegetables, though the cucumbers ripened sour as the summer wore on. The temptation to refill my glass sent me reaching for the milk carton. Then I felt the humid breeze, warm and scented of the outside, and turned to see the front door standing open.

The dog was gone.

THE JOKE—at least it sounded funny in my mind—was that I would call my beast of a dog Uri, or Sergei, or Boris like the spy on one of

BLACK INFINITY • 31

my cartoons. Something Russian, which I thought would be poetic and appropriate, given the story of how he came to be mine. But it was beginning to look as though I needn't have bothered being clever, given the dog's disappearing act.

There hadn't been much to laugh about over that summer. The world had forgotten how to smile. As I traipsed down the flagstone walkway my father built, past the post-and-beam fence in our front yard and across Armstrong Road, whose tired asphalt had been blanched by the sun to the color of comfortable denim, I tried to remember what life was like before the crisis. Unhappiness seemed ready to stay.

So I figured that the dog had found a way out of the house. That maybe my father hadn't properly shut the front door—though he was a stickler for locking it after two men came walking right into our house the previous summer while Theresa and I were eating supper in front of the TV. We figured they were from Massachusetts, had gone to the lake's public beach, were robbing houses and didn't realize we were home until Theresa began to shriek, causing them to run.

Since then, he always locked the doors.

I wandered into the smaller of the two meadows set before the big woods. I decided I should at least make an effort at finding my new friend Rooskie—that was a good name for a gigantic dog, I agreed. Finding my new friend Rooskie.

The hot, green veldt towered over me. I cut past the wood line, where it wasn't uncommon to see tangles of garden snakes sunning themselves, and beneath the shadows of the outlying trees. I knew those woods in the same intimate manner as the shore of Corbett's Lake and instantly sensed the wrongness creeping in an undercurrent from their depths. This was different than the encounter with the lynx; there'd been window and walls between us then. As I drifted farther, I cast a glance up at the Austrian pines and the patches of overcast sky visible

between their scaly boughs. The trees were as tall as skyscrapers, I swore. Vertigo and gravity conspired to drop me to the ground. The scent of pine needles mixed with decaying leaves, all of it cooked up by the summer's heat, grew narcotic. Something buzzed past my ear. Sweat flowed.

Yes, there was a malevolent presence in my woods that hadn't been there before the previous night, and shouldn't be now but was.

Heat lay thick and oppressive around me. My flesh crawled and sweated. A lump formed in my throat. "*Rooskie*," I called, my voice almost not there.

A low, creaking sound tumbled down from the trees. The towering conifers often groaned as they swayed in the wind, only this was different, *other*, part of the wrongness I'd sensed from the start of my arrival. Goosebumps ignited across my arms. I found myself again gazing up and slowly turning around. The trees and sky spun over my head.

I saw the man and, at first, mistook him for a life-sized puppet attached to marionette strings tangled in the upper branches. My turning about ceased. The puppet's face and throat were burned. One of his eyeballs was missing. No, not gone—that was it hanging out of its socket by a thin cable of flesh. The creaking sound resumed, its source the weight of the corpse pulling against those puppet master's strings as it swayed in the balmy breeze.

I screamed.

And screamed.

5

I WAS SEATED on my bed. The red lights of the emergency vehicles dispatched by the airbase, some presently parked in our yard, teased my vision at the periphery, reminding me of blood.

People were speaking outside my bedroom door, their voices reaching me even when whispered. It was a very small house.

"It's the Rooskie pilot, all right," one of the men from the airbase said. "That explains one, but that jet was a two-seater, so where's the other?"

"How's your daughter," another man asked.

"She's fine," my father said.

Like he knew. Like things hadn't been bad enough before I'd gone into the woods in search of my missing dog, which I hadn't even wanted.

I slid off the bed and padded to the door. If they were so concerned about me, why hadn't a single adult checked in for what had seemed an eternity? Eyes looked down, acknowledging my arrival. Theresa detached from the small crowd gathered among our furniture and started toward me.

And as she did, I noticed the dog was back, its body plunked down in the living room before the impotent TV. Right before our glances connected, I had the impression that its eyes and ears were absorbing all being said and acted out.

WE ATE HAM AND CHEESE sandwiches from the food Theresa had moved from the fridge to the cooler following the last blackout. The meat had a funky taste at the edges, as though this was possibly the last hour that it would remain edible. I picked around my sandwich and caught Theresa's disapproval in her next exhale, made loud enough for me to hear. But she didn't scold me. Hard to justify, I supposed, when my father was feeding his dinner to the dog.

"I'm putting in a request at the airbase for some kind of reward or compensation," he said, turning back to the small, round table that accommodated four but had only ever seated three. "Fuel rations, food, cash. After all, we found that dead Soviet pilot."

Rage bubbled up from my guts. The temperature in that corner of the house skyrocketed. "*I* found him," I blurted out before I could censor the words.

My father scowled. "I know you did, but it benefits the entire family. If we could—"

I pushed away from the table hard enough

to jiggle glasses and spill tepid water.

"Mandy," my father barked.

I ignored him and stormed through the porch and out the back door. Tears powered past my defenses. By the time I reached the Elephant and the Rhino, I was sobbing. I'd never felt so alone. Soon after the emotion embraced me, however, I wasn't.

The dog crept past the barrier formed by the Elephant's mica-flecked hide, a vast shadow beyond the veil of my tears. I tensed, swiped at my eyes. The shadow was staring at me.

Mustering the last of my courage, I said, "What do you want?"

For a second, part of me actually expected Rooskie to answer.

"Huh, dog? What are you doing here?"

The giant lowered his head. Golden-green eyes studied me. A chill sliced through the heat encasing my body, because I swore the dog was smiling.

My father called my name. I backed away, between the two boulders deposited thousands of years earlier by receding glaciers. The dog stepped forward, and I was again reminded of the size of his paws. A voice in my head sounded an alarm—*if he wants to, he could eat you!*

"Mandy," my father shouted. "Mandy, you get in here *right now!*"

The dog turned toward the sound of my father's angry voice. I took that moment to run up from the stream's bank, through the backyard, and away from what I now believe would have been my certain death.

I HEARD THE DOG nosing around the house and imagined him walking upright, opening doors with front paws that were really hands. Fear paralyzed my body. What could Rooskie be searching for? Food? My mind flashed back to the miserable dinner, which had culminated with me receiving a stern warning about my attitude. Before that particular humiliation, Theresa had opened a can of beef stew—decent enough food for humans

BLACK INFINITY • 33

during this crisis, but gourmet faire for a dog in any situation. Rooskie had snubbed his nose at the offer.

Time slipped off the normal track of seconds and minutes, transforming one into the other. I heard the front door open. Footsteps pounded outside my bedroom windows, steady and secretive, and again the pattern sounded to my ears as though it was made of two feet, not four. I held my breath. My consciousness slipped into that fugue state as my mind raced.

It's possible that I only dreamed the screaming sounds that came from the direction of Mister Columbus's house.

6

MY FATHER KNOCKED, paced, and knocked again, receiving the same result: no answer.

"If he doesn't hustle soon, we're gonna be late," he said.

I waited beside his bicycle, which had become that summer's only reliable method of transportation around the lake other than legs.

"Daddy," I said, my face hot, my stomach tied in knots.

He shot a look in my direction.

"I think something bad happened to Mister Columbus. Last night, I heard…"

"You heard what?"

My father tested our neighbor's doorknob. It was locked.

Mustering courage, I said, "Daddy, I think the dog hurt Mister Columbus."

"The dog?"

"I don't think it's really a dog. Remember Laika?" My voice hitched with a sob. "She was the first one they sent up into space. On Sputnik 2. They launched her into orbit around the Earth."

Confusion swept across my father's face, along with an obvious note of frustration. "Mandy, what the hell are you babbling on about?"

"The Soviets, experimenting on dogs. That man from the airbase said there were *two*

pilots in the jet. I think the dog's the other one. Only it isn't a dog."

My father sighed, tromped over to where I stood guarding his ride into work, and yanked the bike out of my grasp.

"You know, Mandy, I'm starting to worry about that overactive imagination of yours."

Shaking his head, he rode away, saying nothing more.

7

THE DOG WAS GONE, and nobody but I noticed. They were all so focused on the bigger mystery and crises that they were oblivious to the smaller, no less deadly one taking place around us.

I was right about the dog, or so my gut instinct told me. But I needed proof.

I waded across the stream at its thinnest point and cut through the sedge between Corbett's Lake and the backend of our tiny neighborhood, knowing the muddy traps to avoid. Soon, I'd reached the area where the dog had first appeared. It hadn't rained for a couple of days, and I prayed to whatever god was listening that the evidence I suspected would still be there. To my relief, it was—in the form of a dozen footprints etched into a patch of ground between hillocks. How long I stared, I couldn't be certain. Long enough to attract a swarm of thirsty mosquitoes.

The large prints were staggered in twos, not fours, definitely in the shape of a man's sole. I blinked myself out of the trance and turned toward my house, only to suffer a rush of dizziness. When the world around me again stabilized, I saw the dog standing outside the back porch, staring at me across the distance.

Our eyes connected. The dog blinked, and then he started running toward me.

AS STATED, being alone and lonely had given me license to explore the lush green realm that surrounded my home, and I was intimately acquainted with my remote world. In his haste to reach me, the dog sprinted

34 • **THE NIGHT STALKER**

toward the stream where it ran at its thickest. I raced back in the direction of the spot where it was narrowest. This put me nearer to Mister Columbus's rear door than my own house and, given no option, I ran as fast as I could. I ran for my life.

Water splashed. The pounding of footsteps followed in counterpoint to my desperate sips for breath. It was chasing me, and close. It suddenly dawned on me that the back door to Mister Columbus's house might be locked, like the front. Mercifully, it wasn't. I turned the knob, flew into our neighbor's house uninvited, and slammed the door behind me. Turning the lock seemed to take forever because seconds dragged on with the weight of minutes.

Mister Columbus's bungalow was identical to ours apart from the lack of a back porch, which my father had added on, and the complete absence of a woman's touch. The air smelled stale, like a mixture of mold and sweaty socks, and another odor I couldn't place, not at first.

The house would have been gloomy with the summer sun shining through the windows and the lights turned on. I backed away from the door, into the throat of the short hallway connecting bedrooms and bathroom to a similar though dirtier version of our kitchen/living room combo.

"Mister Columbus?" I called out in vain.

In the back bedroom, the one that was mine in our house, I spied an odd collection of things: men's clothes stacked on a worktable beside guns—my father's hunting rifle among them, a map roughly drawn and showing the lake, airbase, and our neighborhood, and what my imagination identified as a radio cobbled together from a bunch of spare parts. I realized what the dog that wasn't really a dog had been up to at night.

I reached for my father's hunting rifle, going on automatic. Several times that unhappy summer, we'd dined on pheasants hunted out of season. I hated the texture of the butchered meat, swore I could taste the burn from the bullets. The phantom bitterness ignited on my tongue. I raised the rifle and backed out of the room.

My next instinct was to hide. I entered the bigger of the house's two bedrooms, my wet sneakers sloshing across the floor, leaving an accidental roadmap. I found Mister Columbus beside the bed. His throat had been ripped out.

8

POOR LAIKA, left in orbit around the Earth. Her desiccated corpse was still up there, circling our energy-thirsty globe until some future expedition brought her back or a decaying trajectory and the planet's gravity did the same on a fiery pyre. Sputnik was only a couple of years before my birth, the story still fresh, and the cruelty forced on Laika had gotten into my young psyche and would always be there in my private thoughts.

I had no idea of the relationship between that poor canine soul and the monster throwing its mass at the locked backdoor to Mister Columbus's house, but assumed the latter was a Soviet spy sent to infiltrate the airbase. Our neighbor was dead, murdered, his blood the source of that other rank smell I hadn't been able to identify until my arrival to the big bedroom. My blood might soon join his.

I'd fired the gun a few times at the start of the crisis on my father's demand that I be prepared should Soviet soldiers begin dropping out of the sky. I'd laughed at him then, to his considerable annoyance. I wasn't laughing now.

The door burst open and the dog charged in. Dog? I knew it wasn't a dog, not really. The gun lacked silver bullets. I silently prayed conventional ammo would be enough.

The nightmare turned the corner growling, the claws of its big feet scrabbling across the floor. It saw me and, again, I swore it was smiling. Then its wide gold-green eyes recorded the gun. It moved to spring at me. I fired. Thunder rocked the world.

At such close range, my aim was perfect.

BLACK INFINITY • 35

The abomination spilled inelegantly across the floor, hatred clear in its gaze as it labored for breath. The dog exhaled one final time and then, as screams powered past my lips, began to alter.

Before me was the body of a naked man with military-short, fawn-colored hair and golden-green eyes.

"The Night Stalker" first appeared in Blood, Sweat, and Fears: Horror Inspired by the 1970s *(Nosetouch; 2016).*

Raised on a healthy diet of creature double features and classic SF TV, Gregory L. Norris writes regularly for numerous short story anthologies, national magazines, novels, and the occasional episode for TV or film. He novelized the NBC Made-for-TV classic by Gerry Anderson, The Day After Tomorrow: Into Infinity *(as well as a sequel and a forthcoming third entry into the franchise for Anderson Entertainment in the U.K.), a movie he watched as an eleven-year-old sitting cross-legged on the living room floor of the enchanted cottage where he grew up.*

Gregory won HM in the 2016 Roswell Awards in Short SF Writing. He once worked as a screenwriter on two episodes of Paramount's Star Trek: Voyager. *Kate Mulgrew,* Voyager's *"Captain Janeway," blurbed his book of short stories and novellas,* The Fierce and Unforgiving Muse, *stating, "In my seven years on* Voyager, *I don't think I've met a writer more capable of writing such a book—and writing it so beautifully."*

In late 2019, Gregory sold an option on his modern Noir feature film screenplay, Amandine, *to the new Hollywood production company Snark-hunter LLC, owned by actor Dan Lench, a devotee of Gregory's writing. In late 2020,* Snarkhunter *optioned Gregory's tetralogy Horror film based upon four of his short stories,* Ride Along. *That same month, his short story "Water Whispers" (originally appearing in the anthology* 20,000 Leagues Remembered*), was nominated for the Pushcart Prize.*

Gregory lives and writes at Xanadu, a century-old house perched on a hill in New Hampshire's North Country with spectacular mountain views, with his rescue cat and emerald-eyed muse. Follow his further literary adventures at: www.gregorylnorris.blogspot.com

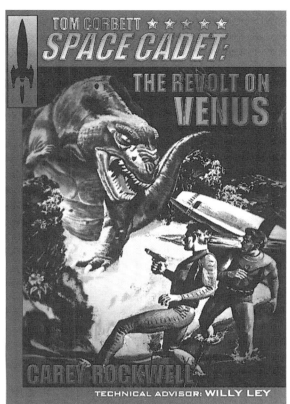

STILL AVAILABLE

TOM CORBETT, SPACE CADET:
THE REVOLT ON VENUS
BOOK 5 IN THE SERIES

On term break from Space Academy, Tom Corbett and Roger Manning accompany their pal Astro to his native planet Venus for a well-deserved rest. There the cadets plan to hunt the biggest game in the star system, but their vacation is soon interrupted when the intrepid crew of the *Polaris* stumble across a secret plot to overthrow the Solar Alliance.

Lost in the Venusian Jungle, unable to contact the Solar Guard, separated from their ship and each other, the hunters have now become the hunted: caught between the heavily armed forces of a would-be tyrant mad for power… and the tyrannosaurus Astro wounded years earlier—thirty tons of terror mad for revenge.

$8.25 ◆ ISBN: 978-0-9966936-6-0

TOM CORBETT, SPACE CADET:
TREACHERY IN OUTER SPACE
BOOK 6 IN THE SERIES

Why has Roger Manning suddenly gone dark? Can his pal Tom Corbett really be dead? What caused the strange trouble on Titan—and how is it connected to a rocket race in outer space?

These are but a few of the mysteries confounding Captain Steve Strong and the big Venusian engineer, Astro, as the Solar Guard races against time to save the mining colony on Saturn's largest satellite. At stake are the lives of hundreds of men, women, and children; the future of the intrepid *Polaris* crew; and quite possibly the fate of the entire star system.

$8.25 ◆ ISBN: 978-1-7324344-0-0

"A beautifully bound, affordably priced keepsake edition of World Fantasy Award-winning illustrator Allen Koszowski's incredible art, featuring over 500 examples of the strange and fantastic worlds of Allen K. HIGHLY RECOMMENDED!"

Tom English, editor of *Nightmare Abbey* and *Black Infinity*

AVAILABLE FROM
Centipede Press
CentipedePress.com

Introduction by
Ramsey Campbell
Stamped cloth binding with ribbon marker
Illustrated endpapers and a gorgeous double-sided
dustjacket. March 2023 ♦ 568 pages ♦ ISBN 978-1-61347-320-7
SPECIAL DISCOUNT AT https://www.centipedepress.com/art/allenkoszowskisale.html

AMOEBOID

by WILLIAM MEIKLE

T**HE TROUBLE STARTED AT 6:00PM ON A QUIET THURSDAY AFTERNOON,** and at first it was so small that it was hardly noticed. The summer of '56 had been a hot one so far, and was showing no signs of relenting, and I had gone in search of some escape from the overpowering sense of being slowly boiled in my tin-roofed office. I tried standing under one of the few trees in the shade while smoking down one of my Capstan's but what little wind there was felt too dry, too hot—and the thought of returning to the oven that enclosed my desk was too much to bear. I took a slow, laborious walk over to the only place I know might give me some respite.

The Rocket Research Group's main laboratory was usually the coolest place in the facility, having the benefit of some new-fangled air conditioning from our American chums. I had sought some solace there just the previous day, so knew a couple of minutes there would rejuvenate me—for a time at least. When I entered I saw that young George Thornton was the only other member of staff present, and his whole attention was on something under his microscope lens.

"What have you got there, lad?" I asked.

"I don't rightly know, Prof," he said. "I was just about to come and fetch you to have a look. It's a sample we got from the high altitude balloon flight—some top layer stratospheric stuff. I know there's not supposed to be anything alive up there—but this sure looks like life to me."

He motioned me over to take a look.

"Just five minutes ago it was only a spore—I took it for a pollen grain at first. But either the heat or from the water on the slide have woken it up—and I've no idea what it is."

I bent over the scope and looked down—it certainly had been a spore at one point—one with a rough, almost hairy outer coat, long fine tendrils that wafted to and fro on the tiny currents caused by the light stage's heat on the fluid under the slide. But now the spore had split, and it had a long swollen finger of protoplasm escaping from the right hand edge at about three o'clock as I looked at it. Even as I watched, it swelled, and oozed

BLACK INFINITY • 39

further across the field of view. It was full of livid colors—greens and blues and gold, and it almost seemed to twinkle in the harsh light. It was escaping from the spore so fast that it filled my field of view completely in a matter of seconds and I had to reduce the magnification twice to keep track of the growth.

"It's certainly making itself at home," I said. "Is there just the one of these spores or are there more?"

George shrugged.

"It came from a scraping I took from the bottom of the sample jar—there was a coating, like a hard crust on the outside of the jar when we brought the balloon down."

"And where's the jar now?"

George stood and bent under the desk.

"Down here in the refrigerator—I thought it best, what with the heat and all."

He opened the fridge door—and the contents, what was left of them, spilled—or rather, oozed out at his feet. There were Petri dishes, glass sample jars, distilled water bottles and what looked like the remains of a jam sandwich, all partially melted—digested—inside what looked like a clear, almost transparent, gelatinous ooze. More of it was already dripping down onto the wooden floor, sending long fat fingers creeping toward George's toes. I saw with some dismay that door of the fridge itself had also been partially dissolved—whatever this was, it was voracious.

And it was clearly growing.

Suddenly I was thinking of infection and contagion.

"Don't think—just go. Get out," I said to George. "Now. Hit the sprinklers and flush the system, while we still can."

I followed the lad out of the lab and we both hit the sprinkler button at the same time. A wash of dilute hydrochloric acid came from the showerhead in the ceiling, sending a fine spray through the whole room. We watched the gelatinous ooze as pustules bubbled and popped across its surface. It pulled itself into a tighter clump, almost the size of a football,

obviously a defensive maneuver, but not enough to save it as the acid fell and, slowly but surely, dissolved it until it was little more than a puddle on the floor by the fridge. A haze rose over the remains, an oily residue that danced in rainbow colors before falling back into the spilled ooze. Beyond the window the laboratory fell quiet.

"That was too close," I said once I was sure it was dead. I turned to George—he looked pale, almost ashen. "What's the matter lad—did you get any of that stuff on you."

"No, Professor," he said. "It's not that—it's just that, when I got the sample jar from the balloon this morning I saw there was more of that crusty stuff on the surface of the balloon itself—a lot more.

The balloon was one of the focal points of our research—our main tool for investigating the realms into which we intended at some point to launch our first test rocket. Anything that might cause a problem for the balloon was going to cause problems—big ones—for the whole unit. George knew that as well as I did, and was out of the door first and beat me to the shed where we kept the kit. He stopped and stood at the door until I approached.

"What do we do if...?" he started, but didn't finish, for neither of us had a ready answer at hand. I stepped past him and opened the door.

This time it was me who had to step back quickly—there was more of the ooze here—much more of it, covering the whole floor of the large storage shed. All that remained of our massive high altitude balloon—so big it normally took six of us to get it out of the shed to prepare it for flight—were a few fragments—already dissolving in a mass of seething protoplasm.

"Fetch some acid, lad," I shouted. The ooze somehow seemed to sense an escape route, and surged toward me, forcing me to slam the door hard on it. I remembered the fridge, and I wondered how long it would be before it melted its way through the wood itself.

George hadn't moved. He was staring at

40 • AMOEBOID

the door. I took him by the shoulders and shook him, hard.

"Acid, Thornton. We need it now."

The lad finally came to his senses.

"How much should I get."

"All of it," I replied, rather too sharply, and then had to stand back. The bottom of the door had gone soft and saggy, threatening to drip. "And best be quick about it. It looks like we don't have much time here."

George left at a run. Other members of our team were, by now, beginning to become aware that something was going on and came out of their huts to investigate. It started to get crowded around the shed door. I sent a couple of the faster lads after George with orders to help him out, but I was beginning to wonder whether they'd be on time—or whether we even had enough acid on the facility to cope with what was clearly a rather large menace.

We could all hear groaning and screeching from inside the shed. The structure lurched heavily to one side, and the roof fell in with a crash, the door falling inward to join it. A mass of ooze slumped over the rubble then seemed to fall in on itself with a moist slither, then disappear from view.

I saw the reason as I stepped gingerly forward—the floor, the roof, the door, the balloon and the slime itself, everything had all fallen through the floor of the shed. I had to step closer still to look down into the resulting hole, and my sense of foreboding got stronger still—there had been a drain in the center of the shed, which was what had collapsed.

Somewhere, far below, I heard a deep, moist gurgling.

Whatever the stuff was, it was now in the sewer system under our base.

GEORGE AND THE OTHER TWO lads returned a minute or two later, wheeling a wonky barrow that had been rather precariously stacked with jars of acid. I had them dump the whole bally lot down the drain in the shed before

they caused another accident, but I feared it was far too little, far too late.

I knew we needed to get down there after it, but before I could organize a proper hunt I had to spend minutes I could ill afford bringing the rest of the team up to date with the matter at hand.

"So exactly what is it?" Jennings, our administrator, accountant and all round worrier asked. He liked to be precise and clear on every matter, but I had no answer that would satisfy him, and young George's reply was as good as any I could have managed.

"Clearly it's some kind of space poo," he said. "Shed eating space poo. There, does naming it make it any better—any more understandable?"

After everyone had a laugh at Jennings' expense I was able to start managing the situation. Jennings provided some answers to my many questions. The first, and most important, was as to the extent and nature of our sewage system—I'd never given it a moment's thought but our administrator seemed intimately familiar with it.

"We're on a main county system," he explained when I asked him. "Something my predecessor insisted on after the war when they were building the site. There's a new sewer right under our feet—an eight-foot diameter brick channel that feeds directly into a main drain that goes through Anchester and down the valley before heading down toward Oxford for processing."

I could see the bally stuff in my mind's eye, slithering down there in the dark, heading for town and something to eat.

"Then we'd best get down there and stop this thing before it gets to that main drain," I said. I split the men up into four three-man teams, each with respirators and bottles of acid, and sent them down the valley to take up watching briefs in case our quarry got that far down the sewer.

Young George outdid himself by knocking up, in the five minutes it took me to find a flashlight, a small knapsack affair that, when

BLACK INFINITY • 41

squeezed under the arm like a bagpipe sac, fed acid down a metal tube to a pistol-grip nozzle that could be fired from my hand. I noted that he had even had time to make one for himself as he and I—with Jennings close behind—went down into the main drain under the shed, picking our way gingerly through the rubble.

THE FIRST THING I NOTED was the smell—even through the respirator mask the tang of the acid I'd had dumped down the hole was strong and acrid, threatening to burn at my nose and throat. We had descended right over the spot where the collapse had happened, but there was no sign of the ooze—although there was a distinct trail on the floor of the sewer to mark its passing that seemed to shine and shimmer in the beam from my flashlight. I motioned to the others that they should follow and I headed, at some speed, deeper into the tunnel.

At least the brickwork was new and hadn't crumbled—for a sewer the tunnel was remarkably clean, and I came to almost be thankful for the stink of acid, for it surely masked many other stenches than might have proved rather more noxious. We were able to make good time—a fact that gave me some pause, for if we were making such rapid progress, then it meant that our quarry was moving just as quickly—and possibly even faster.

The first sign that it was still ahead of us came when my light fell on a partially digested rat. The head end still twitched and squealed in pain but from the ribs to where the tail should have been was just a mess of unregulated protoplasm, bubbling and seething—and growing. I had not considered that the ooze would be able to detach portions of goop and, in effect, multiply more rapidly—and now that I had thought of it, I could think of little else.

The poor beast beside my foot squealed piteously. I squirted acid on it and put it out of its misery with the heel of my boot—but

even as I did so I heard more screams—all too human screams—coming up the tunnel from ahead of us.

I didn't wait for the other two—I ran, full pelt toward the hideous noises, the flashlight beam swinging wildly against the walls of the sewer ahead of me.

I WAS TOO LATE—far too late. The screaming stopped, leaving only the sound of my footsteps splashing in the puddles in the floor of the sewer and my breathing, loud and heavy inside the respirator. I rounded a long curve, then had to stop, all breath leaving me at the sight that awaited in the tunnel.

The ooze—protoplasm—whatever the hell it was, sat under an open manhole, pulled up into a sphere almost six feet in diameter, the bulk of it almost filling the tunnel. One of the crews I'd sent to keep watch were embedded inside it, partially melted, skin and bone and clothes in the process of being assimilated into the matrix, three grown men, all already, thankfully, dead as the flesh sloughed from their bones.

I heard young George bring up his lunch in the tunnel behind me. Someone else—Jennings probably, began to weep quietly, but I forced myself to step closer. I raised the pistol grip, squeezed the bag under my arm, and sprayed the ooze with acid.

The result was immediate—it recoiled, as if struck, a wobble traveling all the way through it. As I had seen before, in the laboratory, it pulled itself into a tighter ball, then started to half-slump, half-roll away down the tunnel. The result of that retreat was that the three partially eaten bodies of my friends were unceremoniously deposited in the sewer at my feet, but I had no time for grief—the ooze was already retreating away from me at some speed.

I stepped over the bodies and headed after it, but as fast as I could spray acid, it could retreat faster. I had at least succeeded in slowing its growth—it was half the size it had been as it disappeared at an alarming

42 • AMOEBOID

haste into the darkness beyond the reach of my light.

Even then I might have followed, had I not heard a cry from behind me. I turned to see Jennings shouting up to someone up above the open drain cover. I was torn between pressing my small advantage and my curiosity. Curiosity—and common sense—won in the end, and I returned back up the tunnel to stand under the manhole.

Jennings was talking animatedly to one of the other search crews I'd sent out. I left him to it and went to young George's aid. Despite his obvious distaste and nausea he was intent on checking the three bodies—obviously intent on trying to save them—but it was clear to me that the men were far gone.

"It's all my fault," the lad was saying, over and over again, trying for a pulse on an arm that was barely attached to the molten remains of what had been a shoulder and rib cage. I had to bodily drag him away, and had Jennings tend to him while I caught up with the men above. In truth, there wasn't much to hear—although what there was chilled me to the bone. This was the last manhole before town—and the slime was now surely on its way there.

I almost felt the blood drain from my face. Anchester wasn't big, but it had a population of almost ten thousand. I looked at the bodies at my feet, and tried to picture that scene, multiplied a hundred fold and more. Seconds later I was running, full pelt, down the tunnel. I was vaguely aware of George and Jennings behind me, also running, calling my name, but I had no thought for them.

George had been wrong on one thing—it wasn't his fault. They were my men—my responsibility. Any fault was mine and mine alone.

And I was not about to let any more people die due to my negligence.

I came to a junction some five minutes after leaving the open manhole. The new red brick tunnel gave way to a much older sewer—dank and wet, dripping with thick slimy moss and lichen, and ankle deep in black water. Now that I no longer had the tang of acid to keep the smell at bay I noticed the stench, thick, almost chewable. Only the respirator mask prevented me from having to stop, and even then I was almost choking as I headed left—downhill—toward Anchester.

I did not have to go far before I once again heard screams—from above me now, in the streets of the town. George and Jennings caught up with me as I was trying to heave a manhole cover aside to give me access up to the road above. Between the three of us we managed to push the heavy circle of iron up and out of the way. If I was worried that we might disrupt traffic I needn't have bothered —traffic was more than adequately disturbed already.

I climbed up out of the sewer into a scene of utter chaos.

THE FIRST THING I SAW was an overturned butcher's van—it had been in collision with a horse and cart in the middle of the main street. Two older ladies tended to the butcher —he was bleeding profusely from a head wound and was clearly in a daze. His livelihood, the meat from his van, was strewn all across the road, as was the contents of the cart—old iron, clothing scraps and books by the look of it. The cart driver had got the worst of things—his body lay, already mostly eaten, in the center of a mass of oozing protoplasm. The poor horse lay beside its master. The bulk of it was partially digested. Thankfully the ooze had caught it at the front end first, so its death would have been quick at least. But the back legs were still kicking, even as flesh sloughed off its back. I looked away, back to the ooze. The horse's head was already little more than sludge and goop; lumps of tissue and blood were visible in the clear protoplasm, clearly being drawn to a spot in the interior of the oozing mass.

The screaming was coming from two children, too frightened to run, too amazed at the sight in the street to take their eyes off it.

BLACK INFINITY • 43

By rights I should have done something to comfort them, but the digestive processes of the ooze had caught my gaze. As I said, it was clearly taking its sustenance down toward a central part of its bulk—and if that was the case, I knew that there must be some sense to its structure, some degree of organization.

And something with organization could become disorganized, in the right circumstances.

I watched the poor horse be digested as first George, then Jennings pulled themselves up out of the sewer to stand beside me.

"We need to focus our attack," I said as George raised his pistol to point it at the ooze. "And we need to coordinate it too. Follow my lead."

The ooze was growing visibly, throbbing and swelling as it assimilated the bulk of the horse and the meat from the van. A crowd had gathered in the street, keeping a discreet distance, the townspeople clearly unsure what to make of this new thing in their midst. Some of the more curious of them were already encroaching perilously close to the protoplasm, and if I did not take charge of matters soon, someone else was going to get hurt—or killed.

"With me, George," I said, and stepped forward. I ignored the closest parts of the ooze and aimed my pistol at the central portion, aiming at the spot where most of the digested matter seemed to be being transported. Blood and pink tissue flowed inward, a grotesque mockery of a circulatory system. I aimed for the central area and squeezed the trigger. George sent a stream of acid almost exactly at the same spot.

I hoped we would be able to end it there and then as the plasm bubbled and hissed, but I had forgotten how speedy the dashed thing could be. It immediately recoiled away from the acid—and from us, heading off down the cobbled street, scattering the watching crowd in front of it, leaving a trail of bloody slime in its wake. I hosed the slimy remains down with acid, remembering the rat, and

how there was life in the ooze, even in the remnants it left behind, then turned my attention to the rapidly departing ooze.

"After it, George, quickly," I called. We can't let it get away." The pair of us, with Jennings close behind, ran in pursuit, leaving the startled townspeople far behind as the chase took us the length of the High Street.

We got close enough on two occasions to send more acid over the bulk of it, but the central portion—the place where a ball of partially digested bloody matter still hung— continued to elude us—and the ooze was capable of moving faster than we could run.

We pursued it through the town, squirting acid at any globs of material it left in its wake, before finally catching up to it on the riverbank near the Rowing Club. It slithered quickly down the jetty and spread out, like a huge cape, across almost the full width of the river. An oily, shimmering glow seemed to rise from the water, even as I squeezed the trigger, over and over again, until the pack was completely empty of acid.

The current flowed past us, and the ooze sank, slowly, out of sight. I raised my gaze from the water and looked downstream.

The city of Oxford lay directly ahead—and the ooze was being taken right to it.

"We're going to need bigger knapsacks," George said.

I WAS KEPT BUSY for the rest of that long day— arranging for everywhere, and everything, the ooze might have touched to be washed down with acid and—a much harder task in the end —attempting to impress on the authorities the seriousness of the situation facing us. It didn't help my case that the thing seemed to have gone to ground, so to speak—all that afternoon I had teams out looking for signs of it up and down the riverbanks, but to no avail. As evidence, I had a butcher with a sore head and a whole lot of bloody, acid scarred, slime— certainly not enough to convince the Ministry to give me any special attention, despite the

44 • AMOEBOID

fact that some of it was the remains of dead members of my team.

"We've got a bally flap on in Gibraltar," the clipped tones on the other end of the phone said. "We don't have the time or the manpower to waste on any blasted jelly from outer space. Please don't be bothering us again unless you've got something that needs our urgent attention. You're a rocket group aren't you? Well just blow the bloody thing up and have an end to it."

Tempting as the idea might be, launching a rocket on the academia in Oxford wasn't really an option. I could only keep a watching brief, prepare as well as I could for any eventuality, and hope that I could control any resultant mayhem without any further loss of life.

At least I had the local constabulary on my side, for two officers had seen what happened on Anchester High Street. One of them, Sergeant Green, was a seasoned veteran and levelheaded enough that his superiors couldn't ignore his story. By the time night fell I had a team of firemen, the Oxford police force and my own staff at my disposal. George and Jennings had arranged, by hook or by crook, for a delivery of industrial acid to be shipped to us. Instead of water the firemen had access to a tanker of acid and a generator to pressurize it in their hoses—the hoses themselves might not survive for long—but I was hoping that they wouldn't have to.

I sat in the main Police station in Oxford, smoked too many cigarettes and drank far too much strong, sweet tea. I racked my brains, knowing that I must have missed something in my preparations, at the same time feeling ever increasing guilt creep up on me over the death of my friends and companions.

When the inevitable call finally came and we had to move, I was actually glad of the action.

IT MUST HAVE BEEN IN THE SEWERS—two manholes, both melted and fused as if eaten away, lay on the cobbles, discarded as it oozed, like toothpaste from a too-strongly squeezed tube, up out of the drains, its bulk slowly filling the parking crescent in front of the railway station. Wherever it had been, it had obviously been feeding—it kept coming, and coming, until it lay in a heap almost six feet tall across an area the size of a soccer penalty box. The clear matrix was shot through with red veins, its transport system for taking food back to the central mass. And as I got closer I saw what it had been feeding on—half a dozen cows and several sheep—or what was left of them—hung suspended in the ooze, none of them much more than bags of skin and semi-digested bone. The whole mass of the plasm shimmered in the moonlight, and again I saw the same colors I had seen under the scope—greens and blues and gold hanging in the air above it like a curtain of fine gauze.

The railway's Stationmaster had been the one to call us, and he was clearly flustered, in a situation he did not know how to control or apply to a timetable. He was addressing Sergeant Green, his voice raised almost in a shout.

"What in blazes are you going to do about this then? I can't have this mess on the concourse—the eight ten from Reading will be coming in any minute now—then what am I going to do?"

The Sergeant had the small man taken back into the station but we could all still hear him, promising that he'd be having "a word with our superiors."

"Good luck with that," I muttered, with what would be the last bit of levity for a while as the ooze started to creep—not toward the station but toward the main road.

We only just got the fire crew in position in time as the ooze advanced, crawling over a parked car and stripping its paint job as if it was sandpaper. Sergeant Green gave the order and two hoses started to send an arc of acid over the top of the protoplasm—I had already told them to seek out the central digestive mass. The ooze bubbled and

BLACK INFINITY • 45

hissed—and once again I thought we had it beat, only to be proved wrong.

It surged—I have no other word to describe it—and moved in one smooth motion. We thought we had it contained between the railway station and the tall wall on the other side of the road but the thing flowed up and away and over before we'd scarcely begun to hose it down.

By the time we got round the other side of the wall there was nothing to be seen but a long trail of what looked like partially burned grass across a once-perfect lawn, and some slime draped over the walls and roof of one of the college buildings. It made the old stone shimmer and radiate as if coated in hot oil and in other circumstances might even have been quite beautiful.

SO BEGAN A LONG NIGHT where we played a dangerous game of hide and seek. The ooze showed up twice more—each time larger than the last, each time arising out of the sewer system, and each time retreating so fast from our acid attack that we were unable to stop it. As dawn approached I realized that the town would be waking up, and with it the chance of many more casualties. I could see no other course of action but to take the fight to where the thing was most comfortable—I was going to have to go down into the main sewer.

The firemen, stout chaps that they were, offered to go down in my place, but I felt the burden of responsibility heavy on my shoulders. I had them show me how to operate the nozzles of their hoses. As I was suiting up into one of their safety suits young George started to do the same beside me.

"It's my fault too, Prof," he said as I made to stop him. "I'm coming, and that's that. If you want to put a note in my jotter later, so be it. But I'm coming."

In truth, I was glad of the company as we went gingerly down one of the main manholes into the sewer under the railway station—the first place we had encountered it earlier in the evening. The two hoses were lowered down

to us and we stood there for several minutes as our eyes accustomed to the gloom. I heard the thrum of the generator overhead—the acid was ready and waiting for when we needed it. I only hoped it would be enough.

"Well, here we are then," George said. "What's the plan, Prof?"

"Keep talking—make some noise," I replied, thinking on my feet. "I think it's attracted by sound—our men in the sewer, the butcher's van, the railway station itself—all noise."

"You mean, we're the bait?"

I laughed—the sound echoed around us in the confines of the sewer.

"If you want to put it that way, yes."

"In that case, I've got just the thing."

George then surprised me by starting to sing, loudly and making up in effort what he lacked in musicality.

"I am the Lord High Executioner, a personage of noble rank and title."

It delighted me so much, there in that dark place, that I joined in with all the gusto I could manage.

We had got as far as the second "I've got a little list" when the light in the tunnel changed—somewhere to our north something shimmered, greens and blues and gold—and it was getting closer. George noticed it, and almost faltered in his singing, but I took up the slack, and belted out another chorus as the protoplasm oozed into view, the bulk of it completely filling the sewer as it came forward, heading straight for us.

George looked over at me and even in the gloom I saw that his eyes had gone wide with fear, but he stood beside me as I hefted the heavy hose at my waist, and he followed suit.

We stopped singing as the tunnel filled with a dancing aurora of color that hissed and buzzed as if in response to our song.

"Ready?" I said.

George nodded, and I twisted the nozzle.

As before, the result was immediate. The protoplasm leapt away from us, retreating back in the tunnel. And even as I stepped forward to follow I realized I had indeed forgotten something—the tang of acid and seared protoplasm threatened to choke me…and I wasn't wearing a respirator mask.

But the ooze was getting away again, and this might be my last chance to prevent early morning chaos in the city above. I walked forward fast, spraying ahead of me, my rubber boots splashing in acid, slime and bubbling, popping pustules of protoplasm. George came along at my side as we chased the thing along the sewer.

I had to hold my breath as I went, as the fumes got too noxious, and I was more than aware that we would run out of length of hose any second—but we were, finally, winning. The ooze stopped retreating and formed into a ball some four feet across, a ball that got smaller and smaller as we washed it in acid, sloughing its surface off, revealing the partially digested material at the center.

I was almost out of breath, and the hose was at its maximum length, but I had enough of both remaining to step forward. I thrust the hose—and my hands along with it, deep in the center of the remaining ooze, and let the acid blow it apart into bubbling drips of slime that gave out one last dancing aurora of color then, finally, fell quiet and dark.

THEY SAY MY BURNS WILL HEAL, although I will always have scars on my hands and feet to forever remind me of the thing that came from the sky. But it is not as if I need much reminding. George is here in the bed beside me in the sanitarium—we are allowed out into the garden for a smoke before bed last thing in the evening, and last night it was a clear, moonless night. We looked up, and there, high above us, the sky was dancing and humming, in greens and blues and gold.

Someday soon, we will go and meet it again.

And this time we will be better prepared for the encounter.

"Amoeboid" first appeared in the author's 2016 collection B.E.M.

William Meikle is a Scottish writer, now living in Canada, with over thirty novels published in the genre press and more than 300 short story credits in thirteen countries. He has books available from a variety of publishers including Crossroad Press, Dark Regions Press, and most recently in Severed Press with his successful S-Squad creature feature series. His work has appeared in a large number of professional anthologies and magazines. He lives in Newfoundland with whales, bald eagles and icebergs for company. When he's not writing he drinks beer, plays guitar, and dreams of fortune and glory.

Gorgo by Allen K.
(British Lion-Columbia, 1961)

THE BALA WORM

By James Dorr

"RIGHT, SIR," THE BARMAID SAID—JANIE, HER NAME WAS—when I came home to my own the first time. The lord of her bed, too, soon enough after. And others of the unmarried women. The village, off the normal tourist routes, was old-fashioned in many ways, including a respect for *Droit du Seigneur*.

Of course, I had had an American education, which made me somewhat of an exotic, as well as being the titular lord. And I did have gold too, or its modern equivalent, money and credit. Possibly not so much as I wanted, but...

Then I met Sylvia.

Every so often a rock band came down from the town of Bala, at the lake's far end, to play in the pub here. No one knew quite why they did—for experience, maybe—since Janie's pub's owner could scarcely pay them anything worthwhile. But with the bands came the normal entourage of young people. Groupies. Contrasting vibrantly with the village folk, even the younger ones like Janie.

But it was something for people to do on a Saturday evening, and so the villagers filled the pub along with the groupies, even if few of them actually danced. And as Earl, I got in free—one of my perquisites.

One among many. I winked at Janie, and several more of the Llangower women, as I pushed my way into the taproom. I thought I might have a few pints first, then join the dancers after I'd watched them for a little. But, as I turned to go back to the main room, its tables and chairs lined against the walls to leave its center free, I caught a flash of long, jet black hair, glistening in the lights from the bandstand, milk white legs underneath a shimmering, lizard-scale mini, a face like—an angel? No. More than an angel, at least to my interest. You have to remember I am a young man. Rather, a face like a *fallen* angel.

I caught her eye. I nodded to Janie as she approached me, but continued my way through the crowd. "Do you dance?" I asked this new woman, no doubt one of the ones who had come in with the musicians.

"Try me," she answered. She tossed her head.

The crowd parted enough to give us room and, when that dance ended, we stayed together for another. At length I invited her back to the taproom, where it would be quieter and, finding a table, I asked her her name.

"Sylvia," she answered.

"My name's Bram. Bram Llangower." I saw her eyes widen at the name. "Yes," I added, "the 'lord' of the village. The twenty-third Earl."

She laughed. "Should I call you 'your grace' then?" she asked. Then she kissed me quickly and, before I quite knew how to react, she'd gotten up and already disappeared into the crowd.

THAT WAS A SATURDAY. Sunday I had to busy myself about the manor house I was trying to get back into livable condition. I wrote checks —I had credit, as I have mentioned, and it was no problem to order materials for the repairs against future income—and, speaking of income, wrote my solicitors in London about an advance on the next quarter's interest. Monday I went back into the village and stopped at the pub to enquire about Janie. I had this notion that she might be angry about my having ignored her Saturday, so I was hoping to make amends to her.

But she wasn't there. "I haven't seen her all afternoon, sir," the publican said. "I called her parents to see if perhaps she was feeling ill, but they said they hadn't seen her either. Still, a young girl—and at an age when they're sometimes wild—I shouldn't worry too much about her."

"What do you mean?" I asked.

The publican shrugged. "Sometimes, you know, they take it in mind to go off to the city. Like Swansea or Cardiff...."

"You mean you think she might have left with the band the other night? But that she'll be back in maybe a few days?"

The publican shrugged again. "I can't say I know about that, sir. She won't be the first girl to just disappear. To go off—who knows? Perhaps to Liverpool, if it was the musicians she followed."

I ordered a stout and sat at the bar, but the publican had no more to tell me. I took his advice, though, and didn't worry. I knew what he meant—at the college I went to, there were certainly young birds enough who weren't really students, but just hung around. Girls—and blokes, too—who'd left their homes, but really had no place else to go to.

Still, it *was* a bother. I am a young man and even a few days without a woman was, for me, annoying. But then when I went to find one of the others that I had courted— courted and coupled with—to my chagrin she was missing as well.

But a third, well, she was still present and ready, and so, by the week's end, I had all but forgotten Janie. Or, with the publican, at least resolved not to worry about her.

But then, the next Monday, I'd gone to the market to fetch a few things and, as I was driving back to the manor, who should I see in the road but Sylvia?

"Hullo!" I shouted. I stopped the car.

"Hello," she called back—"your grace," she added, with a smile. She was dressed the same as she had been that Saturday: black, scale-covered minidress—in the sunlight, I saw the material looked like vinyl—with boots to mid-thigh, thick red waist-cinch the color of dark flame, hair unbound and as black as a raven's wing.

"Want a ride?" I asked. After she'd gotten in, I asked her if the band had come back to town, but she shook her head.

"No," she said. "Actually, I've taken a house here. Or at least near here, in Parc, across the water."

"Ah," I said. "But then you didn't walk here. I mean, Bala Lake is narrow enough,

50 • THE BALA WORM

but it's nearly twelve kilometers long...."

She laughed. "Oh, no. I've hired a motorboat for the lake, and then it's only a short hike up on the other side. It's close enough to still be a part of your late ancestor's domain, I'd imagine. I mean the first Earl—you know, the one who slew the Worm?"

"I beg your pardon?"

"The Bala Worm. Don't you know? The local dragon. That's how he got his land and his title...."

I started to laugh. "Look," I said, "let me invite you to *my* house for dinner. It's on the lake, so we can bring your boat right up to it. Then you can tell me more about the first Earl of Llangower. I mean, I know there is a sort of family legend, but how do *you* know so much about it?"

She started to laugh too, a silvery laugh like bells in the dawn wind that blows up the lake through the Cambrian Mountains. "Actually," she finally said, "I'm a sort of a student."

I DID NOT GET HER to bed that night, although it wasn't for want of trying. We left on good terms and, a few nights later, she came down again from her mountain fastness to join me for dinner, though at the pub this time.

"Say," she asked, when we'd finished eating and were sipping the wine I'd bought us, "where's that blonde waitress? You know, the plump one you waved to that night with the band, just before you approached me to dance?"

"You mean Janie?" I asked. I turned red then. I knew what she thought. "She, uh, kind of disappeared," I finally said. "I mean, I came in the pub the next Monday, after I'd met you, and she wasn't working. Then the publican told me something about how she'd gone with the band to Liverpool or somewhere."

Sylvia's eyes held mine. "Was he sure about that?" she asked. "I mean about Liverpool. Did she write her folks after she got there?"

"I don't think he said she did," I answered. "But I can ask him." A few minutes later, after I'd ordered us more wine as well, I told her the publican said she had not written. And that another village girl had disappeared too, just this past weekend, making it three in all.

I thought about this third disappearance. Her name had been Meg, a freckle-faced brunette with deep blue eyes, though not so spellbinding as Sylvia's eyes were. I thought I had satisfied her well enough that she might stay, but then Sylvia's voice broke in on my thoughts.

"Bram," she said. "These were all young girls? Maybe my age. Or the age of your waitress?"

I blushed again. "Uh, yes," I answered.

She looked in my eyes again. "Bram," she said, "remember what we were talking about the other day, about the first Earl and the Bala Worm? Dragons are long-lived—five hundred, six hundred years, more than that sometimes—and it's well known that, as they become old, they fly down from their caves in the mountains and prey on young people."

"Now wait a minute," I protested. "You mean you're saying these girls might have been eaten by a *dragon*? And it's connected with that story about my ancestor? I don't believe you—and anyway, don't dragons only eat virgins? I know for a fact that...."

My voice trailed off as Sylvia glared at me. "Oh?" she said. She stared at me that way for several seconds, as if to demand of me through her silence how I was so certain about who were virgins and who might not have been. Then she said, "You know, I'm a virgin."

This time *I* said "Oh! Uh, no, I didn't know. But"—I thought fast, to find some way I might take advantage—"but if, I mean, you think you're in danger...."

She laughed. "More from you, maybe, than from the Bala Worm. Still—don't you see?—if the dragon your ancestor slew was an old one, a fully mature male, and if it had time to have had issue before it was killed...."

BLACK INFINITY • 51

I nodded, playing along for the moment. "Then what you're saying is that the timing would be right for this dragon's son to be getting an appetite?" Somehow I thought then about my own issue—or lack of any, unlike with my ancestors, what with even village girls these days knowing all about how to prevent such things. Then about Sylvia. How I should settle down some day and start having my own sons, to carry the line on. But then, I couldn't help it, I added with a leer, "I mean, for the birdies—even if not virgins."

"Look, this is serious," Sylvia answered. "They will eat ordinary people, of either sex, though they *do* have a special thing about virgins. I don't know why—maybe it has to do with the smell of man. Or trust or something. But what's important is that people won't stop disappearing until it's been satisfied."

She paused a moment to sip her wine, then caught my eye again as she added, "Of course, there's also the gold to consider."

"*Gold?*" I spluttered. I'd just taken a drink of my wine too. I may as well confess it now— she was speaking my language. While I did have a modest income, my success with the women often required my buying them trinkets. And even village girls these days seemed to have a certain sophistication.

"Yes," she said. "Don't you know the ballad they wrote about your ancestor? I've only seen parts of it in translation, but it makes clear that the dragon he slew had a hoard of gold somewhere in the mountains. At least *he* believed that. He managed to get some too, some that had stuck to the dragon's body, although he died before he was able to find its lair. He was wounded, you see, in the course of combat...."

"But still," I said, "there *aren't* any dragons. They're mythical creatures. That is, there may be some hidden treasure up in the mountains. Perhaps my ancestor's fight was with robbers—I understand there were quite a few back then, that preyed on travelers—and maybe it was *their* gold he got some of. Maybe later someone exaggerated the story...."

"Maybe," she said. "Look, I want you to come to my house tonight." She suddenly laughed, as if she had virtually read my thoughts. "No, not for *that*, Bram. As far as that goes, I do have a guest room for overnight visitors. But, as I told you before when you asked how I knew about your family, I am a student. A student of dragons."

She finished her wine, then started to get up.

"Bram," she said, "I have some things there that I think I should show you."

"SO THERE IT IS," she said, after we had arrived at her home and she'd shown me into her library. All around us were shelves of books, some musty with age, and boxes and cases of rolled up maps and even manuscripts— God knew how old *they* were. In the center was a long table, piled by now with books and papers. And the one big map of Wales and England.

"You see"—she pointed—"in County Clwyd, this was where the Denbigh Worm was finally destroyed. Some say its bones are still in the church crypt there. And here"—her finger moved east, to Anglesey—"peasants are said to have managed to trick the Worm of Penmynydd into fighting its own reflection. Dragons aren't very smart, or so they say. And then here"—she moved south now, into County Powys—"the Llandeilo-graban Worm lay waste the length of the River Wye, while here"—her finger moved back north, in almost a straight line back toward Denbigh, except that it stopped scarcely twenty-five kilometers southeast of where we now sat—"the Llanrhaidr-ym-Mochnant Worm was sighted on many occasions and some say wounded, again through trickery. Or so the tales go."

"But what is your point?" I asked. "I mean, do you think these might have all been the same dragon? That is, if there *were* dragons."

"Bram," she laughed, "you're so bullheaded. My point is this. With so many reports, whether some were of the same dragon or they were all different ones, it stands to

52 • THE BALA WORM

reason there's *some* truth behind them. And that's just here in Wales." She leaned over the map again and this time she pointed east, across the border. "Here, for instance, still not that far away, were the Bromfield Worm and the Brinsop Worm, the latter one, incidentally, said to have been destroyed by none other than the famous Saint George. And here"—she pointed south, and then southeast—"at Mordiford there were several dragons, and at Deerhurst and Chipping Norton, and here, the Uffington Worm, another of Saint George's victims. I could go on. In Cornwall, for instance...."

"Okay," I said. "I'll go along that far. At least a lot of people at one time *claimed* they saw dragons. And maybe killed them—we may as well add the Bala Worm and my own ancestor. Yet these things all happened in the Middle Ages, and here it's already the twenty-first century. And if they're as big as the stories say, and on top of that they fly around breathing fire and killing people, how come there haven't been any noticed in the time since then?"

"First of all," she said, "they usually stay in their caves in daytime." She'd gotten up and was fumbling with a vellum manuscript, which she now brought, still rolled up, to our table. "And when they do come out at night, since people nowadays don't believe in them, if they see them they usually find other explanations. The fiery breath is a meteor, for instance. Or maybe the whole thing's a UFO. But also, remember, dragons only achieve their full growth in their final years. At birth they're worm-like and very tiny—almost too small to see. Then, as they grow, they shed their skins like snakes, taking different forms with each moulting...."

"Now wait a minute. You mean they disguise themselves? That they don't even look like real dragons until they're almost ready to die?"

"Yes," she said. "At one point, for instance, they almost look human. One of the older legends in England, the Laidly Worm of Spindleston Heugh, even describes a person being turned into a dragon, although the story claims it was by sorcery. And other stories say dragons will sometimes take human wives." She saw the look on my face, I think, because she laughed then. "Of course, fact *does* sometimes get mixed up with fancy."

"I dare say," I said. "But then, how do you know? I mean, how do you separate what you call 'facts' out?"

She smiled. "By comparing common elements in all the legends. You toss out the spurious. As for young dragons appearing human, there is other evidence. In the poem *Beowulf* for example, the monsters there are also described as being human-like, walking on two legs, although at the end of the epic, when Beowulf—or perhaps a descendant—slays one of the old ones for its treasure hoard, it's perfectly clear that what he fights then is a full grown bull dragon."

She paused and looked at me, her hands still on the rolled up parchment. "Now hear me out, Bram," she said. "Most of these stages of growth take decades—sometimes centuries—and during much of the time they stay hidden. A sort of a hibernation, you might say. Yet, when they are active, they have been spotted, although, again, people have tried to find other explanations. Their next transformation, when they first grow wings, may well have given rise to the vampire legends, for instance. Such as the one your own namesake, Bram Stoker, wrote only at the end of the nineteenth century. And here's what's important. Don't you see how these things only come at certain times? All the dragon legends in England, taking place in the Middle Ages, probably within a hundred years or so of each other—unless, like *Beowulf*, what's being recalled took place as long ago before then as the Middle Ages were before our time. Then vampires, practically unknown in literature up until then, suddenly begin to crop up in the 1800s, so fully described you'd almost think Stoker had actually seen one...."

BLACK INFINITY • 53

"Then you think he, and others around his time, really did see one?" I had to admit, she *sounded* convincing, but what she was saying....

"Possibly, yes," she said. "Or they heard stories—again there's a lot of fancy mixed in. About digging up graves, for instance, when even young dragons actually nest in caves, although perhaps sometimes old mausoleums or other manmade cave-like structures might have been meant. In any event, once it's able to fly, there's not that much left to its evolution. Filled with blood—for dragons that's like concentrated food—a dragon's next step is to find a place where it can be sure it won't be disturbed, like up in the mountains. There it will sleep for maybe nearly another century, growing slowly, painfully almost, into its final stage. That's when it mates, Bram. When it starts the cycle over, craving human flesh to maintain its enormous energy. That's where it is now."

"The Bala Worm," I said. "The *new* Bala Worm. You mean it's full grown. Or actually very old, since that's the last stage of its development. All from a—what?—an almost microscopic egg that was laid somewhere just before my ancestor supposedly killed the first one?"

She nodded. "Yes." Then she started to unroll the parchment she'd brought to the table. "This is rather rare," she said. "It's on loan, actually, from the collection at Cymmer Abbey, down near Barmouth. The monks there believe in dragons—in fact they believe that some of the treasure the first Worm hoarded, that which your ancestor spent what was left of his life trying to find, was originally theirs. I promised them that when we kill the new dragon...."

"Hold it!" I said. "What do you mean, when *we* kill it? I...."

"Look," she said. The parchment was flat now, gnawed with holes where mice apparently had gotten to it at one time or another, but there was enough left for me to tell that it was the ballad about the first Earl. A "first

edition," as one might call it.

"It's in Welsh," I said. That was the first thing that struck me about it. But then I started to look at the picture that illuminated the top of the scroll—a dragon coiling up from the margin, half coiled around a man in armor, and, so faded as to be almost forgotten, next to a rock to the left of the dragon....

"The Old Tongue, yes," she said. "Medieval Welsh. Can you read it?"

"A little," I said. My grandmother had insisted, when I was small, that I learn it. "But who's the lady?" I asked, pointing toward the faded figure.

Sylvia giggled. "That's the virgin. Your ancestor wasn't all that noble. He used her as bait. But the thing is, *he* was able to kill it—you see his sword there, sticking into its belly? That's the one place the scales are soft enough to stab through."

I nodded. "Sure. Like I'd be fool enough to face something as big as that thing. I...."

Sylvia suddenly kissed me again. Quickly. Like she had done at the public house, when we had first met.

"Bram," she said. "About the virgin. I'd help you, you know. And, traditionally, there are rewards for dragon slayers beyond just getting to find its treasure."

I must have sighed then. "Sure," I said. "But Sylvia, don't you understand? Despite all your theories. Despite the monks, even, at Cymmer Abbey. The fact remains, there *aren't* any dragons."

"Then look there," she said. "Do you realize it's almost morning?"

I looked at my watch, then out the window where she was pointing. Below us, through the trees, was the lake. The sun was just starting to rise on the other side.

"Look," she whispered. "Above the sun."

Then I saw it. A sudden redness, far in the distance. The color of flame.

"Keep looking," she said. "They move rather quickly."

I saw it again. A definite flame. Much nearer this time. And then a shape, as if it were descending to catch an updraft from the lake, a form of a bat with a sinuous neck, a tail trailing behind it. Flying right toward us.

"Look in its talons," Sylvia whispered. I tried to, but suddenly it was right over us, making the roof shake with the wind it stirred in its passage. I ran out the library, into the hallway, trying to find a room with a window on the other side of the house that I might look out of. But when I had found one, the—the *thing*—was gone.

I went back to where Sylvia was waiting for me, the manuscript with its illustration still flat on the table.

"People will say it's just wind," she said. "Some kind of storm, maybe, those that were even up to see it. Some kind of freak lightning."

"It wasn't." I said.

"No, it wasn't," she echoed. "And, when you get back to Llangower this morning, I think you'll find that yet another young girl will be missing."

I WAS NO HERO. Not then at least. And for killing a dragon, I'd never even been able to have much luck shooting a gun, not and hit anything I tried to aim at. I had fenced in college, but somehow an epee—even if, theoretically, its blade would be thin enough to penetrate a dragon's armor—seemed so inadequate as to be silly. And armor itself, well, even though that seemed to be the traditional costume one wore for such ventures, this was, after all, the beginning of the twenty-first century.

Yet, as Sylvia had predicted, another village girl was missing—this time for all I knew one who might actually have been a virgin, although I'll admit I had had my eye on her. And somehow, hero or not, I found myself being drawn back to Sylvia's library.

Something had clicked in my mind that morning. Some kind of pattern. And something about the Earl's ballad too. The illustration.

I brought a Welsh dictionary with me, to help with obscure terms, and started translating it line by line. Although great parts of the poem were missing, it began to become apparent that some kind of trick was involved in his victory. The problem was what, though. And where he had fought it—the illustration suggested he'd found the dragon's cave and attacked it as soon as it came outside, unable to fly with its wings still folded. But, as the text pointed out, he had been wounded and had to go home because he'd lost too much blood, and, once recovered, when he'd tried to find the cave again he couldn't.

But, on that second score, we at least had maps. And I had an idea. I looked, again and again, at the topographical chart where Sylvia had marked the locations of the medieval legends. With her permission, I took a pencil, connecting the dots with a network of lines.

"What are you doing?" Sylvia asked.

"Eliminating the spurious," I said. "Like you say you do with the legends themselves. Look here, for instance." I pointed to a line I'd just highlighted. "This was a dragon you say had been killed, but suppose the legends exaggerated and it had only been chased away. It went to its lair, one might presume, then reappeared here."

I drew another line. "Also here and here. Let's suppose these were all the same dragon. While this one wasn't"—I scratched an earlier line I'd drawn out—"but rather was connected with these sightings over in England."

"So?" Sylvia asked.

"So, now I draw perpendiculars to them. Here. And here." The new lines began to converge over Bala Lake—no, not quite over. Somewhere over the Cambrian Mountains that rose to the west beyond Sylvia's cottage. Yet not converge perfectly. Not to a single point.

Shrugging, I put my pencil down.

"So nothing," I sighed. "I'd hoped that, maybe, I could pinpoint the Bala Worm's lair. But all we know thus far is it's in the

BLACK INFINITY • 55

mountains. And that much we could have guessed anyway, when it flew over your house that morning—"

"Bram, what is it?"

I'd started to laugh.

"I've forgotten the obvious," I finally gasped. "Our own sighting." I leaned to the map and drew another line, this time between Llangower and Parc, where Sylvia's house was, extending it farther on into the mountains. I marked a series of dots on this new line where it crossed the others I'd already drawn. But still no convergence.

I put my pencil down again. I may as well say it here and now, that while still another girl had disappeared from the village—so much for the notion that even a possible virgin might have appeased the thing's hunger—that wasn't why I'd hoped to pinpoint the cave's location. Rather, my ancestor *had* found it too, even if he had lost it afterwards, and, from what I could translate of the ballad, the treasure he'd seen in it hadn't just been a few trinkets of gold, but rather a fortune. And I needed money. Not just needed it, I *desired* money—even more than I desired Sylvia.

Sylvia, whose perfume filled my nostrils as she leaned closer to look at the lines I'd drawn.

"Wasn't the sun over here?" she asked. She picked up the pencil.

"What?" I asked.

"We saw the dragon above the sun. Directly above it." She marked a dot to the right of Llangower, then another in Bala Lake the same distance right of the line I'd drawn. "I'd say about here."

"Then it flew in a curve?" I asked.

"Maybe," she said. She drew a shallow arc. "Perhaps the wind…."

Of course! I thought. The wind in the valley, up from the coast at Barmouth Bay, just as the sun starts to heat the mountain air. Something as big as what we'd seen couldn't avoid being blown off course. Couldn't avoid having to make corrections.

I took the pencil, then asked for a ruler and a calculator. When Sylvia brought them,

I started changing my other lines, some to a greater extent, some a lesser. I thought about curves. Of course it was still guesswork, but, as I continued, the new lines I drew began coming together.

I thought about curves. Lines that bent instead of straight ones.

"*Arenig Fawr!*" Sylvia suddenly whispered.

"What?" I asked. My mind was wandering—the illustration on the manuscript, still unrolled at the end of the table. I knew about fencing.

"The cave," she said. "If you've drawn these lines correctly, it's on the south slope of Arenig Fawr. You've seen the mountain."

A swordsman's arm sticks straight out when he's attacking—that's what gives it leverage—yet the first Earl's was bent in at his side. And the spikes on his armor—the strangely extended shoulder protectors, the points at his elbows. The dragon, too close to breathe fire at the end without burning itself too. Instead attempting to coil around him, like some great constrictor.

"Bram, are you listening?" Suddenly Sylvia kissed me, hard. "I know where the cave is—at least I think I do. It's in a valley, a sort of hollow, only one or two kilometers away. I've *been* there, Bram. But the cave must be hidden, probably covered by shrubs or bushes. That's why the first Earl couldn't find it again when he looked for it—they'd had a chance to grow back to conceal it."

I heard her. I kissed her back. But I was thinking—my ancestor never attacked the dragon, not with his arm bent, at least not directly. The ballad suggested that there'd been a trick.

And I knew what that trick was.

THE NEXT DAY I called a firm in Glasgow that made reproduction armor. I gave them special specifications, including that it be made of the lightest weight, yet strongest metal, and that it and its accompanying shield be lined with asbestos—my ancestor's wounds had included burns, from what I'd been able to read of the ballad. I borrowed heavily against my income—I had to argue with London about that—and further ordered knives and a sword of the sharpest steel, arranging to have it all completed within the week and air-shipped to a field at Barmouth, and thence by truck up the valley to Parc and Sylvia's cottage.

We made that our base of operations. I slept in the guest room and fitted it up as a sort of gym, bringing in weights and other equipment to build my stamina. Once the fight started, well, that would be something else, but simply getting to where we expected to find the cave, even though not very far on the map, would take enough out of me.

And we went on field trips, while we awaited the armor's arrival. To Cymmer Abbey and Castle Carn Dochan, the latter on foot since it was a local ruin and one that legend said had at one time been damaged by dragons.

We read, ate, and slept dragons. Talked only of dragons. We'd both agreed that calling in the civic authorities would do no good. Who would believe us? Even the parents of the missing girls, two more of whom disappeared within that long week, only clucked and blamed the rock bands that still came through every fortnight or so.

Which left it up to us, I in my armor, she as my helper. The Earl and his squire, the former of whom, to be sure, was aware that if we were successful his desire for gold—for other things gold can buy—would be quite sated.

For other things also. I may as well say it. I'd come to love Sylvia, love the way she moved. Love the way she called my name when the crate from Glasgow finally arrived. How she helped me unpack it.

How, in the lamplight of her library, she helped me lay the full plate armor out on the floor, the spikes and blades of its metal shell gleaming. The knife blades I'd had them weld, points out, onto it, porcupine-like to improve on my ancestor's trickery.

I tried it on right then, that evening. I exercised in it, learning its feel. The next day I rested, conserving my strength, and then, the next morning, we set off into the Cambrian Mountains, to Arenig Fawr, to find the Worm's lair.

The going was rough, as you might well imagine. There was no safe way to carry the armor, so I had to wear it, though Sylvia helped with my shield and sword, my gauntlets and helmet. We rested frequently, I often making sketches of the terrain around us, using a notebook and pencils I'd packed in a sort of *sporran* looped to my waist, so, unlike the first Earl, we'd have no trouble retracing our journey should need arise. While Sylvia, more lightly dressed in a hiking skirt and blouse, made tea on a small stove that she had insisted she take along with us, despite the burdens she already carried.

"We must be civilized, Bram," she had said. I loved her for that. I lusted for her—though not at the moment. But after, I thought, as I'd watch her spring up, clean the stove and repack it, take up the other equipment as handily as any squire and lead on, ever upward.

But after. The dragon killed, then the reward. The thought kept me going until mid-afternoon when, having turned at a standing rock, we passed through a small grove of overgrown bushes and into a bare rock, bowl-like depression.

Sylvia stopped short. She looked about her—another standing rock, a slope upward. Another rock, behind it a shadow.

"Bram," she whispered. She waited until I had caught up to her. "Bram," she said again, still in a low voice. "I think we've found it."

I nodded. I wiped the sweat from my face. I moved to the side to look into the shadow, saw how it opened up into a kind of cave.

"Bram, are you frightened?"

I shook my head. No. Truth to tell, I was too tired by then to be frightened. But I was rewarded—a smile and a kiss.

"Very well, then, Bram," she said. "Are you ready? You'll stand where you are now, where it can see you when it emerges. While I take the standing stone"—she smiled again—"the virgin's part, you know. Where I can cower and hide behind it."

I nodded. "Yes," I said. I held my hands out while she pushed on my gauntlets, then helped me strap the shield on my left arm. She handed my sword to me, then kissed me once more.

"It will be sleeping," she said. "I didn't want to tell you, but last night, while you were asleep too, it took another victim. I heard from the village. At least, though, it won't be hungry when it wakes."

I nodded again, then held my head straight while she placed on my helmet, strapping it down to the hooks on my armor. How had she known? I thought. We'd both been up at dawn. But then I shrugged, as best I could in the armor's stiffness—of course, if she'd been up slightly before me, she might have *seen* its flight back from the village.

"I'll wake it," she whispered. I watched as she took up her post by the standing stone, ready to duck in an instant behind it.

"Okay," I whispered.

I pulled down my visor.

And then I heard her cry. Shrill. Ululating. I heard an answering call from inside the cave.

The cry of dragons.

Sylvia was a student of dragons—of course, I realized. She knew how to call them. I watched, as best I could, through the eye slits of my helmet while, for a long moment, nothing happened.

Then, all of a sudden, the cave's inside was lighted with flame. And I saw the treasure! Heaps and heaps of gold. Glinting with its own fire. Jewels and silver.

Then darkness again, for a moment only.

And then it appeared—head first, then the neck—faster than I had thought something so big *could* move. Snake-like it rushed at me, wings still folded. I thrust at it—once only. Swinging my sword at it. All I had time for.

Then I remembered—I needn't attack it. I

put my shield up instead, warding its flame off, and let it rush to me.

That was the plan. To let it attack me from the start, as the earlier Worm had attacked my ancestor, finally impaling itself on the sword he had purposely braced against his side. Except I had sword points studded all over me.

I let it hit me, holding my ground. Staggering slightly as, too close to use its flame anymore, it arched up its body and whipped it around me.

I felt it coil—harder. Trying to crush me. Hearing the creak as my armor withstood its force. Sank to my knees beneath its weight, but my armor still holding.

And then I heard the Bala Worm's shriek as the knife blades sank into its sides and its belly. Louder, deeper, each time it coiled tighter.

And now I shrieked too, but my whoops were of triumph as the great creature's convulsions slowed. As the Bala Worm slumped down, pulling me with it, onto my own side. That didn't matter.

The Worm was dying.

"Sylvia!" I shouted. Where had she gone to? I struggled to free my arm from the dragon's coils and pushed up my visor.

My other arm still trapped, my legs pinned beneath me, my armor nailed firmly—with me still inside it—within its great bulk, but that didn't matter.

And then I saw Sylvia mounting the back of the still twitching dragon, hiking her skirt up above her knees. I couldn't see everything that she was doing, except that her legs became stained with its blood. I saw her climb down its other side, as if dancing, sliding a circle around me. Saw her sit, finally, in front of the dragon and take its huge head into her lap.

She stroked the head silently for a moment. I saw she was crying.

Then she looked up at me.

"Their breath impregnates us," she said. "I don't know how. But in that sense, I lied

58 • THE BALA WORM

to you—about being a virgin. I just haven't coupled with other humans. In return, though, we receive long life and, after we've laid our eggs successfully, we, too, undergo transformations."

She stood up then, laying the Bala Worm's head gently on the ground. "It's their life cycle. I don't understand it." She started slowly to take off her clothing. "For its completion, we must lay our eggs in our lovers' corpses. To nourish the grubs, you see. So they'll grow quickly."

She laughed then. I shivered. I couldn't help it. "Sylvia," I shouted. "I can't move! Don't you see? I don't care about you and the dragon. Just help me get the weight of it off me so I at least can get out of this armor!"

She had her blouse off now and, as she turned to lay it over the Bala Worm's lifeless head, I caught a glimpse of something...not human.

"You don't understand yet, do you Bram?" she said, reaching down now to loosen her skirt. "Why the old dragons get hungry for human flesh—you do deserve to know. Young women, tender, virgins or not, provide the best nourishment for the young ones after their father's own flesh has absorbed it. But any human flesh will do, especially if it's preserved, undigested." She paused and smiled, then bent to untie her shoes. "Perhaps, especially, if it's cased in metal armor to hold it safely, like meat in a can, until his ... *my* children are ready to eat it."

That's when I screamed. Not at what she said, but, when she turned and tossed her hair and I saw, beneath it, the nubs of wings growing. I saw them sprout quickly, spread out before my eyes, black and bat-like, as black and scale-shimmering as the dress she'd worn when I first met her.

This—that I thought I'd loved?

Lusted for, anyway. That and the dragon's gold.

"Sylvia," I said. I suddenly realized that, lust or no lust, I *had* been a hero. "The dragons' life cycle. If your... if *its* grubs are just hatching out now, at least it will be another five hundred years before they've reached their full growth—before they've grown up enough to start killing people again. So at least it's over. At least for now."

She laughed again, louder. An inhuman sound. She turned to the wind, naked, letting her wings billow.

"Yes, Bram," she said. "*My* grubs will take that long. As for the others...."

"The others?" I asked.

"Yes," she said. "I'm afraid I lied a second time when I let you believe the medieval dragon legends might all have been reports of the same Worm. As if they'd all come from a single sire whose mate laid just one egg. Actually, though, we lay many more than one."

She caught the wind's current then, launching herself in it, laughing and shouting back down to where I lay trapped.

"And I do have sisters."

"The Bala Worm" first appeared in the 2008 anthology Black Dragon, White Dragon, *edited by Robert J Santa.*

James Dorr is a Bloomington, Indiana-based short story writer and poet specializing in dark fantasy and horror with forays into mystery and science fiction. His work includes more than five hundred individual publications in journals and anthologies, along with three collections (one of these, The Tears of Isis, *a 2013 Stoker Award® nominee), one "traditionally thin" poetry volume, and a mosaic novel from Elder Signs Press,* Tombs: A Chronicle of Latter-Day Times of Earth. *Dorr has been a technical writer, an editor on a regional magazine, a full time non-fiction freelancer, and a semi-professional musician. He currently harbors a Goth cat named Triana, and counts among his major influences Ray Bradbury, Edgar Allan Poe, Allen Ginsberg, and Bertolt Brecht.*

COMPLETE YOUR COLLECTION!

THE SPECTRE SPIDERS
By W. J. WINTLE

THE FOG HUNG THICKLY OVER LONDON ONE MORNING IN LATE AUTUMN. It was not the dense compound of smoke and moisture, pea-souplike in color and pungent to eyes and nose, that is known as a "London peculiar"; but a fairly clean and white mist that arose from the river and lay about the streets and squares in great wisps and wreaths and banks.

The passing crowd shivered and thought of approaching winter; while a few optimistic souls looked upward to the invisible sky and predicted a warm day when the sun had grown in strength. A little child remarked to a companion that it smelled like washing day, and the comparison was not without its point. It was as if the motor machinery of the metropolis had blown off steam in preparation for a fresh start.

People passed one another in the mist like sheeted ghosts and did not speak. Friend failed to recognize friend; or, if he did, he took for granted that the other did not. Apart from the steady rumble of the traffic and the long deep note that the great city gives forth to hearing ears all the day long, the world seemed strangely silent and unfriendly.

Certainly this applied with truth to one member of the passing crowd whom business brought abroad that misty morning when home and the fireside gained an added attraction. Ephraim Goldstein was silent by nature and unfriendly by profession. For him language was an ingenious device for the concealment of thought; and when there was no special reason for such concealment, why should he trouble to speak?

It was not as if people were over desirous to hear him speak. He was naturally unattractive; and where nature had failed to complete her task, Ephraim had brought it to perfection. A habit of scowling had effectually removed any trace of amiability that might have survived the handicap of evil eyes and unpleasing features. When strangers saw Ephraim for the first time, they looked quickly around for a pleasant face to act by way of antidote.

We have said that he was unfriendly by

BLACK INFINITY • 61

profession. But the unwary and innocent would never have suspected this from his professional announcements in the personal column of the morning papers. The gentleman of fortune who was wishful, without security or inquiry, to advance goodly sums of money to his less fortunate fellow creatures on nominal terms and in the most delicate manner possible, was surely giving the best of all proofs of a soul entirely immersed in the milk of human kindness.

Yet those who had done business with Ephraim spoke of him in terms not usual in the drawing room: men of affairs who knew the world of finance called him a blood-sucking spider, and Scotland Yard had him noted down as emphatically a wrong 'un. Ephraim was not popular with those who knew him. He had in fact only one point of character that could be commended. He had never changed his name to Edward Gordon or even to Edwin Goldsmith: he was born Ephraim Goldstein—and Ephraim Goldstein he was content to remain to the end. A rose by any other name smells just as sweet—but people did not express it quite like that when Ephraim was under discussion.

He had not always been a gentleman of fortune, nor had he always been wishful to share his fortune with others. People with inconveniently long memories recalled a youth of like name who got into trouble at Whitechapel for selling Kosher fowls judiciously weighted with sand, and there was also a story about a young man who manipulated three thimbles and a pea on Epsom Downs.

But why drag in these scandals of the past? In the case of any man it is unfair to thus search the record of his youth for evidence against him; and in the case of Ephraim it was quite unnecessary. He was a perennial plant: however lurid the past, he blossomed forth afresh every year in renewed vigor and in equally glowing colors.

How fortune had come to him seemed to be known by no one save himself; but certainly it had come, for it is difficult to lend money if you do not possess it. And with its coming Ephraim had migrated from Whitechapel to Haggerston, then to Kilburn, and finally to Maida Vale, where he now had his abode. But it must not be supposed that he indulged in either ambition or luxury. He was content with very modest comfort, and lived a simple bachelor existence; but he found a detached villa with some garden behind it more convenient for his purposes than a house in a terrace with an inquisitive neighbor on either side. His visitors came on business and by no means for pleasure: and privacy was as congenial to them as it was to him.

The business that had brought him out on this foggy morning was of an unusual character in that it had nothing to do with money making. It in fact involved spending money to the extent of two guineas now, with a probability of further sums; and he did not at all relish it. Ephraim was on his way to Cavendish Square to consult a noted oculist.

For some weeks past, he had been troubled with a curious affliction of his sight. He was still on the sunny side of fifty, and hitherto he had been very sharp-sighted in more senses than one. But now something seemed to be going wrong. His vision was perfect during the day, and usually through the evening as well; but twice recently he had been bothered with a curious optical delusion. On each occasion he had been sitting quietly reading after dinner, when something had made him uneasy. It was the same sort of disquiet that he always felt if a cat came into the room. So strong had been this feeling that he had sprung out of his chair without quite knowing why he did it and each time had fancied that a number of shadows streamed forth from his chair and ran across the carpet to the walls, where they vanished. They were evidently nothing but shadows, for he could see the carpet through them; but they were fairly clear and distinct. They seemed to be about the size of a cricket ball. Though he attached no meaning to the coincidence, it was a little odd that on each occasion he had

62 • THE SPECTRE SPIDERS

been reluctantly compelled during the day to insist upon his pound of flesh from a client. And when Ephraim insisted, he did not stick at a trifle. But obviously this could have nothing to do with a defect of vision.

The great specialist made a thorough examination of Ephraim's eyes, but could find nothing wrong with them. So he explored further and investigated the state of his patient's nervous aid digestive systems; but found that these were perfectly sound.

Then he embarked upon more delicate matters, and sought to learn something of the habits of Ephraim. A bachelor in the forties may be addicted to the cup that cheers and occasionally inebriates as well; he may be fond of the pleasures of the table; he may be attracted by the excitement of gambling; in fact he may do a great many things that a man of his years should not do. The physician was a man of tact and diplomacy. He asked no injudicious questions; but he had the valuable gift of inducing conversation in others. Not for years had Ephraim talked so freely and frankly to any man. The result was that the doctor could find no reason for suggesting that the trouble was due to any kind of dietary or other indiscretion.

So he fell back on the last refuge of the baffled physician. "Rest, my dear Sir," he said; "that is the best prescription. I am happy to say that I find no serious lesion or even functional disturbance; but there is evidence of fatigue affecting the brain and the optic nerve. There is no reason to anticipate any further or more serious trouble; but a wise man always takes precautions. My advice is that you drop all business for a few weeks and spend the time in golf or other out-of-door amusement—say at Cromer or on the Surrey Downs. In that case you may be pretty confident that no further disturbance of this kind will occur."

Ephraim paid his two guineas with a rather wry face. He had the feeling that he was not getting much for his money; still it was reassuring to find that there was nothing the matter. Rest! Rubbish! He was not over-worked. Surrey Downs indeed! Hampstead Heath was just as good and a great deal cheaper: he might take a turn there on Sunday mornings. Golf? You would not catch him making a fool of himself in tramping after a ridiculous ball! So he simply went on much the same as before, and hoped that all would be well.

Yet, somehow, things did not seem to be quite right with him. Business was prosperous, if you can speak of business in connection with the pleasant work of sharing your fortune with the less fortunate—always on the most reasonable terms possible. Ephraim would have told you that he lost terribly through the dishonesty of people who died or went abroad or whose expectations did not turn out as well as they should; and yet, in some mysterious way, he had more money to lend than ever. But he was worried.

One evening, after an unusually profitable day, he was sitting in his garden, smoking a cigar that had been given him by a grateful client who was under the mistaken impression that Ephraim's five percent was to be reckoned per year, whereas it was really per week. It was a good cigar; and the smoker knew how to appreciate good tobacco. He was lying back in a hammock chair, and idly watching the rings of smoke as they rose on the quiet air and floated away.

Then he suddenly started and stared. The rings were behaving in a very odd fashion. They seemed to form themselves into globes of smoke; and from each of them protruded eight waving filaments that turned and bent like the legs of some uncanny creature, And it seemed as if these trailing limbs of smoke turned and reached toward him. It was curious and not altogether pleasant. But it was no case of an optical delusion. The evening light was good, and the thing was seen clearly enough. It must have been the result of some unusual state of the atmosphere at the time.

He was aroused by hearing conversation on the other side of the wall. The occupant of

BLACK INFINITY • 63

the next-door house was in his garden with a friend, and their talk was of matters horticultural. It did not interest Ephraim, who paid a jobbing gardener the smallest possible amount to keep the place tidy, and concerned himself no further about it. He did not want to hear of the respective virtues of different local seed vendors. But the talk was insistent, and he presently found himself listening against his will. They were talking about spiders, and his neighbor was saying that he had never known such a plague of them or such large-sized specimens. And he went on to say that they all seemed to come over the wall from Ephraim's side! The listener discovered that his cigar had gone out, and he went indoors in disgust.

It was only a few days later when the next thing happened. Ephraim had gone to bed rather earlier than usual, being somewhat tired, but was unable to sleep. For some hours he tossed about wearily and angrily—for he usually slept well—and then came a spell of disturbed and restless slumber. Dream after dream passed through his mind; and somehow they all seemed to have something to do with spiders. He thought that he fought his way through dense jungles of web; he walked on masses of soft and yielding bodies that crushed and squished beneath his tread; multitudinous hairy legs waved to and fro and clung to him; fanged jaws bit him with the sting of fiery fluids; and gleaming eyes were everywhere staring at him with a gaze of unutterable malignancy. He fell, and the webs wrapped him round in an embrace of death; great woolly creatures flung themselves upon him and suffocated him with their foul stink; unspeakable things had him in their ghastly grip; he was sinking in an ocean of unimaginable horror.

He awoke screaming, and sprang out of bed. Something caught him in the face and clung round his head. He groped for the switch and turned on the light. Then he tore off the bandage that blinded him, and found that it was a mass of silky threads like the web that a giant spider might have spun. And, as he got it clear of his eyes, he saw great shadows run up the walls and vanish. They had grown since he saw them first on the carpet; they were now the size of footballs.

Ephraim was appalled by the horror of it. Unrestful sleep and persistent nightmare were bad enough; but here was something worse. The silky wisps that still clung about his head were not such stuff as dreams are made of. He wondered if he was going mad. Was the whole thing a hallucination? Could he pull himself together and shake it off? He tried; but the bits of web that waved from his fingers and face were real enough. No dream spider could have spun them; mere imagination could not have created them. Moreover, he was not a man of imagination. Quite the opposite. He dealt in realities: real estate was the security he preferred.

A stiff glass of brandy and soda pulled him together. He was not addicted to stimulants— it did not pay in his profession—but this was a case that called for special measures. He shook off the obsession, and thought there might be something in the golf suggestion after all. And when a client called during the morning to negotiate a little loan, Ephraim drove a shrewd bargain that surprised even himself.

The next incident that caused considerable disquiet to the gentleman of fortune seems to have occurred about a month later. He was no lover of animals, but he tolerated the presence of a Scots terrier in the house. It occasionally happened that he had large sums of money on the premises—not often, but sometimes it could not be helped—and the alert little dog was a good protection against the intrusive burglar. So he treated the animal as a sort of confidential servant, and was, after his fashion, attached to it. If he did not exactly love it, he at any rate appreciated and valued it. He did not even grudge the veterinarian charges when it was ill.

At night the terrier had the run of the house, but usually slept on a mat outside

64 • THE SPECTRE SPIDERS

Ephraim's door. On this particular occasion Ephraim dreamed that he had fallen over the dog, and that it gave a loud yelp of pain. So vivid was the impression that it woke him, and the cry of the animal seemed to still linger on his ear. It was as if the terrier outside the door had really cried out. He listened, but all was quiet save for a curious clicking and sucking sound that he heard at intervals. It seemed to come from just outside the door; but that could not be, for the dog would have been roused and would have given the alarm if anything was wrong.

So he presently went to sleep again, and did not wake until his usual time for rising. As he dressed, it struck him as unusual that he heard nothing of the dog, which was accustomed to greet the first sounds of movement with a welcoming bark or two. When he opened his door, the terrier lay dead on the mat.

Ephraim was first shocked, then grieved, and next alarmed. He was shocked because it was simply natural to be shocked under the circumstances; he was grieved because it then dawned upon him that he was more fond of the animal than he could have believed possible; and he was alarmed because he knew that the mysterious death of a watch dog is often the preliminary to a burglary.

He hurried downstairs and made a hasty examination of the doors and windows, and particularly of a safe that was hidden in the wall behind what looked like a solid piece of furniture. But everything was in good order, and there was no sign of any attempt on the premises. Then he went upstairs to remove the body of the dog, wondering the while if it would be worth the expense to have a post-mortem. Ephraim disliked mysteries, especially when they happened in the house.

He picked up the dead terrier, and at once met with a bad shock. It was a mere featherweight, and collapsed in his hands! It was little more than a skeleton, rattling loose in a bag of skin. It had been simply sucked dry!

He dropped it in horror, and as he did so he found some silky threads clinging to his hands. And there were threads waving in the air, for one of them twined itself about his head and clung stickily to his face. And then something fell with a soft thud on the floor behind him, and he turned just in time to see a shadow dart to the wall and disappear. He had seen that shadow form before; but it somehow seemed to be less shadowy and more substantial now.

It seems to have been about this time that a rumor circulated in Maida Vale that a monkey had escaped from the Zoological Gardens in Regent's Park and had been seen climbing on Ephraim's house.

It was first seen early in the morning by a milkman, who mentioned it to a policeman, and soon afterward by a housemaid who was cleaning the steps of a house opposite. It was a rather dark and misty morning, which doubtless accounts for a certain vagueness in the descriptions of the animal. But, so far as they went, all the descriptions agreed.

The monkey was described as a very fat specimen, almost like a football in size and rotundity, with very long arms. It was covered with thick, glossy, black hair, and was seen to climb up the front of the house and enter by an open window. The milkman, who was fond of reading, said that he thought it was a spider monkey; but his only reason for this seems to have been some fancied resemblance to a very large spider.

Later in the morning, the policeman called on Ephraim to mention the matter, and to ask if the monkey was still there. His reception was not polite; and he retired in disorder. Then he rang up the Zoological Gardens, but was informed that no monkeys were missing. The incident was duly recorded at the police station, and there it ended, for no more was ever heard of it.

But another occurrence in the following week gave rise to much more talk, especially among the ladies of the neighborhood. The empty skin of a valuable Persian cat was found in the shrubbery of the house next to Ephraim's—empty, that is, except for the bones of the animal. The skin was quite fresh; as it well might be, for the cat had been seen alive the evening before. The mystery formed a nine days' wonder, and was never solved until an even more shocking mystery came to keep it company. The cat's skin had been sucked dry and the local theory was that a stoat or other beast of prey had escaped from the zoo and done the dire deed. But it was proved that no such escape had occurred, and there the matter had to stop.

Although it seems to have no significance, it may be well to place on record a trifling incident that happened a week or two later. A collector for some charitable institution called upon Ephraim under the mistaken impression that he was a person who wanted to get rid of his money. He was speedily undeceived, and was only in the house for a few minutes. But he told his wife afterward that Mr. Goldstein was evidently a great cat fancier, for he had noticed several fine black Persians curled up asleep in the house. But it was curious that they were all in the darkest and most obscure corners, where they could not be seen very clearly. He had made some passing reference to them to Mr. Goldstein, who did not seem to understand him. Indeed, he stared at him as if he thought him the worse for drink!

Another incident at this time was made the subject of remark among Ephraim's neighbors. For reasons best known to himself, he had long been in the habit of sleeping with a loaded revolver at his bedside; and one morning, about daybreak, the sound of a shot was heard. The police were quickly on the spot and insisted upon entering the house. Ephraim assured them that the weapon had been accidentally discharged through being dropped on the floor; and, after asking to see his gun license, the police departed.

But what had really happened was much more interesting. Ephraim had woke up without apparent cause, but with a vague sense of danger; and was just in time to see a round black body, covered with a dense coat of hair, climb up the foot of his bed and make its way cautiously toward his face. It was a gigantic spider; and its eight gleaming eyes blazed with lambent green light like a cluster of sinister opals.

He was paralyzed with horror; then, summoning all his force of will, he snatched up the revolver and fired. The flash and the noise of the report dazed him for a moment; and when he saw clearly again the spider was gone. He must have hit it, for he fired point blank; but it had left no sign. It was just as well, for otherwise his tale would not have passed muster with the police. But, later in the morning, he found a trail of silky threads running across the carpet from the bed to the wall.

But the end was now very near. Only a few days later, the police were again in the house. This time they had been called in by the gardener, who said that he could not make Mr. Goldstein hear when he knocked at his door, and that he thought he must be ill. The door was locked, and had to be forced.

What the police found had better not be described. At the funeral, the undertaker's men said that they had never carried a man who weighed so little for his size.

🕷 🕷 🕷

"The Spectre Spiders" first appeared in the author's 1921 collection Ghost Gleams.

British journalist, author, and naturalist William J. Wintle (1861–1934) had great and varied interests in zoology, history, and Christianity. He wrote for the Windsor Magazine, *the* Harmsworth Encyclopaedia, *and Britain's Sunday School Union. Wintle maintained an impressive seashell collection, hung out with Benedictine monks, was elected to the Conchological Society of Great Britain and Ireland, converted to Roman Catholicism, and wrote biographies of Florence Nightingale, Queen Victoria, and Christian writer, evangelist, and minister Charles Spurgeon, among others.*

Producer Howard Hawk's
The Thing from Another World
(RKO, 1951)

THE FAMOUS MONSTERS STORY

HOW A MOVIE MONSTER MAGAZINE BECAME A POP CULTURE PHENOMENON

By JOHN M. NAVROTH

IT'S HARD TO IMAGINE THAT THE WORLD'S FIRST MONSTER MOVIE NEWSSTAND PERIODICAL HAD ITS ROOTS IN A MEN'S MAGAZINE, BUT IT'S TRUE.

The unlikely partnership between a former appliance ad man and a literary agent formed the alchemy that turned pulp paper into monster gold. How was it that two people from opposite sides of the country with little in common except for their love of films and the fantastic managed to come up with an idea that has persisted in the fabric of popular culture to this day? The story of how it all happened is one of synchronicity, perseverance, and a generous amount of good old-fashioned luck.

James Warren Taubman was born on July 29, 1930, in Philadelphia. He grew up on the mean streets of South Philly, an area he said, "made the Dead End Kids look like the country club set." Although he lived in a household where both parents allowed him free rein over his interests, he nevertheless had to learn how to toughen up when he was outside, where bullies waited in the schoolyard or around the next corner just to beat up a weaker kid. He later said that it was this environment that prepared him for the cut-throat and competitive world of publishing.

James Warren's love affair with art and the printed page began early. His obsessive doodling and copying drawings from comic books and newspaper cartoons led to him contributing to school publications and printing his own newspaper when he was in middle school. He once quipped that he had "printer's ink in my blood... since I was eight years old. I was an editor at nine and a publisher at ten."

One of his early inspirations was Will Eisner's full-page Sunday comic, *The Spirit*. As a youngster, he not only read and collected comic books, but pored over just about any other magazine or printed material that he found interesting, including

James Warren (r) with AIP's James H. Nicholson.
Opposite: The original, full-frame photo of the Queens, NY Chapter of the Famous Monsters Club by Diane Arbus, 1962. It appeared in FM #28, May 1964 as a cropped image. In 2019, the photo sold at a Sotheby's auction for $50,000.

BLACK INFINITY • 69

model kit instructions! Unfortunately, in 1951 after receiving a medical discharge from the Army, he returned home to find that his mother had thrown out every box that contained his beloved collection! (Sound familiar?)

Now a young man, he was adrift and full of fanciful ideas, but had no particular career in mind. He once explained, "I had not yet found a meaningful outlet for my dubious skills." Having no desire to follow in his father's footsteps as a retail clothing salesman, he instead took advice from his uncle, who owned an advertising agency, and, after dropping the name Taubman, started up his own. During this period, he attended the Philadelphia Museum School of Art, as well as the Charles Morris School of Advertising. He eventually gave up on self-employment and took a job at Caloric, an appliance manufacturer, where he wrote the company's ad materials and newsletter.

In 1954, he discovered a new magazine. It was sophisticated, provocative, and contained top-notch fiction. Oh, and it had photos of beautiful girls in it, too. It was called *Playboy*. He also noticed that scads of imitators were also trying out their own men's magazines. Warren decided to give it a shot, too.

He published the first issue of *After Hours* in 1957. It was considerably less stylish in appearance than its model, but Warren nevertheless got his feet wet in the publishing business. "I worked at it 24 hours a day, seven days a week, and I got my first experience with national magazine distributors and retailers, and with large magazine printing plants. It lasted four issues. It was awful."

For his trouble, Warren was indicted on pornography charges by a Philadelphia D.A. who was looking to win an election. The charge was regarding the centerfold, a photo of the nude and bare-breasted pin-up queen,

Bettie Page. The D.A. was elected. The judge looked at the magazine. The charges were dropped. Three more issues of *After Hours* were published (all in 1957) before it folded.

Not fazed, Warren explained: "I learned a lot. I learned the hard way about Teamsters, truckers, loading docks, slowdowns at printing plants, and bankers who welsh on you. But with the fourth issue, something good happened: A guy named Forrey (*sic*) Ackerman came into my life. Forrey was a Hollywood literary agent. Forrey, who was reading every men's magazine in existence as part of his agency work, saw a new one called *After Hours* and he contacted me through the mail. He wrote that he had some stories to offer me for my magazine. I liked what he submitted and ran it. We were featuring 'Girls of Amsterdam,' 'Girls of Las Vegas,' 'Girls of Singapore,' etc., and he came up with the idea, 'Girls from Science-Fiction Movies.' He sent 8"x10" stills with it and wrote it himself. I saw his writing and thought it had an interesting, offbeat style. The more I read it, the better it became, because nobody can write fantasy movie features like Forrey Ackerman. Nobody. He is the best specialty writer on the face of the Earth, bar none—a writer who is so head and shoulders above all other writers for our genre, that nobody will compare with him 100 years from now."

Forrest James Ackerman (November 24, 1916–December 4, 2008) was born in Los Angeles and was thirteen years Warren's senior. Raised on a steady diet of movies and pulp magazines, he became well-known in the science-fiction community and corresponded with a great number of fellow fans and professionals. He became a literary agent to nearly 200 writers, including Ray Bradbury, Isaac Asimov, and L. Ron Hubbard. Over time, he amassed a huge collection of movie stills, posters and props, which would, of course, come in handy later.

The fourth issue of *After Hours* is where the seeds of a future monster magazine were sown. Ackerman's "Confessions of a Science-Fiction Addict," and "Screamoscope Is Here!" are capsule commentaries on science-fiction and horror movies. The style and content are

BLACK INFINITY • 71

classic Ackerman. *After Hours* #4 will remain in the annals of popular culture as the place where monster magazines were born, and its importance as the placeholder for this momentous occasion cannot be understated. One thing is certain, Ackerman's "offbeat style" stuck with Warren and they went on to make publishing history.

In October 1957, Screen Gems assembled a package of 52 Universal horror and thriller films for distribution to TV stations called, *Shock!* (aka *Shock Theater*). The result was a monster-sized response from viewers as the films were broadcast on TV screens across America. Acutely aware of the phenomenon, Warren and Ackerman hatched an idea to publish a magazine devoted entirely to film monsters. With this and the inspiration from a French film magazine, *Cinema 57*, a special issue on horror films that Ackerman had brought back with him from a trip to France, they went to work. Warren would handle the business end of things, as well as the production of the magazine. Ackerman would edit, write the content and provide the photos from his massive collection of film stills. Initially, he came up with the title, *Wonderama*, but the distributor wanted "monsters" in the title. After several more name changes, Warren decided on *Famous Monsters of Filmland*.

FM #1 was 68-pages long with a color cover, black and white interiors, and a logo designed by Warren. Against a brilliant red background, the striking cover depicted a

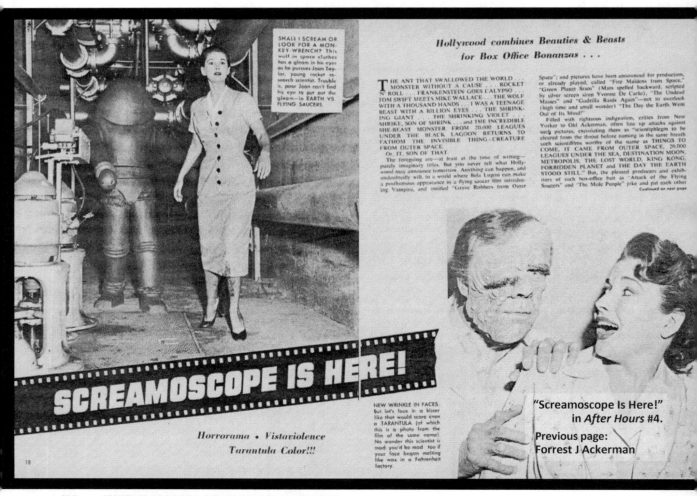

"Screamoscope Is Here!" in *After Hours* #4.
Previous page: Forrest J Ackerman

72 • THE FAMOUS MONSTERS STORY

photo of the Frankenstein monster in a black suit standing next to an attractive blonde wearing an off-the-shoulder dress. It was Warren himself who was under the mask, and the model was credited on the contents page as Marion Moore. Sources have claimed that she was Warren's girlfriend, but Warren disclosed later to a convention audience that Miss Moore was a waitress whom he persuaded to pose with him.

The first issue went on sale on February 27, 1958, and the bellwether for FM's success would be decided in New York where it was primarily distributed. Ironically, New Yorkers were in the middle of a monster snowstorm, but it didn't seem to matter as the magazine nearly sold out.

After wrangling over various problems with the printer, distributor, and wholesalers, Warren managed to hurry out a second printing on March 1, 1958, with the total print run estimated to be between 200,000 and 267,000 copies. Warren would later write: "Somehow, the publisher found a distributor [Kable News]. Somehow, he managed to talk a printer into giving him credit. Somehow, he talked an editor into trusting him for the payment for writing the mag. Somehow, he pasted up the issue himself. And somehow, the issue hit the stands."

Initially planned as a one-shot, on the last page a survey asked readers what they would like to see in the future, a clear indication that Warren was hedging his bets and considering a second issue. Hundreds of letters poured in raving for more, and even though a profit had yet to be seen, forging ahead seemed to be worth the gamble. Warren could have just folded up his tent and gone on to something else, but his gut told him differently. After convincing Ackerman to stay on as editor, he decided to keep publishing.

While the second issue was being prepared, Screen Gems released their *Son of Shock* film package, again bursting with Universal monster movies and thrillers. TV audiences couldn't seem to get enough of the "Monster Mania" that was spreading like an insatiable blob across the American pop culture landscape.

FM #2 appeared on newsstands in September 1958. Warren again was on the cover, this time wearing a werewolf mask and holding up a sign declaring: "2nd Great Issue—First Issue Sold Out!" Still aimed at younger readers (primarily the age-group that was watching *Shock Theater* on TV), the contents offered a thrilling atmosphere, helped along by what would be FM's editorial trademark, Ackerman's inimitable jokes. A number of features were smartly calculated to elicit reader interaction: "Dear Monster" was FM's first letters column, and several recognizable names wrote in, including Robert Bloch and a trio from *Mad* magazine; there was an ad for subscriptions (so there would be no mistaking Warren's intentions now); the first ad for the "Famous Monster Club" encouraged kids to join and share their love of monsters with pen pals (members would include Stephen King and George Lucas); and last but not least was "Monster Mail Order," two pages of novelties and masks for sale, a precursor to Captain Company, which would end up padding an issue with up to 20 pages of merchandise!

Everything seemed to be going well until the returns started coming in from Kable News—the disappointing sales did not meet expectations, especially after the first issue had done so well. What happened? The answer infuriated Warren—he already had not one, but *two* competitors! Suddenly, it looked like he was not the only one looking to profit from the current Monster Craze.

In September, the first issue of *Monster Parade* appeared on newsstands, followed in October by *World Famous Creatures*. Warren boiled over when he learned that the latter magazine was being distributed by Kable News! He was so enraged that he confronted Kable management and voiced his displeasure. Kable collectively shrugged and sent him packing. He responded by suing them—and lost. Ackerman said later: "Warren sued *World Famous Creatures* for what was outrageously,

CONTINUED ON PAGE 76

74 • THE FAMOUS MONSTERS STORY

First advertisement for the Famous Monsters Club, FM #2.

demonstrably plagiarism, but a myopic judge couldn't see the facts before his face."

Warren needn't have worried as neither of the competing magazines lasted long. *Monster Parade* was published by Irwin Stein's Magnum Publications. Stein was a journalist by trade and wrote comic book scripts for both Quality Comics and St. John. He formed Royal Publications, which specialized in men's adventure, detective, and science fiction pulp magazines. When he founded Magnum, he bought the adult magazine *Swank* from Martin "Marvel Comics" Goodman and published titles for mature readers. The cover of the first issue of *Monster Parade* (September 1958) showed a photo of pin-up girl Paula Page (and her cleavage) that was borrowed from a cover of *Swank*, along with a painted-in mummy in the background to make it "monster appropriate." Content-wise, it was tepid fare, with a mix of photo articles, comic book reprints and original fiction. Readers weren't impressed and it lasted only four issues, the last of which was dated March 1959. Stein released a second title in January 1959 called *Monsters and Things*. With contents similar to MP, it disappeared in April after only two issues. Two years later, Stein would enjoy his greatest success in 1961, when he founded the legendary Lancer Books, which introduced the world to Robert E. Howard's Conan.

The second of the competitors, *World Famous Creatures* (a clever cribbing of Warren's title), was a closer copy of FM in contents

Precursor to Captain Company (FM#2).

and appearance. The page layouts were similar and it even added jokes like the ones Ackerman had already been using. Edited by M. Leon Howard, WFC was published by John B. Musacchia's Magsyn Publications, Inc. It looked better than *Monster Parade* due to Musacchia being a commercial artist and illustrator who published how-to art books, celebrity digest magazines, and drew illustrations for 1940s science-fiction pulps. Even with its similarities to FM, *World Famous Monsters* didn't catch on with readers, and

CONTINUED ON PAGE 78

76 • THE FAMOUS MONSTERS STORY

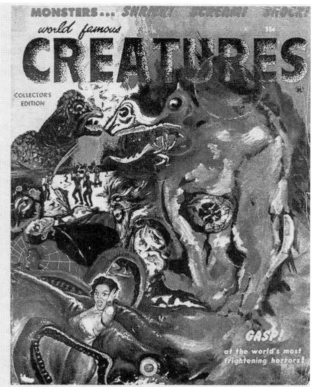
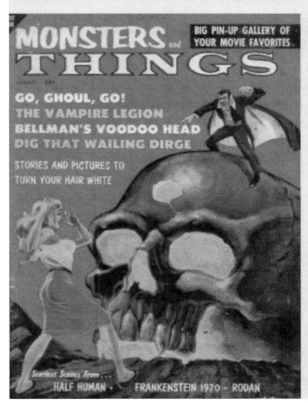

BLACK INFINITY • 77

the last of four issues was published in June 1959. FM was just too fan-friendly at the time and was more appealing to readers who were also devoted viewers of *Shock Theater*. Filmmaker Joe Dante, who would write the article, "Dante's Inferno" in FM #18, hit the coffin-nail on the lid when he remembered: "Oh, my God, we can talk to each other."

When MP and WFC were breathing their last, one more monster magazine crawled onto newsstands in 1959. The one-shot *Journal of Frankenstein* was published by a young monster movie fan by the name of Calvin T. Beck. Beck cut his teeth editing magazines for nutritionist and bodybuilder Joe Weider, and when the Monster Craze hit, he wanted to make a monster magazine of his own. He claimed that Warren "beat him to the punch" at Kable News and had to settle with Acme News as a distributor. Beck's efforts came and went with hardly a blip on the monster magazine screen, but he would be back, as we will see later.

After the relief of changing printers (at the cost of a lower print run), FM #3 was published in April, 1959. Behind the painted cover by Warren, more fan fun was offered in the form of an expanded letters section, a "Reader's Die-Jest" department where readers humorously sounded off with comments regarding their enthusiasm for the magazine, a Famous Monsters Club section with a list of members, and the announcement of a make-up contest along with an ad to buy a makeup kit. It was an issue with two other "firsts": the long-running photo request department, "You Axed for It" (many names were made up by Ackerman so he could choose the movie stills he wanted), and later underground political cartoonist and film designer Ron Cobb's first printed artwork. Other recurring "departments" would appear over the years, such as *Graveyard Examiner*, *Hall of Flame*, *Hidden Horrors*, and *Mystery Photo*. Another popular feature was the Filmbook, comprised of a synopsis accompanied by stills from the movie. One has to remember that this was long before videos, DVDs, and on-demand streaming, so the only way for fans to relive their favorite monster movies was to either hope for re-runs or read the single source at the time, FM.

Things started to pick up in the 1960s with larger print runs and more readers willing to drop their allowances on subscriptions and mail order merchandise. Warren expanded his

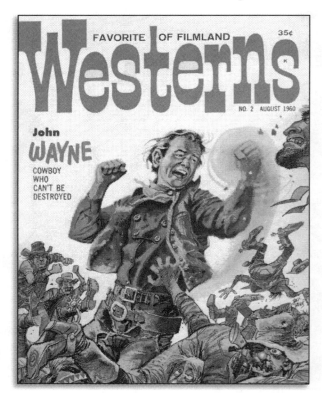

78 • THE FAMOUS MONSTERS STORY

line to generate more income, and in May 1960, he published *Favorite Westerns of Filmland*, the first in what would become a long line of side-titles (FM would always be the flagship). Next came *Help!*, a humor magazine edited by Harvey Kurtzman, who had jumped ship from *Mad* after a disagreement with publisher Bill Gaines. The staff at *Help!* included a stable of future luminaries, including Gloria Steinem, Terry Gilliam, John Cleese, Jay Lynch, and Robert Crumb.

A second Western magazine, *Wildest Westerns*, debuted in October 1960. Sam Sherman, who would become a film producer and team up with cult director Al Adamson, was the editor. In issue #3, Warren changed the name of his mail-order business from General Promotions to *Captain Company* (its first appearance in FM was in issue #15). Mail order sales were his bread and butter during the leaner times, and business was booming. Originally processing orders out of his parent's house, sales grew to a point where he had to move to a larger space in an office building in Philadelphia—and again later to East 32nd Street, New York—to accommodate his increasing staff and the ever-growing inventory of monster merchandise.

Big changes were coming in FM's ninth issue (November 1960) when Warren hired a new cover artist. If anything distinguished FM from other magazines on the newsstand, it was the cover art. The logo and striking images had become FM's trademark. Gone now were the covers he had done himself and those that artist Albert Neutzell had created (issues 4 – 8, and 27). A new artist was to become FM's most popular ever with his first cover, depicting

Above: Basil Gogos made his historic cover art debut with FM #9. Opposite page, top: James Warren poses with members of the Queens, NY Famous Monsters Club; and (bottom) second issue of Warren's *Favorite Westerns of Filmland*.

Vincent Price in Roger Corman's *House of Usher*. Primarily an illustrator for men's adventure magazines popular in the 1950s and '60s, Basil Gogos was hired by Warren, and when he saw his cover of Price, he exclaimed, "This is the best thing I've ever seen! I want more!" Gogos would go on to have his work appear on a whopping 77 Warren covers.

Warren was known for tirelessly promoting his magazine, with one example seen in

CONTINUED ON PAGE 81

Aurora monster model re-issues built and customized by the author.
Opposite page: Advertisement for the national Aurora Monster Model Contest (FM #27).

a monster model-making contest. Entrants from across the country were to build and customize their Aurora monster kits (available from Captain Co., of course!) and enter them in their local participating hobby shop to be judged in a nationwide competition. The winners would receive everything from a complete set of Aurora monster model kits to a trip to Hollywood. A year later, the grand-prize winners would see their assembled and customized kits in FM #32 (March 1965). Warren wasn't done yet, and would further infuse the market with merchandise, such as a trio of FM paperbacks (all reprinted material), calendars, T-shirts, masks, 8mm monster films, and games, just to name a few.

The sixties were also a decade where a tidal wave of monster magazines flooded drugstores and newsstands. The Monster Craze was at its peak, and by that time—thanks in no small part to Warren—was fully fused in popular culture. Monsters seemed to be everywhere: in toy stores, hobby shops, on TV, even in advertising. It made sense that publishers wanted to take advantage of this. New titles included *Horror Monsters* and *Mad Monsters* (both by comics publisher, Charlton), *Fantastic Monsters of the Films* (published by Hollywood special effects man Paul Blaisdell with his pals Ron Haydock and Bob Burns), *For Monsters Only* and *Monster Howls* (monster humor magazines by the folks at *Cracked*), *Monster Mania* (by Warren alumnus and *Creepy*'s first editor, Russ Jones), and *Castle of Frankenstein*, the second run at a monster magazine by Calvin T. Beck, often cited as second best to FM (and sometimes even first!).

It would be remiss not to mention the other seminal magazines Warren published in this decade: *Monster World* (10 issues, 1964–1966), a companion magazine to FM (eventually used as FM numbers 70 to 79 in efforts to get to issue 100 faster), *Creepy* (145 issues, 1964–1983), a full-size comics magazine that re-introduced the shock-ending stories that made EC Comics infamous in the 1950s, *Blazing Combat* (4 issues, 1965–1966), featuring illustrated, thinly-veiled anti-war stories, *Eerie* (139 issues, 1966–1983), a companion magazine to *Creepy*, and *Vampirella* (112 issues, 1969–1983), a sexy, outer-space vampire who hosted tales intended for mature audiences.

FM ushered in the 1970s with an atmospheric cover depicting a scene from *Mark of the Vampire* (1935) by Peter Green. Over the decade, FM appeared to be faltering little by little; one indication was the proliferation of reprint articles that long-time readers had seen not only once, but sometimes more. It soon became apparent that change was in the air. While monster movies were still popular earlier in the decade, a shift in audience interest was taking place, and when *Star Wars* hit the screens in 1977, all heads turned to science fiction. Warren and Ackerman scrambled to keep pace with the new SF and fantasy trend with heavy coverage and by plastering their covers with images from *Star Wars* and similar films that were suddenly dominating the market. As FM's demographics slowly shifted, it suddenly looked like the last original monster magazine standing had finally peaked.   CONTINUED ON PAGE 84

First issues of Charlton's *Mad Monsters*, featuring cover art by Spider-Man co-creator Steve Ditko, and Calvin T. Beck's *Castle of Frankenstein*.

82 • THE FAMOUS MONSTERS STORY

GORGEOUS GOGOS COVER ART ON ISSUES 12, 16, 17, & 20.

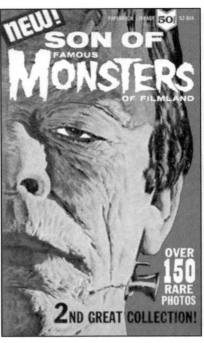

FM gradually faded until it became a shadow of its former, glorious self. Finally, in May 1983, Warren pulled the plug on his empire by declaring bankruptcy and shuttered his doors. The reasons were many: shrinking distribution and readership, rising paper and printing costs, and most of all, debt and lack of cash flow. It was Forrest J Ackerman who made FM live and breathe for its fans, but it was Warren and his relentless drive that had really been running the show.

The last issue was #191, with a cover by Bill Selby depicting a character from *The Dark Crystal*. Ackerman had already resigned his position, and W.R. Mohalley, FM's longtime art director-turned managing editor, assumed the duties. One of its final articles was part two of the last filmbook, *The Time Machine*.

Not to be denied immortality, FM would live on under the ownership of several other publishers and is currently under the wing of Corey Taylor, a member of the band, Slipknot. With all the hopes that it will be successful, one thing is for certain: it will not be the

CONTINUED ON PAGE 86

(Top) Portable Monsters: In 1964 and 1965, Paperback Library published a trio of softcover books reprinting articles from *Famous Monsters of Filmland*. (Left) Forrest J Ackerman buried under paper at his desk.

84 • THE FAMOUS MONSTERS STORY

THE GHOST OF GORGEOUS GOGOS COVER ART ON ISSUES 103, 11, 53, & 108.

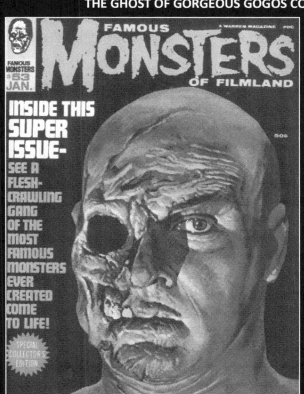

BLACK INFINITY • 85

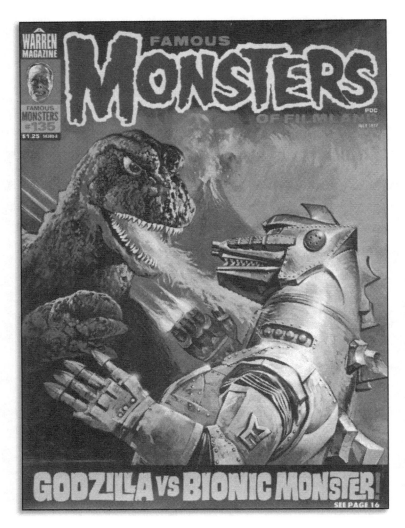

Famous Monsters of Filmland that fans knew and loved, especially the older ones who were there in the beginning.

Author Stephen King summed it up perfectly when he stated: "Ask anyone who has been associated with the fantasy-horror-science fiction genres in the last thirty years about [*Famous Monsters of Filmland*], and you'll get a laugh, a flash of the eyes, and a stream of bright memories."

SELECT REFERENCE

Books:
 Daniel, Dennis, ed. *Famous Monsters Chronicles*, Albany, New York: FantaCo Enterprises, Inc., 1991.
 Horne, David. *Gathering Horror: A Completist Collector's Catalogue and Index for Warren Publishing*, Concord, California: Phrona Press, 2010.
 Roach, David A., ed., Cooke, John B. ed. *The Warren Companion*, Raleigh, North Carolina: TwoMorrows Publishing, 2001.
 Schelly, Bill. *James Warren: Empire of Monsters*, Seattle, Washington: Fantagraphics Books, 2019.
 Skulan, Tom, et al. *Famous Monsters Chronicles II*, Albany, New York: FantaCo Enterprises LLC, 2017.

Periodicals:
 Comic Book Artist; Comic Book Marketplace;
 Little Shoppe of Horrors; Pure Images; Rolling Stone

John Navroth is a writer, film enthusiast, and musician who was born in Los Angeles and has lived for the last 33 years in the Pacific Northwest. He has a lifelong interest in horror movies, makeup and animation since first watching Universal's Dracula on 1960s late night television. As a young Monster Kid, he was lucky enough to visit Forrest J Ackerman's "Ackermansion." His non-fiction work has appeared in Castle of Frankenstein, G-Fan, Mad Doctor, Monsters from the Vault, and We Belong Dead. He also contributed to The Warren Companion. His article, "The Monster in Dressing Room No.5" (Scary Monsters #127) was nominated for a Rondo Award in 2022. He is currently co-authoring a biography of Universal monster makeup master, Jack Pierce. His blog has been published regularly since 2010 at https://monstermagazineworld.blogspot.com

Below: Forrest J Ackerman at home in his "Ackermansion" in Los Angeles.
Opposite page: *Famous Monsters* #135 featured *Godzilla vs. MechaGodzilla* (1974) with cover art by Gogos.

BLACK INFINITY • 87

KOLCHAK: THE NIGHT STALKER   I WALKED WITH A ZOMBIE

NIGHTMARE ABBEY

1

BIG PREMIER ISSUE
RAMSEY CAMPBELL
13 QUESTIONS and THREE TERROR TALES

STEVE DUFFY ♥ GREGORY L. NORRIS   JASON J. McCUISTON
HELEN GRANT ♥ DAVID SURFACE   ALLEN KOSZOWSKI
JOSEPH PAYNE BRENNAN   LYNDA E. RUCKER
JUSTIN HUMPHREYS   DOUGLAS SMITH
HENRY KUTTNER   ROBERT BLOCH
KURT NEWTON   A. M. BURRAGE
JAMES DORR

DON'T MISS
OUR OTHER GREAT
MAGAZINE!

BLACK ICE

by KURT NEWTON

THE WINTER COLD BROUGHT NOTHING BUT A RED-CHEEKED SMILE TO MATTY PELLETIER'S TWELVE YEAR-OLD FACE. The sky was blue; the lake as frozen as Main Street; and he had just scored a goal—his first since he and his buddies began playing pick-up games out on Thompson Lake.

It was dumb luck, really—an errant pass that flew by his teammate, Steve Manneman, somehow threaded through both opposing players, Chad Willis and Josh Burnett, clipped the skate of goalie Kyle Truesdale and rolled lazily into the net. But he'd take it. A goal was a goal. They were still down six goals to two.

Today, Matty was playing defenseman, Steve Manneman was at center, and to round out (so to speak) their three-man team, was Bobby Hilliard in the net. Bobby wore an extra fifty pounds of natural padding and was their slowest skater. But his size made him a natural goalie. Crouched in the center of the net, he nearly filled the small makeshift goal.

"Ready?" shouted the opposing team's goalie. The boy's voice was swallowed up by the cold. Since there were no referees, the two centers stood facing their own goals with the puck already on the ice at their feet. Whichever team had just scored, it was the opposing team's goalie who counted down the face-off.

Matty positioned himself halfway up the ice, his eyes on his teammate.

"Three..."

He watched as Steve Manneman went through his normal routine of shifting back and forth during the count.

"Two..."

A silence descended as each player settled down and dug in their skates.

"One..."

Sticks to the ice.

"Go!"

Whack! Both players' sticks slapped together. Miraculously, Steve got to the puck first and it shot between Josh Burnett's legs toward Matty. Matty picked it up and skated toward the center. "Borque passes to Lemieux..." He flicked the puck to Steve, and Steve picked up both the puck and the commentary.

"Lemieux skates past Roy... he sets... he—"

BLACK INFINITY • 89

"And it's stolen by Gretzky!"

Matty laughed as his teammate, Steve Manneman, got burned royally. Now Josh Burnett raced toward him.

"Block him, Matty!" This came from Bobby, who had already let Josh score five of the six goals against them.

"I got him."

Matty back-skated as Josh closed in. Josh was probably the best skater in the game, if not on the entire lake. Matty tried to check him but didn't even get a chance, as Josh suddenly changed direction, then spun around in a spray of ice, the puck still glued to his stick.

"Gretzky blows past Borque. He shoots..."

Josh slapped the puck with deadly accuracy. Matty stuck his stick out, but he was too late. He could only watch as the puck careened past Bobby's poorly timed block attempt and punched into the net ... and through.

"He scorrrrrrrrrrres! A double hat-trick!"

The black disk skimmed along the ice for another hundred feet, and came to rest against a mound of ice chips piled around an abandoned fisherman's hole. To make matters worse, Bobby had fallen into the net and knocked it free from the ice.

"Nice save, Hil-*lard*." Josh Burnett skated back to his teammates to receive a series of high-fives.

Matty looked at Bobby and shrugged his shoulders. "I should have stopped him," he said. Bobby looked to get a bead on the errant puck. He turned to Matty, his eyes squinting in the sun. "For once I'd like to see that Josh kid miss. Right before he falls through the ice!" A grin spread across the heavyset boy's face.

"Get the friggin' puck, will ya!" This came from Steve Manneman, whose turnover had set the whole score in motion.

Bobby rolled his eyes. "Jeez, my own teammate." He gestured to the dislodged net. "Fix that for me, okay, while I'm getting the *friggin'* puck." He then took off toward the

fishing hole in the distance before any more barbs could be thrown his way.

Matty lifted the leg of the goal and set it back into place. Steve Manneman's dad was a plumber and had made the goals out of PVC and fishing net. The goals stayed up all winter, usually frozen into place. But on sunny days the PVC warmed and the feet had a tendency to pop out if given a good enough jolt.

Matty took the break in play to take in the other activities that were going on around the lake.

Patches of people were gathered here and there along shore. The groups consisted mainly of skate parties and winter barbecues. Farther out were the identifying flagpoles of the ice fishermen. Not much movement with those guys. They had their hotseats and their bottles of whiskey to keep them warm. Even farther out were the ice-sailers, their shark fin sails chasing each other back and forth.

When Matty's gaze returned to the spot where Bobby had gone, Bobby was down on his stomach looking as if he were trying to fish the puck out of the hole.

What the hell is he doing? Matty thought to himself as he watched.

Then Bobby's head went in. His legs began kicking, and before Matty could react, the rest of Bobby disappeared.

Holy sh—!

"Hey!" Matty waved his hands. "Hey, guys, Bobby just fell in!"

Matty took off running. The other boys followed close behind. When they got to the hole, the five of them just stood and stared.

The hole was no larger than a coffee can. The ice was nearly six inches thick and the water inside the hole was slushy but still.

"Good one, Matty," said Steve Manneman.

"What happened? Your goalie run home with his tail between his fat legs?" This came from Josh Burnett. His teammates laughed. "Forfeit. We win."

Matty just stared at the open hole as the boys began to skate away. "Wait! Didn't

90 • BLACK ICE

anybody see? Where you guys going? We have to do something! He's down there!"

Steve Manneman turned around, still skating backwards. "Hang it up, Matty. We lost." He followed the other boys back to pick up their gear.

Matty was left alone. He stared at the open hole, his mind unable to reconcile what he had witnessed. *Couldn't be.* Again, he glanced around the lake.

Same families, same fishermen.

He heard a noise at his feet. A gurgling sound.

His eyes once again stared at the hole in the ice.

The water in the hole was moving, as if an underwater wave had passed by. Then something black floated to the surface.

The puck.

Matty wanted to run, but his legs wouldn't move. He wanted to reach down and grab the puck, rescue it from the lake. At least he could do that much.

He extended a trembling hand toward the open hole. When his fingers were an inch from the puck, he saw an even darker shadow, a larger shadow, move beneath the ice, and the puck was snatched from the slush not with teeth but with long scaly fingers.

It was then Matty ran, his skates biting into the ice, his heart pounding in his chest.

"It happened just like that. Jesus Christ."

"Matthew!" Matty's mother reprimanded.

Detective Johns and Detective Simmons exchanged glances, their notepads unmarked since Matty got to the part where Bobby Hilliard got sucked into a hole the size of a coffee can.

After the incident, Matty told anyone who would listen what had happened, but no one would believe him. It wasn't until the Hilliard boy failed to come home for dinner—a nightly event never missed by the growing youth—that the police were finally called.

"Okay, I think we're done here." The two detectives got to their feet. "Mrs. Pellitier, can we have a word with you?"

"Of course." She turned to her son. "Matthew, don't you have homework?"

Matty looked at the trio. "No. But I get it. You want me to get lost."

"Matthew."

"Whatever."

Matty stormed up the stairs to his room. He turned on his TV and cranked up a music video on YouTube. He then quietly moved down the hall to the top of the stairs to eaves-drop.

"...Ever since his father left, he hasn't been the same."

"I understand, Ma'am."

No, you don't understand! Matty wanted to shout. *There's something in the lake. Bobby didn't just drown, he was...taken.*

"It's possible the Hilliard boy fell through at another location. We've got divers coming first thing in the morning to help with the search. Thank you for your cooperation."

The two detectives left.

Matty sat in his room as the heavy metal beat pounded from the television speakers. All he could see was that clawed hand. It was grey in color, with a coating of soft green fur like the algae that grew on the rocks at the bottom of the lake. He could see it more clearly now in memory than when it had actually happened. Perhaps that was because he wasn't nearly wetting his pants with fear. He knew he wasn't imagining things. He also knew that without any proof, no one would believe him. But what could he do?

He lay back on his bed, closed his eyes, and let the music drown his thoughts.

The following morning, the Worcester Special Diving Unit searched a large portion of Thompson Lake, investigating breaks in the ice large enough to swallow up a child, but not the ice fishing hole that Matty claimed he had seen Bobby disappear into. The sky was clear and the sun was bright, and the on-lookers—which ranged from concerned locals to curious out-of-towners—used the event as

BLACK INFINITY • 91

some kind of social gathering. Nobody really wanted to see a twelve-year-old boy pulled from the freezing water, his body white and bloated, but the chance of that occurring was just too rare to pass up.

While most of his friends were down at the lake watching the spectacle, Matty stayed home. He sat with a blanket on the couch and watched TV instead. Sunday morning programming sucked, nothing but religious services, political discussion, and infomercials, but Matty watched it anyway, snapping out of his zombie-like state long enough to change channels whenever anything closely resembling ice came onto the screen.

For lunch, Matty's mother served him hot soup and a sandwich on a tray. She felt his forehead and treated him as if he were coming down with a cold. "You should go lie down, get some rest," she told him. He simply stared at the television and told her he was okay.

He watched football. Matty liked football. But not as much as he liked hockey. At least, it was his favorite sport up until yesterday. He sat and watched and tried to ignore his conscience until he couldn't take it anymore. He had to do something.

He put on his boots and coat, grabbed his skates and told his mother he'd be back in little while, and was out the door before she could stop him.

By the time he reached the lake, the cars and news crews that had lined the road earlier in the day were all but gone. A cold breeze had kicked up across the lake, and the sun was slowly feeling its way down through the prickly treetops as if to avoid being punctured.

Matty laced up his skates and walked onto the ice.

He skated over to where he and his buddies had played hockey the day before and stood by the goal his friend Bobby had been defending before this nightmare had begun. He stared in the direction of the hole in the ice in the distance, running the images over and over in his mind until his feet grew numb and his eyes began to tear with the cold air. Not far beyond the hole, an ice fisherman had set up shop and was getting his fire started for the long night ahead. Matty skated over to him.

The man was old. His face was deeply lined, and it looked as if he hadn't shaved in several days. The man sat on a stool. He wore a heavy parka, thick wool mittens and insulated boots. A plywood partition surrounded him on three sides to fend off the wind. Directly in front of him, at his feet: the black orifice of the fishing hole he had cut from the ice using a long narrow-bladed saw. The fire Matty had seen him building now burned steadily in a shallow metal pan that sat atop a tripod a foot off the ice. It appeared as if the old fisherman wanted not to be disturbed. But as Matty got closer, the man looked up and his watery blue eyes brightened.

"Hey, young fella."

Matty approached. "Hi. Sorry to bother you—"

"No bother at all. What can I do for you?"

Matty didn't know where to start. "You're old, right?"

The fisherman chuckled. "Yup, I guess I am."

"Sorry—I mean, you've been around here a long time … on the lake … fishing and stuff."

The man nodded sagely. "Been fishing this lake for sixty-two years. Both winter and summer. Get to do it more now that I'm retired."

Matty hesitated, then forged ahead. "Ever see anything … weird?"

"What kind of weird?" The man's face grew more lined.

"I don't know. Weird like—"

Monsters? Matty wanted to say monsters but he just couldn't get it past his lips, because to say it would mean he believed it, and if he believed it, it would be true. "You know, things that aren't supposed to be … like something out of a comic book or a horror movie?"

The old man continued to stare, appearing not to understand.

"You know, something not real, but it had to be real because you know what you saw and you know it wasn't all in your head…but no one believes you…but you keep thinking that if you knew what the thing was and why it did what it did, it would somehow all make sense…"

"Whoa, slow down, you're making my old noggin hurt!"

Matty was on the verge of tears, so he looked away, back toward shore, back toward the place where he had last seen Bobby alive. He didn't want to cry in front of some old guy he didn't even know, but he had to get someone to believe him. If he didn't, he thought he just might go crazy.

"Does this have anything to do with that missing boy?" the old man asked.

Matty took a deep breath. His chest hitched as he spoke. "Bobby Hilliard. His name was Bobby Hilliard. He was my friend."

"So you're the boy who claims that something came out of the lake and got him?"

"Yeah, that's me. But something didn't come out of the lake, Bobby got sucked in. Something pulled him into that hole over there," Matty pointed, "and those stupid rescue people didn't even bother to check it out."

"Your friend got pulled into a fishing hole? In broad daylight?"

Matty nodded.

The old man seemed to consider this for a moment. He stared down at the hole in the ice at his feet as if to gauge its dimensions. The line that ran down into the water tugged slightly, and the old man held up a gloved finger, as if to say, *Shhhh!* Then he relaxed. "Just a nibble," he said. "Okay, you wanted to know if I've ever seen anything weird out here. Well, to be honest, there was only one time. And it was so long ago, I have a hard time remembering it. But parts of it I remember just like it was yesterday.

"I was a boy about your age. My daddy had rented a cottage for the summer. My father fancied himself a big shot businessman and he wanted a place to entertain all his big shot business buddies. My mom spent most of that summer entertaining their wives. Which kind of left me in the lurch. I mean, I was kind of a bookworm back then. Didn't have the size for sports. Didn't have the smooth talk for social events. Which annoyed my daddy to no end. I guess he wanted a son that was more like him than the woman he married. But then the world despises weakness, even if it's just something that appears that way. Anyway, what I'm getting at is that was the summer Michelle Bissonette up and disappeared.

"People called her Shelly. Her parents owned the cottage next to ours. She used to lay out on their floating dock sunning herself like she was something special. And she was. Son, don't ever let the grown-ups tell you you're too young to be in love. Because that Shelly was like a vision in my eyes. She was the sun, the moon *and* the stars. I mean, I was hooked. Hooked bad.

"Of course it was a one-sided thing. Shelly was my age but she had boyfriends who could drive a car and buy liquor. Shelly was a bit too fast for her own good, if you catch my meaning. But she had it all, and she knew it. Knew how to use it, too. There'd be nights I'd be outside fishing off the end of our dock with only a bottle of Coke and a flashlight to keep me company, and I'd hear Shelly's laughter. She had the kind of laugh that melted your insides. Her and one of her many boyfriends would be swimming out to the floating dock, where they'd climb up and then lay down beneath the moon, and all you'd hear after that was a giggle now and then.

"Made me pretty uncomfortable at times. Mainly because I was wishing it were me she was getting all giggly with. One time I was caught staring at her, and her boyfriend yelled over and called me four-eyes and asked if I'd like a knuckle sandwich. But Shelly told him to leave me alone. I think she was the kind of girl who liked having an audience. So when she turned up missing, it was a surprise to some, but not to most."

The fishing line tugged again, and the old man paused. Another false alarm.

"Anyway, to make a long story... After she turned up missing, the authorities searched the lake. Each one of Shelly's boyfriends was brought into town for questioning. In the end, no one was charged. They couldn't find a body. Back then, if you had no body, there was no crime. Shelly was labeled a runaway and that was that.

"You know how water systems work, don't you, son?"

Matty shook his head. He wanted to hear the rest of the old man's story but it was getting late. The sun had set and only its afterglow remained, painting the trees with yellow stripes. The distant fire- and lantern light of other ice fishermen could now be seen dotting the surface of the lake like stars poking through a night sky. The moon was on the rise above the opposite shore. And it was getting cold.

"Well, I've heard it said that all the streams and all the rivers that pour in and out of all the lakes and all the oceans in the world are connected in some way. Some of it over ground. Most of it under. Take Thompson Lake, for instance. Water comes in over at the dam on Route 87 and goes out in a variety of places—Hop River, Buell's Cove, and a dozen other nameless streams, no doubt. So it's conceivable that poor Shelly's body had somehow made it out of the lake and down some stream and ended up God knows where. But by that same token, it's also conceivable that something came into Thompson Lake—something that found a home here and settles deep when the sun is up and rises to the surface when night falls. The same something that grabbed poor Shelly one night when she was out swimming all by her lonesome. The same something that may have grabbed your friend, Bobby."

The old man stared at Matty. The firelight cast strange shadows across the man's weathered features. The watery blue eyes, which seemed so welcoming before, now appeared to dry up and harden. "The only reason I say this," the old man continued, "is because one night I was sitting out at the end of the dock, tossing my line into the black water, thinking about Shelly and what could have happened to her, when up swims the very girl my heart was still pining for. My first thought was that she had come back from wherever she'd run off to, but as she pulled up under my feet and called my name, I knew something was amiss. I mean, this thing had Shelly's face and Shelly's body and Shelly's soft voice, but the look in her eyes was from some deep, dark place that gave me the willies, even though it was one of those warm, muggy summer nights.

"Well, I pulled my legs up right quick and asked her what she wanted. And you know what she said? She said, 'You.' Then she smiled. I told you she had a smile that could melt your heart. And with my daddy trying to look good in front of all his business buddies and my mom just trying to keep up, it was the first time in a long time somebody actually wanted me, for me. And I didn't care what lay behind those black ice eyes or what the next few moments would hold, all I knew was, in that instant, she wanted me, and I wanted her, too."

Darkness had descended fully upon Thompson Lake. The fishing line that ran down into the hole at the old man's feet began to tug furiously, but the old man ignored it. Instead, there was a look in the old man's eye that chilled Matty to the bone. Matty knew he had to get out of there—get out of the old man's reach before he slid one of those thick woolen mittens off and grabbed him with his scaly claw.

With his heart thumping in his chest, Matty planted his skate in the ice and, without as much as a "Good-bye, thanks for the story," he took off toward shore as if he were on a power play.

94 • BLACK ICE

Halfway there, he could have sworn he heard a splash.

Matty turned his skates sideways and skidded to a halt. He looked back.

He could see the fisherman's blind, but he couldn't see the old man anymore.

It must have got him, thought Matty, feeling sick to his stomach. The old guy wasn't going to hurt him. In fact, by running away, he left the old man vulnerable, sitting there so close to that hole in the ice. If he'd stayed a little while longer, maybe he could have done something. The way he could have done something to help Bobby, if only he had reacted sooner.

Once again, Matty turned toward shore—

—and found himself face to face with his friend, Bobby, who stood just two feet away, cast in moonlight, dripping wet but looking the same as he did the day before.

"Why'd you leave me, Matty?"

There was a strange luminescence about his friend's skin, like a photograph not quite developed. "I didn't, Bobby, I tried to tell everybody, but they wouldn't believe me."

"I know. Just kidding." The heavyset boy chuckled—a dead chuckle, like two ice cubes knocking together in an empty glass.

This was like a dream, Matty thought. He couldn't believe Bobby was standing there before him.

"Come on…" Bobby reached out and Matty pulled away. Bobby frowned. "What's the matter?"

That's when Matty noticed that Bobby was standing right next to the fishing hole he had been sucked into the day before. In fact, one of Bobby's skates hovered right over the hole, its outline appearing to blend in with ice. And his eyes—there was something about his eyes that wasn't right.

"C'mon, gimme your hand," Bobby demanded.

"I can't," Matty said, standing his ground. In fact, Matty let himself slide back half a step.

His friend looked at him. "All the pain goes away, Matty, you'll see. Don't you want the pain to go away?"

Bobby had been Matty's friend since kindergarten. Bobby was there when Matty's dad left and his mom fell apart. He was always there with a stupid joke when the seriousness of the moment called for it.

But Bobby was dead. Matty had seen him go into that hole he was now standing over—sucked in the way their science teacher showed them how a boiled egg gets sucked into a milk bottle. He couldn't have survived.

"What do you want?" Matty asked, but he already knew the answer.

Bobby grinned. "You." The word came out as one long hiss. The thing that was Bobby suddenly lost its illusion. It dropped to the ice and thinned into a slick, eel-like creature with spiked fins and a large grinning mouth.

Matty bolted once again, just dodging out of reach of the lunging beast. Matty skated toward shore, then changed direction toward the nearest hockey net. Above the sound of his own skates on the ice, Matty could hear the side-to-side swish of the creature's legless body as it closed the gap behind him.

Matty reached the makeshift goal and struggled to pull it free from the ice. *C'mon, you stupid goal*, Matty's thoughts screamed, but the cold had frozen it back into place.

The creature hissed again as it came hurtling in Matty's direction. Matty kicked at the goal post with his skate. The creature was nearly on top of him when the PVC finally broke free.

As Matty swung the goal around, the creature hit him in the stomach, knocking him backward onto the ice. Matty lay on the ice gasping for air, expecting the worse, expecting the thing that had killed his friend to wrap its snake-like body around him and drag him to the nearest hole and take him down into the cold, watery depths. But all he could hear was the frantic hissing of the beast as it struggled to untangle itself from the goal's netting.

BLACK INFINITY • 95

Matty got to his feet. He didn't want to go near the flailing creature, but somebody had to stand up to this thing. He couldn't let it continue to feed off of the people of the lake. He didn't know if it would work, but this time he could actually do something.

With his skate, Matty kicked at the remaining goal posts until each either broke or broke free from the ice. The creature snapped and hissed and lunged at his ankles, but each time it only succeeded in entangling itself more.

Once free, Matty began to drag the goal and its unusual catch toward shore. He figured there was a reason why this thing was confined to bodies of water. Perhaps it couldn't survive for very long without it.

As Matty reached shore he heard laughter —female laughter. He turned toward the creature in the net, and instead of something hideous, he saw, illuminated by moonlight, the outline of a girl—a beautiful girl—in a bathing suit. *Shelly?*

"Let me out of here, silly," the girl said. Her delicate fingers clung to the netting.

Matty faltered.

"If you set me free, I'll show you why all the boys like me." She reached for her bathing suit strap and peeled it from her shoulder, revealing the pale swell of an adolescent breast.

Matty's legs burned. He was out of breath. He suddenly felt very weak. He wanted to lie down and go to sleep, give in the way his father had given in, the way his mother had given in. It would be so much easier to just believe the illusion and just let this thing have its way. What made him think that he could defeat something that had survived all this time—survived sixty-two years in this lake alone?

"Matty, please, it's so cold." The half-naked girl shivered beneath the netting.

It knew his name. This girl couldn't have known his name. This girl died over sixty years ago.

"Get out of my head!" Matty shouted and began to drag the girl up the embankment to the road. There was no snow on the road, no water—frozen or otherwise—to come into contact with. This had to work. He didn't know what he was going to do if it didn't.

"You're weak," the girl hissed, "you're just like your father! Ow! You're hurting me! Don't... you'll go to jail! You don't know what you're doing!"

Matty's skates dug into the embankment. He yanked the goal and girl up onto the road and dragged the whole entangled mess to the center line...and waited.

Nothing happened. The girl lay still, her chest rising and falling in shallow breaths.

"Come on, die, dammit! You're supposed to die!"

Suddenly there were lights—headlights. The oncoming car came to an abrupt halt, its hi-beams glaring. The driver's-side door opened. Matty held his hand up to see who it was.

"Matthew? What are you doing?"

"Mom?"

"Oh, my God! Is that Bobby?"

Matty looked down at the creature in the net and saw Bobby's frightened face.

"Mrs. Pellitier, help me! Matty's gone crazy —he's trying to kill me!"

"Mom, don't go near him."

"Matthew, why are you doing this? Bobby's your friend."

"Mom, don't!"

Mrs. Pellitier rushed over to the adolescent boy entangled in the net and knelt down beside him.

"It's not Bobby, Mom. Bobby's dead. Now, get away from it!" Matty shoved his mother aside.

Matty could see the surprised—and, yes, frightened—look in his mother's eyes as she sat down hard onto the cold pavement. But that look didn't remain for long as the creature that was trapped in the net could no longer maintain its deceptive appearance.

Illuminated by the car's headlights, Bobby's rosy-cheeked face began to thin, his

96 • BLACK ICE

adolescent pleading suddenly changing to a dry, nasal hiss. In a matter of seconds, the eel-like creature returned, flailing in a last, desperate attempt to free itself. And then, to Matty's amazement, the creature began to change once again.

First, it reclaimed the form of his friend, Bobby. This was then quickly followed by a series of faces and body contortions: the old ice fisherman; Shelly, the promiscuous teen; men, women and children; incarnations too numerous to count; thousands of victims taken over time under cover of night or protected from the sun by thick ice, dating back centuries and spanning continents. And with each ghostly embodiment that was exorcized, the creature surrendered a part of its physical self. Scales began to flake off one by one, segments of its long serpentine tail, portions of its fins. The shapeshifter dried and disintegrated until there was nothing left but a brittle skeleton, as ancient as creation itself. Then even that collapsed under its own weight and was quickly dispersed into the air and the surrounding snow-covered woods like chalk dust blown by a cold breeze.

Matty and his mother sat upon the cold, dry pavement, staring at the now empty hockey goal.

"Now do you believe me?"

Matty's mother nodded, her eyes still wide.

Matty got to his feet, dragged the goal off to the side of the road, then held out his hand for his mother to stand up. When she did, she hugged him harder than he could ever remember. She felt strong. And Matty smiled. "Let's go home," she said.

As they drove away, Matty put his head against the cold window and stared out across the barren, moonlit lake.

The glow of the ice fishermen's lantern lights and makeshift fires flickered in the distant night. And, though he was lucky to be alive and felt good about the evening's events, Matty had to wonder if this was really the end.

Matty sat back and let the car's heater work to warm his cold body. He closed his eyes. He could rest easy.

At least, until spring.

"Black Ice" first appeared in the 2004 anthology Demonicus Grammaticus.

As a child, Kurt Newton was weaned on episodes of The Twilight Zone *and* The Outer Limits, *and* Chiller Theater *(which showed many of the classic sci-fi horror movies of the 1950s and '60s), laying the groundwork for his fertile imagination. His stories have appeared in numerous publications over the last twenty years, including* Weird Tales, Weirdbook, Space & Time, Dark Discoveries, Vastarien, Nightscript, Nightmare Abbey, *and* Cosmic Horror Monthly. *He lives in Connecticut.*

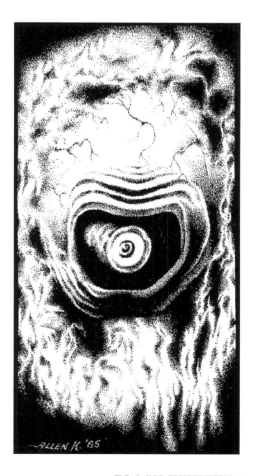

GEORGE PAL: MAN OF TOMORROW

BY JUSTIN HUMPHREYS

FOREWORD BY GEORGE PAL

AUTHORIZED BY THE GEORGE PAL ESTATE

**THE LIFE AND FILMS OF
THE FATHER OF MODERN SCIENCE FICTION CINEMA:
THE TRAILBLAZING PRODUCER, DIRECTOR,
AND ANIMATOR GEORGE PAL**

George Pal classics such as *Destination Moon*, *When Worlds Collide*, *The War of the Worlds*, and *The Time Machine* were a quantum leap forward for the genre's quality, intelligence, and special effects wizardry. When few people in Hollywood— or elsewhere—took science fiction seriously, Pal stood by it, paving the way for SF's enormous future popularity and inspiring generations of filmmakers.

Written and researched with the full cooperation of the George Pal Estate, Justin Humphreys' *George Pal: Man of Tomorrow* involved twenty years of exhaustive research in international archives and private collections, including un- precedented access to the Pal family's archive. This definitive, profusely illustrated biography of this visionary movie futurist includes new interviews with over sixty of Pal's coworkers, family members, and admirers in the film industry, dozens of rare photographs, and gorgeous cover art by renowned science fiction illustrator and historian Vincent Di Fate.   ISBN 9798887710426

"Justin Humphreys is simply as good as film historians get."
— Sam Wasson, NY Times bestselling author of *Fosse* and *The Big Goodbye*

"...A long-term labor of love.... You won't be disappointed...."
— Leonard Maltin

Available at www.Bearmanormedia.com and www.Amazon.com
Signed copies available directly from Justin Humphreys at fivestarfinal@hotmail.com
Signed softcover copies are $60 each ($52 plus $8 shipping in the United States. No international orders.)

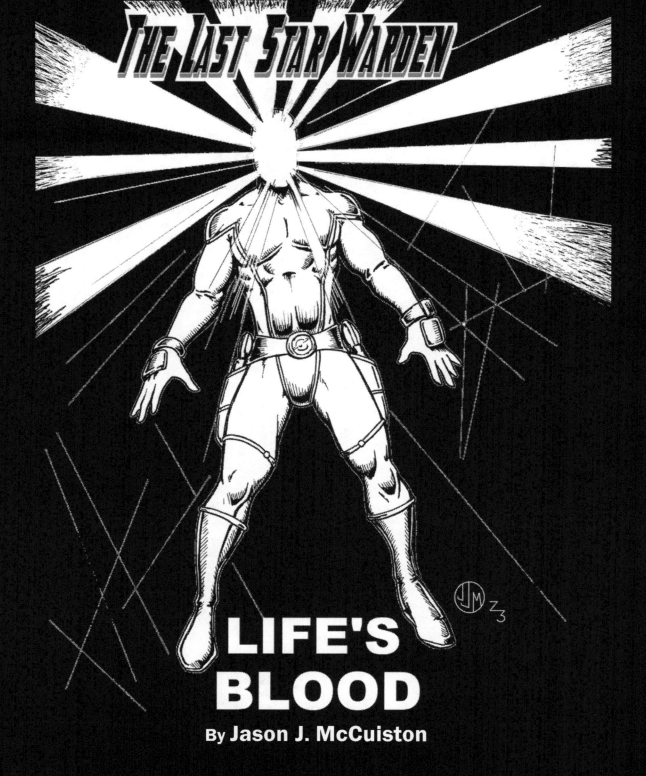

"**H**OLOFERNES OMEGA." THE LAST STAR WARDEN GUIDED THE *RANGER VII* TOWARD THE MOLTEN MOON. The sole surviving planetoid burned like a festering sore amid a spray of lifeless asteroids in the dead system. Several million kilometers away, a dying star gave off a sickly dull glow. "One of the last original and independent mining operations in the Frontier. Volcanic quartz and liquefied metals for PermaSteel, all to keep the U.P.C.'s colonies and ships running."

"It is a good thing we were nearby," Quantum said from the copilot's chair. "The nearest Star Cav ship is three days away by Einstein-Rosen bridge."

The Warden glanced at his blue-skinned Mechtechan friend before hailing the mining station. "Holofernes Omega, this is the Star Warden responding to your S.O.S. What is your status?"

A staticky voice came over the audio. "This is Tara Henning, honcho of this operation. We're in trouble down here. One of my crew has gone nuts and sabotaged a lot of our equipment. He may be homicidal. We're not heavily armed, so we could use your help."

"Copy that. We're on our way." The Warden maneuvered the silvery sleek ship into the moon's hellish atmosphere of high, scorching winds.

"It sounds like a simple case of space madness." Quantum's unblinking black eyes turned to the tiny star at the system's heart. "Humans need far more sunlight than that dwarf provides in order to keep a healthy mental state."

The Warden nodded as the *Ranger VII* touched down on a vacant landing pad. "You're probably right."

As he and Quantum made for the hatch, the Warden pulled on his visored cowl and donned his twin Comet blasters. The ship's sensors said that Holofernes Omega, though deathly hot, somehow maintained a more-or-less Earth-like environment. Donning thermal-regulating overcoats, they stepped out of the ship and into an oven.

Overhead, the expanse of endless night stretched out above the moon's fiery landscape. The heat was a palpable force, reaching in and boiling the Warden's blood in spite of the coat and his spacesuit's thermal safeguards. They were met at the foot of the gangplank by three people dressed in similar thermal suits. The biggest of the group carried an automatic shotgun.

"Warden! Welcome to hell!" Tara Henning's voice came through the Warden's cowl earpieces. She yelled into her wrist chronocom to be heard above the roaring hot winds. "Come on. We'll get to cover!"

They hurried across the landing pad toward a squat, bunker-like structure jutting out of the moon's volcanic surface. Three landers sat on adjacent pads, all showing signs of sabotage—blackened and burned engines and shattered GlasSteel canopies.

Once inside the relative cool of the station's access point, Henning doffed her suit's hood and thermal goggles. Her two crew-members did likewise. The dark-skinned male with the shotgun activated a nic-stick and shared it with a slender, hawk-faced girl. She flashed the big man a smile, then gave the Warden and Quantum an appraising scowl. The five of them stood nearly shoulder-to-shoulder in the tiny room's confines.

"This is Bale M'Gibo, my de facto security guard." Henning rubbed sweat from her nose as she indicated the man. "He's the only other person on the station with a weapon, so he got the job. And this is Chastain, my... machinist." The hawk-faced girl narrowed her amber eyes at the crew chief. "Our medic, Harley Wulf, and our demolitions expert, Rex Cannon, are holed up below."

"You said only *other* person with a weapon. I'm assuming you mean your rogue crewman is also armed?" The Warden studied the auburn-haired woman, seeing the

BLACK INFINITY • 101

premature lines around her hazel eyes, the stern gaze and set jawline of a no-nonsense, hard-working leader.

"Yes. Barkley, our pilot. He's ex-Star Cav, so he's got a service blaster. I thought he kept it more for show, but..." she glanced back in the direction of the landing pads. "You've seen what he did to our landers."

Quantum followed her gaze to the door's narrow window. "Someone is out there."

The Warden turned, seeing the lone figure creep along the shadows of the damaged landers, making for the *Ranger VII*. He knew a hand blaster couldn't do much to his ship's armored hull, but an ex-Star Cav pilot might know other ways to sabotage a hundred-year-old ship. "Let's go!"

The Warden and Quantum bolted from the mine entrance, back into the nightmare heat of Holofernes Omega. The Warden tried to shout at Barkley, but his breath caught in his lungs. Quantum, whose biology differed significantly, managed a deep-throated shout: "Barkley! Stop or we will fire!"

A screeching scarlet blast answered.

The Warden and Quantum ducked and drew their own weapons as they ran across open ground. The saboteur fired again, blazing bolts of plasma cutting through the hot air to explode in volcanic soil. The Warden returned fire. Not to hit the renegade pilot, just to get his attention and keep his head down.

The firefight was short and fierce. Barkley had a single blaster while the Warden and Quantum each wielded a pair. The saboteur was soon outflanked.

"Drop it, Barkley." The Warden stepped around the lander the pilot used for cover. He leveled both Comets at Barkley as the man tried to draw a bead on Quantum, obscured by a haze of steam and vapor.

"They're not who they say they are!" Barkley shouted. He spun and fired. The bolt slashed past the Warden's head.

The Warden fired once.

Barkley jerked with the impact. A shower of sparks erupted from his thermal coat at his right shoulder. The pilot staggered as the blaster fell from his fingers. His mouth moved in a near whisper. "You...can't let it off this moon... It'll take over the galaxy..."

Quantum stepped around the lander as Barkley collapsed. The Warden holstered his weapons and checked the man's slow pulse. "Did you catch that?"

"Every word." Quantum stared back at the mine's entrance. Though the alien was stoic at all times, the Warden sensed wariness on the part of his friend. After securing Barkley's weapon, the Warden carried the wounded pilot back to the mining complex.

"Well," Bale said with a big grin as they entered. "I reckon that's a job well done! Now all we got to do is call for a wreck-and-repair crew to get our landers moving again."

The Warden, Barkley draped across his shoulders, ignored the big man. He turned to Henning. "This investigation isn't over. I want to look into something he said before losing consciousness. We'll need access to your entire crew and your medical facilities."

Henning frowned but gave a curt nod. She turned and led them to a service elevator. "He said something about us not being who we claimed to be, didn't he? He's nuts, Warden. But I reckon if you can figure out what made him that way, it might help keep the rest of us sane."

The Warden suspected this was more than a simple case of space madness. He hadn't seen insanity in Barkley's eyes when he pulled the trigger. Just fear and desperation.

"You have excavated quite deeply," Quantum observed as the creaky elevator continued to drop. The ancient car was a cage-like structure, exposed to the stone walls of the moon's crust, a harsh yellow lamp glowing overhead, a relatively chill draft surging up from below.

Chastain nodded. "This mine has been operational for three generations. My grandfather was one of the first to set boots on this rock." She looked at the Warden. "If what they say about you is true, then you might have known him. Harrison Campbell."

The Warden looked at the girl. "Doesn't ring a bell. But the Frontier is an awful big place. More so back then. But I do recall the newsreels about the Holofernes system being opened for exploration and mining after the first peace treaty with the Tuatha."

The elevator finally came to a jarring halt. The air here was cooler than on the surface, but still warm and humid.

The Warden wondered if the mining operation hadn't stumbled upon something left behind by the ancient and powerful alien race, something dangerous. A nerve toxin, perhaps? He dismissed that possibility. As Chastain had said, the mine had been in operation for over a century, and the Tuatha had ceded the system without a fight.

"Well, as I live and breathe! The Last Star Warden!" A tall man with a red crewcut smiled as the elevator doors opened. He wore an OD jumpsuit, his sweaty, blue-tattooed arms folded across his chest.

The Warden handed the unconscious Barkley to him. "Get him to your medical bay ASAP."

The man blinked and gave Henning a questioning glance.

She nodded. "Get him patched up, Rex. Wulf can take a look at him when he's sober."

Rex Cannon chuckled as he shouldered the bulk of the wounded man. "Good luck with that. Bale, wanna give me a hand here?"

The Warden turned to Quantum. "Go with them. Do what you can for Barkley. Round up the medic. Try to keep everyone together."

Quantum nodded and followed the miners.

The Warden turned to Henning and Chastain. "Care to escort me to Barkley's quarters?"

The two women led the Warden through a cramped, winding maze of hallways more like tunnels, carved out and refined by three generations of miners. Aging fluorescent panels flickered on the low ceiling, cables and conduits hummed along the sides of the narrow walkways, carrying energy and cooled air throughout the complex. Every hundred meters or so, a bulky PlaSteel box jutted from one of the black stone walls. These relay stations maximized energy efficiency by shutting off power to dormant sections of the complex.

"Claustrophobia," the Warden said, "is something that plays at a miner's mind after a while, I imagine."

"You get used to it," Chastain grunted. "Here you are, Casa de Barkley." She waved at a PlaSteel door set in the right-hand wall. The pilot's name was stenciled on a nameplate that looked like it had been used many times.

Henning used her chrono to override the security lock. The door hissed open, releasing a puff of warm, sour-smelling air. The room's automated lights flickered on, revealing a fairly tidy living space: organized desk with personal computer and entertainment center, an opened closet with neatly hung uniforms, a wall covered in framed photos and snapshots, and a black body bag lying on the bunk.

"That explains the smell." Chastain wrinkled her nose as they entered the room.

"Who's missing?" The Warden reached for the bag's zipper. "Have you lost anyone?"

"No." Henning pursed her lips and shook her head. "We're the skeleton crew working the off-season. Just keeping the systems going and automated production up. In a month or so, this place will have almost a hundred folks crawling all over it, getting ready to cut a new vein."

The Warden opened the body bag. A bone-white face stared at him in wide-eyed, frozen horror. Below the face was a ragged, bloodless ruin. The same face had smiled at him just minutes before, on the other side of the complex.

"Rex." Chastain covered her mouth. "That's Rex... but how?"

Henning used her chrono to scan the corpse, shook her head, and looked at the Warden. "It's him... It's definitely him..."

BLACK INFINITY • 103

The Warden raised his own chrono. "Quantum! It's Cannon. Take him down!"

There was no answer. Only static.

He rushed past the two women and headed for the medical bay, hoping he wouldn't get lost, hoping he would reach his friend before it was too late.

The high-pitched whine of blaster fire and the roar of a shotgun sounded as he entered the main corridor near the elevator. Shouts, curses, and a cry of pain followed. The Warden made for the sound of battle.

Rounding a corner, he saw a figure lurch into the narrow corridor. Blood splattered the floor. The sparking overhead light glinted on a red crewcut.

"Halt!" The Warden drew a bead on the fake Rex Cannon. "Stop or I'll shoot!"

The warning cost him his opportunity. The bulking shape of Bale M'Gibo filled the corridor between the Warden and his target. The big man's shotgun roared again, plunging the far end of the hallway into smoke and shadow.

The doppelganger vanished.

"Quantum!" the Warden shouted, edging past the armed miner. "Are you all right?"

The Mechtechan knelt in the center of the cramped medical bay, tending to a short, paunchy man in holo-spectacles with bright red cheeks. Instruments, bunks, and machinery lay scattered about the floor. Barkley sprawled in a corner. Blood, or something like it, splattered the wall beside a shattered specimen cooler.

This caught the Warden's eye. The splatter pattern *moved* like vines seeking sunlight. "What in Sam Hill?"

Quantum turned at the Warden's exclamation. "Interesting. The…entity appears to possess a rather unique and unstable biology. As one might expect from that kind of chromosomal adaptability." Helping the wobbly medic to his feet, Quantum took a sample case from one of the room's drawers and stepped to the tissue-spattered wall.

The Warden knelt beside Barkley, rolled

him over. The pilot was dead. A fresh wound shredded his throat.

"What the hell is going on?" Henning asked as she and Chastain rushed to the doorway. She scanned the chaos before pointing to Bale. "You're hurt. Have Wulf take a look at that."

The big man noticed the wound on his forearm for the first time. "Must've taken some shrapnel when I blasted Rex." His eyes widened and his fingers shook when he tried to activate a fresh nic-stick. "Bastard was trying to *eat* Barkley when me and the blue fellow came in with Doc."

Quantum collected some of the moving tissue in the specimen case. "This entity appears to be quite resilient. I suggest we destroy the rest of its matter while I study this sample."

"You said *entity*." Henning ran her hands over her face. "What is going on here?"

The Warden reloaded his pistols with fresh charges. "The short answer is you've got a bug-hunt on your hands, Miss Henning. The longer answer is this particular bug might be any one of us."

"I will require some time to provide information on the entity's strengths and weaknesses. I recommend we all stay here until several tests can be performed," Quantum said.

The Warden rubbed his chin. "I don't know if we can afford to let this thing have free run of the complex. It acted like the real Cannon, apparently well enough to fool everyone else."

Quantum tilted his head. "I see your point."

"What point?" Fear and frustration filled Chastain's voice.

Henning looked at the younger woman and put her arm around her narrow shoulders. "He means this…*thing* knows what Rex knew. Rex was the demo expert with full access to all the mining charges and detonators."

M'Gibo swore and ran a hand through his short hair.

104 • LIFE'S BLOOD

Harley Wulf blinked, eyes magnified by his holo-specs. Sobered by the encounter, the medic cleared his throat. "Well, we need to find a way to tell who's who. How do we know Cannon was the only one?"

The Warden nodded. "Good point. Get on it. Quantum, run your tests. M'Gibo, you stay here and guard them. I'll retrieve the real Cannon's body for autopsy, and then we can start the hunt." He handed Henning Barkley's blaster. "You know this place better than me, so I'll need your guidance. I'd rather leave you here with the rest but we don't have time for me to learn the lay of the land on the fly."

Chastain raised her chin. "I'm coming too. Before you object, Tara, I'm the best qualified to repair anything Rex... *it* sabotages. That includes disarming any charges it decides to set."

Quantum handed the girl one of his blasters. "Take this."

Henning looked around the room, a hard light in her eyes. Her gaze lingered on the dead pilot. "All right. Let's go. But when I get back, I don't want to see that crawling goop still on the walls. Burn it."

Wulf activated a hand-held plasma torch. "I'm on it."

"So, what's your plan?" Chastain asked the Warden as they left the med bay.

"After we retrieve Barkley's body for autopsy, we secure the demolitions, just to be safe."

Henning led them through the steamy corridors. "You don't sound convinced that the explosives are a priority."

"How long did your chrono say the real Cannon had been dead?"

"About six days."

"Then this...entity has had access to them for at least that long and hasn't done anything. I think it has something more practical in mind."

Chastain frowned. "What?"

They entered the dead pilot's quarters to find an empty body bag. The Warden said, "I think it needs to feed."

"Oh my Cosmos." Chastain covered her mouth.

Henning's face hardened. "Okay. Strike one. After we secure the charges, what's the next part of your plan?"

The Warden forced a smile. "I'm making it up as I go."

"You're a riot." Henning scowled, and led them from the empty room. "Come on. The munitions dump is deeper down. Closer to the active dig."

They hurried through the narrow, winding corridors of volcanic rock. Despite the air conditioning, perspiration glistened on their skin. Deep, ominous shadows loomed inside tunnels and supply-crowded alcoves. By the time they reached the blast-door securing the active dig site, the Warden's jaw ached from clenching. He raised his chrono to check in with Quantum, but there was no signal.

"Iron and quartz deposits play hell with the coms this deep." Chastain shrugged. "There's a hardline station just inside the prep room. You can use that."

The blast-door opened in response to Henning's chrono. A gust of superheated air rushed into the corridor, taking the Warden's breath. Dull red emergency lighting flickered on.

"No sense rerouting power down here when not in use." Henning led them into the muggy gloom. She turned on her suit's integrated lighting, projecting brighter white light from her shoulders.

The Warden drew both Comets and kept his head on a swivel, covering the two women as they moved through the hot cavern. They made for a prefabricated PermaSteel building set into a rough-hewn alcove. The structure looked like it could survive a direct hit from orbital bombardment. It bore the motto DUMP in bright red letters above black skull-and-crossbones. A cartoon balloon beside the skull declared, "Keep your booger hooks off my boom balls!"

"Rex's idea of humor." Chastain checked the security panel on the sealed door with her

BLACK INFINITY • 105

chrono. "Looks like nobody's tried to access the charges in over a week, when Rex last did inventory."

The Warden nodded, still scanning the cavern. "That's good news."

Henning used her chrono to change the access codes. "There. If that thing knew Rex's codes, it's locked out now."

"What was that?" The Warden heard a scratching noise deeper down the tunnel. He tapped his visor, enhancing his vision. There was a flash of movement just before the miners' light beams sparkled on glistening rock.

"There's something there." Henning raised her blaster in a shaky hand.

"Stay behind me and stay together," the Warden said. "But don't shoot unless I do."

The three of them edged down the darkened, winding tunnel, its walls narrowing as it descended. The pale red light behind them faded with each gradual turn.

"It's Rex..." Henning's lights fell on the mangled corpse slumped against the rock wall. The body was in much worse shape than when they'd seen it in Barkley's room, but very little blood.

"Are...you sure that's him?" Chastain looked green in the light of her shoulder rig. "It could be th— that *thing*, right?"

Henning shook her head as she scanned the body again. "No. It's Rex. The bios match his medical records to the tee. Even the Thuban ink in his tattoos."

The Warden noted the corpse's temperature, relative to that of the tunnel. "He hasn't been here long."

Both women raised their pistols, wide eyes probing the darkness.

"I think it's time you made up the next part of your plan, Warden."

"Get back-to-back."

"Warden!" Bale M'Gibo's hoarse voice echoed down the tunnel. "Tara! Chastain! Help me! *Please*!"

"That came from the entrance." Chastain turned and moved that way. "He sounds hurt. Bale! We're coming!"

"Wait!" But the machinist had already vanished around a curve in the tunnel. The Warden and Henning hurried after.

"Chastain!" Henning shouted. "*Stop!*"

The girl's scream filled the tunnel.

The Warden rushed into the red lighting of the staging area. Something that was part Bale M'Gibo and part Rex Cannon stood beside the sealed munitions dump, the twisted and crumpled form of Chastain clutched in its four arms, both mouths buried in the girl's throat and shoulder.

Chastain's amber eyes stared accusingly at the Warden, her mouth wide in mute agony.

Both Comets blazed, filling the humid air with fiery projectiles. The bolts struck the thing's bifurcated legs at the knees, just below Chastain's dangling feet. The creature collapsed with a horrific howl, but did not release its victim.

"*No!*" Henning emerged from the tunnel and froze.

The Warden rushed the creature. It sprang from its kneeling position to grasp the rocky ceiling with a claw-like protuberance from its bulging back.

The entity clung to the girl's body with three of its four arms, the other maneuvering it across the stone ceiling, revealing how it had moved past them in the tunnel.

It glared at the Warden with four mismatched eyes and roared with two bloody mouths.

The Warden blasted the creature until it finally released Chastain's body. His shots were joined by a wide spray from behind him. Henning's bolts hit all around the beast as it moved along the dimly lit ceiling. One of these wild shots blew a chunk of rock away, causing the thing to drop back to the chamber floor.

The creature snarled and howled, appearing to warp and grow. It dived toward the opened entry to the main complex.

"Close the blast door!" The Warden hoped Henning still had the presence of mind to heed him.

The heavy doors slid shut at emergency speed. The thing's rippling bulk darted across the threshold. The doors sliced the creature in two with a sickening wet pop and spray of gore.

The Warden emptied both blasters into the portion inside the chamber. The portion which looked like a half-formed amalgamation of Bale M'Gibo and Chastain. The resulting mess of tissue and carnage continued to move as the Warden reloaded.

"Step back." Henning's voice was cold at his shoulder.

The Warden turned as she hefted a phosphorous charge, the munitions dump open behind her.

"Wait!" But it was too late.

Henning tossed the round device like a softball and watched it roll into the pool of bubbling, steaming matter.

The Warden holstered his weapons, grabbed Henning and pulled her away.

A misshapen tendril coiled around the charge and pulled it into the creature's center mass. Henning activated it with her chrono.

The roaring blast filled the area with a sheet of white flame and steam that lasted a mere second. The Warden and Henning regained their feet, coughing in a cloud of smoke. A black scorch mark marred the blast door where the entity had been. Chastain's smoldering bones lay a few meters away.

Henning fell to her knees beside the blackened corpse, her body wracked with uncontrollable sobs. Leaving the woman to her grief, the Warden stepped to the wall-mounted com box. It had been melted in the blast.

The Warden pulled Henning to her feet. "I'm sorry about Chastain, but we've got to go. You're still the honcho of this dig, and you've got at least one crewman who needs your help. Now come on."

Henning glared through tear-filled eyes. Swatting at her cheeks, she nodded. When they opened the blast door, there was a bloody streak on the tunnel floor leading deeper into the complex. "So, what's your plan now, Warden?"

"We hole up in the med bay until we can get a firm grasp on what this thing is and how it works." The Warden kept his attention focused on the winding, shadowy corridors of the complex, one Comet at the ready.

"Why don't we just get on your ship and get the hell out of here?"

"Because we don't know who could be one of these things, and until we do nobody is getting on the *Ranger VII*." But the question sparked a thought. "Give me a timetable. Was Cannon alone when he did the inventory?"

"Well, yeah. He did the inventory on the charges and made the rounds on the tunnels about a week ago. He and I took turns every other week."

"About the same time your chrono said he died. Yet this thing, in the guise of Cannon, didn't make for the landers?"

"Not as far as I know."

"And when did Barkley start acting suspicious?"

"About the same time... but he didn't sabotage the landers until day before yesterday. Why?"

"I'm working on a theory." The Warden stepped into Barkley's quarters. He wasn't gentle in his search. "You said the operation was about to open a new vein." He tossed the bunk's mattress before taking a closer look at the pinned snapshots. One of them showed Barkley with his arm draped over Rex Cannon's shoulder, both smiling as Rex brandished Barkley's service blaster. "How long since the last dig?"

Henning frowned. "About three weeks, just before we came on shift. What are you looking for?"

The Warden flung drawers open before feeling beneath the desk and finding something taped to the underside. "This, I imagine." He displayed a small data stick. "Come on. Let's get back to the others and see what Barkley knew."

BLACK INFINITY • 107

Reaching medical, the Warden leveled his Comet on Bale M'Gibo. "Drop the weapon."

"What?" the big miner said. He sat on a stool, the shotgun cradled in his lap as he watched the two scientists work. Bale looked to Henning for clarification. "Where's Chas?"

"She's dead." Henning's voice was hard, just like her eyes as she stared at the miner. "Killed by that thing, though it wore your face when it did it. Now put the gun down or I'll shoot you myself." She raised Barkley's blaster.

M'Gibo licked his lips. He eased the shotgun onto the counter and raised his hands.

The Warden noted the fresh bandage on his forearm as Henning retrieved the weapon. "That thing scratched you?"

"No," Wulf answered. "It was a piece of glass from the cooler. I dressed the wound myself. Look, Warden, I get that we're all on edge, but I can vouch for Bale's identity. I ran the test."

The Warden looked at Quantum. His friend nodded confirmation.

Henning stepped beside the Warden and covered the room's other three occupants with the shotgun. "How do we know they aren't all those creatures?"

For a moment, the Warden feared she was right. How could they be certain the entity hadn't made it back here ahead of them? He had seen it split in two after consuming enough tissue to double its mass. Maybe M'Gibo or Wulf were already doppelgängers before he had led Henning and Chastain into the tunnels. Maybe they had killed and copied his friend.

"Because I do not have hemoglobin in my system." Quantum sat back from the instruments and looked at them casually.

The Warden sealed the med bay door and put his back to the wall, blaster still in hand. "Elaborate."

Wulf indicated the workbench's equipment. "We've analyzed the matter left behind when the faux Rex attacked us. My cursory autopsy of Barkley bears out our findings. The thing uses hemoglobin as fuel."

"Fuel?"

Quantum tilted his head. "Yes. Fuel, not food. The entity is not biological in nature."

Henning snapped a glance at the Warden. "But we saw it bleed!"

"Nanobots." Wulf rubbed red-rimmed eyes through his holo spectacles. "The most advanced I've ever seen. An interconnected colony of nanobots programmed to collect DNA from biological beings for the purpose of cataloguing or replication. Done simply by touch—like when Bale helped the faux Rex carry Barkley down here, or any of a hundred other casual contacts since it adopted Rex's identity. The consumption of blood for the hemoglobin is merely the means by which the nanobots maintain and refuel their functions. Given enough hemoglobin, I posit that it could produce more nanobots and, in essence, grow and multiply."

The Warden had seen that in action.

Quantum clarified. "You said this was once a Tuatha system. It is possible that this entity is a weapon developed by that race. Perhaps the Tuatha stored it deep beneath the surface of this lifeless moon, and over time, simply forgot about it."

The Warden lowered the Comet. "That might explain the appearance, but how do these nanobots replicate the memories and personalities of the original?"

Quantum shrugged. "Insufficient data. Possibly something to do with the Tuatha's own nonlinear intelligence, allowing their tech to extrapolate such information from a very small sample size, such as a single cell."

Wulf sighed. "You must admit it's an elegant solution. The perfect saboteur, spy, and assassin. Which begs the question, why didn't they use it to win the war against the U.P.C.?"

"Maybe they feared it." The Warden produced his find from Barkley's room. "Maybe this'll give us a hint."

108 • LIFE'S BLOOD

The medic took the data stick and slid it into a screen. The group gathered to view the contents. It held two files.

The first was a video—dated a week after the crew's arrival—of Barkley training Rex Cannon to use his blaster. The practice range appeared to be somewhere in the mine's depths. The two men joked as they took turns blasting chunks of volcanic rock from the wall of a dead-end tunnel.

The video jerked wildly and the men exchanged surprised curses when a blaster bolt ricocheted back at them. Recovering the dropped camera, Barkley followed Rex to the end of the tunnel to investigate what had caused the errant blast.

"What's this?" Cannon cleared shards from a metallic cylinder buried deep within the wall. "Something carved on it…"

The Warden paused the video. "Those are Tuatha etchings. I can't make out what it says, but I guess that verifies your theory, Quantum. This thing was buried here by the Tuatha."

The video ended with the two men deciding to keep their discovery secret in case the find was valuable. The next file was another video dated the day before the distress call went out. A haggard Barkley sat alone in his room, his drawn face close to the camera.

"I should've known he couldn't wait," the pilot mumbled. "He was my best friend, but he opened that damned container and released whatever was in it."

He picked up the camera and swept the lens across the room to show the body bag on his bed. "And it did that to him. Found him with his throat ripped out down by the empty container. Slipped the baggie outa medical while Wulf was drunk… Now whatever-*it*-is is walking around, wearing Rex's face and acting like it owns the place."

Barkley's bloodshot eyes filled the camera again. "But not me. No, sir. It ain't got me fooled. I seen through it. It ain't got no soul. No light behind the eyes. It might know what Rex knew, but it ain't Rex and never will be.

I reckon it's planning on doing the same to the rest of us, one at a time—if it ain't already started—then it'll be off to another rock or a station or a city, and then it'll never stop until the whole galaxy is just like it."

Barkley raised his blaster into frame. "But I'll fix that. First thing I gotta do is slag those landers, cut off its escape. Then I'll take it down. Right now, I got no way to know who else is real and who's not… I don't know the others so well." The pilot rubbed his watery eyes. "Not until I find more bodies… I guess I'll have to find a better way to tell 'em apart, but for now I gotta take care of those ships."

The video ended.

Henning chewed her lip. "Just think. If it had gone for a ship first thing…"

The Warden nodded. "There was no need. It knew that in a few weeks it would have access to nearly a hundred new sources of hemoglobin and DNA. I think it was biding its time and playing the long game. It just didn't count on Barkley sussing it out so quickly."

Wulf shook his head. "I hope this is the only one the Tuatha left behind. Can you imagine an entire planet of shape-changing vampires?"

The small room plunged into darkness and instant stuffiness.

Bale M'Gibo's deep voice was quiet. "It's shut down the junction box for this section."

Shoulder lighting rigs activated, filling the darkness with narrow lances of bluish light.

The Warden switched his visor to night vision. "Wulf, run the tests on all of us to make sure. Once we're set, we'll make straight for the elevator to the surface, and on to the *Ranger VII*. Once we're away, we'll contact Star Cav and request a quarantine. There may be more containers down there."

The medic hurried through the procedures, his fingers sweating from the growing heat. By the time all the tests were confirmed as legitimate, everyone in the room was soaked, breath straining in the dim light.

BLACK INFINITY • 109

"I'll take the lead." The Warden drew both Comets. "Quantum next, with Henning and Wulf in the middle. M'Gibo, you bring up the rear with the shotgun."

The heated darkness in the corridor was even more intense than that of the infirmary. The Warden rolled his shoulders and moved carefully toward the elevator. His visor painted the narrow hallway in jade and emerald. He knew the entity watched from somewhere just out of sight, waiting to strike.

Every step felt like it might be his last.

A series of turns led them within sight of the elevator.

The Warden exhaled in relief.

Wulf screamed.

The shotgun roared.

The Warden turned, the glare of M'Gibo's shoulder lights dazzling his visor. He heard grunts and scuffling. All but Quantum shouted or screamed. The Warden tapped his visor until vision returned.

"Don't move!" M'Gibo shouted, his smoking shotgun leveled at the two men on the ground at their feet. Quantum and Henning had their blasters aimed at the prone figures as well. The Warden stepped around them in the narrow confines, making use of the side tunnel to his right.

Both men on the ground were Harley Wulf.

"Don't shoot!" one of the medics cried. "It's him! That's the entity!"

"It's lying! I'm me! Kill it!" the other shouted.

They looked identical. The Warden glanced at his companions for some sign of recognition. The horrified expressions on Henning's and M'Gibo's faces declared their own uncertainty. "Quantum?"

The Mechtechan stepped closer, his antennae flexing as his rangy frame knelt for closer inspection. Quantum fell back, clutching his midsection as blue blood splashed in the dim light. M'Gibo fired. Wulf screamed again. The Warden pushed Henning aside as something hit him in the chest. He slammed into the corner, head whipping back with a crack. Stars filled his vision, hot air rushing from his lungs.

The Warden blinked, his nostrils filled with the stink of burnt gunpowder and blood. He shook the fog from his head and reacquired the target. The Wulf-thing swung a claw-tipped tentacle at M'Gibo, forcing the big man to jerk away as he fired. A steaming chunk flew from the tunnel wall in a shower of sparks.

The Warden fired both blasters. The bright red flashes filled the darkness for a moment. The entity recoiled from the wounds, glowing nano-matter splashing across the floor and walls as it bounded down the corridor.

"It's heading for the elevator!" Henning shouted. Her shots slashed around the shadowy thing, filling the hallway with flames and sparks before the weapon's power cell went dry. The Warden used the glow to send another salvo of his own after the entity. More than half his shots hit, but it was too late.

The thing crashed into the metallic framework of the elevator. The horrendous groan of DuraSteel rending and twisting turned into a thunderous roar. The entire cable system and structure collapsed. A huge cloud of dust and debris rushed through the corridor.

For a moment, they all stood in stunned silence.

"Do you think that killed it?" Henning whispered. "Do you think it's dead?"

The Warden holstered his weapons and turned to check on Quantum and Wulf. "I don't know. But I hope you've got another way to the surface, or we will be."

Quantum stood and touched his abdomen. "Just a scratch. It barely pierced my suit."

"Wulf ain't so lucky." M'Gibo knelt beside the medic. The big man fumbled in his jacket for a nic-stick. "I... I think I shot him..."

Quantum checked Wulf's pulse. "He's still alive. Barely. We need to get him back to medical and on a regenerator."

110 • LIFE'S BLOOD

"Without power that's useless," Henning said. "But I can get to the junction box and start it back up. Assuming it isn't destroyed."

The Warden handed her one of his Comets. "You go with the others back to medical. I'll find the junction box."

Henning started to protest, but cast a wary glance at the ruined elevator. "Okay." She held her chrono to the Warden's. "Here's the complex layout. I'm marking the junction box you need to find and uploading my access code. Just get your chrono close to the box and it should take care of the rest. If it's been destroyed, we'll have to relocate to another section."

"Got it." The Warden took off at a jog.

He checked the directions on his chrono every few meters, but still managed to take several wrong turns. He would have brought up the floorplans on his visor's HUD, but wanted nothing obscuring his vision should he run afoul of the entity.

The air grew hotter, harder to breathe. He came to the third dead end and wiped condensation from his visor. "Sam Hill."

"Warden." Quantum's voice came over his chrono as he tried to check the floorplans again. "Wulf will not last much longer without the regenerator. I have done what I can with what we have here, but much of the medication is heat damaged."

"I'm on it." The Warden turned back the way he'd come, praying that Wulf wouldn't perish because he got lost.

"Warden! Over here!" It was Henning's voice from the darkness up ahead.

The Warden drew his remaining Comet. He checked the directions once more, then stepped around the corner.

"Warden!" Henning's eyes widened in the dim blue glow of her shoulder rig. "Glad I found you. I thought you might get lost."

The Warden touched his visor to switch the view to thermal. Henning's heat signature seemed perfectly human. "You should have stayed in medical with the others."

"The only way to save them is to help you." The miner set her jaw. "I'm tired of losing people down here. So let's find that box and get the power back on, huh?"

The Warden twitched the Comet's barrel. "Lead the way."

She scowled, turning to the right and setting a quick pace.

The Warden kept his eyes on the woman. If she was in fact Henning, then all would be fine so long as the entity didn't ambush them again. But if she was the entity, she could be leading him farther from his goal. Wulf would die and the thing would pick them off and replace them one by one. And wait for the main workforce to arrive in a few short weeks.

He checked his chrono, saw the red dot indicating the junction box growing larger on the tiny screen.

"Down here!" Henning made another turn. The junction box, still intact, jutted out of the left-hand wall only a few meters down the corridor. "And just in time. I'm about to boil."

She stepped to the box and raised her chrono.

The Warden cleared his throat. "I'm sorry about Chastain."

Henning didn't pause as she rebooted the junction box. "Me too." Her voice held no emotion.

The overhead lighting panels flickered and hummed back to life.

"You were close, weren't you?"

A dull whoosh announced the cooling units coming back online.

Henning turned, no expression on her face. "I…suppose…"

The Warden fired. The bolt took the left side of Henning's face off in a shower of flaming matter.

The entity lashed out with an arm three times longer than it should have been. The blow struck the Warden in the chest, sent him sliding down the hallway on the moisture-slick floor. The air knocked from his lungs, he fired from his prone position.

The entity morphed grotesquely between shapes as it scrabbled up the side of the

BLACK INFINITY • 111

walls and across the ceiling. Blaster bolts exploded around it and scored flaming hits. The thing had a multitude of eyes and howling mouths, a proliferation of arms and multi-fingered hands, each warped appendage having too many joints.

Springing to his feet, the Warden turned and ran down the corridor leading to the personnel quarters. He continued to fire, but the bolts did little damage. He needed something more devastating, more in line with the phosphorous charge Henning had used in the dig's antechamber. But the munitions dump was several levels below.

The Warden lowered his head and sprinted for the next junction box.

The thing bounded from the ceiling and matched his speed, a howling, writhing abomination of humanoid features and limbs.

The Warden dropped to his knees and slid across the wet floor as he came abreast of the box. A tentacle lashed out, barely missing his head.

The Warden targeted the junction box as the entity reached it. The blaster bolt struck the power coupling in a shower of sparks.

The explosion filled the corridor with electrified plasma. A wall of force flattened the Warden and shattered overhead light panels.

The Warden coughed against the burning heat in his lungs and nostrils as he struggled to his feet. Smoke and steam filled the dim corridor, lit by small fires of burning conduit and nano-matter. He raised his weapon and scanned for a target but his visor was cracked and the HUD was gone.

Removing the visor, the Warden blinked against the stinging smoke. He stayed at the ready until he was sure nothing moved.

"Warden," Henning said over the chrono. "We have power. I think Wulf will make it."

The Warden rolled his aching shoulders and made for the infirmary. "Good. I guess we were due some good news."

👽 👽 👽

"Life's Blood," Jason J. McCuiston's homage to director John Carpenter's film The Thing, *featuring Jason's pulp SF hero The Last Star Warden, debuts in this volume. The title page illustration is by the author*

Jason J. McCuiston has studied under the tutelage of best-selling author Philip Athans. His stories of fantasy, horror, SF, and crime have appeared in numerous anthologies, periodicals, websites, and podcasts, including Nightmare Abbey *and* StoryHack Action & Adventure. *His debut novel, the SF-noir thriller* Project Notebook *is available from Amazon and Audible. He has published two illustrated collections of pulp-style sci-fi action and adventure featuring* The Last Star Warden *with Dark Owl Publishing. You can find most of his publications on his Amazon page at:* www.amazon.com/-/e/B07RN8HT98

Connect with Jason on X (twitter) at: https://twitter.com/JasonJMcCuiston

THE LAST STAR WARDEN

"A rare and refreshing level of pure pulpy fun."
~ Gregory L. Norris, Author of the Gerry Anderson's Into Infinity novels

VOLUME 1

IN PAPERBACK AND ON KINDLE AND KINDLE UNLIMITED

NOVELLA

ON KINDLE VELLA FIRST THREE EPISODES ARE FREE!

VOLUME II

IN PAPERBACK AND ON KINDLE AND KINDLE UNLIMITED

Written and Illustrated by
JASON J. MCCUISTON
Author of Project Notebook

 For more details and to order, visit Dark Owl Publishing
www.darkowlpublishing.com/the-last-star-warden

THE CREATURE FROM THE BLACK LAGOON
UNIVERSAL STUDIOS, 1954

THING FROM A NIGHTMARE

by Tom English

Every night the same dream: outside his bedroom window, the incessant cry of hundreds of crickets and cicadas teeming in the grass and shrubbery below; while inside the room, the soft ticking of the clock on the nightstand, a dull awareness that he's asleep in his bed...and a rising dread of something vaguely familiar taking shape before him.

Against the blackness of the ceiling, a pinhole of silver pierces the darkness, sparkling like a star in the night sky. Slowly it expands, forming a silver cloud in the corner of the room: billowing in an imperceptible breeze, rolling forward, boiling up. Blossoming like a flower, to expose the hideous thing waiting within.

Slowly, ever so slowly, the creature emerges. Just a bit at a time: first the snout, wrinkled, crooked, snarling; then its entire angry head, twisting, struggling to free itself from the cloud of silver mist—like a moth straining from its cocoon—up to its scaly shoulders; squirming until its stubby forearms are free.

Boney fingers claw at the mist clinging to its long torso, as though trying to shave away the rest of the silver smoke that holds it captive. Now it hangs from the ceiling in the corner of the darkened room, half there, half somewhere else, thrashing like an angry insect against an invisible screen.

Bobby knows this is a dream, but it seems so real. He lies quietly in his bed with the sheet pulled up to his nose, trapped halfway between sleep and wakefulness. He tries desperately to be perfectly still while the creature sways from the hole in the ceiling, but his young body is shaking with fear.

His breath catches in his chest. Now he can hear the nauseating sound echoing deep within the creature's larynx: a strange yet familiar noise. A bit like a dog gagging on a chicken bone lodged in its throat; a bit like the gulping sound a water cooler makes when a huge air bubble pushes to the top of the bottle.

Bobby doesn't make these connections. He doesn't have a dog. He's never seen the water cooler in his father's office. He only knows the terror of this thing from a nightmare hovering above the room, threatening to slide down onto his bed.

The monster that haunts his dreams. The thing that comes to him each and every night ...and carries him to the airless summits of his fears. Before Bobby topples over and plunges into darkness, he always manages to wake up—screaming. But after waking, he can

BLACK INFINITY • 115

never remember what frightened him. And in the morning, he can't even remember having a nightmare.

He watches in mute terror as the creature struggles to escape the grip of the silver mist. He can see most of its body now, and then realizes it's never before emerged this far from the cloud. The thing writhes and convulses, twisting back its huge head until it can see Bobby lying frozen on the bed. It leers at him through unblinking yellow eyes, its grotesque head straining closer to where the boy sleeps.

Closer. So near.

The thing curled back its blood-red lips to reveal two long lines of razor-sharp teeth. And Bobby sprang up in his bed screaming.

JOHN MILLER ROLLED OVER onto his back, yawning long and hard as he stretched his legs and arms beneath the bedsheet. The sun was beginning to filter through the drawn blinds. In contrast to the faint light, the grey corners of the room looked gloomy and sullen. He sat up, eased his legs over the side of the bed, and rubbed the back of his neck. *Another horrible night,* he thought. *How much longer?*

He could hear Bobby and Billy giggling in the den downstairs, the sound of carnival music faint in the background. He grabbed his robe. Salvation awaited him downstairs—he could smell it. Sarah had the coffee on and was probably cooking up something special for breakfast.

When he passed through the den on his way to the kitchen, he found the boys lying on their stomachs in front of the television. They were barefooted and still in their pajamas. On the screen an obnoxious-looking clown puppet with a shiny bald head and big red nose was waving a baton over a black box. The puppet was saying something in a squeaky voice that made Bobby and Billy kick their legs up and down and squeal with delight.

"Hi, guys," John said.

"Hi, Daddy," the boys said in unison, not taking their eyes off the TV.

Yeah, it's daddy, John thought. *Nobody special, just the guy who pays the damn cable bill each month.*

He entered the kitchen and took a deep breath. He could smell the pancakes on the griddle.

"Hi, honey," Sarah said cheerfully, as she poured out two small glasses of milk. "I was hoping you'd sleep longer today. How do you feel?"

"Like crap," he said, sinking into a chair at the table. "I'm tired, but I've got things to do today. Besides, I've never been able to lie around the house when it's a nice day outside."

"Well if it happens again tonight, it'll be my turn," she said.

For several moments John gazed pensively out the kitchen window. "Sarah," he said softly, "what are we going to do about these nightmares, anyway?"

Sarah leaned against the counter and brushed back a lock of brown hair. "It's just a phase kids go through. Bobby will grow out of it."

"I don't remember having nightmares like that when I was a kid," John said. His hands were clasped under his chin and there was a far-off gaze in his eyes. "Maybe we should talk to someone…a child psychologist…tell him how long this has been going on."

"It's only been three weeks, John. Things aren't *that* bad."

"I wish the boys would get out of the house more; get some sunshine, fresh air. All they wanna do these days is watch TV. They should be outside running around, playing."

"It's Saturday," Sarah said, "the kid shows are on today. And it's September. All the new shows just started. It's a big deal in a child's life. The boys can play later."

John huffed. "I never watched TV when I was a kid. I was always outside, playing ball, fishing, exploring the woods—or lying under an oak tree with a good book. *The Hobbit.* Or *Horatio Hornblower.* When I was their age—"

116 • THING FROM A NIGHTMARE

"Now you're sounding like your father," Sarah said, smiling.

"Yeah, well maybe Dad was right about *that*. Life's too short. The boys should be out enjoying the day." He pointed a finger in the general direction of the den. "Not watching the idiot box every morning."

"Your father was a Scrooge," Sarah said calmly. "*You* never had a TV because he was too cheap to buy one. Most of his philosophizing was just to justify his stinginess...*and* because he loved to hear himself preach." She ran a hand across John's shoulders. "I'm surprised you made it to adulthood without needing a shrink."

"Well thanks," John said. "Glad I turned out okay."

"Turned out *okay*? You're *amazing*. And I adore you. You can be a grouch when you don't get enough sleep, though," she added. "And sometimes you get all gloomy on me. And then there are days when you—"

"Point taken."

John played absentmindedly with the fork and spoon in front of him. "I just want to do things right. Dad never spent that much time with me. He was always too busy at his feed store. I probably spent more time in the pages of a book than I did with my father." His voice trailed off. "I don't want my kids to feel the way I did when I was growing up. And I sure don't want to look back on things with the same regrets my father had."

"You won't have to," she said. "You're a great dad and the boys absolutely worship you."

"Uh-huh."

"Why don't you take them to the park today. I'll pack a basket for you."

"I'd love that. But..." John stared at the empty plate before him. "Not today. Too much to do around the house. The faucet in the guest bath is still leaking. And I might not get another opportunity to trim the shrubs. How 'bout you, what are you up to today?"

"I'm going to try to get the laundry done while the boys are watching their shows. And I've got some phone calls to make."

He nodded and got up from the table. "I'll tell the boys breakfast is ready."

He walked into the den and sank onto the sofa. On the television the same obnoxious clown puppet was singing in the same squeaky voice, only now it had been joined on screen by a ridiculous dancing dinosaur puppet trying to do the twist, or something like it. Television is so idiotic, he thought. *Such a waste of time...and film?* No, they videotaped the crap these days.

John continued to sit there, watching. He felt too tired from lack of sleep to get up again. *What an ugly clown,* he thought. The puppet had a round, white plastic head, slick and shiny on top except where it was fringed by a half-circle of matted fur. It had strips of thick fur for eyebrows and an over-sized, bulbous, red nose that looked like a blood blister ready to pop from internal pressure. And although it was almost continually jabbering at the audience, it had no visible mouth.

John realized he hated clowns. Something dating back to his childhood, he thought, although he could not say exactly what it was. But he *had* heard that some kids actually had a fear of clowns. There was nothing fearful about this clown, though, despite its nauseating face.

"What's the clown's name?" he asked.

"That's Jolly," Bobby said, eager to show off his profound knowledge. Billy, who was only two and still not very chatty, only giggled and nodded.

"Who's his dinosaur friend?" John asked.

"Klooka's not a dinosaur. He's a dragon!" Bobby said.

"Dwaggin!" Billy said, grinning.

At least he's cute, John thought, as he watched Klooka the dragon doing the wave— *in a creepy sort of way.* The boys looked at each other and snorted with laughter. Then Jolly the clown said: "Okee-dokee, boys and girls, let's see who our special guest is *today*." The clown-puppet pointed to a black video

BLACK INFINITY • 117

monitor, around which Klooka was dancing. The screen of the monitor lit up and appearing on it was a boy about Bobby's age. He was freckle-faced, sandy-haired, and a likely candidate for orthodontic work.

Amazing, John thought. It was no longer enough to *be* on TV. Now they had to *show* the kid on a TV set. They really wanted to drive home the point that this kid was getting to appear on television. It was a perfect tribute to the world's obsession with the boob tube.

When a purple orangutan swung across the screen with a box of Sugar Clumps cereal under its arm, John remembered he was supposed to be rounding up the boys for breakfast. He sat up on the edge of the sofa.

"Hey, Bob-O," he said, "I'm going to the hardware store after breakfast. Would you like to come?"

Bobby started whining, "Do I *haff* to?"

"No, you don't *have* to," John said. "But it's a beautiful day outside. We can drive with the top down. And..." he paused, trying to think of something that would increase the appeal of the outing, "and we'll stop and get a Slurpee."

"I don't wanna!"

"You don't want to be with Daddy?"

Bobby shook his head.

"Don't you love Daddy?"

"I love Klooka," Bobby said, pointing to the television.

John knew he'd asked for it when he'd pressed that last question. He also knew kids often said things that, if taken seriously, could be very hurtful. But he wasn't going to take it seriously. At least, not *too* seriously.

JOHN PULLED THE SHEET up to Billy's chin. "You be a good boy and go to sleep now, Bilbo. Daddy loves you." He kissed his son on the forehead, then tousled the boy's curly hair.

Bobby was sitting up in the middle of his bed, playing with his toes and watching. When John came over and sat on the side of his bed, Bobby smiled and clambered under the sheets.

"How ya doing, Bob-O?" his father whispered.

Bobby whispered in return. "Fine."

"You're getting to be a big fellow," John said. Bobby nodded. "You aren't afraid of the dark, *are you*?"

"Nope," Bobby said with real confidence.

"So we aren't going to have any more nightmares, are we?"

"Nope."

"Because big boys are brave. After all, you're almost five now. And you know Mommy and Daddy are right across the hallway."

Bobby nodded and grinned. John hugged him, and then, before covering him with the sheet, reached out and tickled the boy's ribs. Bobby laughed, grabbed the sheet and pulled it over his head.

THROUGH THE OPEN WINDOW Bobby could hear the rhythmic cry of cicadas in the trees. A full moon cast a pale light into the room and a soft breeze caused the curtains to gently lift and fall as though the night were breathing. He rolled over and lay on his back in the thin darkness, staring at the ceiling. Soon his eyes grew tired and he began to drift in and out of sleep.

At some point the cicadas stopped their hypnotic chittering and the room felt like it was floating on a silent sea. The breeze had gone, too, and evidently the moon had been clouded over because the room was now swallowed up in darkness.

In the far corner of the ceiling a tiny bit of silver stuff began to glimmer, like a tiny pinhole poked through the darkness. Bobby understood what it was—he had seen it before.

He drew the sheet up, tight over his nose and mouth, and watched, half in mute terror, half in fascination, as the blob of silver stuff expanded, slowly evolving, taking the form of a cloud of silver smoke. It billowed out in every direction, bubbling up and folding over upon itself. As the mass grew it also thickened, becoming more defined, more solid.

118 • THING FROM A NIGHTMARE

The cloud bulged from the corner of the ceiling, swollen with the thing forming inside. It slid down the wall and started moving across the room toward the foot of Bobby's bed. Then, like an orchid blooming in a hothouse, layers began to unfold, revealing the writhing form cradled within.

The thing twitched and squirmed within a mass of silver gelatin. Its eyes were still closed. It was sheathed in a grey mucous, but through the slime, Bobby could see the creature's dark, leathery skin. Along its long, muscular torso were perfect rows of scales, or plates, glistening in the faint light like a knight's suit of armor. Down its magnificent back ran a broken ridge of orange fins that were starting to bristle like the fur on a tomcat when it's charged with static.

The creature twisted and stretched in its pool of slime, its great tail thrashing from side to side. Its massive legs kicked out, its bony fingers clawing at the air. And then its eyes opened: yellow, watery eyes that searched the room until they fell upon Bobby's paralyzed frame.

The thing arose, dripping, from the pool of thick, grey fluid, and crouched in the middle of the ruptured sac. From deep within its throat came the strange sound Bobby had heard only in nightmares. But the boy had come to realize this was no dream, for he had never quite fallen asleep.

Not until now had he been able to recognize the thing...to understand the urgency of its call.

The creature sprang forward onto the foot of Bobby's bed and hunched there like a gargoyle, its dorsal fins quivering, the great tail swaying hypnotically in the night air. The crooked snout, still dripping mucous, loomed inches from the boy's face. The cold, lifeless eyes, framed by some evil design, fixed on Bobby's.

The thing exhaled its fetid breath and once again made its guttural noise:

Kloo-kah. Kloo-kah.

Bobby sprang up in bed, his arms held out before him. But not to fend the creature off. This time it wasn't terror that widened his eyes and parted his tiny mouth, but recognition of something with which the boy had grown quite comfortable. Instead of seeing something hideous and horribly wrong, he now saw only the dragon's smiling face and cute, waving tail.

"Klooka!" he said joyously. His arms stretched out to embrace the thing.

THE NEXT MORNING John awoke to screaming as Sarah rushed into their bedroom. "Bobby's gone! I searched all over the house for him— I can't find him anywhere!"

They searched the neighborhood for him, going from door to door a dozen houses down the street in either direction. At each house there were people who joined the search, until there were over fifty people combing the area. They fanned out to the next street over, and then the next, looking through bushes, in drainage ditches behind the houses, anywhere a small boy might wander to.

Then, frantically, John and Sarah called the police, and within fifteen minutes several police cars were slowly moving up and down every street within a two-mile radius of the Miller home.

They could not find Bobby.

AFTER MORE THAN three hours of questioning, telephoning, and checking background records, the police sergeant drove the Millers home and reassured them everything possible would be done to find their little boy.

John and Sarah spent that evening and most of the night pacing back and forth from the living room to Bobby's bedroom. They kept looking out the windows, scanning the darkened street. They would start at the least sound, then run to open the front door. But whenever they threw open the door, no one was there.

Sarah cried the whole night. Several times John broke down, his shoulders shaking violently. Neither of them slept.

BLACK INFINITY • 119

THE NEXT MORNING John pushed himself up from the chair he had occupied for most of the early morning hours. He had watched the sun come up, but it had meant nothing to him. He walked numbly, half dazed, from the living room. Maybe the police would know something by now, he thought. He wanted to call them first thing. Later, he'd call the office and ask for the day off. He needed to stay with Sarah today.

As he shuffled toward the kitchen, he paused at the door to the family room. Inside the dimly lit room, Billy was lying in front of the television, giggling at a clown-puppet. The child was too young to understand the gravity of Bobby's disappearance.

As John stood in the doorway, he realized Billy was watching the same show from Saturday morning. The clown show Bobby took such a delight in. John went in and sagged to the floor next to Billy. On the screen Jolly the clown waved a baton over a video monitor and said: "Okee-dokee boys and girls, let's see who our special guest is *today*."

The screen of the black box lit up, and Billy clapped his little hands and squealed with delight, crying, "Bobby!"

John lurched forward and clutched the sides of the television. "Ohmigod!" he said, "Bobby!"

"Hi, Daddy!" Bobby said, waving his hand on the video monitor. In the background Klooka danced around Bobby, nodding and leering at the camera.

John slowly collapsed in front of the TV. His head was spinning. He felt as though the earth were tilting beneath his body. He knelt there, dazed, unable to comprehend what he was seeing.

Billy was sitting up now, stamping his bare feet up and down, almost hysterical with giggling. John turned and looked at Billy. The laughing child pointed to the screen and said enthusiastically:

"Klooka, Daddy! I *love* Klooka!"

💀 💀 💀

"Thing from a Nightmare" first appeared in the 2018 anthology Fear & Trembling,

Tom English *loves watching old movies, reading vintage comic books, and writing supernatural stories. His work has appeared in books and magazines such as* Haunted House Short Stories *and* Detective Thrillers Short Stories *(both from Flame Tree Publishing);* Gaslight Arcanum: Uncanny Tales of Sherlock Holmes; *and* Weirdbook, *to name a few. Tom edited* Bound for Evil: Curious Tales of Books Gone Bad, *a Shirley Jackson Award finalist for best anthology (2008). He's written five inspirational books with his wife, Wilma Espaillat English, including* Spiritual Boot Camp for Creators & Dreamers, *which BookLife praised as "uniquely thorough, well-written, persuasive, and inspiring." (The BookLife Prize) He resides with Wilma, surrounded by books and beasts, deep in the woods of New Kent, Virginia.*

SMOKE AND SPRITES

BY VONNIE WINSLOW CRIST

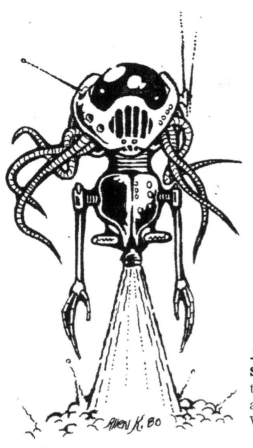

AS SHE APPROACHED THE NORTHERN MARS WASTE DISPOSAL, CALI ADJUSTED THE STRAPS OF HER FACE MASK. Even in her truck, the edges of the apparatus needed to press tight against her skin to seal out the acrid smell of the Waste Zone.

She was in no mood to deal with the stinging eyes and gut-wrenching cough associated with exposure to fumes. Originally scheduled for some down-time, she'd been called in to check the weather phenomenon reported by the facility's workers after Silas cut himself.

"May you get toe rot, Silas Busbeel," she muttered into her mask. Not that she really wished anyone ill, but trying to juggle knives after drinking beer for hours was beyond stupid. Sometimes, it seemed to her that Silas injured himself to avoid leaving home base.

Before her, she saw a skyline of smokestacks sprouting from the NMWD Facility like giant redwood trees. But instead of branches and leaves, the metal chimneys were crowned with clouds of smoke and left-over gases.

As she sped closer, Cali briefly lifted her eyes from the road ahead to study the billowy vapors. Sparks left over from the incineration process glittered at the tops of the smokestacks and tinted vermilion the underbellies of the carbon monoxide and waste gas clouds. At least she hoped still-burning bits were the cause of the bloody discoloration.

Just before she entered a fog of heavy gases which had sunk to ground level, she saw a refuse train pulling under one of the off-loading domes. There, the jumble of garbage would be sorted by machines. The reusable plastics, glasses, papers, and metals that hadn't been removed by scrappers would be taken from the heap. Next, the remaining waste would be funneled to one of the enormous incinerators which not only disposed of garbage, but generated power.

Prompted by the heavy gas dimness, the fog lights on her truck automatically flicked on. Thicker than the usual ground vapors, they limited her visibility, so it took a few minutes before Cali could see the landscape again.

Like most of Mars she'd seen, the red soil here supported stunted trees, straggly grasses, and prickly-looking shrubs. Of course, whatever plants and animals chose to make the Waste their home had to survive without human-made ponds, streams, and reservoirs. She suspected the drought-like conditions were partly responsible for the inhospitable terrain. But no matter what Mars Commercial and Planetary Management, Inc. reported, she knew the gaseous byproducts of the incineration process had to have some impact on the environment.

"Hey, California, you at the site yet?"

Just her luck, thought Cali. Silas was her base contact.

"Yeah. I just drove through the main facility domes and towers. I should be at the Southeast Spur in a few minutes."

"Wanted to let you know a storm's moving in your direction. You might have a chance to see whatever weather phenomenon is spooking the NMWD workers."

"Thanks for the heads up, Silas. California, out."

Cali had added the last phrase to stop any chitchat. She had little tolerance for Silas on a good day. Today, when she was out on a mission he should be working, Cali was sure she'd reel off a series of insults if pushed.

The Southeast Spur, like the main facility and the other NMWD Spurs, was a complex of domes, smokestacks, power lines, and communication towers serviced by a web of train tracks. The facility ran night and day, employing combots and a skeleton crew of humans. Combots, half-robot half-computer machines, did all the labor under the watchful eyes of two human crew members per eight-hour shift. In addition, two facility managers oversaw the crews and arriving train engineers. They also handled the planetary communications, operational reports, and any problems that cropped up.

It was one of those managers who had contacted the Terraforming and Climate Division of MC&PM, Inc. about weird lights in the sky during recent storms. Cali doubted it was more than lightning affected by the various gases released by the Spur's smokestacks. Possibly there was some sort of electrical current from the power generating process charging the atmosphere. But if she had to place a bet, Cali would put her credits on lightning.

Workers at these remote sites tended to go a little buggy after a few years. Almost anyone would begin to imagine things if the only people they saw month after month were five co-workers, two managers, and engineers who just wanted to eat, sleep, and then, leave.

Careful to avoid the machines diligently performing their repetitive tasks, she pulled into the Spur's main dome and tapped her security code in on a virtual keyboard near the entrance.

A man's face appeared on the screen. "What can I do for you?"

"I'm the Terraforming and Climate Division representative sent to evaluate your light anomalies. Am I speaking to Harold Bromski?" Even though it would have been easier for the facilities manager to see her without the mask, Cali refused to lower it and breathe in the stench.

After leaning closer to the screen and squinting, the man responded, "Yeah, I'm Harold. I will be down in a minute. Just have to let the crew know I'll be out of my office for a few hours."

Cali nodded, and then, turned her truck around so it pointed out of the dome. In truth, she didn't like being the only human in the company of hundreds of combots. Although their manufacturers guaranteed their safety, every now and again, a combot suddenly became non-compliant and sometimes violent.

She had finished sending a message to Silas updating him on her status and was checking her data-collection equipment when a loud rap on the passenger's side window of the truck nearly caused her to drop her camera. Cali hit the unlock button, and a gas-masked Harold climbed in.

122 • SMOKE AND SPRITES

"You might want to leave that on," she said when the facility manager started to remove his mask. "At least until we're away from the Spur's smokestacks."

"I forgot the truck wouldn't be airtight," mumbled Harold as he adjusted his mask's straps. He continued, "There's an observation tower about a mile east of here where you should be able to see..." He paused and seemed to be searching for the right word. "The lights. You should be able to see the lights."

Following Harold's directions, Cali wove through the Southeast Spur's buildings, finally arriving at a concrete block tower.

"Need some help?" asked Harold as she gathered various instruments to collect data, her camera, and a handful of spare batteries.

"Nope," she responded. She placed everything in a heavy-weight cloth knapsack, slung it over her shoulder, and followed the manager to the tower's door.

Harold fumbled with several passkeys, located the correct key, and swiped the lock-pad. The lock buzzed and the door swung inward. Lights must have been programmed to turn on when the door was opened, or perhaps when sensors detected humans, because the tower's interior was suddenly illuminated.

"Doesn't feel nearly as spooky, now," Harold said. He forced a nervous laugh. "Not that I'm afraid of a few lights in the sky."

"Never said you were," replied Cali as she brushed past him and began the climb to the observation room.

As soon as she reached the top level of the tower, it was clear Silas's weather forecast was dead on. Nimbus clouds lined up on the horizon like an army of charcoal gray soldiers. Lightning zigzagged from the thunderheads to the ground in an awesome display of electrical power. There must have been mica or some other reflective mineral in the soil, because the bolts appeared to not only strike the planet's surface, but to race across the ground.

"Are those the lights you reported?"

"No," answered Harold with eyes wide.

As Cali set up her Extra Low Frequency radio receivers, low-light camera, and various other instruments, she noted there were sweat beads on Harold's forehead and upper lip.

The storm moved closer, and a pounding rain slammed into the tower's roof. Though it was hard to see through the heavy rainfall, the fierce lightning clearly split the sky, and the thunder seemed to rock the building. As quickly as it had started, the rain slowed to a mist, and what appeared to be flames shot upwards from the clouds.

"TLEs," gasped Cali.

"ETs!" Harold was clearly shocked.

"No, not Extra-Terrestrials." *Certainly, an incorrect nomenclature since we aren't on Earth*, thought Cali. But she knew alien species were still labeled ETs by most people. "TLEs, *Transient Luminous Events*. Sometimes people call them cloud-to-space lightning or upper atmosphere lightning. I think what we have here is a variety called a *sprite*."

The manager stared at her as if waiting for more information.

The phenomenon occurred again. This time, she had the camera pointed in the correct direction and programmed to snap continuous pictures.

"Let's take a look," she said as she plugged the camera into her view-screen. Several finger strokes later, images of TLEs flashed one after the other on the screen.

First, there was a disc-shaped glow above the thunderstorm. Next, a column of red light shot up from the mesosphere and, Cali was sure, into the ionosphere. There appeared to be tendrils of purple and blue coming from the red cylindrical beam and dangling down into the stratosphere, almost touching the clouds.

And then, the upper atmosphere lightning was gone. Within a split second, another red glow occurred, and the sequence began again. Though the sprites seemed to be the same phenomenon repeating itself, Cali knew the radio signature would be unique for each sprite.

Before she could continue her explanation of positive charges and atmospheric layers,

BLACK INFINITY • 123

Harold pointed at the view-screen and whispered, "What is *that*?"

She glanced at the screen. There looked to be a glowing disc-shaped vessel hovering at the base of a sprite. Before she could speak, it dropped groundward in a vivid display of lightning.

"Um, I'm not sure."

The final image was of a glowing disc resting on the planet's surface. She pressed her lips together as the pictures began to repeat.

Cali went to the window, held her binoculars up to her eyes and, using the night-vision setting, scanned the Martian terrain about where the disc should be. She observed the vessel less than two miles from the tower, skimming across the ground in their direction. It was definitely not human in design.

Perhaps the aliens were there to collect the carbon monoxide or other discharged gases from the Waste facility. Perhaps they were observing the sprites, too. Or studying the design of the power-producing incinerators. But there were also many nefarious reasons for ETs to visit a desolate, nearly deserted part of Mars.

Before she had time to wonder about the aliens, Cali saw the vehicle stop about a quarter mile from the tower. A doorway opened in the vessel's side. In the blink of an eye, a ramp shot out, then lowered until it rested on the Martian surface.

Harold, who was also studying the spacecraft with binoculars, gasped.

Although she felt like gasping as well, Cali remained silent as five tall, willowy, glowing bipeds exited the vessel. Even from this distance, the alien's features were easily discernable. Nose slits, wide mouths, and three large eyes were the only dark spots on their pale green bodies. She didn't know if the eerie glow of the creatures was caused by bioluminescent skin, or a spacesuit constructed of a luminous fabric. But more importantly, they each held what appeared to be long-barreled weapons.

As she lowered her binoculars, Cali saw the fear in Harold's eyes. He, too, knew there were rules, negotiations, and notifications if off-worlders wanted to land on Mars. But these ETs had chosen to arrive in secret. And armed. She was certain no good would come of their visit.

Barely able to breathe, she activated her headset. She needed to report what she'd found while investigating the strange lights at the North Mars Waste Disposal Facility to her base contact. She hoped the communication towers still functioned. Hoped there was enough time left to get a warning out.

"Silas, this is California. Please, tell me you're there."

"I'm here for you, Cali. What's shaking?"

If she hadn't been in such a hurry to pack her gear back in her knapsack and get the heck out of there, Cali might have appreciated Silas's attempt at humor. As it was, she was pushing Harold toward the top of the stairs and hoping to make it out of this predicament alive.

"Unidentified alien ship dropped to the ground during a sprite event not far from here. No off-worlder visitors scheduled in this area, are there?"

"I'll check."

Cali and Harold were at the foot of the stairs when Silas spoke again. "No aliens approved for a visit planet-wide at the moment. So I've sent notification of your ETs to MC&PM, Inc.'s Defense Division."

"Roger that. Cutting off communication so the ETs can't trace us. California, out." Cali took off her headset and dropped it into her knapsack with the rest of her gear as she turned to face Harold.

"Can't go out the way we came in," she gestured to the tower's front door with her thumb. "What's below us?"

"I have never been... I mean, I think there might be... that is, if I remember the plans for..."

While the facility's manager mumbled away, Cali scanned the interior of the Southeast Spur's observation tower.

"Is that a basement access door below the steps?" she asked when she noticed a slight variance in the block work. It appeared the tower's builders disguised a metal door by employing an antiquated French painting technique. *Trompe l'oeil* had been expertly applied, creating a convincing illusion of concrete blocks—which might just save their necks.

"Key?" she said to Harold as she stuck her hand out, palm-side up.

"I'm not sure which one unlocks that door," he answered as he dropped the whole ring of keys and passkeys into her hand.

"A traditional key, I imagine," said Cali. "Anything electronic would be scannable, and therefore defeat the purpose of the deceptive paintwork." Seconds later, she held up a skeleton key that looked like it could unlock a treasure chest. "Let's try this one."

After using her fingertips to locate the keyhole in the painted metal door, she pushed the key into the lock, turned it clockwise two turns, then pushed inwards. With a soft scraping sound, the door slid open.

No lights automatically flicked on. So, Cali pulled a small flashlight from her pants pocket, turned it on, and stepped inside the passageway. Almost immediately, within the wall there were steps heading down.

"Come on, Harold. The ETs will be here any second."

Without a word, the facility's manager climbed into the wall beside her, then took several steps down the stairs which Cali surmised led to an underground chamber. She pushed the secreted door closed, used the skeleton key to re-lock it, then pointed her flashlight's beam down the stairwell.

Upon reaching the bottom of the steps, Harold and she found themselves in a subterranean passageway.

"Okay, Harold. Think. Which way should we go?"

"Brom."

"What?"

"People call me, Brom. Not Harold."

Cali paused. A take charge kind of person, she sometimes forgot the personal touch needed for workplace interactions. "Sorry about that. So, Brom, which way should we head in order to avoid the aliens?"

"To the left. There should be a handcar parked on narrow gauge rails in about fifty meters."

As they jogged down the passage, Cali glanced at Brom. Stating his preferred name seemed to have calmed the manager. Perhaps she had misjudged the guy.

When she reached the handcart, Cali loaded her gear onto one side of its platform and climbed aboard the contraption. She'd read about handcarts, but had never actually seen, much less used one. Brom stepped onto the other side of the cart and grabbed the handlebar.

"When I push down, you pull up," he explained. "Then, you push down, and I pull up. Once we get the rhythm, we'll be moving pretty quickly."

"Perfect," she replied as Brom and she, pushing and pulling the hand bars, rolled down the narrow track into the darkness.

After about a minute, Cali took a chance, turned on her flashlight, and pointed it in the direction Brom and she were headed. The beam was quickly swallowed by the blackness.

"Where exactly are we going?" she asked.

"The sub-basement of the Southeast Spur," said Brom. "We should be there soon."

"How do we access the Spur's basement?" Cali wanted a plan in place as soon as possible. So far, it appeared they hadn't been followed by the green glowies. But the handcart's wheels made a rumbling noise as they rolled along, and she had to believe the aliens had discovered the tunnel by now.

"Light!" shouted Brom. "Down the tunnel behind us."

Cali looked over her shoulder.

"It's the aliens," she said. *I hate being right*, thought Cali as the handcart thumped into a bumper.

"We're here," said Brom. He scrambled off

BLACK INFINITY • 125

the cart and tried the handle of a metal door located to the right of the tracks. It was locked.

Cali was two steps behind the facility's manager. She pulled the key ring from her pocket and started trying keys. Finally, a dull silver one fit the lock. A twist to the left, turn of the knob, and hard push later, and the door opened inward. Thankfully, there were motion-activated lights in the sub-basement corridor.

She glanced down the tunnel once more before closing and re-locking the door. The green glowies were now visible.

"Please tell me there's an elevator, because that door isn't going to stop the aliens for long."

"There is," replied Brom. He pointed to a side passage. "And here it is."

Key ring still in her hand, Cali stepped forward. Before she could try the various passkeys to see which unlocked the elevator, the facility manager pointed to a passkey with a red symbol engraved in it.

"That's the one," he said. "Just swipe it."

Cali did as she was told. The elevator took several seconds before it slid its door open.

"I don't think it has ever been used." Brom smiled halfheartedly, then added, "I was afraid it might not work."

"I'm grateful it did," said Cali. And she meant it.

Once they were both in the elevator, it closed its doors. Brom hit the Level Two button, then proceeded to punch in a code on the keypad affixed to the wall beside the control panel.

"Who is this?" asked a gruff voice.

"Harold Bromski and Cali, the MC&PM Terraforming and Climate rep. There are armed aliens in the sub-basement tunnel."

After a mumbled profanity, the man seemed to remember his training. "Sir, has MC&PM's Defense Division been notified?"

"Yes," replied Brom. "But they won't be here for half an hour or longer. So, it's up to us and the combots to defend the Waste Disposal Facility and its equipment until Defense arrives."

Before the man could respond, the elevator stopped, and its doors opened.

Cali found herself inside the Waste Facility with Brom and two nervous crewmen.

"Wake the rest of the crew and meet Cali and me on the first level of the central dome," ordered the facility manager. "The combots there should be willing to assist us."

Once the crewmen had rushed off, she looked at Brom and asked, "Do you really think the combots will help?"

"I have no idea." He closed his eyes for a second. "But if they won't, we're goners."

Cali nodded, then followed Brom down one flight of steps to the Spur's central dome and its army of combots. As she watched him run from combot to combot typing in code then shouting at each bot, "Defend facility," Cali pulled a pulse gun from her backpack.

While she was checking its charge, six crew personnel and the other manager raced down the stairs. All were armed. One carried an extra rifle. No doubt, it was for Harold Bromski.

Now that there were nine people and potentially a throng of combots facing the aliens, Cali felt a little safer. That is until the elevator doors opened and the green glowies rushed out screeching and shooting fireballs from their weapons.

Safety a thing of the past, Cali ducked behind the nearest combot, raised her gun, and pulled the trigger.

"Smoke and Sprites" is a revised and expanded version of a story first appearing in the 2015 anthology Hides the Dark Tower.

Vonnie Winslow Crist, SFWA, HWA, is author of Dragon Rain, Beneath Raven's Wing, The Enchanted Dagger, Owl Light, The Greener Forest, Murder on Marawa Prime, *and other books. Her fiction appears in* Amazing Stories, Cirsova Magazine, Lost Signals: A Terran Republic Anthology, Black Infinity, Planetary Anthology Series: Neptune, Storming Area 51, Worlds, Galactic Goddesses, Insignia 2021: Best Asian Speculative Fiction, *and elsewhere.*

Believing the world is still filled with mystery, magic and miracles, Vonnie strives to celebrate the power of myth in her fiction. For more information: http://www.vonniewinslowcrist.com

I Married a Monster from Outer Space (Paramount, 1958)

BLACK INFINITY • 127

THE STORY THAT INSPIRED THE 1932 UNIVERSAL STUDIOS CLASSIC

THE MUMMY

THE RING OF THOTH
BY SIR ARTHUR CONAN DOYLE

MR. JOHN VANSITTART SMITH, F.R.S., OF 147-A GOWER STREET, WAS A MAN WHOSE ENERGY OF PURPOSE AND CLEARNESS OF THOUGHT MIGHT HAVE PLACED HIM IN THE VERY FIRST RANK OF SCIENTIFIC OBSERVERS. He was the victim, however, of a universal ambition which prompted him to aim at distinction in many subjects rather than preeminence in one.

In his early days he had shown an aptitude for zoology and for botany which caused his friends to look upon him as a second Darwin, but when a professorship was almost within his reach he had suddenly discontinued his studies and turned his whole attention to chemistry. Here his researches upon the spectra of the metals had won him his fellowship in the Royal Society; but again he played the coquette with his subject, and after a year's absence from the laboratory he joined the Oriental Society, and delivered a paper on the Hieroglyphic and Demotic inscriptions of El Kab, thus giving a crowning example both of the versatility and of the inconstancy of his talents.

The most fickle of wooers, however, is apt to be caught at last, and so it was with John Vansittart Smith. The more he burrowed his way into Egyptology the more impressed he became by the vast field which it opened to the inquirer, and by the extreme importance of a subject which promised to throw a light upon the first germs of human civilization and the origin of the greater part of our arts and sciences. So struck was Mr. Smith that he straightway married an Egyptological young lady who had written upon the sixth dynasty, and having thus secured a sound base of operations he set himself to collect materials for a work which should unite the research of Lepsius and the ingenuity of Champollion.[2] The preparation of this *magnum opus* entailed many hurried visits to the magnificent Egyptian collections of the Louvre, upon the last of which, no longer ago than the middle of last October, he became involved in a most strange and noteworthy adventure.

The trains had been slow and the Channel had been rough, so that the student arrived in Paris in a somewhat befogged and feverish condition. On reaching the Hôtel de France, in the Rue Laffitte, he had thrown himself upon a sofa for a couple of hours, but finding that he was unable to sleep, he determined, in spite of his fatigue, to make his way to the Louvre, settle the point which he had come to decide, and take the evening train back to Dieppe. Having come to this conclusion, he donned his greatcoat, for it was a raw rainy day, and made his way across the Boulevard des Italiens and down the Avenue de l'Opéra. Once in the Louvre he was on familiar ground, and he speedily made his way to the collection of papyri which it was his intention to consult.

The warmest admirers of John Vansittart Smith could hardly claim for him that he was a handsome man. His high-beaked nose and prominent chin had something of the same acute and incisive character which distinguished his intellect. He held his head in a birdlike fashion, and birdlike, too, was the pecking motion with which, in conversation, he threw out his objections and retorts. As he stood, with the high collar of his greatcoat raised to his ears, he might have seen from the reflection in the glass-case before him that his appearance was a singular one. Yet it came upon him as a sudden jar when an English voice behind him exclaimed in very audible tones, "What a queer-looking mortal!"

The student had a large amount of petty vanity in his composition which manifested itself by an ostentatious and overdone disregard of all personal considerations. He straightened his lips and looked rigidly at the roll of papyrus, while his heart filled with bitterness against the whole race of traveling Britons.

"Yes," said another voice, "he really is an extraordinary fellow."

"Do you know," said the first speaker, "one could almost believe that by the continual contemplation of mummies the chap has become half a mummy himself?"

"He has certainly an Egyptian cast of countenance," said the other.

John Vansittart Smith spun round upon his heel with the intention of shaming his countrymen by a corrosive remark or two. To his surprise and relief, the two young fellows who had been conversing had their shoulders turned towards him, and were gazing at one of the Louvre attendants who was polishing some brass-work at the other side of the room.

"Carter will be waiting for us at the Palais Royal," said one tourist to the other, glancing at his watch, and they clattered away, leaving the student to his labors.

"I wonder what these chatterers call an Egyptian cast of countenance," thought John Vansittart Smith, and he moved his position slightly in order to catch a glimpse of the man's face. He started as his eyes fell upon it. It was indeed the very face with which his studies had made him familiar. The regular statuesque features, broad brow, well-rounded chin, and dusky complexion were the exact counterpart of the innumerable statues, mummy-cases, and pictures which adorned the walls of the apartment.

The thing was beyond all coincidence. The man must be an Egyptian. The national angularity of the shoulders and narrowness of the hips were alone sufficient to identify him.

---

[2] Prussian Egyptologist, linguist, and modern archaeologist Karl Richard Lepsius (1810–1884); French philologist and orientalist Jean-François Champollion (1790–1832), known primarily as the decipherer of hieroglyphs and a founding figure of Egyptology.

The Uncanny (Boris) Karloff as Imhotep. All photos from *The Mummy* (Universal Studios, 1932)

John Vansittart Smith shuffled towards the attendant with some intention of addressing him. He was not light of touch in conversation, and found it difficult to strike the happy mean between the brusqueness of the superior and the geniality of the equal. As he came nearer, the man presented his side face to him, but kept his gaze still bent upon his work. Vansittart Smith, fixing his eyes upon the fellow's skin, was conscious of a sudden impression that there was something inhuman and preternatural about its appearance. Over the temple and cheek-bone it was as glazed and as shiny as varnished parchment. There was no suggestion of pores. One could not fancy a drop of moisture upon that arid surface. From brow to chin, however, it was cross-hatched by a million delicate wrinkles, which shot and interlaced as though Nature in some Maori mood had tried how wild and intricate a pattern she could devise.

"Où est la collection de Memphis?" asked the student, with the awkward air of a man who is devising a question merely for the purpose of opening a conversation.

"C'est là," replied the man brusquely, nodding his head at the other side of the room.

"Vous êtes un Egyptien, n'est-ce pas?" asked the Englishman.

The attendant looked up and turned his strange dark eyes upon his questioner. They were vitreous, with a misty dry shininess, such as Smith had never seen in a human head before. As he gazed into them he saw some strong emotion gather in their depths, which rose and deepened until it broke into a look of something akin both to horror and to hatred.

"Non, monsieur; je suis Français." The man turned abruptly and bent low over his polishing.

The student gazed at him for a moment in astonishment, and then turning to a chair in a retired corner behind one of the doors he proceeded to make notes of his researches among the papyri. His thoughts, however refused to return into their natural groove. They would run upon the enigmatical attendant with the sphinx-like face and the parchment skin.

"Where have I seen such eyes?" said Vansittart Smith to himself. "There is something

BLACK INFINITY • 131

saurian about them, something reptilian. There's the membrana nictitans of the snakes," he mused, bethinking himself of his zoological studies. "It gives a shiny effect. But there was something more here. There was a sense of power, of wisdom—so I read them—and of weariness, utter weariness, and ineffable despair. It may be all imagination, but I never had so strong an impression. By Jove, I must have another look at them!" He rose and paced round the Egyptian rooms, but the man who had excited his curiosity had disappeared.

The student sat down again in his quiet corner, and continued to work at his notes. He had gained the information which he required from the papyri, and it only remained to write it down while it was still fresh in his memory. For a time his pencil traveled rapidly over the paper, but soon the lines became less level, the words more blurred, and finally the pencil tinkled down upon the floor, and the head of the student dropped heavily forward upon his chest.

Tired out by his journey, he slept so soundly in his lonely post behind the door that neither the clanking civil guard, nor the footsteps of sightseers, nor even the loud hoarse bell which gives the signal for closing, were sufficient to arouse him.

Twilight deepened into darkness, the bustle from the Rue de Rivoli waxed and then waned, distant Notre Dame clanged out the hour of midnight, and still the dark and lonely figure sat silently in the shadow. It was not until close upon one in the morning that, with a sudden gasp and an intaking of the breath, Vansittart Smith returned to consciousness. For a moment it flashed upon him that he had dropped asleep in his study-chair at home. The moon was shining fitfully through the unshuttered window, however, and, as his eye ran along the lines of mummies and the endless array of polished cases, he remembered clearly where he was and how he came there. The student was not a nervous man. He possessed that love of a

novel situation which is peculiar to his race. Stretching out his cramped limbs, he looked at his watch, and burst into a chuckle as he observed the hour. The episode would make an admirable anecdote to be introduced into his next paper as a relief to the graver and heavier speculations. He was a little cold, but wide awake and much refreshed. It was no wonder that the guardians had overlooked him, for the door threw its heavy black shadow right across him.

The complete silence was impressive. Neither outside nor inside was there a creak or a murmur. He was alone with the dead men of a dead civilization. What though the outer city reeked of the garish nineteenth century! In all this chamber there was scarce an article, from the shriveled ear of wheat to the pigment-box of the painter, which had not held its own against four thousand years. Here was the flotsam and jetsam washed up by the great ocean of time from that far-off empire. From stately Thebes, from lordly Luxor, from the great temples of Heliopolis, from a hundred rifled tombs, these relics had been brought. The student glanced round at the long silent figures who flickered vaguely up through the gloom, at the busy toilers who were now so restful, and he fell into a reverent and thoughtful mood. An unwonted sense of his own youth and insignificance came over him. Leaning back in his chair, he gazed dreamily down the long vista of rooms, all silvery with the moonshine, which extend through the whole wing of the widespread building. His eyes fell upon the yellow glare of a distant lamp.

John Vansittart Smith sat up on his chair with his nerves all on edge. The light was advancing slowly towards him, pausing from time to time, and then coming jerkily onwards. The bearer moved noiselessly. In the utter silence there was no suspicion of the pat of a footfall. An idea of robbers entered the Englishman's head. He snuggled up further into the corner. The light was two rooms off. Now it was in the next chamber,

132 • THE RING OF THOTH

and still there was no sound. With something approaching to a thrill of fear the student observed a face, floating in the air as it were, behind the flare of the lamp. The figure was wrapped in shadow, but the light fell full upon the strange eager face. There was no mistaking the metallic glistening eyes and the cadaverous skin. It was the attendant with whom he had conversed.

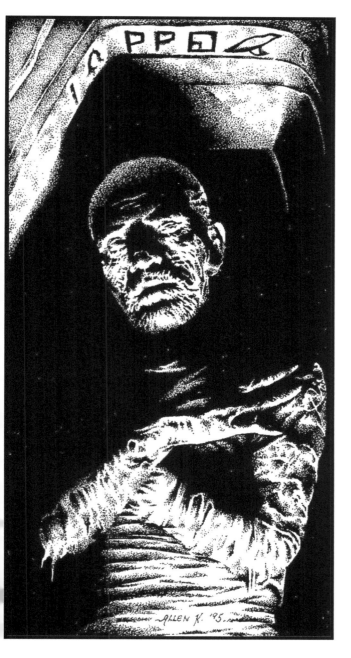

Vansittart Smith's first impulse was to come forward and address him. A few words of explanation would set the matter clear, and lead doubtless to his being conducted to some side door from which he might make his way to his hotel. As the man entered the chamber, however, there was something so stealthy in his movements, and so furtive in his expression, that the Englishman altered his intention. This was clearly no ordinary official walking the rounds. The fellow wore felt-soled slippers, stepped with a rising chest, and glanced quickly from left to right, while his hurried gasping breathing thrilled the flame of his lamp. Vansittart Smith crouched silently back into the corner and watched him keenly, convinced that his errand was one of secret and probably sinister import.

There was no hesitation in the other's movements. He stepped lightly and swiftly across to one of the great cases, and, drawing a key from his pocket, he unlocked it. From the upper shelf he pulled down a mummy, which he bore away with him, and laid it with much care and solicitude upon the ground. By it he placed his lamp, and then squatting down beside it in Eastern fashion he began with long quivering fingers to undo the cerecloths and bandages which girt it round. As the crackling rolls of linen peeled off one after the other, a strong aromatic odor filled the chamber, and fragments of scented wood and of spices pattered down upon the marble floor.

It was clear to John Vansittart Smith that this mummy had never been unswathed before. The operation interested him keenly. He thrilled all over with curiosity, and his birdlike head protruded further and further from behind the door. When, however, the last roll had been removed from the four-thousand-year-old head, it was all that he could do to stifle an outcry of amazement. First, a cascade of long, black, glossy tresses poured over the workman's hands and arms. A second turn of the bandage revealed a low, white forehead, with a pair of delicately arched eyebrows. A

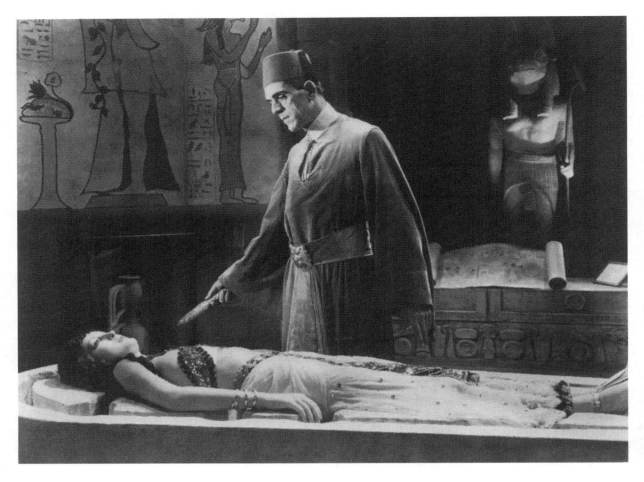

third uncovered a pair of bright, deeply fringed eyes, and a straight, well-cut nose, while a fourth and last showed a sweet, full, sensitive mouth, and a beautifully curved chin. The whole face was one of extraordinary loveliness, save for the one blemish that in the centre of the forehead there was a single irregular, coffee-colored splotch. It was a triumph of the embalmer's art. Vansittart Smith's eyes grew larger and larger as he gazed upon it, and he chirruped in his throat with satisfaction.

Its effect upon the Egyptologist was as nothing, however, compared with that which it produced upon the strange attendant. He threw his hands up into the air, burst into a harsh clatter of words, and then, hurling himself down upon the ground beside the mummy, he threw his arms round her, and kissed her repeatedly upon the lips and brow. *"Ma petite!"* he groaned in French. *"Ma pauvre petite!"* His voice broke with emotion, and his innumerable wrinkles quivered and writhed, but the student observed in the lamplight that his shining eyes were still as dry and tearless as two beads of steel. For some minutes he lay, with a twitching face, crooning and moaning over the beautiful head. Then he broke into a sudden smile, said some words in an unknown tongue, and sprang to his feet with the vigorous air of one who has braced himself for an effort.

In the centre of the room there was a large circular case which contained, as the student had frequently remarked, a magnificent collection of early Egyptian rings and precious

134 • THE RING OF THOTH

stones. To this the attendant strode, and, unlocking it, he threw it open. On the ledge at the side he placed his lamp, and beside it a small earthenware jar which he had drawn from his pocket. He then took a handful of rings from the case, and with a most serious and anxious face he proceeded to smear each in turn with some liquid substance from the earthen pot, holding them to the light as he did so. He was clearly disappointed with the first lot, for he threw them petulantly back into the case, and drew out some more. One of these, a massive ring with a large crystal set in it, he seized and eagerly tested with the contents of the jar. Instantly he uttered a cry of joy, and threw out his arms in a wild gesture which upset the pot and sent the liquid streaming across the floor to the very feet of the Englishman. The attendant drew a red handkerchief from his bosom, and, mopping up the mess, he followed it into the corner, where in a moment he found himself face to face with his observer.

"Excuse me," said John Vansittart Smith, with all imaginable politeness; "I have been unfortunate enough to fall asleep behind this door."

"And you have been watching me?" the other asked in English, with a most venomous look on his corpse-like face.

The student was a man of veracity. "I confess," said he, "that I have noticed your movements, and that they have aroused my curiosity and interest in the highest degree."

The man drew a long flamboyant-bladed knife from his bosom. "You have had a very narrow escape," he said; "had I seen you ten minutes ago, I should have driven this

through your heart. As it is, if you touch me or interfere with me in any way you are a dead man."

"I have no wish to interfere with you," the student answered. "My presence here is entirely accidental. All I ask is that you will have the extreme kindness to show me out through some side door." He spoke with great suavity, for the man was still pressing the tip of his dagger against the palm of his left hand, as though to assure himself of its sharpness, while his face preserved its malignant expression.

"If I thought——" said he. "But no, perhaps it is as well. What is your name?"

The Englishman gave it.

"Vansittart Smith," the other repeated. "Are you the same Vansittart Smith who gave a paper in London upon El Kab? I saw a report of it. Your knowledge of the subject is contemptible."

"Sir!" cried the Egyptologist.

"Yet it is superior to that of many who make even greater pretensions. The whole keystone of our old life in Egypt was not the inscriptions or monuments of which you make so much, but was our hermetic philosophy and mystic knowledge, of which you say little or nothing."

"Our old life!" repeated the scholar, wide-eyed; and then suddenly, "Good God, look at the mummy's face!"

The strange man turned and flashed his light upon the dead woman, uttering a long doleful cry as he did so. The action of the air had already undone all the art of the embalmer. The skin had fallen away, the eyes had sunk inwards, the discolored lips had writhed away from the yellow teeth, and the brown mark upon the forehead alone showed that it was indeed the same face which had shown such youth and beauty a few short minutes before.

The man flapped his hands together in grief and horror. Then mastering himself by a strong effort he turned his hard eyes once more upon the Englishman.

"It does not matter," he said, in a shaking voice. "It does not really matter. I came here tonight with the fixed determination to do something. It is now done. All else is as nothing. I have found my quest. The old curse is broken. I can rejoin her. What matter about her inanimate shell so long as her spirit is awaiting me at the other side of the veil!"

"These are wild words," said Vansittart Smith. He was becoming more and more convinced that he had to do with a madman.

"Time presses, and I must go," continued the other. "The moment is at hand for which I have waited this weary time. But I must show you out first. Come with me."

Taking up the lamp, he turned from the disordered chamber, and led the student swiftly through the long series of the Egyptian, Assyrian, and Persian apartments. At the end of the latter he pushed open a small door let into the wall and descended a winding stone stair. The Englishman felt the cold fresh air of the night upon his brow. There was a door opposite him which appeared to communicate with the street. To the right of this another door stood ajar, throwing a spurt of yellow light across the passage. "Come in here!" said the attendant shortly.

Vansittart Smith hesitated. He had hoped that he had come to the end of his adventure. Yet his curiosity was strong within him. He could not leave the matter unsolved, so he followed his strange companion into the lighted chamber.

It was a small room, such as is devoted to a *concierge*. A wood fire sparkled in the grate. At one side stood a truckle bed, and at the other a coarse wooden chair, with a round table in the centre, which bore the remains of a meal. As the visitor's eye glanced round he could not but remark with an ever-recurring thrill that all the small details of the room were of the most quaint design and antique workmanship. The candlesticks, the vases upon the chimney-piece, the fire-irons, the ornaments upon the walls, were all such as he had been wont to associate with the remote

136 • THE RING OF THOTH

past. The gnarled heavy-eyed man sat himself down upon the edge of the bed, and motioned his guest into the chair.

"There may be design in this," he said, still speaking excellent English. "It may be decreed that I should leave some account behind as a warning to all rash mortals who would set their wits up against workings of Nature. I leave it with you. Make such use as you will of it. I speak to you now with my feet upon the threshold of the other world.

"I am, as you surmised, an Egyptian—not one of the down-trodden race of slaves who now inhabit the Delta of the Nile, but a survivor of that fiercer and harder people who tamed the Hebrew, drove the Ethiopian back into the southern deserts, and built those mighty works which have been the envy and the wonder of all after generations. It was in the reign of Tuthmosis, sixteen hundred years before the birth of Christ, that I first saw the light. You shrink away from me. Wait, and you will see that I am more to be pitied than to be feared.

"My name was Sosra. My father had been the chief priest of Osiris in the great temple of Abaris, which stood in those days upon the Bubastic branch of the Nile. I was brought up in the temple and was trained in all those mystic arts which are spoken of in your own Bible. I was an apt pupil. Before I was sixteen I had learned all which the wisest priest could teach me. From that time on I studied Nature's secrets for myself, and shared my knowledge with no man.

"Of all the questions which attracted me there were none over which I labored so long as over those which concern themselves with

the nature of life. I probed deeply into the vital principle. The aim of medicine had been to drive away disease when it appeared. It seemed to me that a method might be devised which should so fortify the body as to prevent weakness or death from ever taking hold of it. It is useless that I should recount my researches. You would scarce comprehend them if I did. They were carried out partly upon animals, partly upon slaves, and partly on myself. Suffice it that their result was to furnish me with a substance which, when injected into the blood, would endow the body with strength to resist the effects of time, of violence, or of disease. It would not indeed confer immortality, but its potency would endure for many thousands of years. I used it upon a cat, and afterwards drugged the creature with the most deadly poisons. That cat is alive in Lower Egypt at the present moment. There was nothing of mystery or magic in the matter. It was simply a chemical discovery, which may well be made again.

"Love of life runs high in the young. It seemed to me that I had broken away from all human care now that I had abolished pain and driven death to such a distance. With a light heart I poured the accursed stuff into

Zita Johann as Anck-es-en-Amon in *The Mummy*, 1932 (Universal Studios)

see him working with his flasks and his distiller in the Temple of Thoth, but he said little to me as to the result of his labors. For my own part, I used to walk through the city and look around me with exultation as I reflected that all this was destined to pass away, and that only I should remain. The people would bow to me as they passed me, for the fame of my knowledge had gone abroad.

"There was war at this time, and the Great King had sent down his soldiers to the eastern boundary to drive away the Hyksos. A Governor, too, was sent to Abaris, that he might hold it for the King. I had heard much of the beauty of the daughter of this Governor, but one day as I walked out with Parmes we met her, borne upon the shoulders of her slaves. I was struck with love as with lightning. My heart went out from me. I could have thrown myself beneath the feet of her bearers. This was my woman. Life without her was impossible. I swore by the head of Horus that she should be mine. I swore it to the Priest of Thoth. He turned away from me with a brow which was as black as midnight.

my veins. Then I looked round for someone whom I could benefit. There was a young priest of Thoth, Parmes by name, who had won my goodwill by his earnest nature and his devotion to his studies. To him I whispered my secret, and at his request I injected him with my elixir. I should now, I reflected, never be without a companion of the same age as myself.

"After this grand discovery I relaxed my studies to some extent, but Parmes continued his with redoubled energy. Every day I could

"There is no need to tell you of our wooing. She came to love me even as I loved her. I learned that Parmes had seen her before I did, and had shown her that he too loved her, but I could smile at his passion, for I knew that her heart was mine. The white plague had come upon the city, and many were stricken, but I laid my hands upon the sick and nursed them without fear or scathe. She marveled at my daring. Then I told her my secret, and begged her that she would let me use my art upon her.

BLACK INFINITY • 139

"'Your flower shall then be unwithered, Atma,' I said. 'Other things may pass away, but you and I, and our great love for each other, shall outlive the tomb of King Chefru.'

"But she was full of timid, maidenly objections. 'Was it right?' she asked, 'was it not a thwarting of the will of the gods? If the great Osiris had wished that our years should be so long, would he not himself have brought it about?'

"With fond and loving words, I overcame her doubts, and yet she hesitated. It was a great question, she said. She would think it over for this one night. In the morning I should know her resolution. Surely one night was not too much to ask. She wished to pray to Isis for help in her decision.

"With a sinking heart and a sad foreboding of evil I left her with her tirewomen. In the morning, when the early sacrifice was over, I hurried to her house. A frightened slave met me upon the steps. Her mistress was ill, she said, very ill. In a frenzy I broke my way through the attendants, and rushed through hall and corridor to my Atma's chamber. She lay upon her couch, her head high upon the

pillow, with a pallid face and a glazed eye. On her forehead there blazed a single angry purple patch. I knew that hell-mark of old. It was the scar of the white plague, the sign-manual of death.

"Why should I speak of that terrible time? For months I was mad, fevered, delirious, and yet I could not die. Never did an Arab thirst after the sweet wells as I longed after death. Could poison or steel have shortened the thread of my existence, I should soon have rejoined my love in the land with the narrow portal. I tried, but it was of no avail. The accursed influence was too strong upon me. One night as I lay upon my couch, weak and weary, Parmes, the priest of Thoth, came to my chamber. He stood in the circle of the lamplight, and he looked down upon me with eyes which were bright with a mad joy.

"'Why did you let the maiden die?' he asked; 'why did you not strengthen her as you strengthened me?'

"'I was too late,' I answered. 'But I had forgot. You also loved her. You are my fellow in misfortune. Is it not terrible to think of the centuries which must pass ere we look upon her again? Fools, fools, that we were to take death to be our enemy!'

"'You may say that,' he cried with a wild laugh; 'the words come well from your lips. For me they have no meaning.'

"'What mean you?' I cried, raising myself upon my elbow. 'Surely, friend, this grief has turned your brain.' His face was aflame with joy, and he writhed and shook like one who hath a devil.

"'Do you know whither I go?' he asked.

"'Nay,' I answered, 'I cannot tell.'

"'I go to her,' said he. 'She lies embalmed in the further tomb by the double palm-tree beyond the city wall.'

"'Why do you go there?' I asked.

"'To die!' he shrieked, 'to die! I am not bound by earthen fetters.'

"'But the elixir is in your blood,' I cried.

"'I can defy it,' said he; 'I have found a stronger principle which will destroy it. It is working in my veins at this moment, and in an hour I shall be a dead man. I shall join her, and you shall remain behind.'

"As I looked upon him I could see that he spoke words of truth. The light in his eye told me that he was indeed beyond the power of the elixir.

"'You will teach me!' I cried.

"'Never!' he answered.

"'I implore you, by the wisdom of Thoth, by the majesty of Anubis!'

"'It is useless,' he said coldly.

"'Then I will find it out,' I cried.

"'You cannot,' he answered; 'it came to me by chance. There is one ingredient which you can never get. Save that which is in the ring of Thoth, none will ever more be made.

"'In the ring of Thoth!' I repeated; 'where then is the ring of Thoth?'

"'That also you shall never know,' he answered. 'You won her love. Who has won in the end? I leave you to your sordid earth life. My chains are broken. I must go!' He turned upon his heel and fled from the chamber. In the morning came the news that the Priest of Thoth was dead.

"My days after that were spent in study. I must find this subtle poison which was strong enough to undo the elixir. From early dawn to midnight I bent over the test-tube and the furnace. Above all, I collected the papyri and the chemical flasks of the Priest of Thoth. Alas! they taught me little. Here and there some hint or stray expression would raise hope in my bosom, but no good ever came of it. Still, month after month, I struggled on. When my heart grew faint I would make my way to the tomb by the palm-trees. There, standing by the dead casket from which the jewel had been rifled, I would feel her sweet presence, and would whisper to her that I would rejoin her if mortal wit could solve the riddle.

"Parmes had said that his discovery was connected with the ring of Thoth. I had some remembrance of the trinket. It was a large and weighty circlet, made, not of gold, but of a rarer and heavier metal brought from the mines of Mount Harbal. Platinum, you call it. The ring had, I remembered, a hollow crystal set in it, in which some few drops of liquid might be stored. Now, the secret of Parmes could not have to do with the metal alone, for there were many rings of that metal in the Temple. Was it not more likely that he had stored his precious poison within the cavity of the crystal? I had scarce come to this conclusion before, in hunting through his papers, I came upon one which told me that it was indeed so, and that there was still some of the liquid unused.

"But how to find the ring? It was not upon him when he was stripped for the embalmer. Of that I made sure. Neither was it among his private effects. In vain I searched every room that he had entered, every box, and vase, and chattel that he had owned. I sifted the very sand of the desert in the places where he had been wont to walk; but, do what I would, I could come upon no traces of the ring of Thoth. Yet it may be that my labors would have overcome all obstacles had it not been for a new and unlooked-for misfortune.

"A great war had been waged against the Hyksos, and the Captains of the Great King had been cut off in the desert, with all their bowmen and horsemen. The shepherd tribes were upon us like the locusts in a dry year. From the wilderness of Shur to the great bitter lake there was blood by day and fire by night. Abaris was the bulwark of Egypt, but we could not keep the savages back. The city fell. The Governor and the soldiers were put to the sword, and I, with many more, was led away into captivity.

"For years and years I tended cattle in the great plains by the Euphrates. My master died, and his son grew old, but I was still as far from death as ever. At last I escaped upon a swift camel, and made my way back to Egypt. The Hyksos had settled in the land which they had conquered, and their own King ruled over the country. Abaris had been torn down, the city had been burned, and of the great Temple there was nothing left save an unsightly mound. Everywhere the tombs had been rifled and the monuments destroyed. Of my Atma's grave no sign was left. It was buried in the sands of the desert, and the palm-trees which marked the spot had long disappeared. The papers of Parmes and the remains of the Temple of Thoth were either destroyed or scattered far and wide over the deserts of Syria. All search after them was vain.

"From that time I gave up all hope of ever finding the ring or discovering the subtle drug. I set myself to live as patiently as might be until the effect of the elixir should wear away. How can you understand how terrible a thing time is, you who have experience only of the narrow course which lies between the

142 • **THE RING OF THOTH**

cradle and the grave! I know it to my cost, I who have floated down the whole stream of history. I was old when Ilium fell. I was very old when Herodotus came to Memphis. I was bowed down with years when the new gospel came upon earth. Yet you see me much as other men are, with the cursed elixir still sweetening my blood, and guarding me against that which I would court. Now at last, at last I have come to the end of it!

"I have traveled in all lands and I have dwelt with all nations. Every tongue is the same to me. I learned them all to help pass the weary time. I need not tell you how slowly they drifted by, the long dawn of modern civilization, the dreary middle years, the dark times of barbarism. They are all behind me now, I have never looked with the eyes of love upon another woman. Atma knows that I have been constant to her.

"It was my custom to read all that the scholars had to say upon Ancient Egypt. I have been in many positions, sometimes affluent, sometimes poor, but I have always found enough to enable me to buy the journals which deal with such matters. Some nine months ago I was in San Francisco, when I read an account of some discoveries made in the neighborhood of Abaris. My heart leapt into my mouth as I read it. It said that the excavator had busied himself in exploring some tombs recently unearthed. In one there had been found an unopened mummy with an inscription upon the outer case setting forth that it contained the body of the daughter of the Governor of the city in the days of Tuthmosis. It added that on removing the outer case there had been exposed a large platinum ring set with a crystal, which had been laid upon the breast of the embalmed woman. This, then, was where Parmes had hid the ring of Thoth. He might well say that it was safe, for no Egyptian would ever stain his soul by moving even the outer case of a buried friend.

"That very night I set off from San Francisco, and in a few weeks I found myself once more at Abaris, if a few sand-heaps and crumbling walls may retain the name of the great city. I hurried to the Frenchmen who were digging there and asked them for the ring. They replied that both the ring and the mummy had been sent to the Boulak Museum at Cairo. To Boulak I went, but only to be told that Mariette Bey had claimed them and had shipped them to the Louvre. I followed them, and there at last, in the Egyptian chamber, I came, after close upon four thousand years, upon the remains of my Atma, and upon the ring for which I had sought so long.

"But how was I to lay hands upon them? How was I to have them for my very own? It chanced that the office of attendant was vacant. I went to the Director. I convinced him that I knew much about Egypt. In my

eagerness I said too much. He remarked that a Professor's chair would suit me better than a seat in the Conciergerie. I knew more, he said, than he did. It was only by blundering, and letting him think that he had over-estimated my knowledge, that I prevailed upon him to let me move the few effects which I have retained into this chamber. It is my first and my last night here.

"Such is my story, Mr. Vansittart Smith. I need not say more to a man of your perception. By a strange chance you have this night looked upon the face of the woman whom I loved in those far-off days. There were many rings with crystals in the case, and I had to test for the platinum to be sure of the one which I wanted. A glance at the crystal has shown me that the liquid is indeed within it, and that I shall at last be able to shake off that accursed health which has been worse to me than the foulest disease. I have nothing more to say to you. I have unburdened myself. You may tell my story or you may withhold it at your pleasure. The choice rests with you. I owe you some amends, for you have had a narrow escape of your life this night. I was a desperate man, and not to be baulked in my purpose. Had I seen you before the thing was done, I might have put it beyond your power to oppose me or to raise an alarm. This is the door. It leads into the Rue de Rivoli. Good night!"

The Englishman glanced back. For a moment the lean figure of Sosra the Egyptian stood framed in the narrow doorway. The next, the door had slammed, and the heavy rasping of a bolt broke on the silent night.

IT WAS ON THE SECOND DAY after his return to London that Mr. John Vansittart Smith saw the following concise narrative in the Paris correspondence of *The Times*:

"*Curious Occurrence in the Louvre*—Yesterday morning a strange discovery was made in the principal Egyptian Chamber. The *ouvriers* who are employed to clean out the rooms in the morning found one of the attendants lying dead upon the floor with his arms round one of the mummies. So close was his embrace that it was only with the utmost difficulty that they were separated. One of the cases containing valuable rings had been opened and rifled. The authorities are of opinion that the man was bearing away the mummy with some idea of selling it to a private collector, but that he was struck down in the very act by long-standing disease of the heart. It is said that he was a man of uncertain age and eccentric habits, without any living relations to mourn over his dramatic and untimely end."

👽 👽 👽

In addition to creating Mr. Sherlock Holmes, the world's greatest private consulting detective, the prolific author and physician Sir Arthur Conan Doyle (1859–1930) penned adventure novels, supernatural tales, and several books of British military history.

"The Ring of Thoth" first appeared in the author's 1980 collection The Captain of the Polestar and Other Tales, *and is now acknowledged as the obvious source material for* The Mummy. *John L. Balderston, who had scripted the 1931 version of* Dracula, *allegedly adapted a nine-page treatment by Nina Wilcox Putnam and Richard Schayer, called "Cagliostro," in which the magician extends his life 3000 years by injecting nitrates. Right. Not only does Doyle's story contain all of the film's principal themes, attitudes, and elements (the ring of Thoth is changed to a scroll), it also actually includes a mummy!*

144 • THE RING OF THOTH

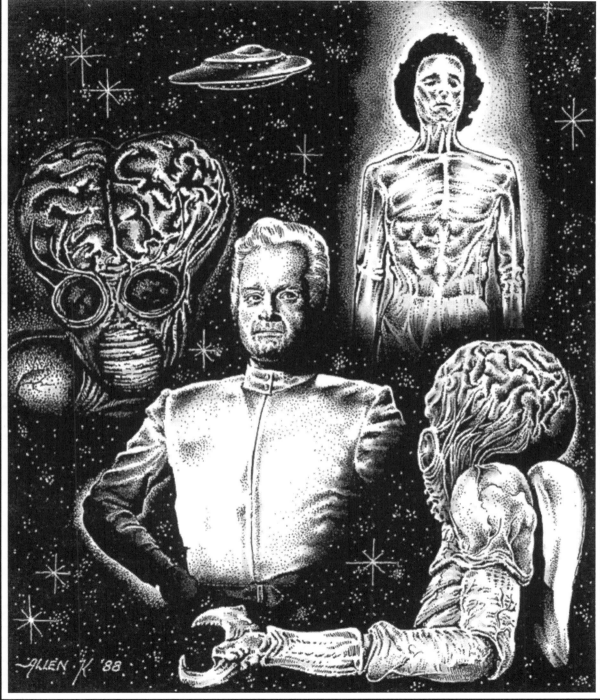

Metaluna scientist Exeter (Jeff Morrow) and an alien mutant from *This Island Earth* (Universal, 1955)

• BLACK INFINITY

GORGONS, AND HYDRAS, AND CHIMERAS—DIRE STORIES OF CELÆNO AND THE HARPIES—MAY REPRODUCE THEMSELVES IN THE BRAIN OF SUPERSTITION—*BUT THEY WERE THERE BEFORE.* THEY ARE TRANSCRIPTS, TYPES—THE ARCHETYPES ARE IN US, AND ETERNAL. HOW ELSE SHOULD THE RECITAL OF THAT WHICH WE KNOW IN A WAKING SENSE TO BE FALSE COME TO AFFECT US AT ALL? IS IT THAT WE NATURALLY CONCEIVE TERROR FROM SUCH OBJECTS, CONSIDERED IN THEIR CAPACITY OF BEING ABLE TO INFLICT UPON US BODILY INJURY? OH, LEAST OF ALL! *THESE TERRORS ARE OF OLDER STANDING. THEY DATE BEYOND BODY*—OR WITHOUT THE BODY, THEY WOULD HAVE BEEN THE SAME.... THAT THE KIND OF FEAR HERE TREATED IS PURELY SPIRITUAL—THAT IT IS STRONG IN PROPORTION AS IT IS OBJECTLESS ON EARTH, THAT IT PREDOMINATES IN THE PERIOD OF OUR SINLESS INFANCY—ARE DIFFICULTIES THE SOLUTION OF WHICH MIGHT AFFORD SOME PROBABLE INSIGHT INTO OUR ANTE-MUNDANE CONDITION, AND A PEEP, AT LEAST, INTO THE SHADOWLAND OF PRE-EXISTENCE.

—CHARLES LAMB, *WITCHES AND OTHER NIGHT-FEARS*

THE DUNWICH HORROR

By H. P. Lovecraft

WHEN A TRAVELER IN NORTH CENTRAL MASSACHUSETTS TAKES THE WRONG FORK AT THE JUNCTION OF THE AYLESBURY PIKE JUST BEYOND DEAN'S CORNERS HE COMES UPON A LONELY AND CURIOUS COUNTRY. The ground gets higher, and the brier-bordered stone walls press closer and closer against the ruts of the dusty, curving road. The trees of the frequent forest belts seem too large, and the wild weeds, brambles, and grasses attain a luxuriance not often found in settled regions. At the same time, the planted fields appear singularly few and barren; while the sparsely scattered houses wear a surprising uniform aspect of age, squalor, and dilapidation. Without knowing why, one hesitates to ask directions from the gnarled, solitary figures spied now and then on crumbling doorsteps or in the sloping, rock-strewn meadows. Those figures are so silent and furtive that one feels somehow confronted by forbidden things, with which it would be better to have nothing to do. When a rise in the road brings the mountains in view above the deep woods, the feeling of strange uneasiness is increased. The summits are too rounded and symmetrical to give a sense of comfort and naturalness, and sometimes the sky silhouettes with especial clearness the queer circles of tall stone pillars with which most of them are crowned.

Gorges and ravines of problematical depth intersect the way, and the crude wooden bridges always seem of dubious safety. When the road dips again there are stretches of marshland that one instinctively dislikes, and indeed almost fears at evening when unseen whippoorwills chatter and the fireflies come out in abnormal profusion to dance to the

BLACK INFINITY • 147

raucous, creepily insistent rhythms of stridently piping bullfrogs. The thin, shining line of the Miskatonic's upper reaches has an oddly serpent-like suggestion as it winds close to the feet of the domed hills among which it rises.

As the hills draw nearer, one heeds their wooded sides more than their stone-crowned tops. Those sides loom up so darkly and precipitously that one wishes they would keep their distance, but there is no road by which to escape them. Across a covered bridge one sees a small village huddled between the stream and the vertical slope of Round Mountain, and wonders at the cluster of rotting gambrel roofs bespeaking an earlier architectural period than that of the neighboring region. It is not reassuring to see, on a closer glance, that most of the houses are deserted and falling to ruin, and that the broken-steepled church now harbors the one slovenly mercantile establishment of the hamlet. One dreads to trust the tenebrous tunnel of the bridge, yet there is no way to avoid it. Once across, it is hard to prevent the impression of a faint, malign odor about the village street, as of the massed mold and decay of centuries. It is always a relief to get clear of the place, and to follow the narrow road around the base of the hills and across the level country beyond till it rejoins the Aylesbury pike. Afterward one sometimes learns that one has been through Dunwich.

Outsiders visit Dunwich as seldom as possible, and since a certain season of horror all the signboards pointing toward it have been taken down. The scenery, judged by any ordinary esthetic canon, is more than commonly beautiful; yet there is no influx of artists or summer tourists. Two centuries ago, when talk of witch-blood, Satan-worship, and strange forest presences was not laughed at, it was the custom to give reasons for avoiding the locality. In our sensible age—since the Dunwich horror of 1928 was hushed up by those who had the town's and the world's welfare at heart—people shun it

without knowing exactly why. Perhaps one reason—though it can not apply to uninformed strangers—is that the natives are now repellently decadent, having gone far along that path of retrogression so common in many New England backwaters. They have come to form a race by themselves, with the well-defined mental and physical stigmata of degeneracy and inbreeding. The average of their intelligence is woefully low, whilst their annals reek of overt viciousness and of half-hidden murders, incests, and deeds of almost unnamable violence and perversity. The old gentry, representing the two or three armigerous families which came from Salem in 1692, have kept somewhat above the general level of decay; though many branches are sunk into the sordid populace so deeply that only their names remain as a key to the origin they disgrace. Some of the Whateleys and Bishops still send their eldest sons to Harvard and Miskatonic, though those sons seldom return to the moldering gambrel roofs under which they and their ancestors were born.

No one, even those who have the facts concerning the recent horror, can say just what is the matter with Dunwich; though old legends speak of unhallowed rites and conclaves of the Indians, amidst which they called forbidden shapes of shadow out of the great rounded hills, and made wild orgiastic prayers that were answered by loud crackings and rumblings from the ground below. In 1747 the Reverend Abijah Hoadley, newly come to the Congregational Church at Dunwich Village, preached a memorable sermon on the close presence of Satan and his imps, in which he said:

It must be allow'd that these Blasphemies of an infernall Train of Dæmons are Matters of too common Knowledge to be deny'd; the cursed Voices of *Azazel* and *Buzrael*, of Beelzebub and Belial, being heard from under Ground by above a Score of credible Witnesses now living. I myself did not more than a Fortnight ago catch a very plain

Discourse of evil Powers in the Hill behind my House; wherein there were a Rattling and Rolling, Groaning, Screeching, and Hissing, such as no Things of this Earth cou'd raise up, and which must needs have come from those Caves that only black Magick can discover, and only the Divell unlock.

Mr. Hoadley disappeared soon after delivering this sermon; but the text, printed in Springfield, is still extant. Noises in the hills continued to be reported from year to year, and still form a puzzle to geologists and physiographers.

Other traditions tell of foul odors near the hill-crowning circles of stone pillars, and of rushing airy presences to be heard faintly at certain hours from stated points at the bottom of the great ravines; while still others try to explain the Devil's Hop Yard—a bleak, blasted hillside where no tree, shrub, or grass-blade will grow. Then, too, the natives are mortally afraid of the numerous whippoorwills which grow vocal on warm nights. It is vowed that the birds are psychopomps lying in wait for the souls of the dying, and that they time their eerie cries in unison with the sufferer's struggling breath. If they can catch the fleeing soul when it leaves the body, they instantly flutter away chittering in demoniac laughter; but if they fail, they subside gradually into a disappointed silence.

These tales, of course, are obsolete and ridiculous; because they come down from very old times. Dunwich is indeed ridiculously old —older by far than any of the communities within thirty miles of it. South of the village one may still spy the cellar walls and chimney of the ancient Bishop house, which was built before 1700; whilst the ruins of the mill at the falls, built in 1806, form the most modern piece of architecture to be seen. Industry did not flourish here, and the Nineteenth Century factory movement proved short-lived. Oldest of all are the great rings of rough-hewn stone columns on the hilltops, but these are more generally attributed to the Indians than to the settlers. Deposits of skulls and bones, found within these circles and around the sizable table-like rock on Sentinel Hill, sustain the popular belief that such spots were once the burial-places of the Pocumtucks; even though many ethnologists, disregarding the absurd improbability of such a theory, persist in believing the remains Caucasian.

2

IT WAS IN THE township of Dunwich, in a large and partly inhabited farmhouse set against a hillside four miles from the village and a mile and a half from any other dwelling, that Wilbur Whateley was born at 5 a.m. on Sunday, the second of February, 1913. This date was recalled because it was Candlemas, which people in Dunwich curiously observe under another name; and because the noises in the hills had sounded, and all the dogs of the countryside had barked persistently, throughout the night before. Less worthy of notice was the fact that the mother was one of the decadent Whateleys, a somewhat deformed, unattractive albino woman of 35, living with an aged and half-insane father about whom the most frightful tales of wizardry had been whispered in his youth. Lavinia Whateley had no known husband, but according to the custom of the region made no attempt to disavow the child; concerning the other side of whose ancestry the country folk might—and did—speculate as widely as they chose. On the contrary, she seemed strangely proud of the dark, goatish-looking infant who formed such a contrast to her own sickly and pink-eyed albinism, and was heard to mutter many curious prophecies about its unusual powers and tremendous future.

Lavinia was one who would be apt to mutter such things, for she was a lone creature given to wandering amidst thunderstorms in the hills and trying to read the great odorous books which her father had inherited through two centuries of Whateleys, and which were fast falling to pieces with age and wormholes.

She had never been to school, but was filled with disjointed scraps of ancient lore that Old Whateley had taught her. The remote farmhouse had always been feared because of Old Whateley's reputation for black magic, and the unexplained death by violence of Mrs. Whateley when Lavinia was twelve years old had not helped to make the place popular. Isolated among strange influences, Lavinia was fond of wild and grandiose daydreams and singular occupations; nor was her leisure much taken up by household cares in a home from which all standards of order and cleanliness had long since disappeared.

There was a hideous screaming which echoed above even the hill noises and the dogs' barking on the night Wilbur was born, but no known doctor or midwife presided at his coming. Neighbors knew nothing of him till a week afterward, when Old Whateley drove his sleigh through the snow into Dunwich Village and discoursed incoherently to the group of loungers at Osborn's general store. There seemed to be a change in the old man —an added element of furtiveness in the clouded brain which subtly transformed him from an object to a subject of fear—though he was not one to be perturbed by any common family event. Amidst it all he showed some trace of the pride later noticed in his daughter, and what he said of the child's paternity was remembered by many of his hearers years afterward.

"I dun't keer what folks think—ef Lavinny's boy looked like his pa, he wouldn't look like nothin' ye expeck. Ye needn't think the only folks is the folks hereabouts. Lavinny's read some, an' has seed some things the most o' ye only tell abaout. I calc'late her man is as good a husban' as ye kin find this side of Aylesbury; an' ef ye knowed as much abaout the hills as I dew, ye wouldn't ast no better church weddin' nor her'n. Let me tell ye suthin'—*someday yew folks'll hear a child o' Lavinny's a-callin' its father's name on the top o' Sentinel Hill!*"

The only persons who saw Wilbur during the first month of his life were old Zechariah Whateley, of the undecayed Whateleys, and Earl Sawyer's common-law wife, Mamie Bishop. Mamie's visit was frankly one of curiosity, and her subsequent tales did justice to her observations; but Zechariah came to lead a pair of Alderney cows which Old Whateley had bought of his son Curtis. This marked the beginning of a course of cattle-buying on the part of small Wilbur's family which ended only in 1928, when the Dunwich horror came and went; yet at no time did the ramshackle Whateley barn seem over-crowded with livestock. There came a period when people were curious enough to steal up and count the herd that grazed precariously on the steep hillside above the old farmhouse, and they could never find more than ten or twelve anemic, bloodless-looking specimens. Evidently some blight or distemper, perhaps sprung from the unwholesome pasturage or the diseased fungi and timbers of the filthy barn, caused a heavy mortality amongst the Whateley animals. Odd wounds or sores, having something of the aspect of incisions, seemed to afflict the visible cattle; and once or twice during the earlier months certain callers fancied they could discern similar sores about the throats of the gray, unshaven old man and his slatternly, crinkly-haired albino daughter.

In the spring after Wilbur's birth, Lavinia resumed her customary rambles in the hills, bearing in her misproportioned arms the swarthy child. Public interest in the Whateleys subsided after most of the country folk had seen the baby, and no one bothered to comment on the swift development which that newcomer seemed every day to exhibit. Wilbur's growth was indeed phenomenal, for within three months of his birth he had attained a size and muscular power not usually found in infants under a full year of age. His motions and even his vocal sounds showed a restraint and deliberateness highly peculiar in an infant, and no one was really unprepared when, at seven months, he began to walk

150 • THE DUNWICH HORROR

unassisted, with falterings which another month was sufficient to remove.

It was somewhat after this time—on Hallowe'en—that a great blaze was seen at midnight on the top of Sentinel Hill where the old table-like stone stands amidst its tumulus of ancient bones. Considerable talk was started when Silas Bishop—of the undecayed Bishops—mentioned having seen the boy running sturdily up that hill ahead of his mother about an hour before the blaze was remarked. Silas was rounding up a stray heifer, but he nearly forgot his mission when he fleetingly spied the two figures in the dim light of his lantern. They darted almost noiselessly through the underbrush, and the astonished watcher seemed to think they were entirely unclothed. Afterward he could not be sure about the boy, who may have had some kind of a fringed belt and a pair of dark blue trunks or trousers on. Wilbur was never subsequently seen alive and conscious without complete and tightly buttoned attire, the disarrangement or threatened disarrangement of which always seemed to fill him with anger and alarm. His contrast with his squalid mother and grandfather in this respect was thought very notable until the horror of 1928 suggested the most valid of reasons.

The next January gossips were mildly interested in the fact that "Lavinny's black brat" had commenced to talk, and at the age of only eleven months. His speech was somewhat remarkable both because of its difference from the ordinary accents of the region, and because it displayed a freedom from infantile lisping of which many children of three or four might well be proud. The boy was not talkative, yet when he spoke he seemed to reflect some elusive element wholly unpossessed by Dunwich and its denizens. The strangeness did not reside in what he said, or even in the simple idioms he used; but seemed vaguely linked with his intonation or with the internal organs that produced the spoken sounds. His facial aspect, too, was remarkable for its maturity; for though he shared his mother's and grandfather's chinlessness, his firm and precociously shaped nose united with the expression on his large, dark, almost Latin eyes to give him an air of quasi-adulthood and well-nigh preternatural intelligence. He was, however, exceedingly ugly despite his appearance of brilliancy; there being something almost goatish or animalistic about his thick lips, large-pored, yellowish skin, coarse crinkly hair, and oddly elongated ears. He was soon disliked even more decidedly than his mother and grandsire, and all conjectures about him were spiced with references to the bygone magic of Old Whateley, and how the hills once shook when he shrieked the dreadful name of *Yog-Sothoth* in the midst of a circle of stones with a great book open in his arms before him. Dogs abhorred the boy, and he was always obliged to take various defensive measures against their barking menace.

3

MEANWHILE, Old Whateley continued to buy cattle without measurably increasing the size of his herd. He also cut timber and began to repair the unused parts of his house—a spacious, peaked-roofed affair whose rear end was buried entirely in the rocky hillside, and whose three least-ruined ground-floor rooms had always been sufficient for himself and his daughter. There must have been prodigious reserves of strength in the old man to enable him to accomplish so much hard labor; and though he still babbled dementedly at times, his carpentry seemed to show the effects of sound calculation. It had really begun as soon as Wilbur was born, when one of the many toolsheds had been put suddenly in order, clapboarded, and fitted with a stout fresh lock. Now, in restoring the abandoned upper story of the house, he was a no less thorough craftsman. His mania showed itself only in his tight boarding-up of all the windows in the reclaimed section—though many declared that it was a crazy thing to bother with the

BLACK INFINITY • 151

reclamation at all. Less inexplicable was his fitting-up of another downstairs room for his new grandson—a room which several callers saw, though no one was ever admitted to the closely-boarded upper story. This chamber he lined with tall, firm shelving; along which he began gradually to arrange, in apparently careful order, all the rotting ancient books and parts of books which during his own day had been heaped promiscuously in odd corners of the various rooms.

"I made some use of 'em," he would say as he tried to mend a torn black-letter page with paste prepared on the rusty kitchen stove, "but the boy's fitten to make better use of 'em. He'd orter hev 'em as well sot as he kin for they're goin' to be all of his larnin'."

When Wilbur was a year and seven months old—in September of 1914—his size and accomplishments were almost alarming. He had grown as large as a child of four, and was a fluent and incredibly intelligent talker. He ran freely about the fields and hills, and accompanied his mother on all her wanderings. At home he would pore diligently over the queer pictures and charts in his grandfather's books, while Old Whateley would instruct and catechize him through long, hushed afternoons. By this time the restoration of the house was finished, and those who watched it wondered why one of the upper windows had been made into a solid plank door. It was a window in the rear of the east gable end, close against the hill; and no one could imagine why a cleated wooden runway was built up to it from the ground. About the period of this work's completion people noticed that the old tool-house, tightly locked and windowlessly clapboarded since Wilbur's birth, had been abandoned again. The door swung listlessly open, and when Earl Sawyer once stepped within after a cattle-selling call on Old Whateley he was quite discomposed by the singular odor he encountered—such a stench, he averred, as he had never before smelt in all his life except near the Indian circles on the hills, and which could not come from anything sane or of this earth. But then, the homes and sheds of Dunwich folk have never been remarkable for olfactory immaculateness.

The following months were void of visible events, save that everyone swore to a slow but steady increase in the mysterious hill noises. On May Eve of 1915 there were tremors which even the Aylesbury people felt, whilst the following Hallowe'en produced an underground rumbling queerly synchronized with bursts of flame—"them witch Whateleys' doin's"— from the summit of Sentinel Hill. Wilbur was growing up uncannily, so that he looked like a boy of ten as he entered his fourth year. He read avidly by himself now; but talked much less than formerly. A settled taciturnity was absorbing him, and for the first time people began to speak specifically of the dawning look of evil in his goatish face. He would sometimes mutter an unfamiliar jargon, and chant in bizarre rhythms which chilled the listener with a sense of unexplainable terror. The aversion displayed toward him by dogs had now become a matter of wide remark, and he was obliged to carry a pistol in order to traverse the countryside in safety. His occasional use of the weapon did not enhance his popularity amongst the owners of canine guardians.

The few callers at the house would often find Lavinia alone on the ground floor, while odd cries and footsteps resounded in the boarded-up second story. She would never tell what her father and the boy were doing up there, though once she turned pale and displayed an abnormal degree of fear when a jocose fish-peddler tried the locked door leading to the stairway. That peddler told the store loungers at Dunwich Village that he thought he heard a horse stamping on that floor above. The loungers reflected, thinking of the door and runway, and of the cattle that so swiftly disappeared. Then they shuddered as they recalled tales of Old Whateley's youth, and of the strange things that are called out of the earth when a bullock is sacrificed at

152 • THE DUNWICH HORROR

the proper time to certain heathen gods. It had for some time been noticed that dogs had begun to hate and fear the whole Whateley place as violently as they hated and feared young Wilbur personally.

In 1917 the war came, and Squire Sawyer Whateley, as chairman of the local draft board, had hard work finding a quota of young Dunwich men fit even to be sent to a development camp. The government, alarmed at such signs of wholesale regional decadence, sent several officers and medical experts to investigate; conducting a survey which New England newspaper readers may still recall. It was the publicity attending this investigation which set reporters on the track of the Whateleys, and caused the *Boston Globe* and *Arkham Advertiser* to print flamboyant Sunday stories of young Wilbur's precociousness, Old Whateley's black magic, the shelves of strange books, the sealed second story of the ancient farmhouse, and the weirdness of the whole region and its hill noises. Wilbur was four and a half then, and looked like a lad of fifteen. His lip and cheek were fuzzy with a coarse dark down, and his voice had begun to break. Earl Sawyer went out to the Whateley place with both sets of reporters and camera men, and called their attention to the queer stench which now seemed to trickle down from the sealed upper spaces. It was, he said, exactly like a smell he had found in the toolshed abandoned when the house was finally repaired, and like the faint odors which he sometimes thought he caught near the stone circles on the mountains. Dunwich folk read the stories when they appeared, and grinned over the obvious mistakes. They wondered, too, why the writers made so much of the fact that Old Whateley always paid for his cattle in gold pieces of extremely ancient date. The Whateleys had received their visitors with ill-concealed distaste, though they did not dare court further publicity by a violent resistance or refusal to talk.

4

FOR A DECADE the annals of the Whateleys sink indistinguishably into the general life of a morbid community used to their queer ways and hardened to their May Eve and All-Hallow orgies. Twice a year they would light fires on the top of Sentinel Hill, at which times the mountain rumblings would recur with greater and greater violence; while at all seasons there were strange and portentous doings at the lonely farmhouse. In the course of time callers professed to hear sounds in the sealed upper story even when all the family were downstairs, and they wondered how swiftly or how lingeringly a cow or bullock was usually sacrificed. There was talk of a complaint to the Society for the Prevention of Cruelty to Animals; but nothing ever came of it, since Dunwich folk are never anxious to call the outside world's attention to themselves.

About 1923, when Wilbur was a boy of ten whose mind, voice, stature, and bearded face gave all the impressions of maturity, a second great siege of carpentry went on at the old house. It was all inside the sealed upper part, and from bits of discarded lumber people concluded that the youth and his grandfather had knocked out all the partitions and even removed the attic floor, leaving only one vast open void between the ground story and the peaked roof. They had torn down the great central chimney, too, and fitted the rusty range with a flimsy outside tin stove-pipe.

In the spring after this event Old Whateley noticed the growing number of whippoorwills that would come out of Cold Spring Glen to chirp under his window at night. He seemed to regard the circumstance as one of great significance, and told the loungers at Osborn's that he thought his time had almost come.

"They whistle jest in tune with my breathin' naow," he said, "an' I guess they're gittin' ready to ketch my soul. They know it's a-goin' aout, an' dun't calc'late to miss it. Yew'll know, boys, arter I'm gone, whether

BLACK INFINITY • 153

they git me er not. Ef they dew, they'll keep up a-singin' an' laffin' till break o' day. Ef they dun't, they'll kinder quiet daown like. I expeck them an' the souls they hunts fer hev some pretty tough tussles sometimes."

On Lammas Night, 1924, Dr. Houghton of Aylesbury was hastily summoned by Wilbur Whateley, who had lashed his one remaining horse through the darkness and telephoned from Osborn's in the village. He found Old Whateley in a very grave state, with a cardiac action and stertorous breathing that told of an end not far off. The shapeless albino daughter and oddly bearded grandson stood by the bedside, whilst from the vacant abyss overhead there came a disquieting suggestion of rhythmical surging or lapping, as of the waves on some level beach. The doctor, though, was chiefly disturbed by the chattering night birds outside; a seemingly limitless legion of whippoorwills that cried their endless message in repetitions timed diabolically to the wheezing gasps of the dying man. It was uncanny and unnatural—too much, thought Dr. Houghton, like the whole of the region he had entered so reluctantly in response to the urgent call.

Toward one o'clock Old Whateley gained consciousness, and interrupted his wheezing to choke out a few words to his grandson.

"More space, Willy, more space soon. Yew grows—an' *that* grows faster. It'll be ready to sarve ye soon, boy. Open up the gates to Yog-Sothoth with the long chant that ye'll find on page 751 *of the complete edition*, an' *then* put a match to the prison. Fire from airth can't burn it nohaow!"

He was obviously quite mad. After a pause, during which the flock of whippoorwills outside adjusted their cries to the altered tempo while some indications of the strange hill noises came from afar off, he added another sentence or two.

"Feed it reg'lar, Willy, an' mind the quantity; but dun't let it grow too fast fer the place, fer ef it busts quarters or gits aout afore ye opens to Yog-Sothoth, it's all over an' no use.

Only them from beyont kin make it multiply an' work.... Only them, the old uns as wants to come back...."

But speech gave place to gasps again, and Lavinia screamed at the way the whippoorwills followed the change. It was the same for more than an hour, when the final throaty rattle came. Dr. Houghton drew shrunken lids over the glazing gray eyes as the tumult of birds faded imperceptibly to silence. Lavinia sobbed, but Wilbur only chuckled whilst the hill noises rumbled faintly.

"They didn't git him," he muttered in his heavy bass voice.

Wilbur was by this time a scholar of really tremendous erudition in his one-sided way, and was quietly known by correspondence to many librarians in distant places where rare and forbidden books of old days are kept. He was more and more hated and dreaded around Dunwich because of certain youthful disappearances which suspicion laid vaguely at his door; but was always able to silence inquiry through fear or through use of that fund of old-time gold which still, as in his grandfather's time, went forth regularly and increasingly for cattle-buying. He was now tremendously mature of aspect, and his height, having reached the normal adult limit, seemed inclined to wax beyond that figure. In 1925, when a scholarly correspondent from Miskatonic University called upon him one day and departed pale and puzzled, he was fully six and three-quarters feet tall.

Through all the years Wilbur had treated his half-deformed albino mother with a growing contempt, finally forbidding her to go to the hills with him on May Eve and Hallowmass; and in 1926 the poor creature complained to Mamie Bishop of being afraid of him.

"They's more abaout him as I knows than I kin tell ye, Mamie," she said, "an' naowadays they's more nor what I know myself. I vaow afur Gawd, I dun't know what he wants nor what he's a-tryin' to dew."

154 • THE DUNWICH HORROR

That Hallowe'en the hill noises sounded louder than ever, and fire burned on Sentinel Hill as usual, but people paid more attention to the rhythmical screaming of vast flocks of unnaturally belated whippoorwills which seemed to be assembled near the unlighted Whateley farmhouse. After midnight their shrill notes burst into a kind of pandemoniac cachinnation which filled all the countryside, and not until dawn did they finally quiet down. Then they vanished, hurrying southward where they were fully a month overdue. What this meant, no one could quite be certain till later. None of the countryfolk seemed to have died—but poor Lavinia Whateley, the twisted albino, was never seen again.

In the summer of 1927 Wilbur repaired two sheds in the farmyard and began moving his books and effects out to them. Soon afterward Earl Sawyer told the loungers at Osborn's that more carpentry was going on in the Whateley farmhouse. Wilbur was closing all the doors and windows on the ground floor, and seemed to be taking out partitions as he and his grandfather had done upstairs four years before. He was living in one of the sheds, and Sawyer thought he seemed unusually worried and tremulous. People generally suspected him of knowing something about his mother's disappearance, and very few ever approached his neighborhood now. His height had increased to more than seven feet, and showed no signs of ceasing its development.

5

THE FOLLOWING WINTER brought an event no less strange than Wilbur's first trip outside the Dunwich region. Correspondence with the Widener Library at Harvard, the Bibliotheque Nationale in Paris, the British Museum, the University of Buenos Aires, and the Library of Miskatonic University at Arkham had failed to get him the loan of a book he desperately wanted; so at length he set out in person, shabby, dirty, bearded, and uncouth of dialect, to consult the copy at Miskatonic, which was the nearest to him geographically. Almost eight feet tall, and carrying a cheap new valise from Osborn's general store, this dark and goatish gargoyle appeared one day in Arkham in quest of the dreaded volume kept under lock and key at the college library —the hideous *Necronomicon* of the mad Arab Alhazred in Olaus Wormius' Latin version, as printed in Spain in the Seventeenth Century. He had never seen a city before, but had no thought save to find his way to the university grounds; where, indeed, he passed heedlessly by the great, white-fanged watchdog that barked with unnatural fury and enmity, and tugged frantically at its stout chain.

Wilbur had with him the priceless but imperfect copy of Dr. Dee's English version which his grandfather had bequeathed him, and upon receiving access to the Latin copy he at once began to collate the two texts with the aim of discovering a certain passage which would have come on the 751st page of his own defective volume. This much he could not civilly refrain from telling the librarian— the same erudite Henry Armitage (A. M. Miskatonic, Ph. D. Princeton, Litt. D. Johns Hopkins) who had once called at the farm, and who now politely plied him with questions. He was looking, he had to admit, for a kind of formula or incantation containing the frightful name *Yog-Sothoth*, and it puzzled him to find discrepancies, duplications, and ambiguities which made the matter of determination far from easy. As he copied the formula he finally chose, Dr. Armitage looked involuntarily over his shoulder at the open pages; the left-hand one of which, in the Latin version, contained such monstrous threats to the peace and sanity of the world.

Nor is it to be thought [ran the text as Armitage mentally translated it] that man is either the oldest or the last of earth's masters, or that the common bulk of life and substance walks alone. The Old Ones were, the Old Ones are, and the Old Ones shall be. Not in the

BLACK INFINITY • 155

spaces we know, but *between* them. They walk serene and primal, undimensioned and to us unseen. *Yog-Sothoth* knows the gate. *Yog-Sothoth* is the gate. *Yog-Sothoth* is the key and guardian of the gate. Past, present, future, all are one in *Yog-Sothoth*. He knows where the Old Ones broke through of old, and where They shall break through again. He knows where They have trod earth's fields, and where They still tread them, and why no one can behold Them as They tread. By Their smell can men sometimes know Them near, but of Their semblance can no man know, *saving only in the features of those They have begotten on mankind*; and of those are there many sorts, differing in likeness from man's truest eidolon to that shape without sight or substance which is *They*. They walk unseen and foul in lonely places where the Words have been spoken and the Rites howled through at their Seasons. The wind gibbers with Their voices, and the earth mutters with Their consciousness. They bend the forest and crush the city, yet may not forest or city behold the hand that smites. Kadath in the cold waste hath known Them, and what man knows Kadath? The ice desert of the South and the sunken isles of Ocean hold stones whereon Their seal is engraven, but who hath seen the deep frozen city or the sealed tower long garlanded with seaweed and barnacles? Great Cthulhu is Their cousin, yet can he spy Them only dimly. *Iä Shub-Niggurath!* As a foulness shall ye know Them. Their hand is at your throats, yet ye see Them not; and Their habitation is even one with your guarded threshold. *Yog-Sothoth* is the key to the gate, whereby the spheres meet. Man rules now where They ruled once; They shall soon rule where man rules now. After summer is winter, and after winter summer. They wait patient and potent, for here shall They reign again.

Dr. Armitage, associating what he was reading with what he had heard of Dunwich and its brooding presences, and of Wilbur Whateley and his dim, hideous aura that stretched from a dubious birth to a cloud of probable matricide, felt a wave of fright as tangible as a draft of the tomb's cold clamminess. The bent, goatish giant before him seemed like the spawn of another planet or dimension; like something only partly of mankind, and linked to black gulfs of essence and entity that stretch like titan fantasms beyond all spheres of force and matter, space and time.

Presently Wilbur raised his head and began speaking in that strange, resonant fashion which hinted at sound-producing organs unlike the run of mankind's.

"Mr. Armitage," he said, "I calc'late I've got to take that book home. They's things in it I've got to try under sarten conditions that I can't git here, an' it 'ud be a mortal sin to let a red-tape rule hold me up. Let me take it along, sir, an' I'll swar they wun't nobody know the difference. I dun't need to tell ye I'll take good keer of it. It wa'n't me that put this Dee copy in the shape it is...."

He stopped as he saw firm denial on the librarian's face, and his own goatish features grew crafty. Armitage, half ready to tell him he might make a copy of what parts he needed, thought suddenly of the possible consequences and checked himself. There was too much responsibility in giving such a being the key to such blasphemous outer spheres. Whateley saw how things stood, and tried to answer lightly.

"Wal, all right, ef ye feel that way abaout it. Maybe Harvard wun't be so fussy as yew be." And without saying more he rose and strode out of the building, stooping at each doorway.

Armitage heard the savage yelping of the great watchdog, and studied Whateley's

156 • THE DUNWICH HORROR

gorilla-like lope as he crossed the bit of campus visible from the window. He thought of the wild tales he had heard, and recalled the old Sunday stories in the *Advertiser*; these things, and the lore he had picked up from Dunwich rustics and villagers during his one visit there. Unseen things not of earth —or at least not of tri-dimensional earth— rushed fetid and horrible through New England's glens, and brooded obscenely on the mountain tops. Of this he had long felt certain. Now he seemed to sense the close presence of some terrible part of the intruding horror, and to glimpse a hellish advance in the black dominion of the ancient and once passive nightmare. He locked away the *Necronomicon* with a shudder of disgust, but the room still reeked with an unholy and unidentifiable stench. "As a foulness shall ye know them," he quoted. Yes—the odor was the same as that which had sickened him at the Whateley farmhouse less than three years before. He thought of Wilbur, goatish and ominous, once again, and laughed mockingly at the village rumors of his parentage.

"Inbreeding?" Armitage muttered half aloud to himself. "Great God, what simpletons! Show them Arthur Machen's *Great God Pan* and they'll think it a common Dunwich scandal! But what thing—what cursed shapeless influence on or off this three-dimensioned earth—was Wilbur Whateley's father? Born on Candlemas—nine months after May Eve of 1912, when the talk about the queer earth noises reached clear to Arkham—what walked on the mountains that May Night? What Roodmas horror fastened itself on the world in half-human flesh and blood?"

During the ensuing weeks Dr. Armitage set about to collect all possible data on Wilbur Whateley and the formless presences around Dunwich. He got in communication with Dr. Houghton of Aylesbury, who had attended Old Whateley in his last illness, and found much to ponder over in the grandfather's last words as quoted by the physician. A visit to Dunwich Village failed to bring out much that was new; but a close survey of the *Necronomicon*, in those parts which Wilbur had sought so avidly, seemed to supply new and terrible clues to the nature, methods, and desires of the strange evil so vaguely threatening this planet. Talks with several students of archaic lore in Boston, and letters to many others elsewhere, gave him a growing amazement which passed slowly through varied degrees of alarm to a state of really acute spiritual fear. As the summer drew on he felt dimly that something ought to be done about the lurking terrors of the upper Miskatonic valley, and about the monstrous being known to the human world as Wilbur Whateley.

6

THE DUNWICH HORROR itself came between Lammas and the equinox in 1928, and Dr. Armitage was among those who witnessed its monstrous prologue. He had heard, meanwhile, of Whateley's grotesque trip to Cambridge, and of his frantic efforts to borrow or copy from the *Necronomicon* at the Widener Library. Those efforts had been in vain, since Armitage had issued warnings of the keenest intensity to all librarians having charge of the dreaded volume. Wilbur had been shockingly nervous at Cambridge; anxious for the book, yet almost equally anxious to get home again, as if he feared the results of being away long.

Early in August the half-expected outcome developed, and in the small hours of the third Dr. Armitage was awakened suddenly by the wild, fierce cries of the savage watchdog on the college campus. Deep and terrible, the snarling, half-mad growls and barks continued; always in mounting volume, but with hideously significant pauses. Then there rang out a scream from a wholly different throat— such a scream as roused half the sleepers of Arkham and haunted their dreams ever afterward—such a scream as could come from no being born of earth, or wholly of earth.

BLACK INFINITY • 157

Armitage hastened into some clothing and rushed across the street and lawn to the college buildings, saw that others were ahead of him; and heard the echoes of a burglar-alarm still shrilling from the library. An open window showed black and gaping in the moonlight. What had come had indeed completed its entrance; for the barking and the screaming, now fast fading into a mixed low growling and moaning, proceeded unmistakably from within. Some instinct warned Armitage that what was taking place was not a thing for unfortified eyes to see, so he brushed back the crowd with authority as he unlocked the vestibule door. Among the others he saw Professor Warren Rice and Dr. Francis Morgan, men to whom he had told some of his conjectures and misgivings; and these two he motioned to accompany him inside. The inward sounds, except for a watchful, droning whine from the dog, had by this time quite subsided; but Armitage now perceived with a sudden start that a loud chorus of whippoorwills among the shrubbery had commenced a damnably rhythmical piping, as if in unison with the last breath of a dying man.

The building was full of a frightful stench which Dr. Armitage knew too well, and the three men rushed across the hall to the small genealogical reading-room whence the low whining came. For a second nobody dared to turn on the light; then Armitage summoned up his courage and snapped the switch. One of the three—it is not certain which—shrieked aloud at what sprawled before them among disordered tables and overturned chairs. Professor Rice declares that he wholly lost consciousness for an instant, though he did not stumble or fall.

The thing that lay half-bent on its side in a fetid pool of greenish-yellow ichor and tarry stickiness was almost nine feet tall, and the dog had torn off all the clothing and some of the skin. It was not quite dead, but twitched silently and spasmodically while its chest heaved in monstrous unison with the mad piping of the expectant whippoorwills outside. Bits of shoe-leather and fragments of apparel were scattered about the room, and just inside the window an empty canvas sack lay where it had evidently been thrown. Near the central desk a revolver had fallen, a dented but undischarged cartridge later explaining why it had not been fired. The thing itself, however, crowded out all other images at the time. It would be trite and not wholly accurate to say that no human pen could describe it, but one may properly say that it could not be vividly visualized by anyone whose ideas of aspect and contour are too closely bound up with the common life-forms of this planet and of the three known dimensions. It was partly human, beyond a doubt, with very manlike hands and head, and the goatish, chinless face had the stamp of the Whateleys upon it. But the torso and lower parts of the body were teratologically fabulous, so that only generous clothing could ever have enabled it to walk on earth unchallenged or uneradicated.

Above the waist it was semi-anthropomorphic; though its chest, where the dog's rending paws still rested watchfully, had the leathery, reticulated hide of a crocodile or alligator. The back was piebald with yellow and black, and dimly suggested the squamous covering of certain snakes. Below the waist, though, it was the worst; for here all human resemblance left off and sheer fantasy began. The skin was thickly covered with coarse black fur, and from the abdomen a score of long greenish-gray tentacles with red sucking mouths protruded limply. Their arrangement was odd, and seemed to follow the symmetries of some cosmic geometry unknown to earth or the solar system. On each of the hips, deep set in a kind of pinkish, ciliated orbit, was what seemed to be a rudimentary eye; whilst in lieu of a tail there depended a kind of trunk or feeler with purple annular markings, and with many evidences of being an undeveloped mouth or throat. The limbs, save for their black fur, roughly resembled the hind legs of prehistoric earth's giant saurians; and

158 • THE DUNWICH HORROR

terminated in ridgy-veined pads that were neither hooves nor claws. When the thing breathed, its tail and tentacles rhythmically changed color, as if from some circulatory cause normal to the non-human side of its ancestry. In the tentacles this was observable as a deepening of the greenish tinge, whilst in the tail it was manifest as a yellowish appearance which alternated with a sickly grayish-white in the spaces between the purple rings. Of genuine blood there was none; only the fetid greenish-yellow ichor which trickled along the painted floor beyond the radius of the stickiness, and left a curious discoloration behind it.

As the presence of the three men seemed to rouse the dying thing, it began to mumble without turning or raising its head. Dr. Armitage made no written record of its mouthings but asserts confidently that nothing in English was uttered. At first the syllables defied all correlation with any speech of earth, but toward the last there came some disjointed fragments evidently taken from the *Necronomicon*, that monstrous blasphemy in quest of which the thing had perished. Those fragments, as Armitage recalls them, ran something like "*N'gai, n'gha'ghaa, bugg-shoggog, y'hah; Yog-Sothoth, Yog-Sothoth....*" They trailed off into nothingness as the whippoorwills shrieked in rhythmical crescendos of unholy anticipation.

Then came a halt in the gasping, and the dog raised his head in a long, lugubrious howl. A change came over the yellow, goatish face of the prostrate thing, and the great black eyes fell in appallingly. Outside the window the shrilling of the whippoorwills had suddenly ceased, and above the murmurs of the gathering crowd there came the sound of a panic-struck whirring and fluttering. Against the moon vast clouds of feathery watchers rose and raced from sight, frantic at that which they had sought for prey.

All at once the dog started up abruptly, gave a frightened bark, and leaped nervously out the window by which it had entered. A cry rose from the crowd, and Dr. Armitage shouted to the men outside that no one must be admitted till the police or medical examiner came. He was thankful that the windows were just too high to permit of peering in, and drew the dark curtains carefully down over each one. By this time two policemen had arrived; and Dr. Morgan, meeting them in the vestibule, was urging them for their own sakes to postpone entrance to the stench-filled reading-room till the examiner came and the prostrate thing could be covered up.

Meanwhile frightful changes were taking place on the floor. One need not describe the *kind* and *rate* of shrinkage and disintegration that occurred before the eyes of Dr. Armitage and Professor Rice; but it is permissible to say that, aside from the external appearance of face and hands, the really human elements in Wilbur Whateley must have been very small. When the medical examiner came, there was only a sticky whitish mass on the painted boards, and the monstrous odor had nearly disappeared. Apparently Whateley had had no skull or bony skeleton; at least, in any true or stable sense. He had taken somewhat after his unknown father.

7

YET ALL THIS WAS ONLY the prologue of the actual Dunwich horror. Formalities were gone through by bewildered officials, abnormal details were duly kept from press and public, and men were sent to Dunwich and Aylesbury to look up property and notify any who might be heirs of the late Wilbur Whateley. They found the countryside in great agitation, both because of the growing rumblings beneath the domed hills, and because of the unwonted stench and the surging, lapping sounds which came increasingly from the great empty shell formed by Whateley's boarded-up farmhouse. Earl Sawyer, who tended the horse and cattle during Wilbur's absence, had developed a woefully acute case of nerves. The officials devised excuses not to enter the noisome boarded place; and were glad to confine their survey of the deceased's living quarters, the newly mended sheds, to a single visit. They filed a ponderous report at the courthouse in Aylesbury, and litigations concerning heirship are said to be still in progress amongst the innumerable Whateleys, decayed and undecayed, of the upper Miskatonic valley.

An almost interminable manuscript in strange characters, written in a huge ledger and adjudged a sort of diary because of the spacing and the variations in ink and penmanship, presented a baffling puzzle to those who found it on the old bureau which served as its owner's desk. After a week of debate it was sent to Miskatonic University, together with the deceased's collection of strange books, for study and possible translation; but even the best linguists soon saw that it was not likely to be unriddled with ease. No trace of the ancient gold with which Wilbur and Old Whateley always paid their debts has yet been discovered.

It was in the dark of September ninth that the horror broke loose. The hill noises had been very pronounced during the evening, and dogs barked frantically all night. Early risers on the tenth noticed a peculiar stench in the air. About 7 o'clock Luther Brown, the hired boy at George Corey's, between Cold Spring Glen and the village, rushed frenziedly back from his morning trip to Ten-Acre Meadow with the cows. He was almost convulsed with fright as he stumbled into the kitchen; and in the yard outside the no less frightened herd were pawing and lowing pitifully, having followed the boy back in the panic they shared with him. Between gasps Luther tried to stammer out his tale to Mrs. Corey.

"Up thar in the rud beyont the glen, Mis' Corey—they's suthin' ben thar! It smells like thunder, an' all the bushes an' little trees is pushed back from the rud like they'd a haouse ben moved along of it. An' that ain't the wust, nuther. They's *prints* in the rud, Mis' Corey—great raound prints as big as barrelheads, all sunk daown deep like a elephant had ben along, *only they's a sight more nor four feet could make.* I looked at one or two afore I run, an' I see every one was covered with lines spreadin' aout from one place, like as if big palm-leaf fans—twict or three times as big as any they is—hed of ben paounded daown into the rud. An' the smell was awful, like what it is araound Wizard Whateley's ol' haouse...."

Here he faltered, and seemed to shiver afresh with the fright that had sent him flying home. Mrs. Corey, unable to extract more information, began telephoning the neighbors; thus starting on its rounds the overture of panic that heralded the major terrors. When she got Sally Sawyer, housekeeper at Seth Bishop's, the nearest place to Whateley's, it became her turn to listen instead of transmit; for Sally's boy Chauncey, who slept poorly, had been up on the hill toward Whateley's, and had dashed back in terror after one look at the place, and at the pasturage where Mr. Bishop's cows had been left out all night.

"Yes, Mis' Corey," came Sally's tremulous voice over the party wire, "Cha'ncey he just come back a-post-in', and couldn't haff talk fer bein' scairt! He says Ol' Whateley's haouse is all blowed up, with the timbers scattered raound like they'd ben dynamite inside; only the bottom floor ain't through, but is all covered with a kind o' tarlike stuff that smells awful an' drips daown offen the aidges onto the graoun' whar the side timbers is blowed away. An' they's awful kinder marks in the yard, tew—great raound marks bigger raound than a hogshead, an' all sticky with stuff like is on the blowed-up haouse. Cha'ncey he says they leads off into the medders, whar a great swath wider'n a barn is matted daown, an' all the stun walls tumbled every which way wherever it goes.

"An' he says, says he, Mis' Corey, as haow he sot to look fer Seth's caows, frighted ez he was; an' faound 'em in the upper pasture nigh the Devil's Hop Yard in an awful shape.

160 • THE DUNWICH HORROR

Haff on 'em's clean gone, an' nigh haff o' them that's left is sucked most dry o' blood, with sores on 'em like they's ben on Whateley's cattle ever senct Lavinny's black brat was born. Seth he's gone aout naow to look at 'em, though I'll vaow he wun't keer ter git very nigh Wizard Whateley's! Cha'ncey didn't look keerful ter see whar the big matted-daown swath led arter it leff the pasturage, but he says he thinks it p'inted towards the glen rud to the village.

"I tell ye, Mis' Corey, they's suthin' abroad as hadn't orter be abroad, an' I fer one think that black Wilbur Whateley, as come to the bad eend he desarved, is at the bottom of the breedin' of it. He wa'n't all human hisself, I allus says to everybody; an' I think he an' Ol' Whateley must a raised suthin' in that there nailed-up haouse as ain't even so human as he was. They's allus ben unseen things araound Dunwich—livin' things—as ain't human an' ain't good fer human folks.

"The graoun' was a'talkin' lass night, an' towards mornin' Cha'ncey he heerd the whippoorwills so laoud in Col' Spring Glen he couldn't sleep none. Then he thought he heerd another faint-like saound over towards Wizard Whateley's—a kinder rippin' or tearin' o' wood, like some big box or crate was bein' opened fur off. What with this an' that, he didn't git to sleep at all till sunup, an' no sooner was he up this mornin', but he's got to go over to Whateley's an' see what's the matter. He see enough, I tell ye, Mis' Corey! This dun't mean no good, an' I think as all the men-folks ought to git up a party an' do suthin'. I know suthin' awful's abaout, an' feel my time is nigh, though only Gawd knows jest what it is.

"Did your Luther take accaount o' whar them big tracks led tew? No? Wal, Mis' Corey, ef they was on the glen rud this side o' the glen, an' ain't got to your haouse yet, I calc'late they must go into the glen itself. They would do that. I allus says Col' Spring Glen ain't no healthy nor decent place. The whippoorwills an' fireflies there never did act like they was creaters o' Gawd, an' they's them as says ye kin hear strange things a-rushin' an' a-talkin' in the air daown thar ef ye stand in the right place, atween the rock falls an' Bear's Den."

BY THAT NOON fully three-quarters of the men and boys of Dunwich were trooping over the roads and meadows between the new-made Whateley ruins and Cold Spring Glen; examining in horror the vast, monstrous prints, the maimed Bishop cattle, the strange, noisome wreck of the farmhouse, and the bruised, matted vegetation of the fields and road-sides. Whatever had burst loose upon the world had assuredly gone down into the great sinister ravine; for all the trees on the banks were bent and broken, and a great avenue had been gouged in the precipice-hanging underbrush. It was as though a house, launched by an avalanche, had slid down through the tangled growths of the almost vertical slope. From below no sound came, but only a distant, undefinable fetor; and it is not to be wondered at that the men preferred to stay on the edge and argue, rather than descend and beard the unknown Cyclopean horror in its lair. Three dogs that were with the party had barked furiously at first, but seemed cowed and reluctant when near the glen. Someone telephoned the news to the *Aylesbury Transcript*; but the editor, accustomed to wild tales from Dunwich, did no more than concoct a humorous paragraph about it; an item soon afterward reproduced by the Associated Press.

That night everyone went home, and every house and barn was barricaded as stoutly as possible. Needless to say, no cattle were allowed to remain in open pasturage. About two in the morning a frightful stench and the savage barking of the dogs awakened the household at Elmer Frye's, on the eastern edge of Cold Spring Glen, and all agreed that they could hear a sort of muffled swishing or lapping sound from somewhere outside. Mrs. Frye proposed telephoning the neighbors,

BLACK INFINITY • 161

and Elmer was about to agree when the noise of splintering wood burst in upon their deliberations. It came, apparently, from the barn; and was quickly followed by a hideous screaming and stamping amongst the cattle. The dogs slavered and crouched close to the feet of the fear-numbed family. Frye lit a lantern through force of habit, but knew it would be death to go out into that black farmyard. The children and the women-folk whimpered, kept from screaming by some obscure, vestigial instinct of defense which told them their lives depended on silence. At last the noise of the cattle subsided to a pitiful moaning, and a great snapping, crashing, and crackling ensued. The Fryes, huddled together in the sitting-room, did not dare to move until the last echoes died away far down in Cold Spring Glen. Then, amidst the dismal moans from the stable and the demoniac piping of late whippoorwills in the glen, Selina Frye tottered to the telephone and spread what news she could of the second phase of the horror.

The next day all the countryside was in a panic; and cowed, uncommunicative groups came and went where the fiendish thing had occurred. Two titan swaths of destruction stretched from the glen to the Frye farmyard, monstrous prints covered the bare patches of ground, and one side of the old red barn had completely caved in. Of the cattle, only about a quarter could be found and identified. Some of these were in curious fragments, and all that survived had to be shot. Earl Sawyer suggested that help be asked from Aylesbury or Arkham, but others maintained it would be of no use. Old Zebulon Whateley, of a branch that hovered about half-way between soundness and decadence, made darkly wild suggestions about rites that ought to be practiced on the hilltops. He came of a line where tradition ran strong, and his memories of chantings in the great stone circles were not altogether connected with Wilbur and his grandfather.

Darkness fell upon a stricken countryside too passive to organize for real defense. In a few cases closely related families would band together and watch in the gloom under one roof; but, in general there was only a repetition of the barricading of the night before, and a futile, ineffective gesture of loading muskets and setting pitchforks handily about. Nothing, however, occurred except some hill noises; and when the day came there were many who hoped that the new horror had gone as swiftly as it had come. There were even bold souls who proposed an offensive expedition down in the glen, though they did not venture to set an actual example to the still reluctant majority.

When night came again the barricading was repeated, though there was less huddling together of families. In the morning both the Frye and the Seth Bishop households reported excitement among the dogs and vague sounds and stenches from afar, while early explorers noted with horror a fresh set of the monstrous tracks in the road skirting Sentinel Hill. As before, the sides of the road showed a bruising indicative of the blasphemously stupendous bulk of the horror; whilst the conformation of the tracks seemed to argue a passage in two directions, as if the moving mountain had come from Cold Spring Glen and returned to it along the same path. At the base of the hill a thirty-foot swath of crushed shrubbery and saplings led steeply upward, and the seekers gasped when they saw that even the most perpendicular places did not deflect the inexorable trail. Whatever the horror was, it could scale a sheer stony cliff of almost complete verticality; and as the investigators climbed around to the hill's summit by safer routes, they saw that the trail ended—or rather, reversed—there.

It was here that the Whateleys used to build their hellish fires and chant their hellish rituals by the table-like stone on May Eve and Hallowmass. Now that very stone formed the center of a vast space thrashed around by the mountainous horror, whilst upon its slightly concave surface was a thick fetid

162 • THE DUNWICH HORROR

deposit of the same tarry stickiness observed on the floor of the ruined Whateley farmhouse when the horror escaped. Men looked at one another and muttered. Then they looked down the hill. Apparently, the horror had descended by a route much the same as that of its ascent. To speculate was futile. Reason, logic, and normal ideas of motivation stood confounded. Only old Zebulon, who was not with the group, could have done justice to the situation or suggested a plausible explanation.

Thursday night began much like the others, but it ended less happily. The whippoorwills in the glen had screamed with such unusual persistence that many could not sleep, and about 3 a.m. all the party telephones rang tremulously. Those who took down their receivers heard a fright-mad voice shriek out, "Help, oh, my Gawd!..." and some thought a crashing sound followed the breaking off of the exclamation. There was nothing more. No one dared do anything, and no one knew till morning whence the call came. Then those who had heard it called everyone on the line and found that only the Fryes did not reply. The truth appeared an hour later, when a hastily assembled group of armed men trudged out to the Frye place at the head of the glen. It was horrible, yet hardly a surprise. There were more swaths and monstrous prints, but there was no longer any house. It had caved in like an eggshell, and amongst the ruins nothing living or dead could be discovered—only a stench and a tarry stickiness. The Elmer Fryes had been erased from Dunwich.

8

IN THE MEANTIME, a quieter yet even more spiritually poignant phase of the horror had been blackly unwinding itself behind the closed door of a shelf-lined room in Arkham. The curious manuscript record or diary of Wilbur Whateley, delivered to Miskatonic University for translation, had caused much worry and bafflement among the experts in languages both ancient and modern; its very alphabet, notwithstanding a general resemblance to the heavily shaded Arabic used in Mesopotamia, being absolutely unknown to any available authority. The final conclusion of the linguists was that the text represented an artificial alphabet, giving the effect of a cipher; though none of the usual methods of cryptographic solution seemed to furnish any clue, even when applied on the basis of every tongue the writer might conceivably have used. The ancient books taken from Whateley's quarters, while absorbingly interesting and in several cases promising to open up new and terrible lines of research among philosophers and men of science, were of no assistance whatever in this matter. One of them, a heavy tome with an iron clasp, was in another unknown alphabet—this one of a very different cast, and resembling Sanskrit more than anything else. The old ledger was at length given wholly into the charge of Dr. Armitage, both because of his peculiar interest in the Whateley matter, and because of his wide linguistic learning and skill in the mystical formulæ of antiquity and the Middle Ages.

Armitage had an idea that the alphabet might be something esoterically used by certain forbidden cults which have come down from old times, and which have inherited many forms and traditions from the wizards of the Saracenic world. That question, however, he did not deem vital; since it would be unnecessary to know the origin of the symbols if, as he suspected, they were used as a cipher in a modern language. It was his belief that, considering the great amount of text involved, the writer would scarcely have wished the trouble of using another speech than his own, save perhaps in certain special formulæ and incantations. Accordingly he attacked the manuscript with the preliminary assumption that the bulk of it was in English.

Dr. Armitage knew, from the repeated failures of his colleagues, that the riddle was

BLACK INFINITY • 163

a deep and complex one, and that no simple mode of solution could merit even a trial. All through late August, he fortified himself with the massed lore of cryptography, drawing upon the fullest resources of his own library, and wading night after night amidst the arcana of Trithemius' *Poligraphia*, Giambattista Porta's *De Furtivis Literarum Notis*, De Vigenere's *Traité des Chiffres*, Falconer's *Cryptomenysis Patefacta*, Davys' and Thicknesse's Eighteenth Century treatises, and such fairly modern authorities as Blair, von Marten, and Klüber's *Kryptographik*. He interspersed his study of the books with attacks on the manuscript itself, and in time became convinced that he had to deal with one of those subtlest and most ingenious of cryptograms, in which many separate lists of corresponding letters are arranged like the multiplication table, and the message built up with arbitrary keywords known only to the initiated. The older authorities seemed rather more helpful than the newer ones, and Armitage concluded that the code of the manuscript was one of great antiquity, no doubt handed down through a long line of mystical experimenters. Several times he seemed near daylight, only to be set back by some unforeseen obstacle. Then, as September approached, the clouds began to clear. Certain letters, as used in certain parts of the manuscript, emerged definitely and unmistakably; and it became obvious that the text was indeed in English.

On the evening of September second, the last major barrier gave way, and Dr. Armitage read for the first time a continuous passage of Wilbur Whateley's annals. It was in truth a diary, as all had thought; and it was couched in a style clearly showing the mixed occult erudition and general illiteracy of the strange being who wrote it. Almost the first long passage that Armitage deciphered, an entry dated November 26, 1916, proved highly startling and disquieting. It was written, he remembered, by a child of three and a half, who looked like a lad of twelve or thirteen:

Today learned the Aklo for the Sabaoth, [it ran] which did not like, it being answerable from the hill and not from the air. That upstairs more ahead of me than I had thought it would be, and is not like to have much earth brain. Shot Elam Hutchins's collie Jack when he went to bite me, and Elam says he would kill me if he dast. I guess he won't. Grandfather kept me saying the Dho formula last night, and I think I saw the inner city at the two magnetic poles. I shall go to those poles when the earth is cleared off, if I can't break through with the Dho-Hna formula when I commit it. They from the air told me at Sabbat that it will be years before I can clear off the earth, and I guess Grandfather will be dead then, so I shall have to learn all the angles of the planes and all the formulas between the Yr and the Nhhngr. They from outside will help, but they can not take body without human blood. That upstairs looks it will have the right cast. I can see it a little when I make the Yoorish sign or blow the power of Ibn Ghazi at it, and it is near like them at May Eve on the Hill. The other face may wear off some. I wonder how I shall look when the earth is cleared and there are no earth beings on it. He that came with the Aklo Sabaoth said I may be transfigured, there being much of outside to work on.

MORNING FOUND Dr. Armitage in a cold sweat of terror and a frenzy of wakeful concentration. He had not left the manuscript all night, but sat at his table under the electric light turning page after page with shaking hands as fast as he could decipher the cryptic text. He had nervously telephoned his wife he would not be home, and when she brought him a breakfast from the house he could scarcely dispose of a mouthful. All that day he read on, now and then halted maddeningly as a reapplication of the complex key became necessary. Lunch and dinner were brought him, but he ate only the smallest fraction of either. Toward the middle of the next night he drowsed off in his chair, but soon woke out of a tangle of nightmares almost as hideous as the truths and menaces to man's existence that he had uncovered.

On the morning of September fourth, Professor Rice and Dr. Morgan insisted on seeing him for a while, and departed trembling and ashen-gray. That evening he went to bed but slept only fitfully. Wednesday—the next day—he was back at the manuscript, and began to take copious notes both from the current sections and from those he had already deciphered. In the small hours of that night he slept a little in an easy-chair in his office, but was at the manuscript again before dawn. Some time before noon his physician, Dr. Hartwell, called to see him and insisted that he cease work. He refused, intimating that it was of the most vital importance for him to complete the reading of the diary, and promising an explanation in due course of time.

That evening, just as twilight fell, he finished his terrible perusal and sank back exhausted. His wife, bringing his dinner, found him in a half-comatose state; but he was conscious enough to warn her off with a sharp cry when he saw her eyes wander toward the notes he had taken. Weakly rising, he gathered up the scribbled papers and sealed them all in a great envelope, which he immediately placed in his inside coat pocket. He had sufficient strength to get home, but was so clearly in need of medical aid that Dr. Hartwell was summoned at once. As the doctor put him to bed he could only mutter over and over again, *"But what, in God's name, can we do?"*

Dr. Armitage slept but was partly delirious the next day. He made no explanations to Hartwell, but in his calmer moments spoke of the imperative need of a long conference with Rice and Morgan. His wilder wanderings were very startling indeed, including frantic appeals that something in a boarded-up farmhouse be destroyed, and fantastic references to some plan for the extirpation of the entire human race and all animal and vegetable life from the earth by some terrible elder race of beings from another dimension. He would shout that the world was in danger, since the Elder Things wished to strip it and drag it away from the solar system and cosmos of matter into some other plane or phase of entity from which it had once fallen, vigintillions of eons ago. At other times he would call for the dreaded *Necronomicon* and the *Dæmonolatreia* of Remigius, in which he seemed hopeful of finding some formula to check the peril he conjured up.

"Stop them, stop them!" he would shout. "Those Whateleys meant to let them in, and the worst of all is left! Tell Rice and Morgan we must do something—it's a blind business, but I know how to make the powder.... It hasn't been fed since the second of August, when Wilbur came here to his death, and at that rate...."

But Armitage had a sound physique despite his seventy-three years, and slept off his disorder that night without developing any real fever. He woke late Friday, clear of head, though sober, with a gnawing fear and tremendous sense of responsibility. Saturday afternoon he felt able to go over to the library and summon Rice and Morgan for a conference, and the rest of that day and evening the three men tortured their brains in the wildest speculation and the most desperate debate. Strange and terrible books were drawn voluminously from the stack shelves and from secure places of storage, and diagrams and formulæ were copied with feverish haste and in bewildering abundance. Of skepticism there was none. All three had seen the body of Wilbur Whateley as it lay on the floor in a room of that very building, and after that not one of them could feel even slightly inclined to treat the diary as a madman's raving.

BLACK INFINITY • 165

Opinions were divided as to notifying the Massachusetts State Police, and the negative finally won. There were things involved which simply could not be believed by those who had not seen a sample, as indeed was made clear during certain subsequent investigations. Late at night the conference disbanded without having developed a definite plan, but all day Sunday Armitage was busy comparing formulæ and mixing chemicals obtained from the college laboratory. The more he reflected on the hellish diary, the more he was inclined to doubt the efficacy of any material agent in stamping out the entity which Wilbur Whateley had left behind him—the earth-threatening entity which, unknown to him, was to burst forth in a few hours and become the memorable Dunwich horror.

Monday was a repetition of Sunday with Dr. Armitage, for the task in hand required an infinity of research and experiment. Further consultations of the monstrous diary brought about various changes of plan, and he knew that even in the end a large amount of uncertainty must remain. By Tuesday he had a definite line of action mapped out, and believed he would try a trip to Dunwich within a week. Then, on Wednesday, the great shock came. Tucked obscurely away in a corner of the *Arkham Advertiser* was a facetious little item from the Associated Press, telling what a record-breaking monster the bootleg whisky of Dunwich had raised up. Armitage, half stunned, could only telephone for Rice and Morgan. Far into the night they discussed, and the next day was a whirlwind of preparation on the part of them all. Armitage knew he would be meddling with terrible powers, yet saw that there was no other way to annul the deeper and more malign meddling which others had done before him.

9

FRIDAY MORNING Armitage, Rice and Morgan set out by motor for Dunwich, arriving at the village about 1 in the afternoon. The day was pleasant, but even in the brightest sunlight a kind of quiet dread and portent seemed to hover about the strangely domed hills and the deep, shadowy ravines of the stricken region. Now and then on some mountain top a gaunt circle of stones could be glimpsed against the sky. From the air of hushed fright at Osborn's store they knew something hideous had happened, and soon learned of the annihilation of the Elmer Frye house and family. Throughout that afternoon they rode around Dunwich, questioning the natives concerning all that had occurred, and seeing for themselves with rising pangs of horror the drear Frye ruins with their lingering traces of the tarry stickiness, the blasphemous tracks in the Frye yard, the wounded Seth Bishop cattle, and the enormous swaths of disturbed vegetation in various places. The trail up and down Sentinel Hill seemed to Armitage of almost cataclysmic significance, and he looked long at the sinister altarlike stone on the summit.

At length the visitors, apprised of a party of State Police which had come from Aylesbury that morning in response to the first telephone reports of the Frye tragedy, decided to seek out the officers and compare notes as far as practicable. This, however, they found more easily planned than performed; since no sign of the party could be found in any direction. There had been five of them in a car, but now the car stood empty near the ruins in the Frye yard. The natives, all of whom had talked with the policemen, seemed at first as perplexed as Armitage and his companions. Then old Sam Hutchins thought of something and turned pale, nudging Fred Farr and pointing to the dank, deep hollow that yawned close by.

"Gawd," he gasped, "I told 'em not ter go daown into the glen, an' I never thought nobody'd dew it with them tracks an' that smell an' the whippoorwills a-screechin' daown thar in the dark o' noonday...."

A cold shudder ran through natives and visitors alike, and every ear seemed strained in a kind of instinctive, unconscious listening.

Armitage, now that he had actually come upon the horror and its monstrous work, trembled with the responsibility he felt to be his. Night would soon fall, and it was then that the mountainous blasphemy lumbered upon its eldritch course. *Negotium perambulans in tenebris....* The old librarian rehearsed the formulæ he had memorized, and clutched the paper containing the alternative ones he had not memorized. He saw that his electric flashlight was in working order. Rice, beside him, took from a valise a metal sprayer of the sort used in combating insects; whilst Morgan uncased the big-game rifle on which he relied despite his colleague's warnings that no material weapon would be of help.

Armitage, having read the hideous diary, knew painfully well what kind of a manifestation to expect, but he did not add to the fright of the Dunwich people by giving any hints or clues. He hoped that it might be conquered without any revelation to the world of the monstrous thing it had escaped. As the shadows gathered, the natives commenced to disperse homeward, anxious to bar themselves indoors despite the present evidence that all human locks and bolts were useless before a force that could bend trees and crush houses when it chose. They shook their heads at the visitors' plan to stand guard at the Frye ruins near the glen; and as they left, had little expectancy of ever seeing the watchers again.

There were rumblings under the hills that night, and the whippoorwills piped threateningly. Once in a while a wind, sweeping up out of Cold Spring Glen, would bring a touch of ineffable fetor to the heavy night air; such a fetor as all three of the watchers had smelled once before, when they stood above a dying thing that had passed for fifteen years and a half as a human being. But the looked-for terror did not appear. Whatever was down there in the glen was biding its time, and Armitage told his colleagues it would be suicidal to try to attack it in the dark.

Morning came wanly, and the night-sounds ceased. It was a gray, bleak day, with now and then a drizzle of rain; and heavier and heavier clouds seemed to be piling themselves up beyond the hills to the northwest. The men from Arkham were undecided what to do. Seeking shelter from the increasing rainfall beneath one of the few undestroyed Frye outbuildings, they debated the wisdom of waiting, or of taking the aggressive and going down into the glen in quest of their nameless, monstrous quarry. The downpour waxed in heaviness, and distant peals of thunder sounded from far horizons. Sheet lightning shimmered, and then a forky bolt flashed near at hand, as if descending into the accursed glen itself. The sky grew very dark, and the watchers hoped that the storm would prove a short, sharp one followed by clear weather.

It was still gruesomely dark when, not much over an hour later, a confused babel of voices sounded down the road. Another moment brought to view a frightened group of more than a dozen men, running, shouting, and even whimpering hysterically. Someone in the lead began sobbing out words, and the Arkham men started violently when those words developed a coherent form.

"Oh, my Gawd, my Gawd!" the voice choked out; "it's a-goin' agin, *an' this time by day*! It's aout—it's aout an' a-movin' this very minute, an' only the Lord knows when it'll be on us all!"

The speaker panted into silence, but another took up his message.

"Nigh on a haour ago Zeb Whateley here heerd the 'phone a-ringin', an' it was Mis' Corey, George's wife that lives daown by the junction. She says the hired boy Luther was aout drivin' in the caows from the storm arter the big bolt, when he see all the trees a-bendin' at the maouth o' the glen—opposite side ter this—an' smelt the same awful smell like he smelt when he faound the big tracks las' Monday mornin'. An' she says he says they was a swishin', lappin' saound, more nor what the bendin' trees an' bushes could make, an' all on a suddent the trees along the rud begun ter git pushed one side, an' they was a awful stompin' an' splashin' in the mud. But mind ye, Luther he didn't see nothin' at all, only jest the bendin' trees an' underbrush.

"Then fur ahead where Bishop's Brook goes under the rud he heerd a awful creakin' an' strainin' on the bridge, an' says he could tell the saound o' wood a-startin' to crack an' split. An' all the whiles he never see a thing, only them trees an' bushes a-bendin'. An' when the swishin' saound got very fur off—on the rud towards Wizard Whateley's an' Sentinel Hill—Luther he had the guts ter step up whar he'd heerd it fust an' look at the graound. It was all mud an' water, an' the sky was dark, an' the rain was wipin' aout all tracks abaout as fast as could be; but beginnin' at the glen maouth, whar the trees bed moved, they was still some o' them awful prints big as bar'ls like he seen Monday."

At this point the first excited speaker interrupted.

"But *that* ain't the trouble naow—that was only the start. Zeb here was callin' folks up an' everybody was a-listenin' in when a call from Seth Bishop's cut in. His haousekeeper Sally was carryin' on fit ter kill—she'd jest seed the trees a-bendin' beside the rud, an' says they was a kind o' mushy saound, like a elephant puffin' an' treadin', a-headin' fer the haouse. Then she up an' spoke suddent of a fearful smell, an' says her boy Cha'ncey was a-screamin' as haow it was jest like what he smelt up to the Whateley rewins Monday mornin'. An' the dogs was all barkin' an' whinin' awful.

"An' then she let aout a turrible yell, an' says the shed daown the rud hed jest caved in like the storm hed blowed it over, only the wind wa'n't strong enough to dew that. Everybody was a-listenin', an' ye could hear lots o' folks on the wire a-gaspin'. All to onct Sally she yelled agin, an' says the front yard picket fence bed jest crumpled up, though they wa'n't no sign o' what done it. Then everybody on the line could hear Cha'ncey an'

ol' Seth Bishop a-yellin', tew, an' Sally was shriekin' aout that suthin' heavy hed struck the haouse—not lightnin' nor nothin', but suthin' heavy agin' the front, that kep' a-launchin' itself agin an' agin, though ye couldn't see nuthin' aout the front winders. An' then...an' then...."

Lines of fright deepened on every face; and Armitage, shaken as he was, had barely poise enough to prompt the speaker.

"An' then...Sally she yelled aout, 'O help, the haouse is a-cavin' in'...an' on the wire we could hoar a turrible crashin', an' a hull flock o' screamin'...jest like when Elmer Frye's place was took, only wuss...."

The man paused, and another of the crowd spoke.

"That's all—not a saound nor squeak over the 'phone arter that. Jest still-like. We that heerd it got aout Fords an' wagons an' raounded up as many able-bodied men-folks as we could get, at Corey's place, an' come up here ter see what yew thought best ter dew. Not but what I think it's the Lord's judgment fer our iniquities, that no mortal kin ever set aside."

Armitage saw that the time for positive action had come, and spoke decisively to the faltering group of frightened rustics.

"We must follow it, boys." He made his voice as reassuring as possible. "I believe there's a chance of putting it out of business. You men know that those Whateleys were wizards—well, this thing is a thing of wizardry, and must be put down by the same means. I've seen Wilbur Whateley's diary and read some of the strange old books he used to read, and I think I know the right kind of a spell to recite to make the thing fade away. Of course, one can't be sure, but we can always take a chance. It's invisible—I knew it would be—but there's a powder in this long-distance sprayer that might make it show up for a second. Later on we'll try it. It's a frightful thing to have alive, but it isn't as bad as what Wilbur would have let in if he'd lived longer. You'll never know what the world has

168 • THE DUNWICH HORROR

escaped. Now we've only this one thing to fight, and it can't multiply. It can, though, do a lot of harm; so we mustn't hesitate to rid the community of it.

"We must follow it—and the way to begin is to go to the place that has just been wrecked. Let somebody lead the way—I don't know your roads very well, but I've an idea there might be a shorter cut across lots. How about it?"

The men shuffled about a moment, and then Earl Sawyer spoke softly, pointing with a grimy finger through the steadily lessening rain.

"I guess ye kin git to Seth Bishop's quickest by cuttin' acrost the lower medder here, wadin' the brook at the low place, an' climbin' through Carrier's mowin' an' the timber-lot beyont. That comes aout on the upper rud mighty nigh Seth's—a leetle t'other side."

Armitage, with Rice and Morgan, started to walk in the direction indicated; and most of the natives followed slowly. The sky was growing lighter, and there were signs that the storm had worn itself away. When Armitage inadvertently took a wrong direction, Joe Osborn warned him and walked ahead to show the right one. Courage and confidence were mounting; though the twilight of the almost perpendicular wooded hill which lay toward the end of their short cut, and among whose fantastic ancient trees they had to scramble as if up a ladder, put these qualities to a severe test.

At length they emerged on a muddy road to find the sun coming out. They were a little beyond the Seth Bishop place, but bent trees and hideously unmistakable tracks showed what had passed by. Only a few moments were consumed in surveying the ruins just around the bend. It was the Frye incident all over again, and nothing dead or living was found in either of the collapsed shells which had been the Bishop house and barn. No one cared to remain there amidst the stench and the tarry stickiness, but all turned instinctively to the line of horrible prints leading on

toward the wrecked Whateley farmhouse and the altar-crowned slopes of Sentinel Hill.

As the men passed the site of Wilbur Whateley's abode they shuddered visibly, and seemed again to mix hesitancy with their zeal. It was no joke tracking down something as big as a house that one could not see, but that had all the vicious malevolence of a demon. Opposite the base of Sentinel Hill the tracks left the road, and there was a fresh bending and matting visible along the broad swath marking the monster's former route to and from the summit.

Armitage produced a pocket telescope of considerable power and scanned the steep green side of the hill. Then he handed the instrument to Morgan, whose sight was keener. After a moment of gazing Morgan cried out sharply, passing the glass to Earl Sawyer and indicating a certain spot on the slope with his finger. Sawyer, as clumsy as most non-users of optical devices are, fumbled a while; but eventually focused the lenses with Armitage's aid. When he did so his cry was less restrained than Morgan's had been.

"Gawd almighty, the grass an' bushes is a-movin'! It's a-goin' up—slow-like—creepin' up ter the top this minute, heaven only knows what fer!"

Then the germ of panic seemed to spread among the seekers. It was one thing to chase the nameless entity, but quite another to find it. Spells might be all right—but suppose they weren't? Voices began questioning Armitage about what he knew of the thing, and no reply seemed quite to satisfy. Everyone seemed to feel himself in close proximity to phases of nature and of being utterly forbidden, and wholly outside the sane experience of mankind.

10

IN THE END the three men from Arkham—old, white-bearded Dr. Armitage, stocky, iron-gray Professor Rice, and lean, youngish Dr. Morgan —ascended the mountain alone. After much patient instruction regarding its focusing and use, they left the telescope with the frightened group that remained in the road; and as they climbed they were watched closely by those among whom the glass was passed around. It was hard going, and Armitage had to be helped more than once. High above the toiling group the great swath trembled as its hellish maker repassed with snail-like deliberateness. Then it was obvious that the pursuers were gaining.

Curtis Whateley—of the undecayed branch —was holding the telescope when the Arkham party detoured radically from the swath. He told the crowd that the men were evidently trying to get to a subordinate peak which overlooked the swath at a point considerably ahead of where the shrubbery was now bending. This, indeed, proved to be true; and the party were seen to gain the minor elevation only a short time after the invisible blasphemy had passed it.

Then Wesley Corey, who had taken the glass, cried out that Armitage was adjusting the sprayer which Rice held, and that something must be about to happen. The crowd stirred uneasily, recalling that this sprayer was expected to give the unseen horror a moment of visibility. Two or three men shut their eyes, but Curtis Whateley snatched back the telescope and strained his vision to the utmost. He saw that Rice, from the party's point of vantage above and behind the entity, had an excellent chance of spreading the potent powder with marvelous effect.

Those without the telescope saw only an instant's flash of gray cloud—a cloud about the size of a moderately large building—near the top of the mountain. Curtis, who had held the instrument, dropped it with a piercing shriek into the ankle-deep mud of the road. He reeled, and would have crumpled to the ground had not two or three others seized and steadied him. All he could do was moan half-inaudibly:

"Oh, oh, great Gawd... *that... that....*"

There was a pandemonium of questioning, and only Henry Wheeler thought to rescue the fallen telescope and wipe it clean of mud. Curtis was past all coherence, and even isolated replies were almost too much for him.

"Bigger 'n a barn... all made o' squirmin' ropes... hull thing sort o' shaped like a hen's egg bigger'n anything, with dozens o' legs like hogsheads that haff shut up when they step ... nothin' solid abaout it—all like jelly, an' made o' sep'rit wrigglin' ropes pushed clost together... great bulgin' eyes all over it... ten or twenty maouths or trunks a-stickin' aout all along the sides, big as stovepipes, an' all a-tossin' an' openin' an' shuttin'... all gray, with kinder blue or purple rings... *an' Gawd in Heaven—that haff face on top!...*"

This final memory, whatever it was, proved too much for poor Curtis, and he collapsed completely before he could say more. Fred Farr and Will Hutchins carried him to the roadside and laid him on the damp grass. Henry Wheeler, trembling, turned the rescued telescope on the mountain to see what he might. Through the lenses were discernible three tiny figures, apparently running toward the summit as fast as the steep incline allowed. Only these—nothing more. Then everyone noticed a strangely unseasonable noise in the deep valley behind, and even in the underbrush of Sentinel Hill itself. It was the piping of unnumbered whippoorwills, and in their shrill chorus there seemed to lurk a note of tense and evil expectancy.

Earl Sawyer now took the telescope and reported the three figures as standing on the topmost ridge, virtually level with the altar-stone but at a considerable distance from it. One figure, he said, seemed to be raising its hands above its head at rhythmic intervals; and as Sawyer mentioned the circumstance the crowd seemed to hear a faint, half-musical sound from the distance, as if a loud chant were accompanying the gestures. The weird silhouette on that remote peak must have been a spectacle of infinite grotesqueness and impressiveness, but no observer was in a mood for esthetic appreciation. "I guess he's sayin' the spell," whispered Wheeler as he

CONTINUED ON PAGE 172

170 • THE DUNWICH HORROR

BLACK INFINITY • 171

snatched back the telescope. The whippoor-wills were piping wildly, and in a singularly curious irregular rhythm quite unlike that of the visible ritual.

Suddenly the sunshine seemed to lessen without the intervention of any discernible cloud. It was a very peculiar phenomenon, and was plainly marked by all. A rumbling sound seemed brewing beneath the hills, mixed strangely with a concordant rumbling which clearly came from the sky. Lightning flashed aloft, and the wondering crowd looked in vain for the portents of storm. The chanting of the men from Arkham now became unmistakable, and Wheeler saw through the glass that they were all raising their arms in the rhythmic incantation. From some farm-house far away came the frantic barking of dogs.

The change in the quality of the daylight increased, and the crowd gazed about the horizon in wonder. A purplish darkness, born of nothing more than a spectral deepening of the sky's blue, pressed down upon the rumbling hills. Then the lightning flashed again, somewhat brighter than before, and the crowd fancied that it had showed a certain mistiness around the altar-stone on the distant height. No one, however, had been using the telescope at that instant. The whippoorwills continued their irregular pulsation, and the men of Dunwich braced themselves tensely against some imponderable menace with which the atmosphere seemed surcharged.

Without warning came those deep, cracked, raucous vocal sounds which will never leave the memory of the stricken group who heard them. Not from any human throat were they born, for the organs of man can yield no such acoustic perversions. Rather would one have said they came from the pit itself, had not their source been so unmistakably the altar-stone on the peak. It is almost erroneous to call them *sounds* at all, since so much of their ghastly, infra-bass timbre spoke to dim seats of consciousness and terror far subtler than the ear; yet one must do so, since their form was indisputably though vaguely that of half-articulate *words*. They were loud—loud as the rumblings and the thunder above which they echoed—yet did they come from no visible being. And because imagination might suggest a conjectural source in the world of non-visible beings, the huddled crowd at the mountain's base huddled still closer, and winced as if in expectation of a blow.

"*Ygnaiih... ygnaiih... thflthkh'ngha... Yog-Sothoth....*" rang the hideous croaking out of space. "*Y'bthnk... h'ehye... n'grkdl'lh....*"

The speaking impulse seemed to falter here, as if some frightful psychic struggle were going on. Henry Wheeler strained his eye at the telescope, but saw only the three grotesquely silhouetted human figures on the peak, all moving their arms furiously in strange gestures as their incantation drew near its culmination. From what black wells of Acherontic fear or feeling, from what unplumbed gulfs of extra-cosmic consciousness or obscure, long-latent heredity, were those half-articulate thunder-croakings drawn? Presently they began to gather renewed force and coherence as they grew in stark, utter, ultimate frenzy.

"*Eh-ya-ya-ya-yahaah... e'yaya-yayaaaa ... ngh'aaaa... ngh'aaaa... h'yuh... h'yuh...* HELP! HELP!...*ff—ff—ff*—FATHER! FATHER! YOG-SOTHOTH!...*"

But that was all. The pallid group in the road, still reeling at the *indisputably English* syllables that had poured thickly and thunderously down from the frantic vacancy beside that shocking altar-stone, were never to hear such syllables again. Instead, they jumped violently at the terrific report which seemed to rend the hills; the deafening, cataclysmic peal whose source, be it inner earth or sky, no hearer was ever able to place. A single lightning bolt shot from the purple zenith to the altar-stone, and a great tidal wave of viewless force and indescribable stench swept down from the hill to all the countryside. Trees, grass, and underbrush

172 • THE DUNWICH HORROR

were whipped into a fury; and the frightened crowd at the mountain's base, weakened by the lethal fetor that seemed about to asphyxiate them, were almost hurled off their feet. Dogs howled from the distance, green grass and foliage wilted to a curious, sickly yellow-gray, and over field and forest were scattered the bodies of dead whippoorwills.

The stench left quickly, but the vegetation never came right again. To this day there is something queer and unholy about the growths on and around that fearsome hill. Curtis Whateley was only just regaining consciousness when the Arkham men came slowly down the mountain in the beams of a sunlight once more brilliant and untainted. They were grave and quiet, and seemed shaken by memories and reflections even more terrible than those which had reduced the group of natives to a state of cowed quivering. In reply to a jumble of questions they only shook their heads and reaffirmed one vital fact.

"The thing has gone forever," Armitage said. "It has been split up into what it was originally made of, and can never exist again. It was an impossibility in a normal world. Only the least fraction was really matter in any sense we know. It was like its father—and most of it has gone back to him in some vague realm or dimension outside our material universe; some vague abyss out of which only the most accursed rites of human blasphemy could ever have called him for a moment on the hills."

There was a brief silence, and in that pause the scattered senses of poor Curtis Whateley began to knit back into a sort of continuity; so that he put his hands to his head with a moan. Memory seemed to pick itself up where it had left off, and the horror of the sight that had prostrated him burst in upon him again.

"Oh, oh, my Gawd, that haff face...that haff face on top of it...that face with the red eyes an' crinkly albino hair, an' no chin, like

BLACK INFINITY • 173

the Whateleys.... It was a octopus, centipede, spider kind o' thing, but they was a haff-shaped man's face on top of it, an' it looked like Wizard Whateley's, only it was yards an' yards acrost...."

He paused exhausted, as the whole group of natives stared in a bewilderment not quite crystallized into fresh terror. Only old Zebulon Whateley, who wanderingly remembered ancient things but who had been silent heretofore, spoke aloud.

"Fifteen year' gone," he rambled, "I heerd Ol' Whateley say as haow someday we'd hear a child o' Lavinny's a-callin' its father's name on the top o' Sentinel Hill...."

But Joe Osborn interrupted him to question the Arkham men anew.

"What was it, anyhaow, an' haowever did young Wizard Whateley call it aout o' the air it come from?"

Armitage chose his words carefully.

"It was—well, it was mostly a kind of force that doesn't belong in our part of space; a kind of force that acts and grows and shapes itself by other laws than those of our sort of Nature. We have no business calling in such things from outside, and only very wicked people and very wicked cults ever try to. There was some of it in Wilbur Whateley himself—enough to make a devil and a precocious monster of him, and to make his passing out a pretty terrible sight. I'm going to burn his accursed diary, and if you men are wise you'll dynamite that altar-stone up there, and pull down all the rings of standing stones on the other hills. Things like that brought down the beings those Whateleys were so fond of—the beings they were going to let in tangibly to wipe out the human race and drag the earth off to some nameless place for some nameless purpose.

"But as to this thing we've just sent back —the Whateleys raised it for a terrible part in the doings that were to come. It grew fast and big from the same reason that Wilbur grew fast and big—but it beat him because it had a greater share of the *outsideness* in it. You needn't ask how Wilbur called it out of the air. He didn't call it out. *It was his twin brother, but it looked more like the father than he did."*

"The Dunwich Horror" first appeared in the April 1929 issue of Weird Tales.

Howard Phillips Lovecraft (1890 – 1937) is best known today for creating the Cthulhu Mythos, a fictional mythology built around a pantheon of ancient god-like aliens, called the Great Old Ones, who once ruled the Earth but lost dominion long before the existence of humankind. Lovecraft gave readers their first glimpse of the mythos in his 1919 story "Dagon" (reprinted in the October 1923 issue of Weird tales*) but did not significantly expand on the idea until his 1926 story "The Call of Cthulhu," (published in the April 1928 issue of* Weird Tales*). With Lovecraft's blessings and encouragement, several of his contemporaries and protégés began incorporating the mythos into their own fiction. One such writer was August Derleth, who is credited for coining the term Cthulhu Mythos (after the aforementioned 1928 story). Derleth eventually started the small press Arkham House to publish and promote Lovecraft's work, and posthumously published the first hardcover collection of HPL stories,* The Outsider and Others, *in 1939.*

Other writers who delved into the Mythos included: Robert E. Howard, creator of Conan the Barbarian; Robert Bloch, whose numerous works of horror fiction (including Psycho) *were frequently adapted for film and television; as well as pulp wordsmiths Henry Kuttner, Frank Belknap Long, Clark Ashton Smith, and Fritz Leiber.*

Today, scores of writers continue to borrow from what has become the most influential shared universe in weird fiction—the dark "Lovecraftian" world of cosmic horror, consisting of monstrous creatures, ancient cults, and arcane rituals—not to mention the quintessential bad book, the Necronomicon.

THE
ARCHAEOLOGY
OF ALIEN:

EXCAVATING THE
CINEMATIC FORERUNNERS OF
RIDLEY SCOTT'S CLASSIC

BY THOMAS
KENT MILLER

ALLEN K. '86

R IDLEY SCOTT'S SCIENCE-FICTION HORROR MASHUP *ALIEN* WAS RELEASED IN 1979, MAKING IT AMONG THE FIRST BIG-BUDGET, seriously-made science-fiction movies that successfully caught the swelling wave that followed the success of *Star Wars* in 1977. Amongst these numerous films were Disney's *Black Hole* (1979), *Star Trek: The Motion Picture* (1979), *Superman: The Movie* (1979), Dino De Laurentiis's *Flash Gordon* (1980), *Blade Runner* (1982), *ET: The Extra-Terrestrial* (1982), *Dune* (1984), and *Lifeforce* (1985), on and on and on, continuing up to the present. (Ironically, Stephen Spielberg's *Close Encounters of the Third Kind* is not eligible to be listed here—because it was being produced concurrently with *Star Wars* and was also released in 1977, and seriously influenced filmmaking thereafter in its own right.)

Alien had no sooner been released on May 25, 1979, than sci-fi movie aficionados began to speculate whether the 1958 United Artist B-film *It! The Terror from Beyond Space* may have been somehow an influence on Scott's film. Indeed, Douglas Brode in his *Fantastic Planets, Forbidden Zones and Lost Continents: The 100 Greatest Science-Fiction Films* tells us that Ronald Shusett, half of *Alien*'s writing team, had been highly impressed by the concept of *It! The Terror from Beyond Space*, while Dan O'Bannon, the other half of the writing team and the man who had initiated the project that became *Alien*, has said in interviews that he used Howard Hawk's *The Thing from Another World* (1951) for inspiration.

When all is said and done, though, there can be no doubt that the essential plots of *It! The Terror from Beyond Space* and *Alien* are virtually identical—taking into account that *Alien* was an $11 million ($47 million in today's dollars) over-the-top visual special effects extravaganza, and the budget for *It!* wouldn't have been much different from the myriad black-and-white sci-fi "quickies" of the 50s and 60s: a bullet-proof blood-thirsty space monster manages to enter a spaceship surreptitiously, uses air vents to access all levels of the ship, and massacres a goodly number of the rather larger-than-traditional-size crew while in search of sorely-needed, essential life-sustaining aspects of, coincidentally for both, the human body. The Martian monster in *It!* requires blood, water, and oxygen and leaves behind dead dry husks, while the creature in *Alien* must have warm, wholesome and nourishing breeding grounds.

Bill Warren in his valuable labor of love *Keep Watching the Skies! American Science Fiction Movies of the Fifties*, says about the relationship between the two films:

> While undeniable story similarities exist, particularly the encounters with the monsters in the ventilator systems, the treatment is different. *Alien* emphasizes: when is it gonna get you? While *It!* emphasizes: how do we get rid of it? In short, *Alien* is primarily a horror and suspense film, while *It!* is a problem film with some tension. Unfortunately, too many SF horror movie fans conclude *Alien* is definitely a rip-off of *It!*.

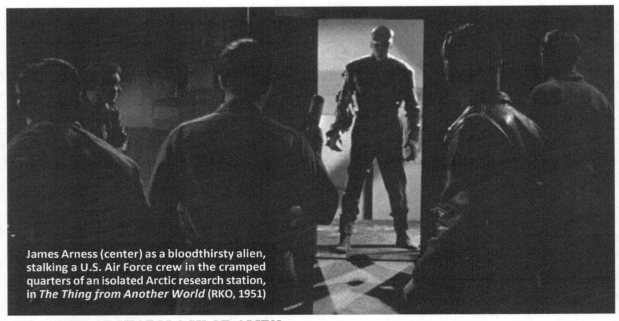

James Arness (center) as a bloodthirsty alien, stalking a U.S. Air Force crew in the cramped quarters of an isolated Arctic research station, in *The Thing from Another World* **(RKO, 1951)**

Major Purdue (Robert Bice) discovers the drained corpse of a crewman stuffed in an airduct, in Edward L. Cahn's *IT! The Terror from Beyond Space* (MGM, 1958)

Below: Captain Dallas (Tom Skerritt) conducts some duct work of his own, in Ridley Scott's *Alien* (20th Century Fox, 1979)

Though it was relatively easy to spot the overt commonalities of the 1958 and 1979 films, these same aficionados above quickly spread their nets a bit farther and began to proclaim that *Alien*'s story was also beholden to two other earlier films: *Planet of the Vampires* (1965) and *Queen of Blood* ('66). Whereas this is definitely true of *Planet of the Vampires*, arguments that try to show *Queen of Blood* as a major influence on *Alien* are much less convincing. *It!* and *Planet* contain much that is replicated in *Alien*, *Queen* is much more of a stretch. While some concepts in *Queen* can be *construed* to have had an influence on, or have similarities to, *Alien*, these connections are far more subtle and abstract. All of which will be detailed below.

IT! THE TERROR FROM BEYOND SPACE AGAINST ALIEN

It! The Terror from Beyond Space opens very nicely. The first thing the audience sees is a wide well-crafted black and white model Mars-scape with a destroyed spaceship in the middle foreground. The sky is full of stars, including a spiral galaxy. While it is impossible to see such a sight from Mars, it is still a charming image, rather like the last shot in *Star Wars: Episode V – The Empire Strikes Back*. *It!*'s title races out from the center of the screen in mock 3D, and the credits roll over this Mars-scape. But as soon as "Directed by Edward L. Cahn" fades from sight, the camera pans right and finally we see a second and brand new spacecraft also in the foreground. All and all, this opening scene is pulled off very nicely. As the camera pans, we hear the voice of Colonel Edward Carruthers explaining that he is the only

BLACK INFINITY • 179

survivor from the first flight to Mars, and the second ship was sent to return him back to earth for court martial. Cut to the inside of the ship, which falls well into the category of "hard" science fiction due to the prevalence of much hardware and is, therefore, quite believable for the most part.

Two plot points are provided immediately: First, that a monster has snuck onto the ship because one of the astronauts was careless and left an airlock open. Gary Gerani, in his book *Top 100 Sci-Fi Movies*, lists *It!* as number 87 and states that the makers of *It!* invented an "ingeniously simple premise for a sci-fi thriller, famously used in *Alien*." Furthermore, Gary Westfahl, in his book *The Spacesuit Film: A History, 1918-1969*, supports that *It!* is "an obvious precursor of Ridley Scott's *Alien* (1979)."

The second plot point established at the start is that the captain of the rescue ship is 100 percent convinced that Carruthers murdered his nine crewmates in order to stretch out the supplies on the broken ship for ten years. For his part, Carruthers insists that he is innocent and that some sort of monster had grabbed his friends in a sandstorm.

It is not long before the stowaway creature begins killing the crew one by one, somehow draining every bit of blood, water, and oxygen from them, leaving behind desiccated corpses (effectively proving that Carruthers was telling the truth). The creature is unrelenting and unstoppable. It crashes through every improvised protective barrier the crew hastily assembles.

Despite fans' gravitation to *It! The Terror from Beyond Space* as being the source of *Alien*, Jerome Bixby, the scriptwriter of *It! The Terror from Beyond Space*, when questioned, has explained that his inspiration was Howard Hawk's *The Thing from Another World*. Sci-Fi authority Jon Abbott, in his *Space Travel in 1950s Cinema*, says that this film

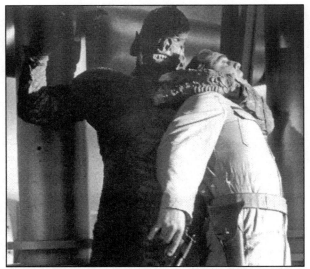

Special photo juxtaposition © 2016–2017 by Thomas Kent Miller

is "very much a brazen copy of *The Thing from Another World*"; nevertheless, the coincidences between *It!* and *Alien* abound: the two creatures board the ship surreptitiously, in *It!*, through a hatch door accidentally left open by a careless crewman, and, in *Alien*, by inserting an embryonic alien into the living body of an unsuspecting crewman. Once each creature gets its bearings, it uses the ship's air vents to move around at will. The human crew of each film's ship is significantly larger than the human crews of earlier spaceship pictures—no doubt to provide a grander buffet from which the creatures can pick and choose. (Most films of this era peopled their rockets with crews of four or five: *Destination Moon* (1950), *Rocketship X-M* ('50), *Flight to Mars* ('51), *Conquest of Space* ('55) (though *Conquest* includes a stowaway), and *Angry Red Planet* (1959).) In both *It!* and *Alien*, separating all the oxygen that's available to the creature succeeds in killing it.

There are two women aboard *It!*'s spaceship. One is portrayed as a busy and competent doctor, while the other's role onboard is vague. Nevertheless, they both make and serve coffee for the men and cook and serve their meals. A shipboard romance blooms between Curruthers and the empathetic but non-medical woman. The third party in a lovers triangle is the ship's captain, who is

resentful at first, then becomes noble. Hope is nearly lost as the creature is smashing through their last protective barrier, the hatch that covers the stairs leading from the level

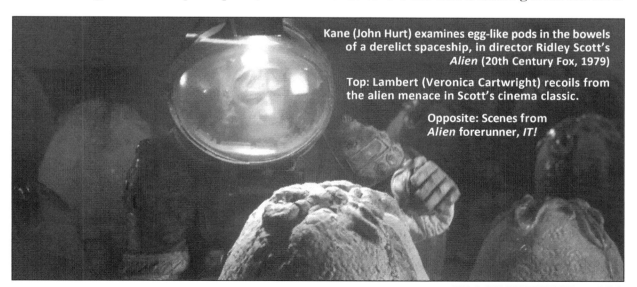

Kane (John Hurt) examines egg-like pods in the bowels of a derelict spaceship, in director Ridley Scott's *Alien* (20th Century Fox, 1979)

Top: Lambert (Veronica Cartwright) recoils from the alien menace in Scott's cinema classic.

Opposite: Scenes from *Alien* forerunner, *IT!*

BLACK INFINITY • 181

below, when Carruthers notices that some gauges registering a disproportionate amount of oxygen in use, which can only mean that the creature is dependent on oxygen to survive. They all put on spacesuits and let the air out of the ship, killing the creature.

Following in the footsteps of William Castle's *Macabre* (1958), which affixed some variant of the following statement on virtually all its advertising—"The Producers of the film MACABRE, undertake to pay the sum of ONE THOUSAND DOLLARS in the event of the death by fright of any member of the audience during the performance. Insured by Lloyds of London"—the makers of *It!* take a page out of this marketing ploy and blast from its advertising, "$50,000 Guaranteed! By a world-renowned insurance company to the first person who can prove 'IT!' is not on Mars now!" Such a bold statement most likely did get some people into the movie theaters.

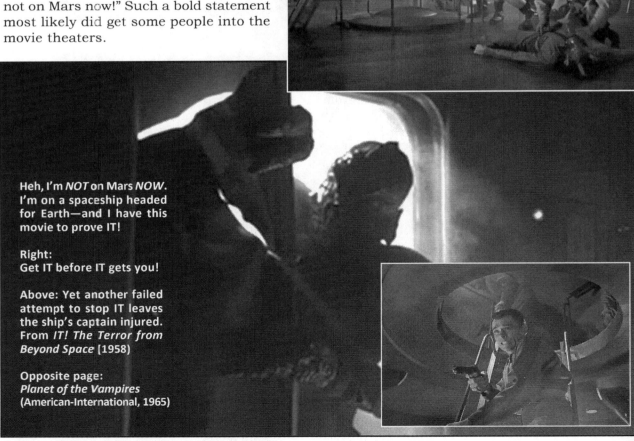

Heh, I'm *NOT* on Mars *NOW*. I'm on a spaceship headed for Earth—and I have this movie to prove IT!

Right:
Get IT before IT gets you!

Above: Yet another failed attempt to stop IT leaves the ship's captain injured. From *IT! The Terror from Beyond Space* (1958)

Opposite page:
Planet of the Vampires
(American-International, 1965)

182 • THE ARCHAEOLOGY OF *ALIEN*

PLANET OF THE VAMPIRES AGAINST ALIEN

Alien emulates just as much from *Planet of the Vampires* as it does from *It!*. The similarities of *Alien* and *Planet of Vampires* are startling. In both films, the crew unexpectedly receives an alien electromagnetic transmission that may or may not be an SOS. The captain of each ship reluctantly chooses to respond to the transmission and veers away from his original course to investigate. They land on the planet near the wreck of a derelict alien spacecraft that is the source of the transmission. The landscapes on which the two ships land are rugged and full of towering stones, similar in shape and size to Earth's termite mounds. The main difference is that the *Planet of the Vampires* landscape is colorfully lit, recalling the three seasons of the original *Star Trek*, wherein the artistry of principal Director of Photography, Gerald Finnerman, frequently casts colored highlights on the background walls, corridors, and ceilings using orange, violet, blue, green, and red filters. *Alien*'s alien landscape, on the other hand, is treacherous and mist-enveloped. When each crew enters their respective derelict spaceship, the first thing they encounter in *Planet of the Vampires* is a giant humanoid skeleton sitting at a desk, while in *Alien* the boarding party rounds a bend and sees another giant humanoid skeleton sitting in a huge central command chair. I sometimes fantasize that if the first half of *Planet of the Vampires* up to finding the skeletons, was edited onto the beginning of *It!*, the result would be a fair representation of *Alien*.

Danish film director Nicolas Winding Refn writes on the Web's Courtesy Cannes Classics about how *Alien* creators Ridley Scott and Dan O'Bannon "stole" from Mario Bava's *Planet of the Vampires* to make *Alien*:

When you look at the two movies, it's not just similarities. It's lifted structure, scenes, characters, dilemmas, themes that are very apparent...one can clearly see the DNA of *Planet of the Vampires* in *Alien*... Both revolve around a space-crew (consisting of

Planet of the Vampires (1965)
Opposite: *Alien* (1979)

mostly men and two women)...There is an entire sequence in *Planet of the Vampires* which is copied shot-for-shot in *Alien*. In both films, the protagonists leave their spaceship—walking...through the foreign planet's foggy barren landscape to investigate the origin of the [mysterious] call they received. Yet as the sequence continues and the characters enter their respective unknown spaceships, the commonalities begin to increase.... As the spacemen...locate the centre of the ship, *we see the thing that* proves *either Ridley Scott or Dan O'Bannon saw* Planet of the Vampires *at some point in their lives—a skeleton. But not just any skeleton—a giant alien skeleton.* [italics mine]

As I described above, when *entering* their respective derelict spaceships, in *Planet* the first thing out-of-the-ordinary they encounter is a giant humanoid skeleton sitting at a desk, while in *Alien*, an equivalent scene is the boarding party finding a bigger giant humanoid skeleton sitting in a huge central chair.

In retrospect, it may be that the inclusion of the giant alien skeleton in the derelict spaceship in *Planet of the Vampires* was the brainchild of its co-writer, Ib Melchior, in which case, his impact, consciously or unconsciously, but certainly belatedly, contributed a whole new trope to cinema's vocabulary, insofar as *Alien*'s co-optation of that giant skeleton reappears more than three decades later as an important plot element in *Prometheus*, another of Ridley Scott's *Alien* adventures. When the co-opted *Planet of the Vampires*'

giant skeleton was included in the first *Alien,* it was no more than an exotic, over-the-top, and colorful image, one of many that populate the film. It could have remained in stasis forever. However, it was indeed resurrected for *Prometheus*, and everything changed; the giant skeleton character unexpectedly morphed into a foundational aspect of the whole *Alien* franchise; in other words, that first *Planet of the Vampires* appearance of the skeleton, its very concept, evolved, becoming part of the over-arching *Alien* mythology, if you will. What I'm trying to say is that that first appearance of the giant skeleton in *Planet* was fresh, something new under the sun, precedent-creating—for which Melchior is entitled to a feather in his cap. Melchior was also director and co-writer of the 1959 roller-coaster special-visual-effects marathon, *The Angry Red Planet*; and originator and co-writer of *Robinson Crusoe on Mars* ('64), without doubt amongst the finest Mars exploration films; and director and co-writer of the well-regarded *The Time Travelers* (1964). In fact, the director of *Planet of the Vampires*, Mario Brava, was so pleased with Ib Melchior's work on the picture that he wrote a letter to the film's producer, American International Pictures' co-founder Samuel Z. Arkoff, in which he was expressly laudatory of Melchior's collaboration and abilities on *Planet of the Vampires*.

Opposite page: *Prometheus* (20th Century Fox, 2012)
Here and below: scenes from *Queen of Blood*
with Don Eitner and John Saxon (MGM, 1965)

QUEEN OF BLOOD AGAINST ALIEN

The Earth is at peace and science has advanced. Earth is virtually a utopia. A message is received from another galaxy. The aliens wish to get to know us better and are sending a ship with their emissaries, but the embassy ship crash lands on Mars. Learning of the aliens' desperate situation from an SOS capsule that crashes into the sea, a rescue mission is sent from earth. The ship encounters solar flares, which uses precious fuel that would otherwise be used for landing and take-off maneuvers. The earth crew of three, including Laura James, lands on Mars. They locate the alien spacecraft with one crew member dead at his post. There had to be others. Where are they? The Earth crew's problem is that they used so much fuel avoiding the solar flares that they don't have enough to cruise around the planet looking for more alien astronauts.

Two earth astronauts, who were not selected for this initial trip, provide the

BLACK INFINITY • 187

chief scientist with a plan. They will take a smaller ship to Mars, distribute several reconnaissance satellites in orbit around the planet, land on Phobos, then use their two-passenger rescue craft to go down to the planet to join their fellow astronauts. However, following their landing on Phobos, they must launch the tiny two-man rescue craft within 29 minutes or they will have to wait a week until Phobos and Mars are lined up properly. They look out their porthole and, incredibly, see an alien vessel—their alien visitors' escape pod that had ejected, crashing into Phobos.

The two astronauts search the pod, find an unconscious green female survivor, and get back to their own ship, all within the 29 allotted minutes. Since the rescue ship is small, one of the astronauts must stay behind. They flip a coin to decide who stays behind to be picked up when the next earth ship arrives in a week.

The rescue craft enters the Martian atmosphere and gets lost in a sandstorm, crashing far from the earth ship. Our brave astronaut, Brenner, carries the alien woman for miles through the blowing, ripping gales of abrasive sand. When everyone is together, they take off for Earth. When the alien awakens, she displays great dislike for needles and for Laura James, the woman in the earth crew. In short order, one of the men winds up dead with his blood drained from his body. Now they understand what the creature is. She's a vampire with hypnotic powers. She drains another victim dry and is starting on a third when Laura James spots her and they engage in a cat fight, wherein the alien is

Isn't it best to let sleeping dogs lie? Astronauts Brenner and Barrata (Saxon and Eitner) with the titular *Queen of Blood* (Florence Marly)

188 • **THE ARCHAEOLOGY OF** *ALIEN*

scratched. In the end, all her blood drains out, and she promptly dies. She was a hemophiliac. As they reach home, they discover that the alien had laid her pulsating green and red gelatinous naval-orange-sized eggs by the dozens hidden all over the ship, which the scientists are uncommonly excited about and carefully remove from the ship to be studied.

As I said from the get-go, there are many arguments that try to show *Queen of Blood* as a major influence on *Alien* that I don't find convincing. Which isn't to say that many another fan finds strong connections. For example, while researching background on *Queen of Blood* relative to *Alien*, I've encountered a plethora of websites and blogs and two documentary films—titled *The Beast Within: The Making of 'Alien'* (2003) and *Memory: The Origins of Alien* (2019)—in which interviewed subjects are convinced that *Queen of Blood* was an important influence on *Alien*. Indeed, Jason Henderson of Castle of Horror thinks of "*Queen of Blood* as the *Alien* movie before *Alien*" and claims that it is "the *undeniable* blueprint for Ridley Scott's *Alien*." [italics mine]

In other words, a great deal of energy has been spent to show that 1966's *Queen of Blood* unequivocally bears an uncanny resemblance to Ridley Scott's *Alien* and appears to have had no small influence on Scott's film.

But as I said above, I don't see it.

Arguments that try to show *Queen of Blood* as a major influence on *Alien* are unconvincing. Though *It!* and *Planet of the Vampires* contain much that seems, or is in fact, replicated in *Alien*, finding such copiable artifacts or incidents in *Queen* is much more of a stretch. While some concepts in *Queen* can be *construed* to have had an influence on *Alien*, these connections are entirely generalized and are far more subtle and abstract. For instance, obviously, there are the journeys through space in spaceships. There is the SOS message, but it is here used in a context totally different than in *Planet of the Vampires* and *Alien*; commentators are always saying,

over and over, that the alien signals in both the *Planet of the Vampires* and *Alien* films are "distress calls," but both films clearly and emphatically indicate that the nature of the signals is unknown (at least through the first two acts of *Alien*). Naturally, a blood-thirsty monster is crucial. The woman astronaut defeats the monster. And alien eggs are discovered. These are the only elements in *Queen* that could possibly have influenced the 1979 movie. As I say, it's a stretch.

However, whether or not *Queen of Blood* was an influence on *Alien*, it does come equipped with a specially interesting pedigree. In the mid-1960s, American International Pictures and filmmaker and producer Roger Corman gained access to three amazingly well-crafted high-budget science fiction epics

John Hurt discovers eggs by the dozens, in *Alien*.
Top: *Queen of Blood*'s Judi Meredith;
and *Alien*'s Sigourney Weaver.

190 • THE ARCHAEOLOGY OF *ALIEN*

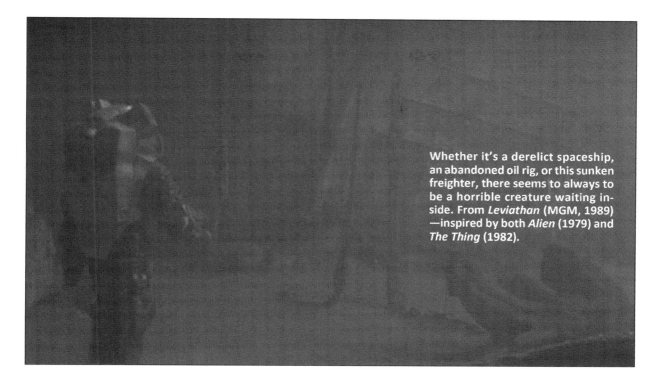

Whether it's a derelict spaceship, an abandoned oil rig, or this sunken freighter, there seems to always to be a horrible creature waiting inside. From *Leviathan* (MGM, 1989)—inspired by both *Alien* (1979) and *The Thing* (1982).

made by the then Soviet Union—including one titled *Mechte Navstrechu*. Corman gave instructions to his staff that all three films needed to be refashioned for American audiences. The job of reworking *Mechte Navstrechu* fell to Curtis Harrington. He salvaged some—though not much, basically some establishing long shots—of the extremely colorful, almost psychedelically rich, footage from the original (pity he did not use more), shot the movie largely from scratch with American actors, changed the story, and assembled *Queen of Blood*, stitching together his new footage with the Soviet footage.

Where the original film focused on a friendly first contact between beings from different worlds, Harrington integrates some visual effects from the Soviet original into an outer-space sci-fi horror movie, matching costumes, spacesuits and helmets. Cutting from the American planet-surface scenes to the Soviet scenes and vice versa were practically seamless, especially since Corman had provided Harrington with only $35,000 and an 8-day shooting schedule.

SOME FINAL THOUGHTS

Nothing described above is news. Filmmakers such as George Lucas, James Cameron, Sergio Leone, Quentin Tarantino, Roger Corman, and countless others have built their careers and filmographies on such practices. While Star Wars relied heavily on Flash Gordon on serials, westerns, war movies, ad infinitum, its follow-up clones relied heavily on Star Wars—*Battlestar Galactica*, *The Black Hole*, *Battle Beyond the Stars*, and *The Last Starfighter* among them. The aftermath of James Cameron's 1989 underwater epic *The Abyss* resulted in *DeepStar Six*, *Leviathan*, *The Evil Below*, *Lords of the Deep*, and *The Rift* and others that depended on Cameron's movie for inspiration. Going back in time, it was in fact the success of 1953's *The Beast from 20,000 Fathoms* that brought into the world 1954's *Gojria* and *Godzilla, King of the Monsters*.

Further, *Beast* was also more-or-less again cloned to create *Them!*, which resulted in the long and marvelous profusion of giant bug movies! It's just the way the system, or the movie industry, works.

Though no expert in either field, Thomas Kent Miller delights in Victorian and Edwardian ghost stories—stories with a malevolent and odious ghost. He is also fond of Hudson River School landscape paintings, of which he has written "these landscapes were astonishingly photographic; every aspect was rendered in minute detail, while at the same time interpreting nature in such romanticized and noble hues, with such immaculate emphasis on light and atmosphere, that the paintings are like windows into paradise." He has written Mars in the Movies: A History *(2016), the first movie book entirely about Mars films. His novels are a Victorian pastiche series including* Sherlock Holmes on the Roof of the World *(1987),* The Great Detective at the Crucible of Life *(2005), and* The Sussex Beekeeper at the Dawn of Time *(2013), all currently available from MX Publishers as Kindle Books, Audible Books, and trade paperbacks. He is a member of The Friends of Arthur Machen as well as The Rider Haggard Society. He has written for* The Ghosts & Scholars M. R. James Newsletter, Faunus: The Journal of the Friends of Arthur Machen, Wormwood, *MX Publishers,* Crypt of Cthulhu, *Airship27 New Pulp Publishers, Belanger Books, and Hippocampus Press. Reading and home theater with multiple devices are his joys these days.*

GORGO (1961)

"Wonderful...from the beloved to the obscure, Miller holds great love for the genre and many of the films featured. If there was not already a book on this subject, there needed to be one. Miller has written it...and the definitive one, at that." —*Flick Attack*

MARS in the MOVIES

A HISTORY

Thomas Kent Miller

FOREWORD BY MICHAEL STEIN

The Ymir
20 Million Miles to Earth
(Columbia Pictures, 1957)

Dracula's Guest

"Adapted" by Universal Studios as *Dracula's Daughter*, the sequel to the 1931 cinema classic with Bela Lugosi

By Bram Stoker

WHEN WE STARTED FOR OUR DRIVE THE SUN WAS SHINING BRIGHTLY ON MUNICH, and the air was full of the joyousness of early summer. Just as we were about to depart, Herr Delbrück (the maître d'hôtel of the Quatre Saisons, where I was staying) came down, bareheaded, to the carriage and, after wishing me a pleasant drive, said to the coachman, still holding his hand on the handle of the carriage door:

"Remember you are back by nightfall. The sky looks bright but there is a shiver in the north wind that says there may be a sudden storm. But I am sure you will not be late." Here he smiled, and added, "for you know what night it is."

Johann answered with an emphatic, "Ja, mein Herr," and, touching his hat, drove off quickly. When we had cleared the town, I said, after signaling to him to stop:

"Tell me, Johann, what is tonight?"

He crossed himself, as he answered laconically: "Walpurgis nacht." Then he took out his watch, a great, old-fashioned German silver thing as big as a turnip, and looked at it, with his eyebrows gathered together and a little impatient shrug of his shoulders. I realized that this was his way of respectfully protesting against the unnecessary delay, and sank back in the carriage, merely motioning him to proceed. He started off rapidly, as if to make up for lost time. Every now and then the horses seemed to throw up their heads and sniffed the air suspiciously. On such occasions I often looked round in alarm. The road was pretty bleak, for we were traversing a sort of high, wind-swept plateau. As we drove, I saw a road that looked but little used, and which seemed to dip through a little, winding valley. It looked so inviting that, even at the risk of offending him, I called Johann to stop—and when he had pulled up, I told him I would like to drive down that road. He made all sorts of excuses, and frequently crossed himself as he spoke. This somewhat piqued my curiosity, so I asked him various questions. He answered fencingly, and repeatedly looked at his watch in protest. Finally I said:

"Well, Johann, I want to go down this road. I shall not ask you to come unless you like; but tell me why you do not like to go, that is all I ask." For answer he seemed to throw himself off the box, so quickly did he reach the ground. Then he stretched out his hands appealingly to me, and implored me not to go. There was just enough of English mixed with the German for me to understand the drift of his talk. He seemed always just about to tell me something—the very idea of which evidently frightened him; but each time he pulled himself up, saying, as he crossed himself: "Walpurgis-Nacht!"

I tried to argue with him, but it was difficult to argue with a man when I did not know his language. The advantage certainly rested with him, for although he began to speak in English, of a very crude and broken kind, he always got excited and broke into his native tongue—and every time he did so, he looked at his watch. Then the horses became restless and sniffed the air. At this he grew very pale, and, looking around in a frightened way, he suddenly jumped forward, took them by the bridles and led them on some twenty feet. I followed, and asked why he had done this. For answer he crossed himself, pointed to the spot we had left and drew his carriage in the direction of the other road, indicating a cross, and said, first in German, then in English: "Buried him—him what killed themselves."

I remembered the old custom of burying suicides at cross-roads: "Ah! I see, a suicide. How interesting!" But for the life of me I could not make out why the horses were frightened.

Whilst we were talking, we heard a sort of sound between a yelp and a bark. It was far away; but the horses got very restless, and it took Johann all his time to quiet them. He was pale, and said, "It sounds like a wolf—but yet there are no wolves here now."

"No?" I said, questioning him; "isn't it long since the wolves were so near the city?"

"Long, long," he answered, "in the spring and summer; but with the snow the wolves have been here not so long."

Whilst he was petting the horses and trying to quiet them, dark clouds drifted rapidly across the sky. The sunshine passed away, and a breath of cold wind seemed to drift past us. It was only a breath, however, and more in the nature of a warning than a fact, for the sun came out brightly again. Johann looked under his lifted hand at the horizon and said:

"The storm of snow, he comes before long time." Then he looked at his watch again, and straightway holding his reins firmly—for the horses were still pawing the ground restlessly and shaking their heads—he climbed to his box as though the time had come for proceeding on our journey.

I felt a little obstinate and did not at once get into the carriage.

"Tell me," I said, "about this place where the road leads," and I pointed down.

Again he crossed himself and mumbled a prayer, before he answered, "It is unholy."

"What is unholy?" I enquired.

"The village."

"Then there is a village?"

"No, no. No one lives there hundreds of years." My curiosity was piqued, "But you said there was a village."

"There was."

"Where is it now?"

Whereupon he burst out into a long story in German and English, so mixed up that I could not quite understand exactly what he said, but roughly I gathered that long ago, hundreds of years, men had died there and been buried in their graves; and sounds were heard under the clay, and when the graves were opened, men and women were found rosy with life, and their mouths red with blood. And so, in haste to save their lives (aye, and their souls!—and here he crossed himself) those who were left fled away to other places, where the living lived, and the dead were dead and not—not something. He was evidently afraid to speak the last words. As he proceeded with his narration, he grew more and more excited. It seemed as if his imagination had got hold of him, and he ended in a perfect paroxysm of fear—white-faced, perspiring, trembling and looking round him, as if expecting that some dreadful presence would manifest itself there in the bright sunshine on the open plain. Finally, in an agony of desperation, he cried:

"Walpurgis nacht!" and pointed to the carriage for me to get in. All my English blood rose at this, and, standing back, I said:

"You are afraid, Johann—you are afraid. Go home; I shall return alone; the walk will do

196 • DRACULA'S GUEST

me good." The carriage door was open. I took from the seat my oak walking-stick—which I always carry on my holiday excursions—and closed the door, pointing back to Munich, and said, "Go home, Johann—Walpurgis-nacht doesn't concern Englishmen."

The horses were now more restive than ever, and Johann was trying to hold them in, while excitedly imploring me not to do anything so foolish. I pitied the poor fellow, he was deeply in earnest; but all the same I could not help laughing. His English was quite gone now. In his anxiety he had forgotten that his only means of making me understand was to talk my language, so he jabbered away in his native German. It began to be a little tedious. After giving the direction, "Home!" I turned to go down the cross-road into the valley.

With a despairing gesture, Johann turned his horses towards Munich. I leaned on my stick and looked after him. He went slowly along the road for a while: then there came over the crest of the hill a man tall and thin. I could see so much in the distance. When he drew near the horses, they began to jump and kick about, then to scream with terror. Johann could not hold them in; they bolted down the road, running away madly. I watched them out of sight, then looked for the stranger, but I found that he, too, was gone.

With a light heart I turned down the side road through the deepening valley to which Johann had objected. There was not the slightest reason, that I could see, for his objection; and I daresay I tramped for a couple of hours without thinking of time or distance, and certainly without seeing a person or a house. So far as the place was concerned, it was desolation itself. But I did not notice this particularly till, on turning a bend in the road, I came upon a scattered fringe of wood; then I recognized that I had been impressed unconsciously by the desolation of the region through which I had passed.

I sat down to rest myself and began to look around. It struck me that it was considerably colder than it had been at the commencement of my walk—a sort of sighing sound seemed to be around me, with, now and then, high overhead, a sort of muffled roar. Looking upwards I noticed that great thick clouds were drifting rapidly across the sky from North to South at a great height. There were signs of coming storm in some lofty stratum of the air. I was a little chilly, and, thinking that it was the sitting still after the exercise of walking, I resumed my journey.

The ground I passed over was now much more picturesque. There were no striking objects that the eye might single out; but in all there was a charm of beauty. I took little heed of time and it was only when the deepening twilight forced itself upon me that I began to think of how I should find my way home. The brightness of the day had gone. The air was cold, and the drifting of clouds high overhead was more marked. They were accompanied by a sort of far-away rushing sound, through which seemed to come at intervals that mysterious cry which the driver had said came from a wolf. For a while I hesitated. I had said I would see the deserted village, so on I went, and presently came on a wide stretch of open country, shut in by hills all around. Their sides were covered with trees which spread down to the plain, dotting, in clumps, the gentler slopes and hollows which showed here and there. I followed with my eye the winding of the road, and saw that it curved close to one of the densest of these clumps and was lost behind it.

As I looked there came a cold shiver in the air, and the snow began to fall. I thought of the miles and miles of bleak country I had passed, and then hurried on to seek the shelter of the wood in front. Darker and darker grew the sky, and faster and heavier fell the snow, till the earth before and around me was a glistening white carpet the further edge of which was lost in misty vagueness. The road was here but crude, and when on

BLACK INFINITY • 197

the level its boundaries were not so marked, as when it passed through the cuttings; and in a little while I found that I must have strayed from it, for I missed underfoot the hard surface, and my feet sank deeper in the grass and moss. Then the wind grew stronger and blew with ever increasing force, till I was fain to run before it. The air became icy-cold, and in spite of my exercise I began to suffer. The snow was now falling so thickly and whirling around me in such rapid eddies that I could hardly keep my eyes open. Every now and then the heavens were torn asunder by vivid lightning, and in the flashes I could see ahead of me a great mass of trees, chiefly yew and cypress all heavily coated with snow.

I was soon amongst the shelter of the trees, and there, in comparative silence, I could hear the rush of the wind high overhead. Presently the blackness of the storm had become merged in the darkness of the night. By-and-by the storm seemed to be passing away: it now only came in fierce puffs or blasts. At such moments the weird sound of the wolf appeared to be echoed by many similar sounds around me.

Now and again, through the black mass of drifting cloud, came a straggling ray of moonlight, which lit up the expanse, and showed me that I was at the edge of a dense mass of cypress and yew trees. As the snow had ceased to fall, I walked out from the shelter and began to investigate more closely. It appeared to me that, amongst so many old foundations as I had passed, there might be still standing a house in which, though in ruins, I could find some sort of shelter for a while. As I skirted the edge of the copse, I found that a low wall encircled it, and following this I presently found an opening. Here the cypresses formed an alley leading up to a square mass of some kind of building. Just as I caught sight of this, however, the drifting clouds obscured the moon, and I passed up the path in darkness. The wind must have grown colder, for I felt myself shiver as I walked; but there was hope of shelter, and I groped my way blindly on.

I stopped, for there was a sudden stillness. The storm had passed; and, perhaps in sympathy with nature's silence, my heart seemed to cease to beat. But this was only momentarily; for suddenly the moonlight broke through the clouds, showing me that I was in a graveyard, and that the square object before me was a great massive tomb of marble, as white as the snow that lay on and all around it. With the moonlight there came a fierce sigh of the storm, which appeared to resume its course with a long, low howl, as of many dogs or wolves. I was awed and shocked, and felt the cold perceptibly grow upon me till it seemed to grip me by the heart. Then while the flood of moonlight still fell on the marble tomb, the storm gave further evidence of renewing, as though it was returning on its track. Impelled by some sort of fascination, I approached the sepulchre to see what it was, and why such a thing stood alone in such a place. I walked around it, and read, over the Doric door, in German:

COUNTESS DOLINGEN OF GRATZ
IN STYRIA
SOUGHT AND FOUND DEATH.
1801.

On the top of the tomb, seemingly driven through the solid marble—for the structure was composed of a few vast blocks of stone —was a great iron spike or stake. On going to the back, I saw, graven in great Russian letters:

"The dead travel fast."

There was something so weird and uncanny about the whole thing that it gave me a turn and made me feel quite faint. I began to wish, for the first time, that I had taken Johann's advice. Here a thought struck me, which came under almost mysterious circumstances and with a terrible shock. This was Walpurgis Night!

Walpurgis Night, when, according to the belief of millions of people, the devil was abroad—when the graves were opened and the dead came forth and walked. When all evil things of earth and air and water held revel. This very place the driver had specially shunned. This was the depopulated village of centuries ago. This was where the suicide lay; and this was the place where I was alone —unmanned, shivering with cold in a shroud of snow with a wild storm gathering again upon me! It took all my philosophy, all the religion I had been taught, all my courage, not to collapse in a paroxysm of fright.

And now a perfect tornado burst upon me. The ground shook as though thousands of horses thundered across it; and this time the storm bore on its icy wings, not snow, but great hailstones which drove with such violence that they might have come from the thongs of Balearic slingers—hailstones that beat down leaf and branch and made the shelter of the cypresses of no more avail than though their stems were standing-corn. At the first I had rushed to the nearest tree; but I was soon fain to leave it and seek the only spot that seemed to afford refuge, the deep Doric doorway of the marble tomb. There, crouching against the massive bronze door, I gained a certain amount of protection from the beating of the hailstones, for now they only drove against me as they ricocheted from the ground and the side of the marble.

As I leaned against the door, it moved slightly and opened inwards. The shelter of even a tomb was welcome in that pitiless tempest, and I was about to enter it when there came a flash of forked-lightning that lit up the whole expanse of the heavens. In the instant, as I am a living man, I saw, as my eyes were turned into the darkness of the tomb, a beautiful woman, with rounded cheeks and red lips, seemingly sleeping on a bier. As the thunder broke overhead, I was grasped as by the hand of a giant and hurled out into the storm. The whole thing was so sudden that, before I could realize the shock,

moral as well as physical, I found the hailstones beating me down. At the same time, I had a strange, dominating feeling that I was not alone. I looked towards the tomb. Just then there came another blinding flash, which seemed to strike the iron stake that surmounted the tomb and to pour through to the earth, blasting and crumbling the marble, as in a burst of flame. The dead woman rose for a moment of agony, while she was lapped in the flame, and her bitter scream of pain was drowned in the thunder-crash. The last thing I heard was this mingling of dreadful sound, as again I was seized in the giant-grasp and dragged away, while the hailstones beat on me, and the air around seemed reverberant with the howling of wolves. The last sight that I remembered was a vague, white, moving mass, as if all the graves around me had sent out the phantoms of their sheeted-dead, and that they were closing in on me through the white cloudiness of the driving hail.

GRADUALLY THERE CAME a sort of vague beginning of consciousness; then a sense of weariness that was dreadful. For a time I remembered nothing; but slowly my senses returned. My feet seemed positively racked with pain, yet I could not move them. They seemed to be numbed. There was an icy feeling at the back of my neck and all down my spine, and my ears, like my feet, were dead, yet in torment; but there was in my breast a sense of warmth which was, by comparison, delicious. It was as a nightmare—a physical nightmare, if one may use such an expression; for some heavy weight on my chest made it difficult for me to breathe.

This period of semi-lethargy seemed to remain a long time, and as it faded away I must have slept or swooned. Then came a sort of loathing, like the first stage of sea-sickness, and a wild desire to be free from something—I knew not what. A vast stillness enveloped me, as though all the world were asleep or dead—only broken by the low panting as of some animal close to me. I felt a

BLACK INFINITY • 199

warm rasping at my throat, then came a consciousness of the awful truth, which chilled me to the heart and sent the blood surging up through my brain. Some great animal was lying on me and now licking my throat. I feared to stir, for some instinct of prudence bade me lie still; but the brute seemed to realize that there was now some change in me, for it raised its head. Through my eyelashes I saw above me the two great flaming eyes of a gigantic wolf. Its sharp white teeth gleamed in the gaping red mouth, and I could feel its hot breath fierce and acrid upon me.

For another spell of time, I remembered no more. Then I became conscious of a low growl, followed by a yelp, renewed again and again. Then, seemingly very far away, I heard a "Holloa! holloa!" as of many voices calling in unison. Cautiously I raised my head and looked in the direction whence the sound came; but the cemetery blocked my view. The wolf still continued to yelp in a strange way, and a red glare began to move round the grove of cypresses, as though following the sound. As the voices drew closer, the wolf yelped faster and louder. I feared to make either sound or motion. Nearer came the red glow, over the white pall which stretched into the darkness around me. Then all at once from beyond the trees there came at a trot a troop of horsemen bearing torches. The wolf rose from my breast and made for the cemetery. I saw one of the horsemen (soldiers by their caps and their long military cloaks) raise his carbine and take aim. A companion knocked up his arm, and I heard the ball whizz over my head. He had evidently taken my body for that of the wolf. Another sighted the animal as it slunk away, and a shot followed. Then, at a gallop, the troop rode forward—some towards me, others following the wolf as it disappeared amongst the snow-clad cypresses.

As they drew nearer I tried to move, but was powerless, although I could see and hear all that went on around me. Two or three of the soldiers jumped from their horses and knelt beside me. One of them raised my head and placed his hand over my heart.

"Good news, comrades!" he cried. "His heart still beats!"

Then some brandy was poured down my throat; it put vigor into me, and I was able to open my eyes fully and look around. Lights and shadows were moving among the trees, and I heard men call to one another. They drew together, uttering frightened exclamations; and the lights flashed as the others came pouring out of the cemetery pell-mell, like men possessed. When the further ones came close to us, those who were around me asked them eagerly:

"Well, have you found him?"

The reply rang out hurriedly:

"No! no! Come away quick—quick! This is no place to stay, and on this of all nights!"

"What was it?" was the question, asked in all manner of keys. The answer came variously and all indefinitely as though the men were moved by some common impulse to speak, yet were restrained by some common fear from giving their thoughts.

"It—it—indeed!" gibbered one, whose wits had plainly given out for the moment.

"A wolf—and yet not a wolf!" another put in shudderingly.

"No use trying for him without the sacred bullet," a third remarked in a more ordinary manner.

"Serve us right for coming out on this night! Truly we have earned our thousand marks!" were the ejaculations of a fourth.

"There was blood on the broken marble," another said after a pause—"the lightning never brought that there. And for him—is he safe? Look at his throat! See, comrades, the wolf has been lying on him and keeping his blood warm."

The officer looked at my throat and replied: "He is all right; the skin is not pierced. What does it all mean? We should never have found him but for the yelping of the wolf."

"What became of it?" asked the man who was holding up my head, and who seemed the least panic-stricken of the party, for his hands were steady and without tremor. On his sleeve was the chevron of a petty officer.

"It went to its home," answered the man, whose long face was pallid, and who actually shook with terror as he glanced around him fearfully. "There are graves enough there in which it may lie. Come, comrades—come quickly! Let us leave this cursed spot."

The officer raised me to a sitting posture, as he uttered a word of command; then several men placed me upon a horse. He sprang to the saddle behind me, took me in his arms, gave the word to advance; and, turning our faces away from the cypresses, we rode away in swift, military order.

As yet, my tongue refused its office, and I was perforce silent. I must have fallen asleep; for the next thing I remembered was finding myself standing up, supported by a soldier on each side of me. It was almost broad daylight, and to the north a red streak of sunlight was reflected, like a path of blood, over the waste of snow. The officer was telling the men to say nothing of what they had seen, except that they found an English stranger, guarded by a large dog.

"Dog! that was no dog," cut in the man who had exhibited such fear. "I think I know a wolf when I see one."

The young officer answered calmly: "I said a dog."

"Dog!" reiterated the other ironically. It was evident that his courage was rising with the sun; and, pointing to me, he said, "Look at his throat. Is that the work of a dog, master?"

Instinctively I raised my hand to my throat, and as I touched it I cried out in pain. The men crowded round to look, some stooping down from their saddles; and again there came the calm voice of the young officer:

"A dog, as I said. If aught else were said we should only be laughed at."

I was then mounted behind a trooper, and we rode on into the suburbs of Munich. Here we came across a stray carriage, into which I was lifted, and it was driven off to the Quatre Saisons—the young officer accompanying me, whilst a trooper followed with his horse, and the others rode off to their barracks.

When we arrived, Herr Delbrück rushed so quickly down the steps to meet me, that it was apparent he had been watching within. Taking me by both hands he solicitously led me in. The officer saluted me and was turning to withdraw, when I recognized his purpose, and insisted that he should come to my rooms. Over a glass of wine I warmly thanked him and his brave comrades for saving me. He replied simply that he was more than glad, and that Herr Delbrück had at the first taken steps to make all the searching party pleased; at which ambiguous utterance the maître d'hôtel smiled, while the officer pleaded duty and withdrew.

"But Herr Delbrück," I enquired, "how and why was it that the soldiers searched for me?"

He shrugged his shoulders, as if in depreciation of his own deed, as he replied:

"I was so fortunate as to obtain leave from the commander of the regiment in which I served, to ask for volunteers."

"But how did you know I was lost?" I asked.

"The driver came hither with the remains of his carriage, which had been upset when the horses ran away."

"But surely you would not send a search-party of soldiers merely on this account?"

"Oh, no!" he answered; "but even before the coachman arrived, I had this telegram from the Boyar whose guest you are," and he took from his pocket a telegram which he handed to me, and I read:

BISTRITZ.

Be careful of my guest—his safety is most precious to me. Should aught happen to him, or if he be missed, spare nothing to find him and ensure his safety. He is English and therefore adventurous. There are often dangers from snow and wolves and night. Lose not a moment if you suspect harm to him. I answer your zeal with my fortune. —Dracula.

As I held the telegram in my hand, the room seemed to whirl around me; and, if the attentive maître d'hôtel had not caught me, I think I should have fallen. There was something so strange in all this, something so weird and impossible to imagine, that there grew on me a sense of my being in some way the sport of opposite forces—the mere vague idea of which seemed in a way to paralyze me. I was certainly under some form of mysterious protection. From a distant country had come, in the very nick of time, a message that took me out of the danger of the snow-sleep and the jaws of the wolf.

Written in 1897, "Dracula's Guest" was intended as a chapter of Bram Stoker's novel Dracula. *The publisher omitted the material to shorten the novel, but the chapter was later repurposed as a standalone story. As such, it first appeared in the author's posthumous, 1914 collection* Dracula's Guest and Other Weird Stories. *It was loosely "adapted" for the movie* Dracula's Daughter, *the 1936 sequel to the 1931 Universal Studios' classic. The completed film, however, bears little resemblance to Stoker's story.*

Irish author Bram Stoker (1847–1912) is best remembered today for codifying the lore of vampirism into a single groundbreaking novel. But that novel and its undead antagonist, Dracula, didn't achieve immortality until Carl Laemmle Jr., Universal Studios' head of production from 1928–1936, essentially created the monster movie genre, adding the vampire to its stable of cool creatures.

During his lifetime, Bram Stoker was better known as the personal assistant to the stage actor Sir Henry Irving, than as the author of one of the greatest novels in English literature—or as the creator of one of the most recognizable characters in the world.

THE PURPLE TERROR

BY FRED M. WHITE

LIEUTENANT WILL SCARLETT'S INSTRUCTIONS WERE DEVOID OF PROBLEMS, physical or otherwise. To convey a letter from Captain Driver of the *Yankee Doodle*, in Porto Rico Bay, to Admiral Lake on the other side of the isthmus, was an apparently simple matter.

"All you have to do," the captain remarked, "is to take three or four men with you in case of accidents, cross the isthmus on foot, and simply give this letter into the hands of Admiral Lake. By so doing we shall save at least four days, and the aborigines are presumedly friendly."

The aborigines aforesaid were Cuban insurgents. Little or no strife had taken place along the neck lying between Porto Rico and the north bay where Lake's flagship lay, though the belt was known to be given over to the disaffected Cubans.

"It is a matter of fifty miles through practically unexplored country," Scarlett replied, "and there's a good deal of the family quarrel in this business, sir. If the Spaniards hate us, the Cubans are not exactly enamored of our flag."

Captain Driver roundly denounced the whole pack of them.

"Treacherous thieves to a man," he said. "I don't suppose your progress will have any brass bands and floral arches to it. And they tell me the forest is pretty thick. But you'll get there all the same. There is the letter, and you can start as soon as you like."

"I may pick my own men, sir?"

"My dear fellow, take whom you please. Take the mastiff, if you like."

"I'd like the mastiff," Scarlett replied, "as he is practically my own, I thought you would not object."

Will Scarlett began to glow as the prospect of adventure stimulated his imagination. He was rather a good specimen of West Point naval dandyism. He had brains at the back of his smartness, and his geological and botanical knowledge were going to prove of considerable service to a grateful country when said grateful country should have passed beyond the rudimentary stages of colonization. And there was some disposition to envy Scarlett on the part of others floating for the past month on the liquid prison of the sapphire sea.

A warrant officer, Tarrer by name, *plus* two A.B.'s of thews and sinews, to say nothing of the dog, completed the exploring party. By the time that the sun kissed the tip of the feathery hills they had covered some six miles of their journey. From the first Scarlett had been struck by the absolute absence of the desolation and horror of civil strife. Evidently the fiery cross had not been carried here; huts and houses were intact; the villagers stood under sloping eaves, and regarded

204 • **BLACK INFINITY**

the Americans with a certain sullen curiosity.

"We'd better stop for the night here," said Scarlett.

They had come at length to a village that boasted some pretensions. An adobe chapel at one end of the straggling street was faced by a wine-house at the other. A padre, with hands folded over a bulbous, greasy gabardine, bowed gravely to Scarlett's salutation. The latter had what Tarrer called "considerable Spanish."

"We seek quarters for the night," said Scarlett. "Of course, we are prepared to pay for them."

The sleepy padre nodded towards the wine-house.

"You will find fair accommodation there," he said. "We are friends of the Americanos."

Scarlett doubted the fact, and passed on with florid thanks. So far, little signs of friendliness had been encountered on the march. Coldness, suspicion, a suggestion of fear, but no friendliness to be embarrassing.

The keeper of the wineshop had his doubts. He feared his poor accommodation for guests so distinguished. A score or more of picturesque, cut-throat-looking rascals with cigarettes in their mouths lounged sullenly in the bar. The display of a brace of gold dollars enlarged mine host's opinion of his household capacity.

"I will do my best, señors," he said. "Come this way."

So it came to pass that an hour after twilight Tarrer and Scarlett were seated in the open amongst the oleanders and the trailing gleam of the fireflies, discussing cigars of average merit and a native wine that was not without virtues. The long bar of the wine-house was brilliantly illuminated; from within came shouts of laughter mingled with the ting, tang of the guitar and the rollicking clack of the castanets.

"They seem to be happy in there," Tarrer remarked. "It isn't all daggers and ball in this distressful country."

A certain curiosity came over Scarlett.

"It is the duty of a good officer," he said, "to lose no opportunity of acquiring useful information. Let us join the giddy throng, Tarrer."

Tarrer expressed himself with enthusiasm in favor of any amusement that might be going. A month's idleness on shipboard increases the appetite for that kind of thing wonderfully. The long bar was comfortable, and filled with Cubans who took absolutely no notice of the intruders. Their eyes were turned towards a rude stage at the far end of the bar, whereon a girl was gyrating in a dance with a celerity and grace that caused the wreath of flowers around her shoulders to resemble a trembling zone of purple flame.

"A wonderfully pretty girl and a wonderfully pretty dance," Scarlett murmured, when the motions ceased and the girl leapt gracefully to the ground. "Largesse, I expect. I thought so. Well, I'm good for a quarter."

The girl came forward, extending a shell prettily. She curtsied before Scarlett and fixed her dark, liquid eyes on his. As he smiled and dropped his quarter-dollar into the shell a coquettish gleam came into the velvety eyes. An ominous growl came from the lips of a bearded ruffian close by.

"Othello's jealous," said Tarrer. "Look at his face."

"I am better employed," Scarlett laughed. "That was a graceful dance, pretty one. I hope you are going to give us another one presently——"

Scarlett paused suddenly. His eyes had fallen on the purple band of flowers the girl had twined round her shoulder. Scarlett was an enthusiastic botanist; he knew most of the gems in Flora's crown, but he had never looked upon such a vivid wealth of blossom before.

The flowers were orchids, and orchids of a kind unknown to collectors anywhere. On this point Scarlett felt certain. And yet this part of the world was by no means a difficult one to explore in comparison with New Guinea and

BLACK INFINITY • 205

Sumatra, where the rarer varieties had their homes.

The blooms were immensely large, far larger than any flower of the kind known to Europe or America, of a deep pure purple, with a blood-red center. As Scarlett gazed upon them he noticed a certain cruel expression on the flower. Most orchids have a kind of face of their own; the purple blooms had a positive expression of ferocity and cunning. They exhumed, too, a queer, sickly fragrance. Scarlett had smelt something like it before, after the Battle of Manila. The perfume was the perfume of a corpse.

"And yet they are magnificent flowers," said Scarlett. "Won't you tell me where you got them from, pretty one?"

The girl was evidently flattered by the attention bestowed upon her by the smart young American. The bearded Othello alluded to edged up to her side.

"The señor had best leave the girl alone," he said, insolently.

Scarlett's fist clenched as he measured the Cuban with his eyes. The Admiral's letter crackled in his breast-pocket, and discretion got the best of valor.

"You are paying yourself a poor compliment, my good fellow," he said, "though I certainly admire your good taste. Those flowers interested me."

The man appeared to be mollified. His features corrugated in a smile.

"The señor would like some of those blooms?" he asked. "It was I who procured them for little Zara here. I can show you where they grow."

Every eye in the room was turned in Scarlett's direction. It seemed to him that a kind of diabolical malice glistened on every dark face there, save that of the girl whose features paled under her healthy tan.

"If the señor is wise," she began, "he will not——"

"Listen to the tales of a silly girl," Othello put in, menacingly. He grasped the girl by the arm, and she winced in positive pain.

"*Pshaw*, there is no harm where the flowers grow, if one is only careful. I will take you there, and I will be your guide to Port Anna, where you are going, for a gold dollar."

All Scarlett's scientific enthusiasm was aroused. It is not given to every man to present a new orchid to the horticultural world. And this one would dwarf the finest plant hitherto discovered.

"Done with you," he said; "we start at daybreak. I shall look to you to be ready. Your name is Tito? Well, good-night, Tito."

As Scarlett and Tarrer withdrew the girl suddenly darted forward. A wild word or two fluttered from her lips. Then there was a sound as of a blow, followed by a little, stifled cry of pain.

"No, no," Tarrer urged, as Scarlett half turned. "Better not. They are ten to one, and they are no friends of ours. It never pays to interfere in these family quarrels. I daresay, if you interfered, the girl would be just as ready to knife you as her jealous lover."

"But a blow like that, Tarrer!"

"It's a pity, but I don't see how we can help it. Your business is the quick dispatch of the Admiral's letter, not the squiring of dames."

Scarlett owned with a sigh that Tarrer was right.

II

IT WAS QUITE A DIFFERENT Tito who presented himself at daybreak the following morning. His insolent manner had disappeared. He was cheerful, alert, and he had a manner full of the most winning politeness.

"You quite understand what we want," Scarlett said. "My desire is to reach Port Anna as soon as possible. You know the way?"

"Every inch of it, señor. I have made the journey scores of times. And I shall have the felicity of getting you there early on the third day from now."

"Is it so far as that?"

"The distance is not great, señor. It is idle

206 • THE PURPLE TERROR

passage through the woods. There are parts where no white man has been before."

"And you will not forget the purple orchids?"

A queer gleam trembled like summer lightning in Tito's eyes. The next instant it had gone. A time was to come when Scarlett was to recall that look, but for the moment it was allowed to pass.

"The señor shall see the purple orchid," he said; "thousands of them. They have a bad name amongst our people, but that is all nonsense. They grow in the high trees, and their blossoms cling to long, green tendrils. These tendrils are poisonous to the flesh, and great care should be taken in handling them. And the flowers are quite harmless, though we call them the devil's poppies."

To all of this Scarlett listened eagerly. He was all-impatient to see and handle the mysterious flower for himself. The whole excursion was going to prove a wonderful piece of luck. At the same time he had to curb his impatience. There would be no chance of seeing the purple orchid today.

For hours they fought their way along through the dense tangle. A heat seemed to lie over all the land like a curse—a blistering, sweltering, moist heat with no puff of wind to temper its breathlessness. By the time that the sun was sliding down, most of the party had had enough of it.

They passed out of the underwood at length, and, striking upwards, approached a clump of huge forest trees on the brow of a ridge. All kinds of parasites hung from the branches; there were ropes and bands of green, and high up, a fringe of purple glory that caused Scarlett's pulses to leap a little faster.

"Surely that is the purple orchid?" he cried.

Tito shrugged his shoulders contemptuously.

"A mere straggler or two," he said, "and out of our reach in any case. The señor will have all he wants and more tomorrow."

"But it seems to me," said Scarlett, "that I could——"

Then he paused. The sun like a great glowing shield was shining full behind the tree with its crown of purple, and showing up every green rope and thread clinging to the branches with the clearness of liquid crystal. Scarlett saw a network of green cords like a huge spider's web, and in the center of it was not a fly, but a human skeleton!

The arms and legs were stretched apart as if the victim had been crucified. The wrists and ankles were bound in the cruel web. Fragments of tattered clothing fluttered in the faint breath of the evening breeze.

"Horrible," Scarlett cried, "absolutely horrible!"

"You may well say that," Tarrer exclaimed, with a shudder. "Like the fly in the amber or the apple in the dumpling, the mystery is how he got there."

"Perhaps Tito can explain the mystery," Scarlett suggested.

Tito appeared to be uneasy and disturbed. He looked furtively from one to the other of his employers as a culprit might who feels he has been found out. But his courage returned as he noted the absence of suspicion in the faces turned upon him.

"I can explain," he exclaimed, with teeth that chattered from some unknown terror or guilt. "It is not the first time that I have seen the skeleton. Some plant-hunter doubtless who came here alone. He climbed into the tree without a knife, and those green ropes got twisted round his limbs, as a swimmer gets entangled in the weeds. The more he struggled, the more the cords bound him. He would call in vain for anyone to assist him here. And so he must have died."

The explanation was a plausible one, but by no means detracted from the horror of the discovery. For some time, the party pushed their way on in the twilight, till the darkness descended suddenly like a curtain.

"We will camp here," Tito said; "it is high, dry ground, and we have this belt of trees above us. There is no better place than this for miles around. In the valley the miasma is dangerous."

As Tito spoke he struck a match, and soon a torch flamed up. The little party were on a small plateau, fringed by trees. The ground was dry and hard, and, as Scarlett and his party saw to their astonishment, littered with bones. There were skulls of animals and skulls of human beings, the skeletons of birds, the frames of beasts both great and small. It was a weird, shuddering sight.

"We can't possibly stay here," Scarlett exclaimed.

Tito shrugged his shoulders.

"There is nowhere else," he replied. "Down in the valley there are many dangers. Further in the woods are the snakes and jaguars. Bones are nothing. *Peuf*, they can be easily cleared away."

They had to be cleared away, and there was an end of the matter. For the most part the skeletons were white and dry as air and sun could make them. Over the dry, calcined mass the huge fringe of trees nodded mournfully. With the rest, Scarlett was busy scattering the mocking frames aside. A perfect human skeleton lay at his feet. On one finger something glittered—a signet ring. As Scarlett took it in his hand he started.

"I know this ring!" he exclaimed; "it belonged to Pierre Anton, perhaps the most skilled and intrepid plant-hunter the *Jardin des Plantes* ever employed. The poor fellow was by way of being a friend of mine. He met the fate that he always anticipated."

"There must have been a rare holocaust here," said Tarrer.

"It beats me," Scarlett responded. By this time a large circle had been shifted clear of human and other remains. By the light of the fire loathsome insects could be seen scudding and straddling away. "It beats me entirely. Tito, can you offer any explanation? If the bones were all human I could get some grip of the problem. But when one comes to birds and animals as well! Do you see that the skeletons lie in a perfect circle, starting from the center of the clump of trees above us? What does it mean?"

Tito professed utter ignorance of the subject. Some years before a small tribe of natives invaded the peninsula for religious rites. They came from a long way off in canoes, and wild stories were told concerning them. They burnt sacrifices, no doubt.

Scarlett turned his back contemptuously on this transparent tale. His curiosity was aroused. There must be some explanation, for Pierre Anton had been seen of men within the last ten years.

"There's something uncanny about this,"

208 • THE PURPLE TERROR

he said, to Tarrer. "I mean to get to the bottom of it, or know why."

"As for me," said Tarrer, with a cavernous yawn, "I have but one ambition, and that is my supper, followed by my bed."

III

SCARLETT LAY IN THE LIGHT of the fire looking about him. He felt restless and uneasy, though he would have found it difficult to explain the reason. For one thing, the air trembled to strange noises. There seemed to be something moving, writhing in the forest trees above his head. More than once it seemed to his distorted fancy that he could see a squirming knot of green snakes in motion.

Outside the circle, in a grotto of bones, Tito lay sleeping. A few moments before his dark, sleek head had been furtively raised, and his eyes seemed to gleam in the flickering firelight with malignant cunning. As he met Scarlett's glance, he gave a deprecatory gesture and subsided.

"What the deuce does it all mean?" Scarlett muttered. "I feel certain, yonder rascal is up to some mischief. Jealous still because I paid his girl a little attention. But he can't do us any real harm. Quiet, there!"

The big mastiff growled and then whined uneasily. Even the dog seemed to be conscious of some unseen danger. He lay down again, cowed by the stern command, but he still whimpered in his dreams.

"I fancy I'll keep awake for a spell," Scarlett told himself.

For a time, he did so. Presently he began to slide away into the land of poppies. He was walking amongst a garden of bones which bore masses of purple blossoms. Then Pierre Anton came on the scene, pale and resolute as Scarlett had always known him; then the big mastiff seemed in some way to be mixed up with the phantasm of the dream, barking as if in pain, and Scarlett came to his senses.

He was breathing short, a beady perspiration stood on his forehead, his heart hammered in quick thuds—all the horrors of nightmare were still upon him. In a vague way as yet he heard the mastiff howl, a real howl of real terror, and Scarlett knew that he was awake.

Then a strange thing happened. In the none too certain light of the fire, Scarlett saw the mastiff snatched up by some invisible hand, carried far on high towards the trees, and finally flung to the earth with a crash. The big dog lay still as a log.

A sense of fear born of the knowledge of impotence came over Scarlett; what in the name of evil did it all mean? The smart scientist had no faith in the occult, and yet what did it all mean?

Nobody stirred. Scarlett's companions were soaked and sodden with fatigue; the rolling thunder of artillery would have scarce disturbed them. With teeth set and limbs that trembled, Scarlett crawled over to the dog.

The great, black-muzzled creature was quite dead. The full chest was stained and soaked in blood; the throat had been cut apparently with some jagged, saw-like instrument away to the bone. And, strangest thing of all, scattered all about the body was a score or more of the great purple orchid flowers broken off close to the head. A hot, pricking sensation travelled slowly up Scarlett's spine and seemed to pass out at the tip of his skull. He felt his hair rising.

He was frightened. As a matter of honest fact, he had never been so horribly scared in his life before. The whole thing was so mysterious, so cruel, so bloodthirsty.

Still, there must be some rational explanation. In some way the matter had to do with the purple orchid. The flower had an evil reputation. Was it not known to these Cubans as the devil's poppy?

Scarlett recollected vividly now Zara's white, scared face when Tito had volunteered to show the way to the resplendent bloom; he remembered the cry of the girl and the blow that followed. He could see it all now. The girl had meant to warn him against some nameless horror to which Tito, was leading the

BLACK INFINITY • 209

small party. This was the jealous Cuban's revenge.

A wild desire to pay this debt to the uttermost fraction filled Scarlett and shook him with a trembling passion. He crept along in the drenching dew to where Tito lay, and touched his forehead with the chill blue rim of a revolver barrel. Tito stirred slightly.

"You dog!" Scarlett cried. "I am going to shoot you."

Tito did not move again. His breathing was soft and regular. Beyond a doubt the man was sleeping peacefully. After all he might be innocent; and yet, on the other hand, he might be so sure of his quarry that he could afford to slumber without anxiety as to his vengeance.

In favor of the latter theory was the fact that the Cuban lay beyond the limit of what had previously been the circle of dry bones. It was just possible that there was no danger outside that pale. In that case it would be easy to arouse the rest, and so save them from the horrible death which had befallen the mastiff. No doubt these were a form of upas tree, but that would not account for the ghastly spectacle in mid-air.

"I'll let this chap sleep for the present," Scarlett muttered.

He crawled back, not without misgivings, into the ring of death. He meant to wake the others and then wait for further developments. By now his senses were more alert and vigorous than they had ever been before. A preternatural clearness of brain and vision possessed him. As he advanced he saw suddenly falling a green bunch of cord that straightened into a long, emerald line. It was triangular in shape, fine at the apex, and furnished with hooked spines. The rope appeared to dangle from the tree overhead; the broad, sucker-like termination was evidently soaking up moisture.

A natural phenomenon evidently, Scarlett thought. This was some plant new to him, a parasite living amongst the tree-tops and drawing life and vigor by means of these green, rope-like antennae designed by Nature to soak and absorb the heavy dews of night.

For a moment the logic of this theory was soothing to Scarlett's distracted nerves, but only for a moment, for then he saw at regular intervals along the green rope the big purple blossoms of the devil's poppy.

He stood gasping there, utterly taken aback for the moment. There must be some infernal juggling behind all this business. He saw the rope slacken and quiver, he saw it swing forward like a pendulum, and the next minute it had passed across the shoulders of a sleeping seaman.

Then the green root became as the arm of an octopus. The line shook from end to end like the web of an angry spider when invaded by a wasp. It seemed to grip the sailor and tighten, and then, before Scarlett's affrighted eyes, the sleeping man was raised gently from the ground.

Scarlett jumped forward with a desire to scream hysterically. Now that a comrade was in danger he was no longer afraid. He whipped a jack-knife from his pocket and slashed at the cruel cord. He half expected to meet with the stoutness of a steel strand, but to his surprise the feeler snapped like a carrot, bumping the sailor heavily on the ground.

He sat up, rubbing his eyes vigorously.

"That you, sir?" he asked. "What is the matter?"

"For the love of God, get up at once and help me to arouse the others," Scarlett said, hoarsely. "We have come across the devil's workshop. All the horrors of the inferno are invented here."

The bluejacket struggled to his feet. As he did so, the clothing from his waist downwards slipped about his feet, clean cut through by the teeth of the green parasite. All around the body of the sailor blood oozed from a zone of teeth-marks.

Two-o'clock-in-the-morning courage is a virtue vouchsafed to few. The tar, who would have faced an ironclad cheerfully, fairly shivered with fright and dismay.

"What does it mean, sir?" he cried. "I've been——"

"Wake the others," Scarlett screamed; "wake the others."

Two or three more green tangles of rope came tumbling to the ground, straightening and quivering instantly. The purple blossoms stood out like a frill upon them. Like a madman Scarlett shouted, kicking his companions without mercy.

They were all awake at last, grumbling and moaning for their lost slumbers. All this time Tito had never stirred.

"I don't understand it at all," said Tarrer.

"Come from under those trees," said Scarlett, "and I will endeavor to explain. Not that you will believe me for a moment. No man can be expected to believe the awful nightmare I am going to tell you."

Scarlett proceeded to explain. As he expected, his story was followed with marked incredulity, save by the wounded sailor, who had strong evidence to stimulate his otherwise defective imagination.

"I can't believe it," Tarrer said, at length. They were whispering together beyond earshot of Tito, whom they had no desire to arouse for obvious reasons. "This is some diabolical juggling of yonder rascally Cuban. It seems impossible that those slender green cords could——"

Scarlett pointed to the center of the circle.

"Call the dog," he said, grimly, "and see if he will come."

"I admit the point as far as the poor old mastiff is concerned. But at the same time, I don't—however, I'll see for myself."

By this time a dozen or more of the slender cords were hanging pendent from the trees. They moved from spot to spot as if jerked up by some unseen hand and deposited a foot or two farther. With the great purple bloom fringing the stem, the effect was not unlovely save to Scarlett, who could see only the dark side of it. As Tarrer spoke he advanced in the direction of the trees.

"What are you going to do?" Scarlett asked.

"Exactly what I told you. I am going to investigate this business for myself."

Without wasting further words Scarlett sprang forward. It was no time for the niceties of an effete civilization. Force was the only logical argument to be used in a case like this, and Scarlett was the more powerful man of the two.

Tarrer saw and appreciated the situation.

"No, no," he cried; "none of that. Anyway, you're too late."

He darted forward and threaded his way between the slender emerald columns. As they moved slowly and with a certain stately deliberation there was no great danger to an alert and vigorous individual. As Scarlett

BLACK INFINITY • 211

entered the avenue, he could hear the soak and suck as the dew was absorbed.

"For Heaven's sake, come out of it," he cried.

The warning came too late. A whip-like trail of green touched Tarrer from behind, and in a lightning flash he was in the toils. The tendency to draw up anything and everything gave the cords a terrible power. Tarrer evidently felt it, for his breath came in great gasps.

"Cut me free," he said, hoarsely; "cut me free. I am being carried off my feet."

He seemed to be doomed for a moment, for all the cords there were apparently converging in his direction. This, as a matter of fact, was a solution of the whole sickening, horrible sensation. Pulled here and there, thrust in one direction and another, Tarrer contrived to keep his feet.

Heedless of possible danger to himself Scarlett darted forward, calling to his companions to come to the rescue. In less time than it takes to tell, four knives were at work ripping and slashing in all directions.

"Not all of you," Scarlett whispered. So tense was the situation that no voice was raised above a murmur. "You two keep your eyes open for fresh cords, and cut them as they fall, instantly. Now then."

The horrible green spines were round Tarrer's body like snakes. His face was white, his breath came painfully, for the pressure was terrible. It seemed to Scarlett to be one horrible dissolving view of green, slimy cords and great weltering, purple blossoms. The whole of the circle was strewn with them. They were wet and slimy underfoot.

Tarrer had fallen forward half unconscious. He was supported now by but two cords above his head. The cruel pressure had been relieved. With one savage sweep of his knife Scarlett cut the last of the lines, and Tarrer fell like a log unconscious to the ground. A feeling of nausea, a yellow dizziness, came over Scarlett as he staggered beyond the dread circle. He saw Tarrer carried to a place of safety, and then the world seemed to wither and leave him in the dark.

"I feel a bit groggy and weak," said Tarrer an hour or so later: "but beyond that this idiot of a Richard is himself again. So far as I am concerned, I should like to get even with our friend Tito for this."

"Something with boiling oil in it," Scarlett suggested, grimly. "The callous scoundrel has slept soundly through the whole of this business. I suppose he felt absolutely certain that he had finished with us."

"Upon my word, we ought to shoot the beggar!" Tarrer exclaimed.

"I have a little plan of my own," said Scarlett, "which I am going to put in force later on. Meanwhile we had better get on with breakfast. When Tito wakes a pleasant little surprise will await him."

Tito roused from his slumbers in due course and looked around him. His glance was curious, disappointed, then full of a white and yellow fear. A thousand conflicting emotions streamed across his dark face. Scarlett read them at a glance as he called the Cuban over to him.

"I am not going into any unnecessary details with you," he said. "It has come to my knowledge that you are playing traitor to us. Therefore we prefer to complete our journey alone. We can easily find the way now."

"The señor may do as he pleases," he replied. "Give me my dollar and let me go."

Scarlett replied grimly that he had no intention of doing anything of the kind. He did not propose to place the lives of himself and his comrades in the power of a rascally Cuban who had played false.

"We are going to leave you here till we return," he said. "You will have plenty of food, you will be perfectly safe under the shelter of these trees, and there is no chance of anybody disturbing you. We are going to tie you up to one of these trees for the next four-and-twenty hours."

All the insolence died out of Tito's face. His knees bowed, a cold dew came out over the ghastly green of his features. From the shaking of his limbs he might have fared disastrously with ague.

"The trees," he stammered, "the trees, señor! There is danger from snakes, and—and from many things. There are other places——"

"If this place was safe last night, it is safe today," Scarlett said, grimly. "I have quite made up my mind."

Tito fought no longer. He fell forward on his knees, he howled for mercy, till Scarlett fairly kicked him up again.

"Make a clean breast of it," he said, "or take the consequences. You know perfectly well that we have found you out, scoundrel."

Tito's story came in gasps. He wanted to get rid of the Americans. He was jealous. Besides, under the Americanos would Cuba be any better off? By no means and assuredly not. Therefore it was the duty of every good Cuban to destroy the Americanos where possible.

"A nice lot to fight for," Scarlett muttered. "Get to the point."

Hastened to the point by a liberal application of stout shoe-leather, Tito made plenary confession. The señor himself had suggested death by medium of the devil's poppies. More than one predatory plant-hunter had been lured to his destruction in the same way. The skeleton hung on the tree was a Dutchman who had walked into the clutch of the purple terror innocently. And Pierre Anton had done the same. The suckers of the devil's poppy only came down at night to gather moisture; in the day they were coiled up like a spring. And anything that they touched they killed. Tito had watched more than one bird or small beast crushed and mauled by these cruel spines with their fringe of purple blossoms.

"How do you get the blooms?" Scarlett asked.

"That is easy," Tito replied. "In the daytime I moisten the ground under the trees. Then the suckers unfold, drawn by the water. Once the suckers unfold one cuts several of them off with long knives. There is danger, of course, but not if one is careful."

"I'll not trouble the devil's poppy any further at present," said Scarlett, "but I shall trouble you to accompany me to my destination as a prisoner."

Tito's eyes dilated.

"They will not shoot me?" he asked, hoarsely.

"I don't know," Scarlett replied. "They may hang you instead. At any rate, I shall be bitterly disappointed if they don't end you one way or the other. Whichever operation it is, I can look forward to it with perfect equanimity."

"The Purple Terror" first appeared in the September 1899 issue of the Strand Magazine, *accompanied by illustrations by Paul Hardy (1862–1942).*

The exceedingly prolific British author and journalist Fred Merrick White (1859 – 1935) published over a hundred novels—and twice as many short stories. Several of his stories deal with the fantastic, including six early examples of disaster fiction, collected in The Doom of London *(1903), in which the Victorian city is imperiled by a killer fog, a deadly snowstorm, a fatal epidemic of diphtheria, and other widespread menaces. The Master of Disaster, producer-director Irwin Allen (of* The Towering Inferno *and* The Poseidon Adventure *fame) would have loved this guy!*

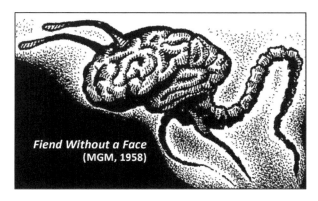

Fiend Without a Face (MGM, 1958)

BLACK INFINITY • 215

TOGETHER THEY FED ON THE SPOILS OF THE DEPTHS...

EVEN THE BIGGEST OF THE SEA'S CREATURES, THE MAMMOTH SPERM WHALES, WERE BUT A MOUTHFUL EACH FOR THE GIGANTIC REPTILIAN MONSTERS!

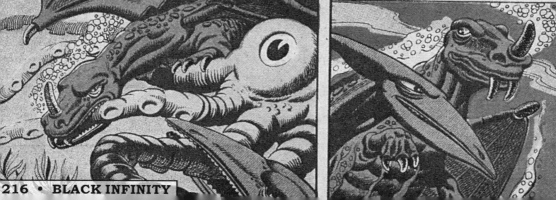

AND THE SEAS FIERCEST DENIZENS, OCTOPI, GIANT SQUID, SHARKS AND KILLER WHALES WERE HELPLESS BEFORE THE ATTACK OF THE MONSTERS FROM THE PAST!

TIME PASSED AS THEY COASTED THROUGH AND DESPOILED THE SEA DEPTHS; THEN THERE CAME A STIRRING WITHIN THE MAMMOTH, SNAKE-LIKE BODIES OF THE TERRIBLE PAIR!

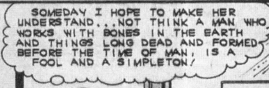

FOOD WAS PLENTIFUL...

AND THE FEMALE OF THIS MONSTROUS PAIR OF CREATURES THAT SHOULD HAVE LONG BEEN EXTINCT, BUILT HER NEST IN THE OOZING SLIME OF THE SWAMP!

WHILE REPTISAURUS STOOD GUARD, AS HIS INSTINCT BADE HIM, AGAINST TERRORS OF THE PAST THAT WERE LONG SINCE DEAD, CREATURES THAT HAD DIED IN THE MISTS OF TIME WHEN THE GREAT ICE AGE CAME TO THIS EARTH!

THERE WAS MOIST PEACE AND QUIET IN THAT STEAMING JUNGLE...BUT ON THE COAST OF THAT SAME CONTINENT THERE WAS...WAR!

BLACK INFINITY • 221

222 BLACK INFINITY

BUT THEY CURBED THEIR ABYSMAL ANGER AND, PRODDED BY ANCESTRAL MEMORY, BEGAN TO REPAIR THE CRACKED EGGS WITH SALIVA FROM GLANDS ON EACH SIDE OF THEIR HUGE JAWS!

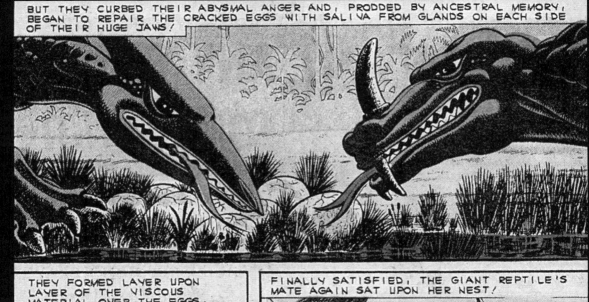

THEY FORMED LAYER UPON LAYER OF THE VISCOUS MATERIAL OVER THE EGGS, SEALING THE SLIGHT CRACKS TO KEEP THE AIR FROM ENTERING AND DESTROYING THE EMBRYOS WITHIN!

FINALLY SATISFIED, THE GIANT REPTILE'S MATE AGAIN SAT UPON HER NEST!

ONLY THEN DID REPTISAURUS GIVE VENT TO HIS FULL RAGE, AND HE ROSE ON MIGHTY WINGS, HIS SCALE-STUDDED, SNAKE-LIKE BODY GLISTENING IN THE SUN, INTENT, IN HIS MINDLESS RAGE, ON WREAKING REVENGE UPON SOMETHING...ANYTHING!

HE FLEW TOWARD THE COAST...

AND, IN KATANGA PROVINCE U.N. SOLDIERS STOOD GUARD...

THE SITUATION WAS TENSE...AND THERE WERE THOSE WHO MADE THEIR PLANS TO CAUSE THE INCIDENT THAT WOULD BRING THE FLOOD...

NOW IS THE TIME! ANY LITTLE THING WILL BEGIN IT...AND WE WILL SUPPLY THAT LITTLE THING!

BLACK INFINITY • 233

IT CAME FROM BENEATH THE SEA
(Columbia Pictures, 1955)

WHAT'S IN STORE FOR READERS NEXT ISSUE? THAT WOULD BE TELLING. BUT WE THINK YOU'LL WANT TO BE HERE FOR IT!

Made in the USA
Middletown, DE
21 June 2024

55863911R00130